Expecting Beowulf

Tom Holt

edited by Deb Geisler

The NESFA Press
Post Office Box 809
Framingham, MA 01701
2002

FIRST EDITION, February 2002

International Standard Book Number:
1-886778-36-1

Printing history

Expecting Someone Taller was first published in Great Britain by
Macmillan London Limited. St. Martin's Press edition
published 1987. Ace edition published September 1990.
Original work © 1987 by Tom Holt.

Who's Afraid of Beowulf was first published in Great Britain by
Macmillan London Limited. St. Martin's Press edition
published 1989. Ace edition published September 1991.
Original work © 1988 by Tom Holt.

Both novels appear by permission of the author.

Contents

holt on holt

Tom Holt is a short, fat, middle-aged bearded guy who sounds like someone doing a rather bad Hugh Grant impression. He was born in a suburb of London in 1961. His father worked in the shoe trade, and his mother helped edit an anthropological journal.

Holt had his fifteen minutes of fame at age thirteen, when a book of his poetry was published, attracting a certain amount of media attention. Holt has spent the last 27 years hunting down and destroying every known copy of this youthful indiscretion; however, if anybody's got one he'll be delighted to sign it, in the owner's blood.

After leaving school, Holt spent seven years at Oxford, playing pool, fixing small, temperamental motorcycle engines and dreaming up excuses for not studying Greek, Latin and Ancient History, the latter subject to postgraduate level (although he failed to attain a postgraduate qualification after his thesis entitled "Did Economic Factors Significantly Affect the Development of Democracy in Fifth-Century Athens?" was found to consist of the single word "No.")

On being slung out of university, Holt realised that he was too old to get a proper job, and accordingly qualified as a lawyer. After seven years in practice, specialising in death and taxes, he resolved to go straight in 1995 and took to writing full-time.

Holt is a shy, nocturnal creature whose working day starts around 9 p.m. and continues till around 4:30 a.m., unless he falls asleep at the keyboard. He's a keenly inept amateur blacksmith and machinist, and is one of the few people ever to have managed to ruin a 400-lb. anvil beyond economic repair. He's married, with one daughter, and lives in a small town in the west of England, just down the road from an extremely smelly meat processing plant.

Holt is easily recognised by his unkempt appearance, startled expression and missing front teeth. Do try not to stare.

Expecting Someone Taller

1

After a particularly unrewarding interview with his beloved, Malcolm was driving home along a dark, winding country lane when he ran over a badger. He stopped the car and got out to inspect the damage to his paintwork and (largely from curiosity) to the badger. It was, he decided, all he needed, for there was a small but noticeable dent in his wing, and he had been hoping to sell the car.

"Damn," he said aloud.

"So how do you think I feel?" said the badger.

Malcolm turned round quite slowly. He had had a bad day, but not so bad that he could face talking badgers—talking *dead* badgers— with equanimity. The badger was lying on its side, absolutely still. Malcolm relaxed; he must have imagined it, or perhaps the bump had accidentally switched on the car radio. Any connection was possible between the confused chow mein of wires under his dashboard.

"You're not the one who's been run over," said the badger, bitterly.

This time, Malcolm turned round rather more quickly. There was the black and white corpse, lying across the road like a dead zebra crossing; yet he could have sworn that human speech had come from it. Was some rustic ventriloquist, possibly a Friend of the Earth, playing tricks on him? He nerved himself to examine his victim. A dead badger, nothing more, nothing less; except that there was some sort of wire contraption wrapped round its muzzle—a homing device, perhaps, attached by a questing ecologist.

"Did you say something?" said Malcolm, nervously.

"So you're not deaf as well as blind," said the badger. "Yes, I did say something. Why don't you pay more attention when people talk to you?"

Malcolm felt rather embarrassed. His social equipment did not include formulae for talking to people he had just mortally wounded, or badgers, let alone a combination of the two. Nevertheless, he felt it incumbent upon him to say something, and his mind hit upon the word designed for unfamiliar situations.

"Sorry," he said.

"You're sorry," said the badger. "The hell with you."

There was a silence, broken only by the screech of a distant owl. After a while, Malcolm came to the conclusion that the badger *was* dead, and that during the collision he had somehow concussed himself without noticing it. Either that, or it was a dream. He had heard about people who fell asleep at the wheel, and remembered that they usually crashed and killed themselves. That did not cheer him up particularly.

"Anyway," said the badger, "what's your name?"

"Malcolm," said Malcolm. "Malcolm Fisher."

"Say that again," said the badger. "Slowly."

"Mal-colm Fi-sher."

The badger was silent for a moment. "Are you sure?" it said, sounding rather puzzled.

"Yes," said Malcolm. "Sorry."

"Well, Malcolm Fisher, let's have a look at you."

The badger twisted its head painfully round, and looked at him in silence for a while. "You know," it said at last, "I was expecting someone rather taller."

"Oh," said Malcolm.

"Fair-haired, tall, muscular, athletic, without spectacles," went on the badger. "Younger, but also more mature, if you see what I mean. Someone with presence. Someone you'd notice if you walked into a room full of strangers. In fact, you're a bit of a disappointment."

There was no answer to that, except Sorry again, and that would be a stupid thing to say. Nevertheless, it was irritating to have one's physical shortcomings pointed out quite so plainly twice in one evening, once by a beautiful girl and once by a dying badger. "So what?" said Malcolm, uppishly.

"All right," said the badger. "Sorry I spoke, I'm sure. Well, now you're here, you might as well get it over with. Though I'm not sure it's not cheating hitting me with that thing." And it waved a feeble paw at Malcolm's aged Renault.

"Get what over with?" asked Malcolm.

"Don't let's play games," said the badger. "You've killed me, you needn't mess me around as well. Take the Ring and the Tarnhelm and piss off."

"I don't follow," said Malcolm. "What are you talking about?"

The badger jerked violently, and spasms of pain ran through its shattered body. "You mean it was an *accident?*" it rasped. "After nearly a thousand years, it's a bloody accident. Marvellous!" The dying animal made a faint gasping noise that might just have been the ghost of laughter.

"Now you have lost me," said Malcolm.

"I'd better hurry up, then," said the badger, with weary resignation in its voice. "Unless you want me dying on you, that is, before I can tell you the story. Take that wire gadget off my nose."

Gingerly, Malcolm stretched out his fingers, fully expecting the beast to snap at them. Badgers' jaws, he remembered, are immensely strong. But the animal lay still and patient, and he was able to pull the wire net free. At once the badger disappeared, and in its place there lay a huge, grey-haired man, at least seven feet tall, with cruel blue eyes and a long, tangled beard.

"That's better," he said. "I hated being a badger. Fleas."

"I'd better get you to a hospital," said Malcolm.

"Don't bother," said the giant. "Human medicine wouldn't work on me anyway. My heart is in my right foot, my spine is made of chalcedony, and my intestines are soluble in aspirin. I'm a Giant, you see. In fact I am—was—the last of the Giants."

The Giant paused, like a television personality stepping out into the street and waiting for the first stare of recognition.

"How do you mean, Giant, exactly? You're very tall, but..."

The Giant closed his eyes and moaned softly.

"Come on," said Malcolm, "there's a casualty department in Taunton. We can get there in forty minutes."

The Giant ignored him. "Since you are totally ignorant of even basic theogony," he said, "I will explain. My name is Ingolf, and I am the last of the Frost-Giants of the Elder Age."

"Pleased to meet you," said Malcolm instinctively.

"Are you hell as like. I am the youngest brother of Fasolt and Fafner the castle-builders. Does that ring a bell? No?"

"No."

"You didn't even see the opera?" said Ingolf, despairingly.

"I'm afraid I'm not a great fan of opera," said Malcolm, "so it's unlikely."

"I don't believe it. Well, let's not go into all that now. I'll be dead in about three minutes. When you get home, look up the Ring Cycle in your *Boy's Book of Knowledge*. My story starts with the last act of *Götterdämmerung*. The funeral pyre. Siegfried lying in state. On his belt, the Tarnhelm. On his finger, the Nibelung's Ring." Ingolf paused. "Sorry, am I boring you?"

"No," Malcolm said. "Go on, please."

"Hagen snatches the Ring from Siegfried's hand as Brunnhilde plunges into the heart of the fire. At once, the Rhine bursts its banks—I'd been warning them about that embankment for years, but would they listen?—and the Rhinedaughters drag Hagen down into the depths of the river and drown him. For no readily apparent reason, Valhalla catches fire. Tableau. The End. Except," and Ingolf chuckled hoarsely through his tattered lungs, "the stupid tarts dropped the ring while they were drowning Hagen, and guess who was only a few feet away, clinging to a fallen tree, as I recall. Me. Ingolf. Ingolf the Neglected, Ingolf the Patient, Ingolf, Heir to the Ring! So I grabbed it, pulled the Tarnhelm from the ashes of the pyre, and escaped in the confusion. To here, in fact, the Vale of Taunton Deane. Last place God made, but never mind."

"Fascinating," said Malcolm after a while. "That doesn't explain why you were a badger just now, and why you aren't one any longer."

"Doesn't it?" Ingolf groaned again. "The Tarnhelm, you ignorant child, is a magic cap made by Mime, the greatest craftsman in history. Whoever wears it can take any shape or form he chooses, animate or inanimate, man, bird, or beast, rock, tree, or flower. Or he can be invisible, or transport himself instantaneously from one end of the earth to the other, just by thinking. And this idiot here thought, Who would come looking for a badger? So I turned myself into one and came to this godforsaken spot to hide."

"Why?"

"Because it's godforsaken, and I'd had about as much of the Gods as I could take. They were after me, you see. In fact, they probably still are. Also the Volsungs. And the Rhinemaidens. And Alberich. The whole bloody lot of them. It hasn't been easy, I can tell you. Luckily, they're all so unbelievably *stupid*. They've spent the last thousand odd years searching high and low for a ninety-foot dragon with teeth like standing stones and an enormous tail. Just because my brother Fafner—a pleasant enough chap in his way, but scarcely imaginative—disguised *himself* as a dragon when he had the perishing thing. I could have told him that a ninety-foot dragon was scarcely inconspicuous, even in the Dawn of the World, but why should I help him? Anyway, I very sensibly became a badger and outsmarted them all."

"Hang on," said Malcolm, "I'm a bit confused. Why did you have to hide?"

"Because," said Ingolf, "they wanted the Ring."

"So why didn't you give it to them—whoever they were—and save yourself all the bother?"

"Whoever owns the Ring is the master of the world," said Ingolf, gravely.

"Oh," said Malcolm. "So you're..."

"And a fat lot of good it's done me, you might very well say. Who did you think ruled the world, anyway, the United bloody Nations?"

"I hadn't given it much thought, to be honest with you. But if you're the ruler of the world..."

"I know what you're thinking. If I'm master of the world, why should I have to hide in a copse in Somerset disguised as a badger?"

"More or less," said Malcolm.

"Uneasy lies the head that wears a crown," said the Giant sagely. "Looking back, of course, I sometimes wonder whether it was all worth it. But you will learn by my mistakes."

Malcolm furrowed his brow. "You mean you're leaving them all to me?" he asked. "The Ring and the—what did you say it was called?"

"Tarnhelm. It means helmet of darkness, though why they describe it as a helmet when it's just a little scrap of wire I couldn't tell you. Anyway, take them with my blessing, for what that's worth."

Ingolf paused to catch his breath.

"To gain inexhaustible wealth," he continued, "just breathe on the Ring and rub it gently on your forehead. Go on, try it."

Ingolf eased the plain gold ring off his finger and passed it to Malcolm, who accepted it rather as one might accept some delicacy made from the unspeakable parts of a rare amphibian at an embassy function. He did as Ingolf told him, and at once found himself knee-deep in gold. Gold cups, gold plates, gold brooches, bracelets, anklets, pectorals, cruets and sauce-boats.

"Convinced?" said Ingolf. "Or do you want a metallurgist's report?"

"I believe you," said Malcolm, who was indeed firmly convinced that he was dreaming, and vowed never to eat Stilton cheese late at night again.

"Leave them," said Ingolf. "Plenty more where that came from. The Nibelungs make them in the bottomless caverns of Nibelheim, the Kingdom of the Mists. They'll be glad of the warehouse space."

"And the Tarnhelm—that works too, does it?"

Ingolf finally seemed to lose patience. "Of course it bloody works," he shouted. "Put it on and turn yourself into a human being."

"Sorry," said Malcolm. "It's all been rather a shock."

"Finally," said Ingolf, "cut my arm and lick some of the blood."

"I'd rather not," said Malcolm, firmly.

"If you do, you'll be able to understand the language of the birds."

"I don't particularly want to be able to understand the language of the birds," said Malcolm.

"You'll understand the language of the birds and like it, my lad," said Ingolf severely. "Now do as you are told. Use the pin on one of those brooches there."

The blood tasted foul and was burning hot. For a second, Malcolm's brain clouded over; then, faintly in the distance, he heard the owl hoot again, and realised to his astonishment that he could understand what it was saying. Not that it was saying anything of any interest, of course.

"Oh," said Malcolm. "Oh, well, thank you."

"Now then," said the Giant. "I am about to go on my last journey. Pile up that gold around my head. I must take it with me to pay the ferryman."

"I thought it was just a coin on the eyes or something."

"Inflation. Also, I'll take up rather a lot of room on the boat." He scowled. "Get on with it, will you?" he said. "Or do you want a receipt?"

Malcolm did as he was told. After all, it wasn't as if it was real gold. Was it?

"Listen," said Ingolf, "listen carefully. I am dying now. When I am dead, my body will turn back into the living rock from which Lord Ymir moulded the race of the Frost-Giants when the world was young. Nothing will grow here for a thousand years, and horses will throw their riders when they pass the spot. Pity, really, it's a main road. Oh, well. Every year, on the anniversary of my death, fresh blood will well up out of the earth and the night air will be filled with uncanny cries. That is the Weird of the Ring-Bearer when his life is done. Be very careful, Malcolm Fisher. There is a curse on the Nibelung's Ring—the curse of Alberich, which brings all who wear it to a tragic and untimely death. Yet it is fated that when the Middle Age of the world is drawing to a close, a foolish, godlike boy who does not understand the nature of the Ring will break the power of Alberich's curse and thereby redeem the world. Then the Last Age of the world will begin, the Gods will go down for ever, and all things shall be well." Ingolf's eyes were closing, his breath was faint, his words scarcely audible. But suddenly he started, and propped himself up on one elbow.

"Hold on a minute," he gasped. "A foolish, godlike boy who does not understand...who does not understand..." He sank down again, his strength exhausted. "Still," he said, "I was expecting someone rather taller."

He shuddered for the last time, and was as still as stone. The wind, which had been gathering during his last speech, started to scream, lashing the trees into a frenzy. The Giant was dead; already his shape was unrecognisable as his body turned back into grey stone, right in the middle of the Minehead to Bridgwater trunk road. All around him,

Malcolm could hear a confused babble of voices, human and animal, living and dead, and, like the counterpoint to a vast fugue, the low, rumbling voices of the trees and the rocks. The entire earth was repeating the astonishing news: Ingolf was dead, the world had a new master.

Just then, two enormous ravens flapped slowly and lazily over Malcolm's head. He stood paralysed with inexplicable fear, but the ravens flew on. The voices died away, the wind dropped, the rain subsided. As soon as he was able to move, Malcolm jumped in his car and drove home as fast as the antiquated and ill-maintained engine would permit him to go. He undressed in the dark and fell into bed, and was soon fast asleep and dreaming a strange and terrible dream, all about being trapped in a crowded lift with no trousers on. Suddenly he woke up and sat bolt upright in the darkness. On his finger was the Ring. Beside his bed, between his watch and his key-chain, was the Tarnhelm. Outside his window, a nightingale was telling another nightingale what it had had for lunch.

"Oh my God," said Malcolm, and went back to sleep.

The Oberkasseler Bridge over the Rhine has acquired a sinister reputation in recent years, and the two policemen who were patrolling it knew this only too well. They knew what to look for, and they seldom had to look far in this particular area.

A tall man with long grey hair falling untidily over the collar of his dark blue suit leaned against the parapet eating an ice cream. Although impeccably dressed, he was palpably all wrong, and the two policemen looked at each other with pleasant anticipation.

"Drugs?" suggested the first policeman.

"More like dirty books," said the other. "If he's armed, it's my turn."

"It's always your turn," grumbled his companion.

The first policeman shrugged his shoulders. "Oh, all right then," he said. "But I get to drive back to the station."

But as they approached their prey, they began to feel distinctly uncomfortable. It was not fear but a sort of awe or respect that caused them to hesitate as the tall man turned and stared at them calmly through his one eye. Suddenly, they found that they were having difficulty breathing.

"Excuse me, sir," said the first policeman, gasping slightly, "can you tell me the time?"

"Certainly," said the tall man, without looking at his watch, "it's just after half-past eleven."

The two policemen turned and walked away quickly. As they did so, they both simultaneously looked at their own watches. Twenty-eight minutes to twelve.

"He must have been looking at the clock," said the first policeman.

"What clock?" inquired his companion, puzzled.

"I don't know. Any bloody clock."

The tall man turned and gazed down at the brown river for a while. Then he clicked his fingers, and a pair of enormous ravens floated down and landed on either side of him on the parapet. The tall man broke little pieces off the rim of his cornet and flicked them at the two birds as he questioned them.

"Any luck?" he asked.

"What do you think?" replied the smaller of the two.

"Keep trying," said the tall man calmly. "Have you done America today?"

The smaller raven's beak was full of cornet, so the larger raven, although unused to being the spokesman, said Yes, they had. No luck.

"We checked America," said the smaller raven, "and Africa, and Asia, and Australia, and Europe. Bugger all, same as always."

"Maybe you were looking in the wrong place," suggested the tall man.

"You don't understand," said the smaller raven. "It's like looking for..." the bird racked its brains for a suitably graphic simile "...for a needle in a haystack," it concluded triumphantly.

"Well," said the tall man, "I suggest you go and look again. Carefully, this time. My patience is beginning to wear a little thin."

Suddenly he closed his broad fist around the cornet, crushing it into flakes and dust.

"You've got ice cream all over your hand," observed the larger raven.

"So I have," said the tall man. "Now get out, and this time concentrate."

The ravens flapped their broad, drab wings and floated away. Frowning, the tall man clicked the fingers of his clean hand and took out his handkerchief.

"I've got a tissue if you'd rather use it," said a nervous-looking thin man who had hurried up to him. The tall man waved it away.

"How about you?" he asked the thin man. "Done any good?"

"Nothing. I did Toronto, Lusaka, and Brasilia. Have you ever been to Brasilia? Last place God made. Oh, I'm sorry. I didn't mean..."

"The more I think about it," said the tall man, ignoring this gaffe, "the more convinced I am that he's still in Europe. When Ingolf went to ground, the other continents hadn't even been discovered."

The thin man looked puzzled. "Ingolf?" he said. "Haven't you heard?"

The tall man turned his head and fixed him with his one eye. The thin man started to tremble slightly, for he knew that expression well.

"Ingolf is dead," continued the thin man. "I thought you'd have known."

The tall man was silent. Clouds, which had not been there a moment before, passed in front of the sun.

"I'm only the King of the Gods, nobody ever bothers to tell me anything," said the tall man. "So?"

"He died at a quarter to midnight last night, at a place called Ralegh's Cross in the West of England. He was knocked down by a car, and..."

Rain was falling now, hard and straight, but the thin man was sweating. Oddly enough, the tall man wasn't getting wet.

"No sign of the Ring," said the thin man nervously. "Or the helmet. I've checked all the usual suspects, but they don't seem to have heard or seen anything. In fact, they were as surprised as you were. I mean..."

Thunder now, and a flicker of distant lightning.

"I got there as quickly as I could," said the thin man, desperately. "As soon as I felt the shock. But I was in Brasilia, like I said, and it takes time..."

"All the usual suspects?"

"All of them. Every one."

Suddenly, the tall man smiled. The rain stopped, and a rainbow flashed across the sky.

"I believe you," said the tall man, "thousands wouldn't. Right, so if it wasn't one of the usual suspects, it must have been an outsider, someone we haven't dealt with before. That should make it all much easier. So start searching."

"Any where in particular?"

"Use your bloody imagination," growled the tall man, irritably, and the rainbow promptly faded away. The thin man smiled feebly, and soon was lost to sight among the passers-by. Wotan, the great Sky-God and King of all the Gods, put his handkerchief back in his pocket and gazed up into the sky, where the two enormous ravens were circling.

"Got all that?" Wotan murmured.

Thought, the elder and smaller of the two messenger ravens who are the God's eyes and ears on earth, dipped his wings to show that he had, and Wotan walked slowly away.

"Like looking for a needle in a haystack," repeated Thought, slid-

ing into a convenient thermal. His younger brother, Memory, banked
steeply and followed him.

"This is true," replied Memory, "definitely."

"You know the real trouble with this business?" said Memory,
diving steeply after a large moth.

"What's that, then?"

"Bloody awful industrial relations, that's what. I mean, take Wotan.
Thinks he's God almighty."

"He is, isn't he?"

Memory hovered for a moment on a gust of air. "I never thought
of that," he said at last.

"Well, you wouldn't," said Thought, "would you?"

2

The next morning, Malcolm thought long and hard before waking up, for he had come to recognise over the past quarter of a century that rather less can go wrong if you are asleep.

But the radiant light of a brilliant summer morning, shining in through the window in front of which he had neglected to draw the curtains, chased away all possibility of sleep, and Malcolm was left very much awake, although still rather confused. Such confusion was, however, his normal state of mind. Without it, he would feel rather lost.

Confusion is the only possible result of a lifetime of being asked unanswerable questions by one's parents and relatives, such as "What *are* we going to do with you?" or "Why can't you be more like your sister?" To judge by the frequency with which he encountered it, the latter problem was the truly significant one, to which not even the tremendous intellectual resources of his family had been able to find an answer. Malcolm himself had never made any sort of attempt to solve this problem; that was not his role in life. His role (if he had one, which he sometimes doubted) was to provide a comparison with his elder sister Bridget. Rather like the control group in the testing process for a new medicine, Malcolm was there to ensure that his parents never took their exceptional daughter for granted. If ever they were misguided enough to doubt or underestimate that glorious creature, one look at Malcolm was enough to remind them how lucky they were, so it was Malcolm's calling to be a disappointment; he would be failing in his duty as a son and a brother if he was anything else.

When Bridget had married Timothy (a man who perfectly exemplified the old saying that all work and no play makes Jack a management consultant) and gone to turn the rays of her effulgence on Sydney, Australia, it was therefore natural that her parents, lured by the prospect of grandchildren to persecute, should sell all they had and follow her. They had muttered something about Malcolm presumably coming too, but their heart was not really in it; he was no longer needed, now that the lacklustre Timothy could take over the mantle of unworthiness. So Malcolm had decided that he would prefer to stay in England. He disliked bright sunlight, had no great interest in the cinema, opera, tennis or seafood, and didn't particularly want to go on getting under people's feet for the rest of his life. He was thus able to add ingratitude and lack of proper filial and brotherly affection to the already impressive list of things that were wrong with him but not with his sister.

After a great deal of enjoyable agonising, Mr. and Mrs. Fisher decided that Malcolm's only chance of ever amounting to anything was being made to stand on his own two feet, and allowed him to stay behind. Before they left, however, they went to an extraordinary amount of trouble and effort to find him a boring job and a perfectly horrible flat in a nasty village in the middle of nowhere. So it was that Malcolm had come to leave his native Derby, a place he had never greatly cared for, and go into the West, almost (but not quite) like King Arthur. Taking with him his good suit, his respectable shirts, his spongebag and his two A-levels, he had made his way to Somerset, where he had been greeted with a degree of enthusiasm usually reserved for the first drop of rain at a Wimbledon final by his parents' long-suffering contacts, whose tireless efforts had made his new life possible. Malcolm took to the trade of an auctioneer's clerk like a duck to petrol, found the local dialect almost as inscrutable as the locals found his own slight accent, and settled down, like Kent in *King Lear,* to shape his old course in a country new.

The fact that he hated and feared his new environment was largely beside the point, for he had been taught long ago that what he thought and felt about any given subject was without question the least important thing in the world. Indeed he had taken this lesson so much to heart that when the Government sent him little pieces of card apparently entitling him to vote in elections, he felt sure that they had intended them for somebody else. He told himself that he would soon get used to it, just as he had always been told that he would grow into the grotesquely outsized garments he was issued with as a child. Although two years had now passed since his arrival in the West Country, the sleeves of his new life, so to speak, still reached down to his fingernails. But that was presumably his fault for not growing. Needless to say, it was a remark of his sister Bridget's that best summed up his situation; to be precise, a joke she used to make at the age of seven. "What is the difference," she would ask, "between Marmalade [the family cat] and Malcolm?" When no satisfactory answer could be provided by the admiring adults assembled to hear the joke, Bridget would smile and say, "Daddy isn't allowed to shout at Marmalade."

So it seemed rather strange (or counter-intuitive, as his sister would say) that Malcolm should have been chosen by the badger to be the new master of the world. Bridget, yes; she was very good indeed at organising things, and would doubtless make sure that the trains ran on time. But Malcolm—"only Malcolm," as he was affectionately known to his family—that was a mistake, surely. Still, he reflected as he put the Ring back on his finger, since he was surely imagining the whole thing, what did it matter?

Without bothering to get out of bed, he breathed on the Ring and rubbed it on his forehead. At once, countless gold objects materialised in the air and fell heavily all around him, taking him so completely by surprise that all he could think was that this must be what the Americans mean by a shower. Gold cups, gold plates, gold chalices, torques, ashtrays, pipe-racks, cufflinks, bath-taps, and a few shapeless, unformed articles (presumably made by apprentice Nibelungs at evening classes under the general heading of paperweights) tumbled down on all sides, so that Malcolm had to snatch up a broad embossed dish and hold it over his head until the cascade had subsided in order to avoid serious injury.

Gathering the shreds of his incredulity around him, Malcolm tried to tell himself that it probably wasn't real or solid gold; but that was a hard hypothesis. Only a complete and utter cheapskate would go to the trouble of materialising copper or brass by supernatural means. No, it was real, it was solid, it existed, and it was making the place look like a scrapyard, as his mother would undoubtedly say were she present. Having wriggled out from under the hoard, Malcolm found some cardboard boxes and put it all neatly away. That alone was hard work. Malcolm shook his head, yawned, and wiped the sweat from his forehead with the back of his hand, thus accidentally starting off the whole process all over again...

"For Christ's sake!" he shouted, as a solid gold ewer missed him by inches, "will you stop that?"

The torrent ceased, and Malcolm sat down on the bed.

"Well, I'm damned," he said aloud, as he removed a gold tie-pin that had fallen into his pyjama pocket. "Ruler of the world..."

Try as he might, he couldn't get the concept to make sense, so he put it aside. There was also the Tarnhelm to consider. Very, very tentatively, he put it on and stood in front of the mirror. It covered his head —it seemed to have grown in the night, or did it expand and contract automatically to fit its owner?—and was fastened under the chin by a little buckle in the shape of a crouching gnome.

So far as he could remember, all he had to do was think of something he wanted to be, or a place he wanted to go to, and the magic cap did all the rest. As usual when asked to think of something, Malcolm's mind went completely blank. He stood for a while, perplexed, then recalled that the helmet could also make him invisible. He thought invisible. He was.

It was a strange sensation to look in the mirror and not see oneself, and Malcolm was not sure that he liked it. So he decided to reappear and was profoundly relieved when he saw his reflection in the glass once more. He repeated the process a couple of times, appearing and disappearing like a trafficator, now you see me, now you don't, and so on. Childish, he said to himself. We must take this thing seriously or else go stark staring mad.

Next, he must try shape-changing proper. He looked round the room for inspiration, and his eye fell on an old newspaper with a photograph of the Chancellor of the Exchequer on the front page. The thought crossed his mind that his mother had always wanted him to make something of himself, and now if he wanted to, he could be a member of the Cabinet...

In the mirror, he caught sight of the Chancellor of the Exchequer, looking perhaps a trifle eccentric in blue pyjamas and a chain-mail cap, but nevertheless unmistakable. Even though he had done his best to prepare his mind for the experience of shape-changing, the shock was terrifying in its intensity. He looked frantically round the room to see if he could see himself anywhere, but no sign. He had actually changed shape.

He forced himself to look at the reflection in the mirror, and it occurred to him that if he was going to do this sort of thing at all, he might as well do it properly. He concentrated his mind and thought of the Chancellor in his customary dark grey suit. At once, the reflection changed, and now the only jarring note was the chain-mail cap. That might well be a problem if it insisted on remaining visible all the time. He could wear a hat over it, he supposed, but that would be tricky indoors, and so few people wore hats these days. Malcolm thought how nice it would be if the cap could make itself invisible. At once, it disappeared, giving an excellent view of the Chancellor's thinning grey hair. So the thing worked. Nevertheless, he reflected, it would be necessary to think with unaccustomed precision when using it.

Once he had overcome his initial fear of the Tarnhelm, Malcolm set about testing it thoroughly. Had anyone been sufficiently inquisitive, or sufficiently interested in Malcolm Fisher, to be spying on him with a pair of binoculars, they would have seen him change himself into the entire Cabinet, the King of Swaziland, Theseus, and Winston

Churchill, all in under a minute. But it then occurred to him that he need not restrict himself to specific people. The only piece of equipment with similar potential he had ever encountered was a word-processor, and there was not even a manual he could consult. How would it be if the Tarnhelm could do Types?

"Make me," he said aloud, "as handsome as it is possible to be."

He closed his eyes, not daring to look, then opened his right eye slowly. Then his left eye, rather more quickly. The result was pleasing, to say the least. For some reason best known to itself, the Tarnhelm had chosen to clothe this paradigm in some barbaric costume from an earlier era—probably to show the magnificent chest and shoulders off to their best advantage. But England is a cold place, even in what is supposed to be summer... "Try that in a cream suit," he suggested, "and rather shorter hair. And lose the beard."

He stood for a while and stared. The strange thing was that he felt completely comfortable with this remarkable new shape; in fact, he could not remember exactly what he actually looked like, himself, in propria persona. The first time he had ever been aware of his own appearance (so far as he could recall) was when he appeared in a school nativity play, typecast as Eighth Shepherd, at the age of five. He had had to stand in front of a mirror to do up his cloak, and had suddenly realised that the rather ordinary child in the glass was himself. Quite naturally, he had burst out crying, refusing to be comforted, so that the Second King had had to go on for him and say his one line (which was, he seemed to recall, "Oh look!").

"I'll take it," he said to the mirror, and nodded his head to make the reflection agree with him. He then hurried through every permutation of clothes and accessories, just to make sure. There was no doubt about it; the Tarnhelm had very good taste. "We'll call that one Richard" (he had always wanted to be called Richard). He resumed his own shape (which came as a bitter disappointment) then said "Richard," firmly. At once, the Most Handsome Man reappeared in the mirror, which proved that the Tarnhelm had a memory, like a pocket calculator.

"How about," he said diffidently, "the most beautiful *woman* in the world? Just for fun," he added quickly.

Contrary to all his expectations, the Tarnhelm did as it was told, and the mirror was filled with a vision of exquisite loveliness, so that it took Malcolm some time to realise that it was him. In fact the extraordinary thing was that all this seemed perfectly natural. Why shouldn't he be what he wanted to be, and to hell with the laws of physics?

The next stage was to test the cap's travel mode. Ingolf had told him that he could enjoy instantaneous and unlimited travel, and although this sounded rather like a prize in a game show or an advertisement for a season ticket, he was fully prepared to believe that it was possible. If he was going out, however, he ought to get dressed, for he was still in his pyjamas. He looked around for some clean socks, then remembered that it wasn't necessary. He could simply think himself dressed, and no need to worry about clean shirts. In fact, he could now have that rather nice cashmere sweater he had seen in that shop in Bridgwater, and no problem about getting one in his size, either.

For his first journey it would be advisable not to be too ambitious, just in case there were complications. "The bathroom," he thought, and there he was. No sensation of rushing through the air or dissolving particle by particle; he was just there. Rather a disappointment, for Malcolm enjoyed travel, and it is better to travel hopefully than to arrive (or at least that had always been his experience). "The High Street," he commanded.

It was cold out in the street, and he had to call for an overcoat, which came at once, slipping imperceptibly over his shoulders and doing up its buttons of its own accord. "Back," he thought, and he was sitting on his bed once again. Suddenly, this too seemed intensely real, and it was the ease with which he managed it that made it seem so; no difficulty, as one might expect from a conjuring-trick or a sleight of hand. He transformed himself and travelled through space as easily as he moved the fingers of his hand, and by exactly the same process; he willed it to happen and it happened. In the same way, it seemed to lose its enchantment. Just because one is able to move one's arms simply by wanting to, it does not follow that one continually does so just for the fun of it. He felt somehow disillusioned, and had to make a conscious effort to continue with the experiment.

It occurred to him that he had not actually specified where he wanted to be put down in the High Street. This could lead to problems. If he were to say "Jamaica" or "Finland" without specifying where exactly in those particular countries he wished to end up, he might find himself standing on the surface of a lake or the fast lane of a motorway. He tried the High Street again, and found that he was exactly half-way up it, and standing safely on the pavement. He repeated the procedure three times, and each time ended up in the same spot. Then he tried a few of the neighbouring towns and villages. A distinct pattern emerged. The Tarnhelm put him as close as it reasonably could to the centre of the town, and in every instance in a place of safety where he could materialise without being noticed.

Could he combine shape-changing and travel? "Bristol and a postman," he cried, and a postman in the centre of Bristol he became. This was enjoyable. He rattled through the capital cities of the world (as many as he could remember; he had done badly at geography at school) in a variety of disguises, pausing only for a moment in each place to find a shop-window in which to see his reflection. The only failure—relative failure—in this procession was Washington, which he had elected to visit in the guise of a computer programmer. He forgot to specify which Washington, and the Tarnhelm, doubtless on the principle of *difficilior lectio,* had sent him to Tyne and Wear.

He had almost forgotten in all this excitement that he was also supposed to be able to understand the language of the birds. When he had returned to Nether Stowey, he overheard snatches of conversations outside the window, which worried him until he realised that it was in fact a pair of seriously-minded crows who were discussing the world situation, with special reference to the death of Ingolf. This reminded Malcolm that he really ought to find out a little more about the background to his new possessions. So he went, invisibly and instantaneously, to the library and spent an hour or so reading through the libretti of Wagner's operas.

Rather than wade through the text, which was German poetry translated into some obscure dialect of Middle English, he read through the synopses of the plot, and highly improbable he found it all. The fact that it was all (apparently) true did little to improve matters. Malcolm had never been greatly inclined to metaphysical or religious speculation, but he had hoped that if there was a supreme being or divine agency, it would at least show the elements of logic and common sense in its conduct. Seemingly, not so. On the other hand, the revelation that the destiny of the world had been shaped by a bunch of verbose idiots went some way towards explaining the problems of human existence.

For one could attribute any sort of illogical folly to a god who orders a castle to be built for him by a couple of Frost-Giants in the full knowledge that the price he is expected to pay for his new home is his sister-in-law. But this, apparently, was what Wotan, the great Sky-God and King of the Gods, had seen fit to do, promising his wife's sister Freia to the Giants Fasolt and Fafner. Arguably an arrangement by which one gains a castle and disposes of a relative by marriage at one and the same time is a bargain in anybody's terms; but Wotan, if this was at the back of his omniscient mind, had apparently overlooked the fact that this Freia was the guardian of the golden apples of youth, through whose power the Gods not only kept the doctor away but also maintained their immortality. Without Freia to supply them with gold-en apples, they would all dry up and perish, and the Giants, who ap-peared to have at least an elementary grounding in politics, philoso-phy and economics, were well aware of this when they struck the bar-gain.

Something of a dilemma for the everlasting Gods. But to their aid comes the clever Fire-God, Loge, who persuades the Giants that what they really need is not the most beautiful woman in the world, who also happens to be the guardian of the secret of eternal youth, but a small, plain gold ring that belongs to somebody else. The Ring is, in fact, the property of Alberich, a sulphur-dwarf from the underground caverns of Nibelheim.

Alberich had stolen some magic gold from the River Rhine, wherein dwelt (presumably before the river became polluted) three rather pretty girls, the Rhinedaughters, who owned the magic gold. This gold, if made into a ring by someone who vowed to do without Love (some of us, Malcolm reflected bitterly, have no choice in the matter), would confer upon its owner the control of the world, in some concrete but ill-defined way. Alberich had originally set out with the intention of chatting up one of the Rhinedaughters; having failed in this, he cursed Love, stole the gold, and made the Ring. By its power, he found that he was able to compel all his fellow sulphur-dwarves to mine and work gold for him in unlimited quantities, this apparently being what sul-phur-dwarves do best. With this wealth, it was his intention to sub-vert the world and make himself its master.

Before he can get very far with this project, Wotan steals the Ring from him and uses it to pay off the Giants, who immediately start fight-ing over who should have it. Fafner kills Fasolt, and transforms himself into a dragon before retiring to a cave in a forest in the middle of no-where, this apparently being preferable in his eyes to retiring to a cave in a forest with the Goddess Freia. It takes all sorts.

Wotan is understandably concerned to get hold of the Ring for him-self. Once again, Malcolm was moved to wonder at the stupidity, or at least the obscurity, of the King of the Gods; evidently the sort of person who, if asked to rescue a cat from a roof, would tackle the problem by burning the house down. Wotan sets about securing the ring by having an affair with Mother Earth, the result of which is nine noisy daughters called Valkyries, and a son and a daughter called Volsungs. The latter obviously take after their father, for all they manage to do before meeting with horrible deaths is commit incest and produce a son.

This son is Siegfried, a muscular but stupid youth who kills the dragon Fafner. From the pile of gold on top of which the dragon has been sleeping for a hundred years (rather uncomfortable, Malcolm thought), Siegfried picks out the Ring and the Tarnhelm, not knowing what they are for. He only discovers the secret of these articles when, led by a woodbird, he wakes up the Number One Valkyrie, Brunnhilde, who has been sleeping on a fiery mountain for twenty years after a quarrel with her father.

Brunnhilde, who is of course Siegfried's *aunt,* is also the first woman he has ever seen, and the two of them fall in love at first sight. Brunnhilde tells Siegfried all about the Ring and the terrible curse that Alberich had placed on it which brings all who own it to a horrible and untimely death. Siegfried, not being a complete idiot, gives it to her as a present. This is, of course, all in accordance with Wotan's plan ("Sounds more like coincidence to me," said Malcolm to himself, "but never mind") since Brunnhilde is the embodiment of Wotan's will, and because Wotan is forbidden by his intermittent but ferocious conscience to touch the perishing thing himself, Brunnhilde getting it is the nearest he can come to controlling it.

In a logical world, that would be that. But Siegfried goes off into the world to continue his career as a professional Hero, and falls in with some very dubious people called the Gibichungs. They manage to persuade Siegfried to take the Ring back from Brunnhilde and marry their horse-faced sister Gutrune. Brunnhilde is naturally livid, and conspires with Hagen (a Gibichung and also, would you believe, Alberich's son) to kill Siegfried and get the Ring back. Hagen kills Siegfried, and Brunnhilde immediately changes her mind (so like a woman). She hurls herself onto Siegfried's funeral pyre, clutching the Ring, and is burnt to a crisp. As she does so, the Rhine fortuitously bursts its banks and floods Germany, allowing the Rhinedaughters to snatch the Ring from Brunnhilde's charred finger and drown Hagen. Meanwhile, the castle of the Gods (which had caused the whole mess in the first place) has caught fire and burns down, the Gods rather foolishly neglecting to leave it while it does so, and the curtain falls on a carbonised heaven and a flooded earth, or, in other words, a typical operatic Happy Ending. Or so Wagner thought...

Having finally come to the end of this narrative, Malcolm was left with two abiding impressions: first, that Fafner the dragon, instead of keeping his money under the mattress like everyone else, had kept his mattress under the money; second, that humanity generally gets the Gods it deserves. He shook his head sadly and transported himself to the pub.

Over a pint of beer and a chicken sandwich, he went over the story in his mind. The logical flaws and inconsistencies that riddled the tale, far from making him doubt its veracity, finally convinced him that it might indeed be true; for life is like that. He also wrote down on a beer-mat the names of all the Gods and monsters who might come looking for him, and turned his attention to more pressing matters.

First, there was the problem of turning the Nibelung's gold into folding money. He resolved to try the straightforward approach, and so transported himself to Bond Street, where he found an old-established jeweller's shop. He assumed a grave and respectable appearance and approached the counter holding two heavy gold chalices selected at random from the gold he had materialised that morning. The jeweller studied them for a moment in silence.

"That's odd," he said, turning one of them over in order to study the outlandish script on the rim, "they aren't on the list."

"What list?"

"The list of stolen gold and silver we get from the police each month. Or did you nick them recently?"

"I didn't steal them," said Malcolm truthfully, "they're mine."

"Tell that to the inspector, chum," said the jeweller. A burly assistant stood in front of the door, as the jeweller lifted the telephone and started to dial.

"You people never learn," he said sadly. "You come in off the street expecting me to buy five grand's worth of gold..."

"As much as that?"

"That's the value of the metal. Add a couple of grand for the workmanship, if it's genuine. I expect the owner will be glad to get it back."

"Oh, that's all right, you can keep them," Malcolm said, and vanished.

3

As he put the kettle on back in Nether Stowey, Malcolm worked out a way in which he could turn the Nibelung hoard into mastery of the world. First, he would have to find some way of contacting an unscrupulous gold dealer—not too difficult; all he need do would be request the Tarnhelm, in its travel mode, to take him to an unscrupulous gold dealer's house and there he would be—and sell off a reasonable quantity of gold with no questions asked. With the money thus obtained, he could start buying shares—lots of shares in lots of big companies. Then sell more gold, then buy more shares. Sooner or later, he would flood the gold market, which would be a pity; but by then, he ought to have enough shares to enable him to do without the gold per se. After about a decade of buying as many shares as he could, he would be in a position to start seizing control of major international companies. Through these (and massive corruption) he could in turn gain influence over the Governments of the countries of the free world.

With the free world in his pocket, he could patch up a workable detente with the Communist bloc to the extent that he could start infiltrating them. By a combination of bribery, economic pressure and, where necessary, military force, he could in about thirty-five years gain unseen but effective control of the world, and probably about a hundred ulcers to go with it. It all sounded perfectly horrible and no fun at all, and Malcolm wanted no part of it. In a way he was relieved. Control of the world, as he had imagined it would be when Ingolf first mentioned the subject, would have entailed responsibilities as well as benefits. As it was, he could perfectly well throw the Ring away—back into the Rhine, if the Rhinedaughters had not long since died of sewage poisoning—and keep the Tarnhelm for his own amusement. He could get a job as an express messenger...

"Idiot," said a voice.

He looked around, startled. There was nobody to be seen...then he remembered. The voice had come from a rather bedraggled pigeon perched on his window ledge.

"I beg your pardon?" he said.

"You're an idiot, Malcolm Fisher," said the pigeon. "Open the window and let me in."

Although he was beginning to tire of being insulted and ordered about by dumb animals, Malcolm did as he was told.

"Sorry," said the pigeon, "it was rude of me. But I felt it was my duty to tell you. You see, I'm a woodbird, like the woodbird who advised Siegfried all those years ago."

"No, you're not," said Malcolm. "You're a pigeon."

"Correct. I'm a woodpigeon. And we care about things."

That was presumably meant to be logical. Certainly, it made about as much sense as everything else Malcolm had heard during the past forty-eight hours. "So why am I an idiot?" he asked. "What have I done now?"

"The Ring you've got there," said the pigeon, its beak full of crumbs from Malcolm's table, "you don't understand what it is, do you? I mean, you've heard the story and you've read the book..."

"When do I get to see the film?"

"It's not a toy, you know," said the pigeon, sternly, "and before you ask, I know all this because I'm a bird."

"Thank you."

"You're welcome. You see," continued the pigeon, preening its ruffled feathers, "the Ring has other powers beyond creating wealth that were not even guessed at—good crumbs these, by the way. I'm into healthy scavenging—guessed at when it was forged. Have you heard today's news?"

Malcolm looked at his watch; it was five o'clock, and he leaned forward to switch on the radio. But even before he touched the set, the voice of the newsreader became clearly audible.

"That's handy," said Malcolm.

"Giant's blood," replied the pigeon. "Of course, it's selective; you can only hear the broadcasts if you make a conscious decision to do so. Otherwise you'd go mad in a couple of minutes, with all those voices jabbering away in a hundred different languages. And yes, it does work with telephones."

"Don't tell me," said Malcolm, to whom a sudden revelation had been made, "you birds can do it as well."

The pigeon did not speak. Nevertheless Malcolm heard it clearly in his mind's ear. Although the bird did not open its beak, it was exactly the same as hearing a voice, rather like having a conversation with someone with their back to you. Even the pigeon's faint Midlands accent was preserved.

"And you can do everything that we can do, as well or even better. For instance you can read thoughts, like you're doing now—selectively, of course. But in your case, you can blot them out and hear nothing if you want to. We can't."

One distinct advantage of this conversation without speech was that these communications, which would have taken several seconds to say out loud, flashed through Malcolm's mind in no time at all. To give an illustration: an actor reciting the whole of *Paradise Lost* by thought-transfer would detain his audience for no more than six minutes. As Malcolm opened his mind to the concept, he found that he could hear the pigeon's thoughts even when it wasn't trying to communicate them.

"Same to you," he said (or thought) irritably.

"Sorry," said the bird. "I forgot you could hear. That's why we birds never evolved very far, I suppose, despite our considerable intelligence. We have to spend all our time and energy watching what we think, and so we can never get around to using our brains for anything useful. You humans only have to watch what you say. You're lucky."

"Where was I?"

"Listening to the radio."

"Oh, yes."

This entire conversation had taken up the time between the second and third pips of the Greenwich time signal. Malcolm, whose mind had grown used to working at a faster speed, found the wait for the next pip unendurably dull, as whole seconds of inactivity ticked by. When the newsreader started speaking, her words were at first almost incomprehensible, like a recording slowed right down.

The announcer seemed rather harassed, for her beautiful BBC voice was distinctly strained as she went through the catalogue of natural and man-made disasters that had struck the planet since about one o'clock that morning.

"When you killed the Giant," said the pigeon.

There had been earthquakes all across North and South America, a volcano had erupted in Italy, and a swarm of locusts bigger than any previously recorded had formed over North Africa. Seven Governments had been violently overthrown, the delicate peace negotiations in the Middle East had collapsed, the United States had broken off diplomatic relations with China, and England had lost the First Test by an inning and thirty-two runs.

"That's awful," said Malcolm. aloud.

"Listen," urged the pigeon.

Amazingly enough, said the announcer (and her voice palpably

quavered) in all these disasters nobody had been killed or even seriously injured, anywhere in the world, although the damage to property had been incalculable. Meanwhile, at London Zoo Za-Za the Giant
Panda...

Malcolm dismissed the voice from his mind. "So what's going on?"

The pigeon was silent and its mind was blank. "Is it my fault?"
Malcolm demanded impatiently. "Did I do all that?"

"No, not exactly. In fact, I would say it was sort of a tribute to
your integrity, like."

"My what?"

"Integrity. You see, because of the curse Alberich put on it, the
Ring can't help causing destruction. Every day it continues to exist, it
exercises power on the world, and unless this power is channelled
deliberately into positive and constructive things, which is impossible
anyway, it just sort of crashes about, causing damage and breaking
things."

"What sort of things?"

"The earth's crust. Governments. You name it. Why do you think
the world's been such a horrible place for the last thousand years? Ingolf
couldn't care less what happened to the world so long as he was all
right, and over the past century and a bit, when his temper wasn't
improved by perpetual toothache, he actively encouraged the Ring by
thinking unpleasant thoughts. Hence wars, progress and all the rest of
it."

Malcolm shook his head in disbelief. "But...but what about the
Gods, then? I mean, I've only just found out they exist. What do they
do?"

"What they like, mostly. Wotan—he's the only one who matters—
is omnipotent; well, omnipotent up to a point. The only thing he can't
compete with is the Ring, which is far more powerful than he is. That's
why he wants it so badly. But it doesn't really interfere with his being
all-powerful. You see, no-one can control the Ring, or make it do what
they want it to. That's the point..."

The pigeon's thought tailed off into the blank. Something had
obviously occurred to it that it could not even put into thoughts, let
alone words. It made an effort and continued.

"Needless to say," said the pigeon, "when the Ring changes hands,
it gets very temperamental. Nobody likes being killed, and all the bad
vibes that went through Ingolf's mind as he died last night won't have
made things any better. You see, bad thoughts give the Ring something to get its teeth into. Hence all those earthquakes."

Once again, the pigeon's thoughts tailed away. It walked round the table, pecked at a Biro, and then stopped dead in its tracks.

"And nobody got killed," it said. "That's strange, don't you think? Did you put the Ring on straight away?"

"Yes."

"I don't know if this is even possible, but maybe you *were* controlling the Ring in some way or other, stopping it from actually killing anyone. God knows how. I mean, even Siegfried couldn't control it, and he was much more..."

"I know, so everyone keeps telling me."

"Anyway, he couldn't stop the curse, although he was probably the only one so far who had the potential—he was Wotan's grandson, but no longer in his power. But perhaps it's not the curse... Anyway, he couldn't do a thing with it. And look at you..."

"In that case," said Malcolm, "all I have to do to end this whole curse business and make the world safe, all I have to do is throw the Ring back into the Rhine. It was the Rhine, wasn't it?"

The pigeon flapped its wings and flew round the room to relieve its feelings. It didn't work.

"Idiot!" it shouted. "You haven't been listening to a word I've thought, have you? That's the worst possible thing you could do."

"But it said in the book: The waters of the Rhine will wash away Alberich's curse."

"How quaintly you put it, I'm sure. You haven't grasped the point I've been trying to make. The curse isn't like that. In fact... Sorry." The pigeon fluttered up from the table and perched forgivingly on Malcolm's head. "I forgot, you aren't used to reading thoughts. Only it's just occurred to me that the curse is nothing to do with it. It's just a curse, that's all. It just brings all the owners of the Ring to a horrible and untimely death. But the Ring was powerful *before* Alberich put the curse on it. If you were to throw the Ring into the Rhine..."

"Would you please stop pecking at my head?"

"Sorry. It's instinct, I'm afraid. We birds are martyrs to instinct. Where was I? If you were to throw the Ring into the Rhine, there's no guarantee that the Rhinedaughters would be able to control its nasty habits any more than Ingolf could. And even if they could and they wanted to, they can't be expected to be able to guard it properly against the bad guys—Wotan and Alberich and that lot. Let alone any new contenders. They have no power, you see, they can only offer an alternative."

"What alternative?"

"Think about it." The pigeon chuckled. "In the Dark Ages, of course, it was inconceivable that anyone would prefer unlimited wealth to a bit of fun with a pretty Rhinedaughter—that's what all that stuff about forswearing Love was about—but that was a thousand years ago. What could you buy a thousand years ago that was worth having? The ultimate in consumer goods was a rowing-boat or a goatskin hat, and the ideal home was a damp log cabin with no chimney. These days, everything has changed. These days, most people would forswear Love for a new washing-machine, let alone the entire world. No, if you throw the Ring into the Rhine, you'll make everything much worse."

Malcolm buried his head in his hands, causing the pigeon to lose its balance. "Watch out," it said.

"But Wagner said..."

"Forget Wagner, this is real life."

"Where did he get the story from, by the way?"

"A little bird told him."

Malcolm sat for a moment in silence, while the pigeon tried to eat his diary.

"This is terrible," he said at last. "Now I'm going to be personally responsible for every catastrophe in the world. And I thought it was only my mother who blamed me for everything."

"Not necessarily," said the pigeon, soothingly. "Perhaps—I say per-haps—you can stop all these terrible things from happening. Don't ask me how, but you stopped I don't know how many people from being killed today."

"Did I?"

"Well, if you didn't, then who the hell did? Let me put it to you this way." The pigeon buried its beak in its feathers and thought hard for a moment. "By and large, all things considered, you wouldn't ac-tually want to kill anyone, now would you?"

"No," replied Malcolm, "certainly not."

"But when you hear about disasters in other countries, it doesn't spoil your day. You think, Hard luck, poor devils, but you don't burst out crying all over the place."

"True."

"Whereas a disaster in this country would affect you rather more deeply, wouldn't it?"

"Yes, I suppose it would."

"That follows. All these disasters, you see, happened abroad. The only bit of local disaster was that England lost a cricket match, and the way things are nowadays, that would probably have happened anyway. I remember when I was feeding in the outfield at Edgbaston in nineteen fifty-six..."

"Get on with it," said Malcolm irritably.

"The way I see it," said the pigeon, picking up a crumb of stale cheese it had previously overlooked, "the Ring is being guided by your will. A certain number of momentous things have to happen when the Ring changes hands. It's like a volcano: all that force and violence has to go somewhere. But your will protected Britain..."

"Do you mind not using that word? It makes it sound like my last will and testament."

"All right then, you protected Britain, because you care more about it than about other countries. All subconsciously, of course. And you refused to let the Ring kill anybody, because you instinctively don't approve of people being killed. When you think about it, that's pretty remarkable. Have you got any more of that cheese anywhere?"

Malcolm was rather taken aback. "You mean I really can make the world do what I want?"

"Not in the way you think. The Ring won't take orders from your *conscious* mind. But you can prevent it from destroying the world, if you're sufficiently strong-minded."

"But that can't be right."

"It does seem odd, I agree. After all, Wotan couldn't do it. Fafner couldn't do it. Even Siegfried couldn't do it and he was much more..."

"Siegfried was an idiot. Or did Wagner get that wrong, too?"

"Yes, he did. Siegfried wasn't an idiot, not by a long way. He just didn't know what was going on. But then, neither did you." The pigeon fell silent again.

"How come I can't read your thoughts?" Malcolm asked. "You've done this two or three times now."

"I'm not so much thinking as communing."

"What with?"

"How should I know?" snapped the pigeon in a sudden flurry of bad temper. "Mother Earth, I've always assumed. Go on, you try it."

Malcolm tried it, opening his mind to everything in the world. There was a perfectly horrible noise and he switched it off. "Nothing," he said, "just a lot of voices."

"Oh," said the pigeon, and Malcolm could sense unease, even awe, in its thoughts. "Oh, I *see.*"

"You mean it's me you're communing with?" Malcolm was so amazed that he turned himself into a stone without intending to.

"That's the way it's looking," said the pigeon. "Sir," it added.

"Go ahead," said Malcolm bitterly. "You and my Immortal Soul have a nice chat, don't mind me."

"I'm sorry," said the pigeon, "I suppose it must be very frustrating for you, especially since it's so good, you'd enjoy it if you could hear it, you really would."

"What did it say last?"

"Well, it suggested that you may not be wise or noble or fearless or brave or cunning or anything like that..."

"That sounds like me talking."

"...But you're probably the only *nice* person in history to own the wretched thing."

"Nice?"

"Nice."

"You really think I'm nice?" said Malcolm, blushing.

"Where I come from," said the pigeon, "that's not a compliment. Anyway, I didn't say it, you did, only you couldn't hear yourself think. But if by nice you mean decent, inoffensive, wouldn't hurt a fly, yes, I think you probably are. And all the other Ring-Bearers have been right bastards in one way or another."

"Even Siegfried?"

"Siegfried had a wicked temper. If his porridge wasn't just right, he'd throw it all round the hall."

Malcolm rubbed his eyes. "And my niceness is going to save the world, is it?"

"Could do, who knows? Just try saying to yourself over and over again, I don't want anything bad to happen to anyone anywhere to-day. See if that makes any difference." The pigeon turned its head and looked at the sun, which was starting to shine with the evening light. "Time I was on my way," it said. "There's a field of oilseed rape out there I want to look in on as I go home. They've got one of those machines that go bang every ten minutes, but who cares? I like it round here. Always wanted to retire to the seaside."

"So that's it, is it? Think nice thoughts?"

"Try it. If it doesn't work, try something else. Well, take care, won't you? It's been a privilege meeting you, I suppose. But watch out for the Gods and the Volsungs for a while. They'll be after you by now."

"Can they read thoughts too?"

"No, but Wotan has a couple of clever ravens. I don't think they can find you easily, though. The Tarnhelm masks your thoughts, except at very short range, and the world's a very big place. You've got the advantage, having the Tarnhelm. But if I were you, I'd be a bit more discreet in future. It's not clever to go around looking like people who have been dead for a thousand years."

"You mean Theseus?"

"Who's that? No, I mean Siegfried. And Brunnhilde, come to that."
The pigeon flapped its wings, said, "Thanks for the crumbs," and was
gone.

For a moment, Malcolm did not understand what the pigeon had
said about Siegfried and... He had only turned himself into one female character today. He stood in front of the mirror.

"Quick," he ordered, "Siegfried, then Brunnhilde."

Once again, the images of the Most Handsome Man and the Most
Beautiful Woman flashed across the glass. He sat down on the bed and,
for some reason or other, began to cry.

4

Apotheosis can be rather unnerving. Even the most hardened and cynical Royal visitor to remote islands is taken aback to find the islanders worshipping his framed photograph, and he at least has the consolation of knowing that he isn't really a God. Malcolm had no such consolation as he faced up to the fact that his mind controlled the world.

"If only," he kept on saying to himself, "Mr. Scanlon knew." Mr. Scanlon had tried to teach him Physics at school, and if his assessment of Malcolm's mental capacities had been correct, the world was in deep trouble. For his part, Malcolm had always been inclined to share his teacher's opinion; certainly, the weight of the evidence had always seemed to be on Mr. Scanlon's side. Nevertheless, it was necessary to make the best of a bad job. Malcolm now had literally no-one to blame but himself, and the Daily Service on the radio seemed to be directly addressed to him. Especially one line, which Malcolm took it upon himself to paraphrase slightly:

"For there is none other that fighteth for us, but only thou. Oh, *God!*"

But the news from the outside world gave him grounds for cautious optimism. The disasters that had marked his accession cleared themselves up with embarrassing speed. The United Nations, for example, held a special session in New York and unanimously voted to levy an unprecedented contribution from all its members to relieve the suffering of the victims of the catastrophe. The various coups and revolutions resolved themselves into benign democracies as if that had been their intention all along. Peace negotiations in the Middle East were resumed, America and China started playing each other at ping-pong again, and the swarm of locusts was devoured by a huge flock of migrating birds. Admittedly, England lost the Second Test as well, but Malcolm knew that he could not be expected to work miracles. The only disaster that had been reported was the destruction by volcanic forces of a small, uninhabited atoll in the middle of the Pacific Ocean; and even that had its good side, as the residents of the neighbouring

atoll had always complained that it was an eyesore and spoilt their view
of the sunset.

It needed no ghost come from the grave, and no visitation of pro-
phetic birds to tell Malcolm that this was all the result of being nice.
He had rigorously excluded from his mind all unpleasant, spiteful or
angry thoughts for the best part of a fortnight (the strain was beginning to show), and the result had been a quite unparalleled upturn in
the fortunes of the human race. "And all that," Malcolm reflected smugly, "was me."

But it was extremely frustrating to have to keep all this to oneself.
Malcolm had never achieved anything before, except third prize in a
village flower show when he was nine (three people had entered that
particular category), and the wish to be congratulated was very strong.
His sister, for example, had achieved many things, but she had never
stopped a war or disposed of a swarm of locusts. But the Ring seemed
to cut him off from the rest of the human race. Although he was the
master of the Tarnhelm, he scarcely went out at all. This was partly
laziness, partly caution; for if he was to remain nice and keep his mind
free of malice or resentment, it would not be advisable for him to see
any of his friends or relatives. He was also beginning to feel extremely
hungry. All the food lying about the flat (some of which had been there
for a considerable time) was long since finished, he had no money left,
and he could see little prospect of getting any more. Even if his job
still existed (and after two weeks' unexplained absence, that seemed
unlikely) he knew that for the sake of mankind he could not go back
to it. One cannot work as a clerk in a provincial auction room without
entertaining some fairly dark thoughts, any one of which, given his
present position, could blot out a major city. The obvious alternative—
theft, using the power of the Tarnhelm—was open to the same objection. If he were to start stealing things, who could tell what the consequences might be?

He contemplated the problem, turning himself into Aristotle in
the hope that the transformation might assist his powers of reasoning.
During the past two weeks, metamorphosis had been virtually his only
occupation, and had kept him moderately amused. He had always
rather wanted to know what various characters from history and fiction really looked like, especially the girls described by the poets. He
also took the trouble to assume the shapes of all his likely assailants—
Wotan and Alberich and Loge—so as to be able to recognise them
instantly, and had frightened himself half to death in the process.

The outward shape of Aristotle seemed to inspire him, and he went
through the various ways in which he could sell gold for money with-

out actually getting involved himself. Having dismissed the notion of putting an advertisement in the Classified section of the *Quantock Gazette*, he hit upon what seemed to be an acceptable notion. Armed with a large suitcase, he commanded the Tarnhelm to take him to some uninhabited vault in the Bank of England where he might find plenty of used banknotes. On arrival, he filled the suitcase (more of a small trunk) with ten- and twenty-pound notes, then started to materialise gold to a roughly equivalent value. By the time he had finished, his forehead was quite sore with rubbing and the floor of the vault was covered in exquisite treasures. He removed himself and the suitcase and tried the equivalent banks in France, America, Australia and other leading countries (for it would be unfair if only one or two countries suddenly found themselves linked to the gold standard). With the immense wealth he gathered in this way, he opened a large number of bank accounts in various names—a terrifying business, full of unforeseen complications—and bought himself the house he had always wanted, a huge and extremely attractive manor house near Taunton, which happened to be for sale.

As he had anticipated, no mention was made by any of the financial institutions with which he had done business of the sudden disappearance of large sums of money or the equally unexpected appearance of a fortune in gold. The price of the metal fluctuated wildly for a day or so, then went considerably higher than it had been for some time. Intrigued, Malcolm revisited his favourite banks, invisible and carrying two suitcases. All the gold had gone, and there were plenty more banknotes, neatly packaged up for ease of transportation. In the national bank of Australia there was even a piece of card with "Thanks; Please Call Again" written on it, propped up on a shelf.

Now that he was a multi-millionaire on both sides of the Iron Curtain, Malcolm turned his attention to furnishing his new house. It seemed likely that he would have to spend a great deal of time in it, on his own, and since money was no object, he decided to have the very best of everything. It was obvious that he could not risk appearing there in his own shape—what would Malcolm Fisher be doing buying Combe Hall?—and so he designed for himself a new persona to go with his new life. In doing so, he made a terrible mistake; but by the time he realised what he had done, it was too late.

It was simple carelessness on his part that caused the trouble. He had been so excited at the prospect of owning Combe Hall that he had gone to the estate agents who were handling the sale in his own shape. He was shown into an office and asked to wait while the senior partner came down to see him, and as the door opened to admit this gentleman, Malcolm caught sight of his own, original face in the mirror and realised his mistake. He commanded the Tarnhelm to change him into someone else, but did not have time to specify who. To his horror, he saw that the face in the mirror was that of the Most Handsome Man; but the estate agent had seen him now, so he could not change into anything less conspicuous. He had stuck like it, just as his mother had warned him he would.

Thus it was that Malcolm found himself condemned to embark on his new life with the face and body of Siegfried the Dragon-Slayer, also known as the Most Handsome Man. He could not help remembering the pigeon's warning about this, but it was too late now. Not that Malcolm objected in principle to being the most handsome man who had ever lived; but the sight of ravens (or crows, or blackbirds; he was no ornithologist) filled him with horror.

Meanwhile, he fleshed out his new character and by deviousness and contrivance of which he had not thought himself capable acquired the necessary documents and paperwork. In order to give his new self a history (multi-millionaires do not simply appear from nowhere) he had to Tarnhelm himself at dead of night into the computer rooms of half the public records offices in the country, and since he knew next to nothing about twentieth-century machines, he accidentally erased the life histories of several hundred people before getting the result he wanted. Finally, however, he ended up with everything he needed to be Herr Manfred Finger of Düsseldorf, the name and identity he had chosen. Again, the German aspect was ill-advised and unintentional; he had wanted to be a foreigner of some sort (since in Somerset it is understood that all foreigners are mad, and allowances for eccentric or unusual behaviour are made accordingly) and had chosen a country at random. That he should have chosen Germany was either yet more carelessness or else the Ring trying to get its own back on him for making it do good in the world. He was not sure which, but was inclined to the first explanation, as being more in keeping with his own nature.

Herr Finger was soon familiar to all the inhabitants of Combe, who were naturally curious to know more about their new neighbour. As local custom demanded, they soon found a nickname for the new Lord of the Manor. The various members of the Booth family who had owned the Hall from the early Tudor period onwards had all been known by a variety of affectionate epithets—Mad Jack, or Drunken George—and the periphrasis bestowed on Malcolm was "that rich foreign bastard." Such familiarity did not, however, imply acceptance. Although it was generally admitted that Herr Finger was not too bad on the surface and no worse than the last of the Booths (Sir William, or Daft Billy), it went without saying that there was something wrong about him. He was, it was agreed, a criminal of some sort; but whether he was an illegal arms dealer or a drug smuggler, the sages of Combe could not be certain. The only thing on which everyone was unanimous was that he had murdered his wife. After all, none of them had ever seen her in the village...

"And what time," said Wotan, "do you call this?"

Loge, his hands covered in oil, climbed wearily off his motorcycle and removed his helmet. "It broke down again," he said. "Just outside Wuppertal. Plugs."

Wotan shook his head sadly. Admittedly, it had been on his orders that the immortal Gods had traded in their eight-legged horses and chariots drawn by winged cats for forms of transport more suited to the twentieth century, but he expected his subordinates to be both punctual and properly turned out. Cleanliness, he was fond of asserting, is next to godliness.

"Well, you're here now," he said. "So what do you make of *that?*"

Loge looked about him. There was nothing to see except cornfields. He said so.

"Well done," growled Wotan. "We are unusually observant this morning, are we not? And what do you find unusual about the corn in these corn-fields?"

Loge scratched his head, getting oil on his hair. "Dunno," he said. "It looks perfectly normal to me."

"Normal for August?"

"Perfectly."

"It's June."

Loge, who had spent an hour wrestling with a motorcycle engine beside a busy autobahn, did not at first appreciate the significance of this remark. Then the pfennig dropped. "It's two months in advance, you mean?"

"Precisely." Wotan put his arm around Loge's shoulder. "Good, wouldn't you say?"

"I suppose so."

"It's bloody marvellous, considering the weather they've been having this year. And why do you suppose the crops are doing so very, very well? In fact, why is everything in the world doing so very, very well? Answer me that?"

Loge instinctively looked up at the sky. Thunder-clouds were beginning to form.

"Someone's been interfering?" he suggested.

"Correct!" Wotan shouted, and the first clap of thunder came in, dead on cue. "Someone's been interfering. Now who could that be? Who on earth could be responsible for this new golden age?"

From his tone, Loge guessed that it couldn't have been Wotan himself. Which left only one candidate. "You mean the Ring-Bearer?"

"Very good. The only force in the Universe capable of making things happen so quickly and so thoroughly. But isn't that a trifle strange in itself? Wouldn't you expect the Ring to do nasty things, not nice ones? Left to itself, I mean?"

Loge agreed that he would.

"So you would agree that anyone capable of making the Ring do what it doesn't want to do is likely to be a rather special person?"

Wotan had picked up this irritating habit of asking leading questions from the late and unlamented Socrates. Loge hated it.

"In fact, someone so remarkable that even if he didn't have the Ring he would present a serious danger to our security. And since he does have the Ring..."

Wotan was trembling with rage, and the rain was falling fast, beating down the standing corn. "We have to find him, quickly," he roared. "Otherwise, we are in grave danger. To be precise, *you* have to find him. Do you understand?"

Loge understood, but Wotan wanted to make his point. "And if I were you, my friend, I would spare no effort in looking for him. I would leave no stone unturned and no avenue unexplored. And do you know why? Because if you don't, you might very well find yourself spending the rest of Eternity as a waterfall. You wouldn't like that, now would you?"

Loge agreed that he wouldn't, and Wotan was about to develop this theme further when it stopped raining. The clouds dispersed, and the sun shone brightly, pitching a vivid rainbow across the blue sky.

"Who said you could stop raining?" screamed Wotan. "I want lightning. Now!"

The sky took no notice, and Loge went white with fear. Everyone has his own particular phobia, and Loge was terrified of fish. As a waterfall, he would have salmon jumping up him all day long. He would have prayed for rain if he wasn't a God himself. But the sky remained cloudless.

"That does it!" Wotan smashed his fist into the palm of his left hand. "When I'm not even allowed to rain my own rain because it damages the crops, it's time for positive action." He stood still for a moment, then turned to Loge.

"Are you still here?" he asked savagely.

"I'm on my way," Loge replied, jumping desperately on the kick-start of his motorcycle. "I'll find him, don't you worry."

Loge sped off into the distance, and Wotan was left alone, staring angrily at the sun. Two coal-black ravens floated down and settled on the fence.

"Nice weather we're having," said Thought.

For some reason, this did not go down well. "Any result?" Wotan snapped.

"Nothing so far, boss," said Memory.

"Where have you been looking?"

"Everywhere, boss. But you know we can't find the Ring-Bearer. We can't see him, or read his thoughts, or anything like that."

"God give me strength!" Wotan clenched his fist and made an effort to relax. "Then what you do, you stupid bird, is go through all the people of the world, one by one, and when you find one whose thoughts you can't read and who you can't see, that's him. I'd have thought that was obvious."

Thought looked at Memory. Memory looked at Thought.

"But that'll take weeks, boss," said Memory.

"So what else were you planning to do?"

The two ravens flapped their wings and launched themselves into the air. They circled for a moment, then floated over the world. All day they flew, sweeping in wide circles across the continents, until Memory suddenly swooped down and landed beside the banks of the Rhine.

"Stuff this," he said to Thought. "Why don't we ask the girls?"

"Good idea," said Memory. "Wish I'd thought of that."

"It must have slipped your mind." The two birds took off again, but this time they flew only a mile or so, to a spot where, about a thousand years ago, a certain Alberich had stopped and watched three beautiful women swimming in the river. The ravens landed in a withered tree and folded their wings.

Under the tree, three young girls were sunbathing, and for them the Sun Goddess had saved the best of the evening light, for she was their friend.

"Flosshilde," said one of the girls, "there's a raven in that tree looking at you."

"I hope he likes what he sees," replied the Rhinedaughter lazily.

Wellgunde, the eldest and most serious of the three, rolled onto her stomach and lifted her designer sunglasses.

"Hello, Thought," she said, "hello, Memory. Found him yet, then?"

The ravens were silent, ruffling their coarse feathers with their beaks, and the girls giggled.

"But you've been looking for simply ages," said Woglinde, the youngest and most frivolous of the three. "It must be *somewhere.*"

"I'm always losing things," said Flosshilde. "Where do you last remember seeing it?"

"You sure it's not in your pocket?"

"You've put it somewhere safe and you can't remember where?"

Wotan's ravens had been putting up with this sort of thing for a thousand years, but it still irritated them. The girls laughed again, and Memory blushed under his feathers.

"If you don't find him soon," yawned Flosshilde, combing her long, golden hair, "he'll slip through your claws, just like clever old Ingolf did. By the way, fancy Ingolf being a badger!"

"He'll get the hang of the Tarnhelm and then no-one will ever find him," purred Woglinde. "What a shame that would be."

"Good luck to him," said Wellgunde. "Who wants the boring old Ring, anyway?"

"Dunno what you're being so bloody funny about," said Memory. "Supposed to be your Ring we're looking for."

"Forget it," said Woglinde, waving her slender arms. "It's a lovely day, the sun is shining, the crops are growing..."

Memory winced at this. Flosshilde giggled.

"...And it's been so long since Alberich took the beastly thing that we don't really care any more, do we?" Woglinde wiggled her toes attractively, in a way that had suggested something far nicer than measureless wealth for thousands of years. "What do we want with gold when we have you to entertain us?"

"Save it for the human beings," said Memory.

"I wonder what he looks like," said Wellgunde. "I bet you he's handsome."

"And strong."

"And noble. Don't forget noble."

"I never could resist noble," said Woglinde, watching the ravens carefully under her beautiful eyelashes.

"We came to tell you that we'd heard something," said Thought. "But since you're not interested any more..."

Wellgunde yawned, putting her hand daintily in front of her mouth. "You're right," she said. "We're not." She turned over onto her back and picked up a magazine.

"Something interesting, we've heard," said Memory.

"Oh, all right," said Flosshilde, smiling her most dazzling smile. "Tell us if you must."

Even Wotan's ravens, who are (firstly) immortal and (secondly) birds, cannot do much against the smiles of Rhinedaughters. But since Memory was bluffing, there was nothing for him to do.

"I didn't say we were going to tell you what we'd heard," he said, archly, "only that we'd heard it." It is not easy for a raven to be arch, but Memory had been practising.

"Oh go away," said Flosshilde, throwing a piece of orange peel at the two messengers. "You're teasing us, as usual."

"You wait and see," said Memory, lamely, but the three girls jumped up and dived into the water, as elegantly as the very best dolphins.

"We know something you don't know," chanted Flosshilde, and the Sun-Goddess made the water sparkle around her floating hair. Then she disappeared, leaving behind only a stream of silver bubbles.

"I dunno," said Thought. "Women."

The ravens flapped their heavy wings, circled morosely for a while, and flew away.

By a strange coincidence, a few moments after Flosshilde dived down to the bed of the Rhine, three identical girls hopped out of the muddy, fetid waters of the River Tone, at the point where it runs through the centre of Taunton. A few passers-by stopped and stared, for the three girls were far cleaner than anyone who had recently had anything to do with the Tone has any right to be. But the girls' smiles wiped such thoughts from their minds, and they went on their way whistling and wishing that they were twenty years younger. Had they realised that what they had just seen were the three Rhinedaughters, Flosshilde, Wellgunde and Woglinde, they might perhaps have taken a little more notice.

5

One of the things that slightly worried Malcolm was the fact that he was becoming decidedly middle-aged. For example, the ritualised drinking of afternoon tea had come to mean a lot to him, not simply because it disposed of an hour's worth of daylight. He had chosen half-past four in the afternoon as the best time for reading the daily papers, and from half-past four to half-past five (occasionally a quarter to six) each day he almost made himself feel that he enjoyed being extremely nice and bored stiff, for he knew that all the good news that filled the papers was, in one way or another, his doing.

Today, there was any amount of good news from around the world. Malcolm could sense the frustration and despair of the editors and journalists as they forced themselves to report yet more bumper harvests, international accords and miraculous cures. Admittedly, there had been a freak storm in Germany (banner headlines in the tabloids) and some crops had been damaged in a few remote areas. Nevertheless, he noted with satisfaction, this minor disaster was not entirely a bad thing, since it had prompted the EEC to draft and sign a new agreement on compensating farmers for damage caused by acts of God. So every cloud, however small, had a silver lining, although these days it was beginning to look as though only a very few silver linings had clouds.

Malcolm tried to work out what could have caused the freak storm in the first place. He picked up the *Daily Mirror* ("German farmers in rain horror") and observed that the storm had started at three o'clock their time, which was two o'clock our time, which was when Malcolm's new secretary had finally managed to corner him and force him to sign five letters. He resolved to be more patient with her in future, and not call her a whatsisname under his breath.

His tea was stone cold, but that didn't matter; it was, after all, Only Him. That was a marvellous phrase, and one that he had come to treasure. When one has suddenly been forced into the role of the Man of Sorrows, self-pity is the only luxury that remains. In fact, Malcolm had no objection whatsoever to taking away the sins of the world, but it was useful to keep an option on self-pity just in case it came in useful later. He poured the cold tea onto the lawn and watched it soak into the ground. In the crab-apple tree behind him, a robin perched and sang excitedly, but he ignored it, closing his mind to its persistent chirping. He had found that the little birds liked to come up to him and confide their secrets that they could not share with other birds, and at first he had found this extremely flattering. But since the majority of these confidences were extremely personal and of interest only to a trained biologist, he had decided that it would be best not to encourage them. After a while, the robin stopped singing and went away. Malcolm rose to his feet and walked slowly into the house.

Combe Hall was undoubtedly very beautiful, but it was also very big. It had been built in the days when a house-holder tended to feel claustrophobic if he could not accommodate at least one infantry regiment, including the band, in his country house. Its front pediment was world famous. Its windows had been praised and reviled in countless television series. Its kitchens were enormous and capable of being put to any use except the convenient preparation of food. It was very grand, very magnificent, and very empty.

Malcolm had always fancied living at Combe Hall on the strict understanding that his wish was never to come true. Now that he was its owner and (apart from the legion of staff) its only resident, he felt rather like a bewildered traveller at an international airport. The house was bad enough, but the staff were truly awful. There was no suave, articulate butler and no pretty parlourmaids; instead, Malcolm found himself employing an army of grimly professional contract cleaners and an incomprehensible Puerto Rican cook, whom he was sure he was shamelessly exploiting in some way he could not exactly understand. After a week, Malcolm left them all to it and retreated to one of the upstairs drawing-rooms, which he turned into a nicely squalid bedsit.

As a result, he felt under no obligation to assume the role of country gentleman. With the house had come an enormous park, some rather attractive gardens, into which Malcolm hardly dared go for fear of offending the gardeners, and the Home Farm. Ever since he could remember, Malcolm had listened to the Archers on the radio—not from choice, but because they had always been there in his childhood, and so had become surrogate relatives—and his mental picture of agriculture had been shaped by this influence. But the farm that he owned (now *there* was a thought!) whirred and purred with machines and clicked and ticked with computers, filling its owner with fear and amazement. Yet when he suggested to the farm manager that the whole thing might perhaps be rearranged on more picturesque lines and to hell with the profits, which nobody really needed, the farm manager stared at him as if he were mad. Since then, he had kept well away from it.

But with his new property came certain ineluctable responsibilities, the most arduous of which was coping with his new secretary. On the one hand, the woman was invaluable, for she ran the place and left him alone for most of the time. Without the irritations and petty nuisances of everyday life to contend with, he could keep his temper and make the maize grow tall all over Africa. But for this freedom from care he had to pay a severe price: his secretary, who was American and in her middle forties, had clearly made a resolution to be more English than anyone else in the history of the world. Her convert's passion for all things English gave her the zeal of a missionary, and it was obvious that she intended to Anglicise young Herr Finger if it killed her. And, like many missionaries, she was not above a little persecution in the cause of the communication of Enlightenment.

Apart from avoiding his staff and his secretary and anything else that might tend to irritate or annoy, however, Malcolm found that he had very little to do. Even as a small boy, he had never had a hobby of any kind, and he had always found making friends as difficult as doing jigsaw puzzles, and even less rewarding. As for the comfort and solace of his family, Malcolm knew only too well that that was out of the question. If, by some miracle, he could persuade his kin to believe this ludicrous tale of rings and badgers, he knew without having to think about it what their reaction would be. "Malcolm," his mother would say, "give that ring back to Bridget *this instant*"—the implication being that it had been meant for her all along.

Not that the possibility had not crossed his mind. Surely, he had reflected, his talented and universally praised sister would make a far better job of all this than he would; she had five A-levels and had been to Warwick University. But somehow he felt sure that Bridget was not the right person for the job. For a start, she did not suffer fools gladly, and since a large percentage of the people of the world are fools, it was possible that she might not give them the care and consideration they needed. Throughout its history, Malcolm reflected, the Ring had been in the possession of gifted, talented, exceptional people, and look what had happened...

One morning, when Malcolm was listening (rather proudly) to the morning news, the English Rose, as he had mentally christened her, came hammering on his door. She seemed to have an uncanny knack of knowing where he was.

She informed him that the annual Combe Show was to be held in the grounds of the Hall in a fortnight's time. Malcolm, who loathed all such occasions from the bottom of his heart, tried to protest, but without success.

"Oh, but I've been talking to the folks from the village, and they all say that it's the social event of the year, buzzed the Rose. "It's one of the oldest surviving fairs in the country. According to the records I consulted..."

Malcolm saw that there was no hope of escape. His secretary, apart from having the persistence of a small child in pursuit of chocolate, was an outstanding example of true Ancestor Worship (although it was not her own ancestors that she worshipped; her name was Weinburger) and anything remotely traditional went to her head like wine. In fact, Malcolm was convinced, if she could revive the burning of witches, with all its attendant seventeenth-century pageantry, she probably would.

"But will it not be—how is it in English?—a great nuisance to arrange?" he suggested. That was, of course, the wrong thing to say. The Rose thrived on challenges.

"Herr Finger," she said, looking at him belligerently over the top of her spectacles, "that is not my attitude and well you know it. It will be truly rewarding for me to make all the necessary social arrangements for the proposed event, and Mr. Ayres, who is the Chairman of the Show Committee, will be calling on you to discuss all the practicalities. There will be the usual livestock competition, of course, and I presume that the equestrian events will follow their customary pattern. I had hoped that we might prevail upon the Committee to revive the Jacobean Sheriff's Races, but Mr. Ayres has, at my request, performed a feasibility study and feels that such a revival could not be satisfactorily arranged in the limited space of time left to us before the Show. So I fear that we will have to content ourselves with a gymkhana situation..."

Although Malcolm had acquired the gift of tongues from the blood of the Giant, he still had occasional difficulty in understanding his secretary's English. The name Ayres, however, was immediately recognisable. It was a name he was only too familiar with; indeed, he knew virtually all the words in the language that rhymed with it, for Liz Ayres was the girl he loved. Mr. William Ayres, the Chairman of the Show Committee, was her father, and a nastier piece of work never read a Massey-Ferguson catalogue. But thoughts of malice or resentment were no longer available to Malcolm, and so finally he agreed. The English Rose scuttled away, no doubt to flick through Debrett (after Sir Walter Elliot, she was its most enthusiastic reader) and Malcolm resigned himself to another meeting with possibly his least favourite person in the world.

William Ayres could trace his ancestry back to the early fifteenth century; his namesake had won the respect of his betters at the battle of Agincourt by throwing down his longbow and pulling a fully armed French knight off his horse with his bare hands. The present William Ayres undoubtedly had the physical strength to emulate his ancestor's deed and, given his unbounded ferocity, would probably relish the opportunity to try. So massively built was he that people who met him for the first time often wondered why he bothered with tractors and the like on his sprawling farm at the top of the valley. Surely he could save both time and money by drawing the plough himself, if necessary with his teeth. Compared to his two sons, however, Mr. Ayres was a puny but sunny-tempered dwarf, and Malcolm could at least console himself with the reflection that he would not be confronted with Joe or Mike Ayres at this unpleasant interview.

Malcolm decided that in order to face Mr. Ayres it would be necessary for him to be extremely German, for his antagonist had strong views about rich foreigners who bought up fine old houses in England.

"It's a tremendously important occasion," said Mr. Ayres, "one of the high points of the year in these parts. It's been going on for as long as I can remember, certainly. When Colonel Booth still had the Hall..."

Mr. Ayres was a widower, and Malcolm toyed with the idea of introducing him to the English Rose. They would have so much in common...

"I am most keen on your English traditions, *natürlich*. Let us hope that we can make this a show to be remembered."

Mr. Ayres winced slightly. He disliked the German race, probably because they had thoughtlessly capitulated before he had been old enough to get at them during the War.

"Then perhaps you would care to invite some of the local people to the Hall," he replied. "It would be a splendid opportunity for you to get to know your neighbours."

"Delighted, *das ist sehr gut.*" Mr. Ayres did not like the German language, either. "*Aber*—who shall I invite? I am not yet well acquainted with the local folk."

"Leave that to me," said Mr. Ayres. "I'll send you a list, if you like." He drank his tea brutally—everything he did, he seemed to do brutally. "It should be a good show this year, especially the gymkhana."

"What is gymkhana?" Malcolm asked innocently. "In my country we have no such word."

"So I believe," said Mr. Ayres, who had suspected as much from the start. He did his best to explain, but it was not easy; anyone would have difficulty in explaining such a basic and fundamental concept, just as it would be difficult to explain the sun to a blind man. In the end, he was forced to give up the struggle.

"I'll get my daughter to explain it to you," he said brightly. "She and her fiancé—they haven't announced it yet, but it'll be any day now—I expect they'll be taking part in the main competition. And far be it from me, but I think they're in with a good chance. Well, not Liz perhaps, but young Wilcox—that's her fiancé..."

Malcolm fought hard to retain his composure, and as he struggled, slight earth tremors were recorded in California. For all that he had never expected anything to come of his great love for Elizabeth Ayres, the news that she was soon to be engaged and married made him want to break something. Fortunately for the inhabitants of San Francisco he managed to get a grip on himself.

"Ah, that is good," he said mildly. "So you will make the necessary arrangements with my secretary, yes? So charmed to have met you. *Auf Wiedersehen.*"

"Good day, Mr. Finger." Mr. Ayres stood up, for a moment blotting out the sun, and extended an enormous hand. Malcolm cringed as he met it with his own; he had shaken hands with Mr. Ayres once before, and was convinced that the farmer's awesome grip had broken a small bone somewhere. To his surprise, however, he was able to meet the grip firmly and without serious injury, and he suddenly realised that his arm—the arm of Siegfried the Dragon-Slayer, give or take a bit—was as strong or possibly stronger. This made him feel a little better, but not much.

As soon as Mr. Ayres had gone, Malcolm sat down heavily and relieved his feelings by tearing up a newspaper. They hadn't announced it yet, but it would be any day now. Soon there would be a coy paragraph in the local paper, followed by a ceremony at the beautiful church with the possibly Saxon font: then a reception at the Blue Boar—the car park full of Range-Rovers, champagne flowing freely (just this once) and minced-up fish on tiny biscuits—and so the line of the bowman of Agincourt would force its way on into the twenty-first century.

Fortune, Malcolm suddenly remembered, can make vile things

precious. Like all her family, Liz was obsessed with horses. It might yet be a gymkhana to remember.

When the day came the drive to Combe Hall resembled a plush armoured column, so crowded was it with luxury four-wheel-drive vehicles. Large women in hats and large men in blazers, most of whom Malcolm had last seen making nuisances of themselves at the auction rooms in Taunton, strolled through the garden, apparently oblivious of the scowls of the gardeners, or peered through the windows of the house to see what atrocities its new, foreign owner had perpetrated. Malcolm, dressed impeccably and entirely unsuitably in a dark grey suit and crocodile shoes (courtesy of the Tarnhelm; Vorsprung durch Technik, as they say on the Rhine) was making the best job he could of being the shy, charming host, while the English Rose was having the time of her life introducing him to the local gentry. He had provided (rather generously, he thought) a cold collation on the lawn for all the guests on Mr. Ayres' list, which they had devoured down to the last sprig of parsley, apparently unaware of the maxim that there is no free lunch.

When the last strand of flesh had been stripped off the last chicken leg, the guests swept like a tweed river into the Park, where the Show was in full swing. A talentless band made up of nasty old men and surly children was playing loudly, but not loudly enough to drown the high-pitched gabble of the Quality, as deafening and intimidating as the buzzing of angry bees. There were innumerable overweight farm animals in pens, inane sideshows, vintage traction engines, and a flock of sheep, who politely but firmly ignored the efforts of a number of sheepdogs to make them do illogical things. All as it should be, of course, and the centrepiece of this idyll was the show-jumping.

As he surveyed his gentry-mottled grounds, Malcolm was ambushed by the Ayres clan: William, Michael, Joseph, and, of course, Elizabeth. He was introduced to the two terrifying brothers, who rarely made any sound in the presence of their father, and to the daughter of the family. A beautiful girl, Miss Ayres; about five feet three, light brown hair, very blue eyes and a smile you could read small print by. Malcolm, whose mind controlled the world, smiled back, displaying the Dragon-Slayer's geometrically perfect teeth. The two brightest smiles in the world, more dazzling than any toothpaste advertisement, and all this for politeness' sake. Malcolm managed to stop himself shouting, "Look, Liz, it's me, only much better-looking," and listened attentively as the girl he loved desperately in his nebulous but wholehearted way explained to him, as by rote, the principles of the gymkhana. To this explanation Malcolm did not listen, for he was using the power he had gained by drinking Giant's blood to read her thoughts. It was easily done and, with the exception of one or two of his school reports, Malcolm had never read anything so discouraging. For although the Tarnhelm had made him the most handsome man in the world, it was evident that Miss Ayres did not judge by appearances. For Liz was wondering who this boring foreigner reminded her of. Now, who was it? Ah, yes. That Malcolm Fisher...

He smiled, wished the family good luck in the arena, and walked swiftly away. When he was sure no-one was watching, he turned himself into an apple tree and stood for a moment in one of his own hedges, secure in the knowledge that apple trees cannot weep. But even apple trees can have malicious thoughts (ask any botanist) and if the consequences for the world were unfortunate, then so be it. One of Malcolm's few remaining illusions had been shattered: he had always believed that his total lack of attractiveness to the opposite sex was due simply to his unprepossessing appearance, a shortcoming (as he argued) that was in no respect his fault, so that his failure in this field of human endeavour reflected badly not on him but on those who chose to make such shallow and superficial judgements.

The natural consequence of the destruction of this illusion was that Malcolm wanted very much to do something nasty and spiteful, and he wanted to do it to Philip Wilcox, preferably in front of a large number of malicious people. He shrugged his branches, dislodging a blackbird, and resumed his human shape.

Thanks to the blood of the Giant Ingolf, Malcolm could understand all languages and forms of speech, even the curious noises coming out of the tannoy. The competitors in the main event were being asked to assemble in the collecting ring. With the firm intention of turning himself into a horse-fly and stinging Philip Wilcox's horse at an appropriate moment, Malcolm made his way over to the arcade of horseboxes that formed a temporary mews under the shade of a little copse in the west corner of the Park. He recognised the Wilcox family horsebox, which was drawn up at the end of the row. There was the horse, just standing there.

An idea, sent no doubt by the Lord of the Flies, suddenly came into Malcolm's mind. How would it be if...? No-one was watching; the attention of the whole world seemed to be focused on a fat child in jodhpurs and his long-suffering pony. Malcolm made himself invisible, and with extreme apprehension (for he was terrified of horses) he led Philip Wilcox's steed out of its box and into the depths of the tangled copse, where he tied it securely to a tree. Then, with his nails pressed hard into the palms of his hands, he changed himself into an exact copy of the animal and transported himself back to the horsebox. This would be hard work, but never mind.

"And have you met the new owner?" asked Aunt Marjorie, settling herself comfortably on a straw bale. "I never thought I'd live to see the day when a foreigner..."

"Just for a few minutes," replied Liz Ayres. She had learnt over the years the art of separating the questions from the comments in her aunt's conversation, and slipping in answers to them during pauses for breath and other interruptions.

"What's he like? The trouble with most Germans..."

"I don't know. He seemed pleasant enough, in a gormless sort of way, but I only said a few words to him."

"Well, I suppose we should all be very grateful to him for letting us put a water-jump in the middle of his Park, not that I imagine he minds anyway, or he wouldn't have. Colonel Booth never let us have one, but he was just plain difficult at times. I remember..."

"I don't think he's terribly interested in the Hall, actually." Liz wondered if Aunt Marjorie had ever finished a sentence of her own free will in her life. Probably not. "I'm told he doesn't *do* anything, just stays indoors all day. Daddy said...oh look, there's Joe."

Elizabeth Ayres' loyalties were sadly divided in the jump-off for the main event, since the two competitors most likely to win it were her brother Joe and her fiancé. Joe was the better rider, but Philip's horse seemed to have found remarkable form just at the right moment. Only last week, Philip had been talking of selling it; perhaps it had been listening (at times, they seem almost human) for today it was sailing over the jumps like a Harrier. Even Aunt Marjorie, who in matters of showjumping was a firm believer in entropy, had admitted that the animal wasn't too bad.

"My money's on your boyfriend," said Aunt Marjorie. "What's that horse of his called? It's playing a blinder today. Almost as if it *understood.*"

She had a point. Intelligence, so Philip had always maintained, had never been one of old Mayfair's attributes. Any animal capable of taking a paper bag or a rusting Mini for a pack of wolves and acting accordingly was unlikely ever to win Mastermind, and this lack of mental as opposed to physical agility had prompted one of Philip's brightest sayings. Even if you led Mayfair to water, he would say, it probably wouldn't even occur to him to drink. But today, Mayfair hadn't put a foot wrong, in any sense.

"Mr. Joseph Ayres and Moonbeam," said the tannoy. A hush fell over the crowd, for it seemed wrong that Joe should be riding the horse instead of the other way round. Joe was obviously the stronger of the two, just as Moonbeam was clearly the more intelligent. Aunt Marjorie, who was, like so many of her class, a sort of refined Centaur, leaned forward and fixed her round, bright eyes on horse and rider. "Look at his knees," she muttered. "Just *look* at them."

Joe did his best, but the consensus of opinion was that his best was not going to be good enough. "Twelve faults," said the tannoy, and Aunt Marjorie shook her head sadly. "Why wasn't the idiot using a martingale?" she said. "When I was a girl..."

"Excuse me," said one of the three rather pretty girls who had just made their way to the front. "You obviously know all about this sort of thing. Could you tell us what's going on? We're terribly ignorant about horse-racing."

"It isn't racing, it's jumping," said Aunt Marjorie, not looking round.

"Oh," said the youngest of the three girls. "Oh I *see.*"

"Haven't you been to a show before?" Liz asked, kindly.

"No," chorused the girls, and this was true. There are no shows and very few gymkhanas at the bottom of the River Rhine, where these three girls, the Rhinedaughters Flosshilde, Wellgunde, and Woglinde, had spent the last two thousand years. They have trout races, but that is not quite the same.

"Well," said Aunt Marjorie patiently, as if explaining to a Trobriand Islander how to use a fork, "the idea is to make the horse jump over all the obstacles."

"Why?" asked Flosshilde. Woglinde scowled at her.

"Because if you don't, you get faults," said Aunt Marjorie, "and if you get more faults than everyone else, you lose."

"That explains a great deal," said Flosshilde, brightly. "Thank you."

"Mr. Philip Wilcox on Mayfair," said the tannoy.

Aunt Marjorie turned to the Rhinemaidens, who were amusing themselves by making atrocious puns on the word "fault." "Watch this," she urged them. "He's very good."

The Rhinedaughters put on their most serious expressions (which were not very serious, in absolute terms) and paid the strictest attention as Philip Wilcox and his tired but determined horse entered the ring. As the horse went past her, Flosshilde suddenly started forward, but Wellgunde nudged her and she composed herself.

"You see," said Aunt Marjorie, "he's building up his speed nicely, he's timed it just right, and—oh."

"Why's he stopped?" asked Woglinde. "I thought you said he was going to jump over that fence thing."

Aunt Marjorie, raising her voice above the gasps and whispers of the spectators, explained that that was called a refusal.

"Does he lose marks for that?"

"Yes," said Liz, crisply.

"He's still got points in hand," said Aunt Marjorie, trying to stay calm in this crisis. "I expect he'll go round the other way now. Yes, I thought he would."

"He's stopped again," said Woglinde.

"So he has," said Liz. "I wonder why?"

"Is he allowed to hit his horse with that stick?" asked Flosshilde. "It must hurt an awful lot."

"I think it's cruel," said Wellgunde.

"I think he's going to try the gate this time," said Aunt Marjorie nervously. "Oh dear, not *again...*"

"I think it's his fault for hitting the horse with that stick," said Wellgunde. "If I was the horse, I'd throw him off."

"Thirty-three faults," sniggered the tannoy.

"Is that a lot?" asked Flosshilde. Aunt Marjorie confirmed that it was, rather.

Philip Wilcox was obviously finding it hard to think straight through the buzz of malicious giggling that welled up all around him. About the only jump he hadn't tried yet was the water-jump. He pulled Mayfair's head round, promised him an apple if he made it and the glue factory if he didn't, and pressed with his heels in the approved manner. Mayfair began to move smoothly, rhythmically towards the obstacle.

"Come on, now," Aunt Marjorie hissed under her breath, "plenty of pace. Go on..."

There is nothing, nothing in the world that amuses human beings more than the sight of a fully grown, fully clothed man falling into water, and sooner or later the human race must come to terms with this fact. But, to the Rhinedaughters (who are not human, but were created by a unique and entirely accidental fusion of the life-forces) it seemed strange that this unfortunate accident should produce such gales of laughter from everyone present, including the tannoy. Even Wellgunde, who thought it served him right for hitting the horse with the stick, was moved to compassion. She looked around to see if she was the only person not laughing, and observed that at least the girl sitting next to the fat woman did not seem to be amused. In fact, she appeared to be perfectly calm, and her face was a picture of tranquillity, like some Renaissance Madonna. Perhaps, thought the Rhinedaughter, she's an immortal too. Or perhaps she's just annoyed.

"I'm so glad Joe won in the end," said Liz, getting to her feet. "Shall we go and find some tea?"

Restored to human shape once more, Malcolm crawled into the house and collapsed into a chair. He was utterly exhausted, his mouth was bruised and swollen, his back and sides were aching, and he had pulled a muscle in his neck when he had stopped so suddenly in front of the water-jump. The whole thing had probably hurt him just as much as it had hurt Philip Wilcox, and he had a terrible feeling that it hadn't been worth it. A minute or so of unbridled malice on his part was probably the worst thing that could happen to the universe, and his original argument, that anything that humiliated Philip Wilcox was bound to be good for the world, seemed rather flimsy in retrospect. He could only hope that the consequences would not be too dire.

With an effort, he rose to his feet and stumbled out into the grounds. The show was, mercifully, drawing to a close and, within an hour or so, all the cars that were hiding his grass from the sun would be winding their way home, probably, since this was Somerset, at fifteen miles an hour behind a milk tanker. All he had to do now was present the prizes. This would, of course, mean standing up in public and saying something coherent, and for a moment he stopped dead in his tracks. He should be feeling unmitigated terror at the prospect of this ordeal, but he wasn't. He tried to feel frightened, but the expected reaction refused to materialise. He raised his eyebrows and said "Well, I'm damned" to himself several times.

As he stood on the platform handing out rosettes, the three Rhine-daughters studied him carefully through their designer sunglasses.

"No, don't tell me," whispered Flosshilde. "I'll remember in a minute."

"Siegfried," said Wellgunde. "It's Siegfried. What a nerve!"

"Why shouldn't he be Siegfried if he wants to?" whispered Woglinde. "I think it suits him."

"Oh, well." Flosshilde shrugged her slim shoulders. "Here we go again."

Malcolm was shaking Joe Ayres by the hand and saying "Well done." Joe Ayres winced as he withdrew his hand; he suspected that the German's ferocious grip had dislocated one of his knuckles.

"It could have been worse," said Flosshilde, "considering..." She stopped suddenly and poked Wellgunde's arm. "Look," she hissed, "over there, by the pear tree. Look who it is!"

"No!" Wellgunde's eyes were sparkling with excitement as she followed Flosshilde's pointing finger, and a pear on the tree ripened prematurely as a result. "I don't believe it."

"He doesn't look a day older," said Woglinde, fondly.

The other two made faces at her.

Malcolm recognised Alberich at once. As the Prince of the Nibelungs approached him, Malcolm's heart seemed to collapse. Not that the Nibelung was a terrifying sight; a short, broad, grey-haired man in a dark overcoat, nothing more. There was no point in running away, and Malcolm stood his ground as Alberich approached and extended his hand for a handshake. Malcolm closed his fist around the Ring and put his hands behind his back.

"I'm sorry," said Alberich in German. "I thought you were someone else."

"Oh, yes?"

"Someone I used to know in Germany, as a matter of fact. You look very like him, from a distance. But perhaps he was a little bit taller."

"I don't think so," said Malcolm without thinking.

· Alberich laughed. "How would you know? But you're right, actually. He wasn't."

"My name is Manfred Finger," Malcolm managed to say. "I own the Hall."

"Hans Albrecht." Alberich smiled again. "I'm afraid I don't know many people in England. But perhaps you know a friend of mine who lives near here."

"I'm afraid I don't know many people either," said Malcolm, forcing himself to smile. "I've only been here a short while myself."

"Well, this friend of mine is a very remarkable person, so perhaps you do know him. Malcolm Fisher. Familiar?"

"Any friend of Malcolm's is a friend of mine," said Malcolm truthfully. "But I don't remember him mentioning you."

"That's so like him." Alberich was massaging the fourth finger of his right hand as if it was hurting. "Arthritis," he explained. "Anyway, if you see him before I do, you might remind him that he's got something of mine. A gold ring, and a hat. Both valueless, but I'd like them back."

"I'm afraid Malcolm hasn't been quite himself lately," said Malcolm. "But I'll remind him if I see him before you do."

"Would you? That's very kind. And do give him my best wishes." Alberich turned to go, then stopped. "Oh, and by the way," he said in English. "Well done. I liked your horse. Goodbye."

As if that wasn't bad enough, Malcolm heard on the late news that two airliners had missed each other by inches over Manchester that afternoon. Had they collided, said the announcer, more than five hundred people would probably have lost their lives. An inquiry was being held, but the probable cause of the incident was human error.

6

Against the dark blue night sky above the Mendip Hills, someone with bright eyes might have been able to make out two tiny black dots, which could conceivably have been ravens, except of course that they were far too high up.

"It was around here somewhere," said Thought.

"That's what you said last time," said Memory. His pinions were aching, and he hadn't eaten for sixteen hours. During that time, he and his colleague had been round the world twenty-four times. Anything the sun could do, it seemed, they could do better.

"All right, then," said Thought, "don't believe me, see if I care. But he's down there somewhere, I know he is. I definitely heard the Ring calling."

"That was probably Radio Bristol," said Memory. Exhaustion had made him short-tempered.

They flew on in silence, completing a circuit of the counties of Somerset, Avon and Devon. Finally, they could go no further, and swooped down onto the roof of a thatched barn just outside Dulverton.

"How come you can hear the Ring, anyway?" said Memory. "I can't."

"Nor me, usually. It just sort of happens, once in a while. But it never lasts long enough for me to get an exact fix on it."

A foolhardy bat fluttered towards them, curious to know who these strangers might be. The two ravens turned and stared at it, frightening it out of its wits.

"If it's about the radio licence," said the bat, "there's a cheque in the post."

"Get lost," said Memory, and the bat did its best to obey. Being gifted with natural radar, however, it did not find it easy.

"Wotan's in a terrible state these days," said Thought. "Not happy at all."

"So what's new?"

"He's been all over the shop looking for clues. Went down a tin-mine in Bolivia the other day, came out all covered in dust."

"I could have told him he'd do no good in Bolivia," said Memory. "Perhaps it would be better if we split up. That way we could cover more ground. You take one hemisphere, I take the other, sort of thing."

Thought considered this for a moment. "No, wouldn't work. You couldn't think where to go, and I couldn't remember where I'd been. Waste of everybody's time."

"Please yourself."

"You want to go off on your own then, or what?"

"Forget it."

Thought was about to say something, but stopped. "Listen," he whispered. "Did you hear that?"

"What?"

"It's the Ring again. Somewhere over there." He pointed with his wing to the east. "Not too far away, either."

"How far?"

"Dunno, it's stopped again."

Memory shook his head. "I'm thinking of packing all this in," he said.

"How do you mean?" said Thought.

"All this flying about, and that. I mean, where's it getting me?"

"It's a living, though."

"Is it?" Memory leaned forward and snapped up a moth. It tasted sour. "You take my brother-in-law. Talentless little git if you ask me. Used to run errands for the Moon-Goddess. Then they got one of those telexes, and he was out on his ear. So he set up this courier service—five years ago, give or take a bit—and look at him now. Nest in the tallest forest in Saxony, another in the Ardennes for the winter, and I bet he isn't eating moths."

"Nests aren't everything," said Thought. "There's job satisfaction. There's travel. There's service to the community."

"I know," said Memory. "Instead of all this fooling about, why don't we keep an eye on the girls, or Alberich? Maybe they know something we don't."

Thought considered this. "Could do," he said, "it's worth a try..." He stopped, and both birds were silent for a moment "There it goes again. Definitely over there somewhere."

"Stuff it," said Memory. "Let's find the Rhinedaughters."

Malcolm found it difficult to sleep that night. He had managed to get the thought of the two airliners out of his mind, but the meeting with Alberich was not so lightly dismissed. He had been afraid, more so than ever before, and the terrible thing was that he could not understand why. He was taller and stronger than the Nibelung, and he had the ability to make himself taller and stronger yet if the need arose. That was the whole point of the Tarnhelm. But the Nibelung had something else that made his own magic powers seem irrelevant; he had authority, and that was not something Malcolm could afford to ignore.

He looked at his watch; it was half-past two in the morning. He toyed with the idea of transporting himself to Los Angeles or Adelaide, where it would be light and he could get a cup of coffee without waking up the housekeeper. He was on the point of doing this when he heard a noise in the corridor outside.

Combe Hall was full of unexplained noises, which everyone he asked attributed to the plumbing. But something told Malcolm that plumbing made gurgling noises, not stealthy creeping noises. Without understanding why, he knew that he was in danger, and something told him that it was probably the right time for him to become invisible.

His bedroom door was locked, and he stood beside it. Outside, he could hear footsteps, which stopped. There was a scrabbling sound, a click and the door opened gently. He recognised the face of Alberich, peering into the room, and for a moment was rooted to the spot. Then it occurred to him that he was considerably bigger than Alberich, and also invisible. The Nibelung crept into the room and tiptoed over to the bed. As he bent over it, Malcolm kicked him hard.

It would be unfair to Malcolm to say that he did not know his own strength. He knew his own strength very well (or rather his lack of it) but as yet he had not come to terms with the strength of Siegfried the Dragon-Slayer. As a result, he hit Alberich very hard indeed. The intruder uttered a loud yelp and fell over.

Malcolm was horrified. His first reaction was that he must have killed Alberich, but a loud and uncomplicated complaint from his victim convinced him that that was not so. His next reaction was to apologise.

"Sorry," he said. "What the hell do you think you're doing?"

"You clumsy idiot," said the Prince of the Nibelungs, "you've broken my leg."

It occurred to Malcolm that this served Alberich right, and he said so. In fact, he suggested, Alberich was extremely lucky to get off so lightly, since presumably he had broken in with the intention of committing murder.

"Don't be stupid," said Alberich. "I only wanted the Ring."

He made it sound as if he had just dropped by to borrow a bowl of sugar. "Now, about my broken leg..."

"Never mind your broken leg."

"I mind it a lot. Get a doctor."

"You're taking a lot for granted, aren't you?" said Malcolm sternly. "You're my deadliest enemy. Why shouldn't I...well, dispose of you, right now?"

Alberich laughed. "You?" he said incredulously. "Who do you think you are, Jack the Ripper?"

"I could be if I wanted to," said Malcolm. The Nibelung ignored him.

"You wouldn't hurt a fly," he sneered. "That's your trouble. You'll never get anywhere in this world unless you improve your attitude. And did no-one ever tell you it's bad manners to be invisible when someone's talking to you?"

"You sound just like my mother," said Malcolm.

He reappeared, and Alberich glowered at him. "Still pretending to be who you aren't, I see," he said.

"I'll be who I want to be. I'm not afraid of you any more."

"Delighted to hear it. Perhaps you'll fetch a doctor now."

"And the police," said Malcolm, to frighten him. "You're a burglar."

"You wouldn't dare," replied Alberich, but Malcolm could see he was worried. This was remarkable. A few minutes ago, he had been paralysed with fear. Now he found the whole thing vaguely comic. Still, it would be as well to call a doctor. He went to the telephone beside his bed.

"Not that sort of doctor," said Alberich, irritably. "What do you think I am, human?"

"So what sort of doctor do you want?" Malcolm asked.

"A proper doctor. A Nibelung."

"Fine. And how do you suggest I set about finding one, look in the Yellow Pages?"

"Don't be facetious. Use the Ring."

"Can I do that?" Malcolm was surprised by this.

"Of course you can. Just rub the Ring against your nose and call for a doctor."

Feeling rather foolish, Malcolm did what he was told. At once, a short, stocky man with very pale skin materialised beside him, wearing what appeared to be a sack.

"You called?" said the Nibelung.

"Where did you come from?" Malcolm asked.

"Nibelheim, where do you think? So where's the patient?"

The doctor did something to Alberich's leg with a spanner and a jar of ointment, and disappeared as suddenly as he had come.

"That's handy," Malcolm said. "Can I just summon Nibelungs when I want to?"

"Of course," said Alberich. "Although why you should want to is another matter. By and large, they're incredibly boring people."

Malcolm shrugged his shoulders. "Anyway, how's your leg?" he asked.

"Very painful. But it's healed."

"Healed? But I thought you said it was broken."

"So it was," replied Alberich, calmly. "And now it's unbroken again. That's what the doctor was for. It'll be stiff for a day or so, of course, but that can't be helped. If you will go around kicking people, you must expect to cause anguish and suffering."

Malcolm yawned. "In that case, you can go away and leave me in peace," he said. "And don't let me catch you around here again, or there'll be trouble."

This bravado didn't convince anyone. Alberich made no attempt to move, but sat on the floor rubbing his knee, until Malcolm, unable to think of anything else to do, offered him a drink.

"I thought you'd never ask," said Alberich. "I'll have a large schnapps, neat."

"I don't think I've got any of that," said Malcolm.

"You're supposed to be a German. Oh well, whatever comes to hand, so long as it isn't sherry. I don't like sherry."

So it was that Malcolm found himself sharing a bottle of gin with the Prince of Nibelheim at three o'clock in the morning. It was not something he would have chosen to do, especially after a tiring day, but the mere fact that he was able to do it was remarkable enough. Alberich made no further attempt to relieve him of the Ring; he didn't even mention the subject until Malcolm himself raised it. Instead, he talked mostly about his health, or to be precise, his digestion.

"Lobster," he remarked more than once, "gives me the most appalling heartburn. And gooseberries..."

In short, there was nothing to fear from Alberich, and Malcolm found himself feeling rather sorry for the Nibelung, who, by his own account at least, had had rather a hard time.

"It wasn't the gold I wanted," he said. "I wanted to get my own back on those damned women."

"Which women?"

"The Rhinedaughters. I won't bore you with all the details. Not a nice story." Alberich helped himself to some more gin. "There I was, taking a stroll beside the Rhine on a pleasant summer evening, and these three girls, with no more clothes on than would keep a fly warm..."

"I know all that," said Malcolm.

"Do you?" said Alberich, rather disappointed. "Oh well, never mind. But it wasn't the power or the money I wanted—well, they would have been nice, I grant you, I'm not saying they wouldn't—but it's the principle of the thing. You know how it is when someone takes something away from you without any right to it at all. You feel angry. You feel hard done by. And if that thing is the control of the world, you feel very hard done by indeed. Not that I *want* to control the world particularly—I imagine I'd do it very badly. But it's like not being invited to a party, you feel hard done by even if you wouldn't have gone if they'd asked you. I know I'm not explaining this very well... You can get obsessive about it, you know? Especially if you've thought about nothing else for the last thousand years."

"Couldn't you have done something else, to take your mind off it? Got a job, or something?"

"This may seem strange, but having been master of the world for forty-eight hours—that's how long they let me keep the Ring, you know—doesn't really qualify you for much. And they threw me out of Nibelheim."

"Did they?"

"They did. You can't really blame them. I had enslaved them and made them mine gold for me. They weren't best pleased."

"So what have you been doing ever since?"

"Moping about, mostly, feeling sorry for myself. And looking for the Ring, of course. And a bit of freelance metallurgy, just to keep the wolf from the door. My card."

He took a card from his wallet. "Hans Albrecht and partners," it read, "Mining Engineers and Contractors, Est. AD 900."

"Most people think the date's a misprint," said Alberich, "but it's not. Anyway, that's what I've been doing, and a thoroughly wretched time I've had, too."

"Have another drink," Malcolm suggested.

"You're too kind," said Alberich. "Mind you, if I have too much to drink these days, it plays hell with my digestion. Did I tell you about that?"

"Yes."

Alberich shook his head sadly. "I'm boring you, I can tell. But let me tell you something useful. Even if you won't give me the Ring, don't let Wotan get his hands on it."

"I wasn't planning to," said Malcolm. "Another?"

"Why not? And then I must be going. It's late, and you've been a horse all afternoon. That's tiring, I know. Now, about Wotan. I don't know how you've managed it, but you've got the Ring to do what you want it to. Not what I had intended when I made it, let me say. In fact, I can't remember what I intended when I made it. It's been a long time. Anyway. Is there any tonic left?"

"No. Sorry."

"Doesn't matter. About Wotan. He's devious, very devious, but if you've got the Ring on your side..."

Malcolm thought of something incredibly funny. "I haven't got the Ring on my *side,*" he said, "I've got it on my *finger.*"

They had a good laugh over that. "No, but seriously," said Alberich, "if you can make the Ring do what you want it to, then there's nothing Wotan can do to you unless you want him to."

"But I don't want him to do anything to me. I want him to go away."

"That's what you think. Like I said, Wotan's devious. Devious devious *devious.* He'll get you exactly where he wants you unless you're very careful, I assure you."

"How?"

"That, my friend, remains to be seen. The days of armed force and violence are long gone, I'm sorry to say. It's cleverness that gets results. It's the same in the mining industry. Did I tell you about that?"

"Yes," Malcolm lied. "Go on about Wotan."

Alberich looked at the bottom of his glass. Unfortunately, there was nothing to obscure his view of it. He picked up the bottle, but it was empty.

"I am going to have raging indigestion all tomorrow," he said sadly. "Don't let them tell you there's no such thing as spontaneous combustion. I suffer from it continually. Wotan can't take the Ring from you, but he can make you give it to him of your own free will. And before you ask me, I don't know how he'll do it, but he'll think of something. Have you got any Bisodol?"

"I can get you a sandwich."

"A sandwich? Do you want to kill me as well as breaking my leg? No, don't you let go of the Ring, Malcolm Fisher. If I can't have it, you might as well keep it. It'll be safe with you until you're ready to give it to me."

Malcolm looked uncomfortable at this. Alberich laughed.

"Of your own free will, I mean. But that won't happen until it isn't a symbol of power any more, only a bit of old jewellery. It'll happen, though, you mark my words. See how it ends."

"How do you know?"

"I don't." Alberich rose unsteadily to his feet. "Time I was going."

"How's your leg?"

"My leg? Oh, that's fine, it's my stomach I'm worried about. I'm always worried about my stomach. We sulphur-dwarves were created out of the primal flux of the earth's core. We have always existed, and we will always exist, in some form or other. You can kill us, of course, but unless you do, we live for ever. The problem is, if you're made largely of sulphur, you are going to suffer from heartburn, and there's nothing at all you can do about it. Over the past however many it is million years, I have tried absolutely every remedy for dyspepsia that has ever been devised, and they're all useless. All of them. In all the years I've been alive, there was only one time I didn't have indigestion. You know when that was? The forty-eight hours when I had the Ring. Good night."

"You can stay here if you like," said Malcolm.

"That's kind of you, but I've got a room over at the Blue Boar. The fresh air will clear my head. I'll see myself out."

"That reminds me. How did you get in here?"

"Through the front door. I have a way with locks."

"And how did you find me in the first place?"

"Easy. I smelt the Ring. Once you started using it, that was no problem."

Alberich went to the door, then turned. "Do you know something, Malcolm Fisher?" he said. "It goes against the grain saying this, but I like you. In a way. Up to a point. You can keep the Ring for the time being. I like what you're doing with it."

Malcolm wanted to say something but could think of nothing.

"And if ever there's anything... Oh, forget it. Good luck."

A few minutes later, Malcolm heard the front door slam. He got back into bed and switched off the light. It was nearly morning, and he was very tired.

Two ravens were perched on the telegraph pole outside the Blue Boar in Combe.

"It's definitely coming from near here somewhere," said Thought.

Memory had been listening for the Voice all day, and he no longer believed in it. "You've been overdoing it," he said. "Maybe you should take a couple of days off. We can't hear the Ring, either of us. It's not possible."

In the road below, a short, heavily-built man was waiting for the night porter to open the door of the hotel. Thought flapped his wings to attract his partner's attention.

"Look," he whispered, "down there."

"It's Alberich," replied Memory. "What's he doing here?"

"I told you," said Thought. "I told you and you wouldn't..."

"All right, all right," said Memory uneasily. "Doesn't prove anything, does it? I mean, he could be here for some totally different reason."

"Such as?"

Memory stared blankly at his claws. "Dunno," he said. "But it still doesn't mean..."

"Come on," said Thought, "we've found him. He's somewhere in this village. We'd better tell Wotan."

"Oh no." Memory shook his head. "You can if you like. If we're wrong, and Wotan comes flogging out here on a fool's errand..."

"So what do we do?"

They racked their brains for a moment, but in vain. Then Thought had a sudden inspiration. "I know," he said. "We'll tell Loge. Then it'll be his duty to pass the message on to the Boss."

The two ravens laughed, maliciously.

7

Alberich woke up next morning with a thick head, a weary heart, and indigestion. He took a taxi to Taunton, only to find that he had missed the London train, and was faced with an hour in one of the dreariest towns he had ever come across in the course of a very long life.

The only possible solution was a cup or two of strong, drinkable coffee, and he set off to find it. As he sat in a grimly coy coffee shop in Kingston Road, he tried to turn over in his mind the various courses of action still open to him, but found that rational thought was not possible in his state of health and the centre of Taunton. He gave it up, and as he did so became aware of a familiar voice behind him:

"Really," it was saying, "nobody's worn that shade of blue since the twelfth century. I *couldn't* go out looking like that."

"You should have thought of that earlier," said another voice, just as familiar. "You're impossible sometimes."

The last time Alberich had heard those two voices, and the third voice that broke in to contradict them both, was in the depths of the Rhine, about a thousand years ago. He turned round slowly.

"What are you three doing here?" he asked.

Flosshilde smiled sweetly at him, with the result that the milk in his coffee turned to cream. "Hello, Alberich," she said. "How's the digestion?"

"Awful. What are you doing here?"

"Drinking coffee. What about you?"

"Don't be flippant."

"But that's what we do best," said Woglinde, also smiling. There was little point to this, except pure malice, for Alberich had forsworn Love and was therefore immune to all smiles, even those of Rhine-daughters. But Woglinde smiled anyway, as a sportsman who can find no pheasants will sometimes take a shot at a passing crow. "We're too set in our ways to change now."

"What are you doing here?" Alberich asked.

"That would be telling," said Wellgunde, twitching her nose like a rabbit. "How about you?"

"Tourism," said Albench with a shudder. "I like grim, miserable places where there's nothing at all to do."

"You would," said Flosshilde. That, so far as she was concerned, closed the subject. But Wellgunde was rather more cautious.

"We're out shopping," she said artlessly. "Everyone's looking to Taunton for colours this season."

"In fact," said Flosshilde, "Taunton is the place where it's all happening these days." She giggled, and Wellgunde kicked her under the table.

Alberich shook his head, which was a rash move on his part. "You'll find it harder than you imagine," he said. "You won't be able to trap him easily."

"Trap who?"

Alberich ignored her. "What you fail to take into account," he continued, "is his extreme lack of self-confidence. Even if he does fall in love with one or all of you, he's highly unlikely to feel up to doing anything about it. He'll just go home and feel miserable. And then what will you have achieved?"

"We're not like that," said Woglinde. "We're good at dealing with shy people."

Alberich laughed and rose to his feet. "I wish you luck," he said.

"No, you don't," said Wellgunde shrewdly.

"Let me rephrase that. You'll need luck. Lots of it. See you in another thousand years."

"Not if we see you first," said Flosshilde cheerfully. "Have a nice day."

One of the few luxuries that Malcolm had indulged in since his acquisition of limitless wealth was a brand new sports car. He had always wanted one, although now that he had it he found that he was rather unwilling to go above thirty miles an hour in it. The whole point of having a car, however, as any psychologist will tell you, is that it represents Defended Space, where no-one can get at you, and Malcolm always felt happier once he was behind the wheel. There were risks, of course; driving in Somerset, that county of narrow lanes and leisurely tractors, can cause impatience and bad temper, which Malcolm was in duty bound to avoid.

Once his headache had subsided, Malcolm thought it would make a change to go into Taunton and look at the shops. He had been an enthusiastic window-shopper all his life, and now that he could afford to buy not only the things in the shop-windows but the shops themselves if he wanted to, he enjoyed this activity even more. Not that he ever did buy anything, of course; the habits of a lifetime are not so easily broken.

For example, he stood for quite five minutes outside the fishing-tackle shop in Silver Street looking at all the elegant and attractive paraphernalia in the window. At least two rivers, possibly three, ran through the grounds of the Hall, and fishing was supposed to be a relaxing occupation which soothed the nerves and the temper. Not that he particularly wanted to catch or persecute fish; but it would at least be an interest, with things to learn and things to buy. For the same reason, he had a good look at the camera shop in St. James Street, and he only stopped himself from going inside by reflecting that he had nobody to take pictures of, except perhaps the English Rose.

He walked by the auction-rooms, and wondered who was doing his old job now. Inside there would be Liz, cataloguing something or other, and Philip Wilcox, training, not very energetically, to be an auctioneer. Again, he felt a strong temptation to go inside and look at them, and that would be perfectly reasonable, since they both knew him only as the rich German who had bought the Hall. He could now afford to buy everything in the sale if he wanted to. But the sale today was of antique clocks, and he already knew only too well how slowly the time passed. Besides, there was no point in buying anything for himself (it was, after all, Only Him) and he had no-one else to buy things for.

As he walked down North Street towards what passes for a centre, he noticed a shop that he could not recall having seen before. It was one of those art and craft places, selling authentic pottery and ethnic clothes (hence no doubt its name, Earth 'n' Wear). But shops of that kind are always springing up and disappearing like mayflies in upwardly-mobile towns, and Taunton is nothing if not upwardly-mobile. In fact, as they will be delighted to tell you, Taunton is no longer a one-horse town; these days, they have a bicycle as well...

Entirely out of curiosity, since he was safe in the knowledge that there would not be anything in a shop of this sort that he could conceivably want to buy, Malcolm opened the door, which had goat-bells behind it, and went in. The place was empty, except for a ghostly string quartet playing Mozart, a large cat asleep on a pile of Indian cotton shirts, and an astoundingly pretty girl with red hair sitting behind the till. As soon as Malcolm walked through the door, she looked up from the poem she was writing in a spiral-bound notebook with a stylised cat on the cover and smiled at him.

Malcolm had always been of the opinion that pretty girls should not be allowed to smile at people unless they meant something by it, for it gives them an unfair advantage. He now felt under an obligation to buy something. That presumably was why the owner had installed a pretty girl in the shop in the first place, and Malcolm did not approve. It was exploitation of the worst sort.

"Feel free to look around," said the girl.

Malcolm walked briskly to the back of the shop and tried to appear profoundly interested in beeswax candles. Although he had his back to her, he felt sure that the girl was still looking at him, and he remembered that he was the most handsome man in the world, which might account for it. A smirk tried to get onto his face, but he sent it away. He was, he assured himself, only imagining it, and even if he wasn't, there was bound to be a catch in it all somewhere. This was Taunton, not Hollywood.

For her part, Wellgunde was rather dismayed. Either her smile had gone wrong since she checked it that morning, or else this young man was immune to smiles, which would be a pity. She had gone to the trouble of materialising this shop and all its contents just in order to be able to have somewhere to smile at the Ring-Bearer. A shop, the Rhinedaughters had decided, made an ideal trap for ensnaring unwary Ring-Bearers. Perhaps they had underestimated him, Wellgunde thought. Certainly it had seemed a very straightforward project when they discussed it that morning. From all they had learnt about him, Ingolf's Bane was a foolish, sentimental and susceptible young man who would as instinctively fall in love with a pretty girl who smiled at him as a trout snaps at a fly. The only point at issue in their planning session had been which one of them should have the dubious privilege of being the fly. They had tried drawing lots, but Woglinde would insist on cheating. They had tried tossing for it, but Flosshilde had winked at the coin, and it kept coming down in her favour. So finally they had decided to make a game of it: whoever captivated the Ring-Bearer first would have to see the job through, but the others would buy her lunch at Maxim's.

To make it a fair contest, they had materialised three shops in the centre of Taunton. It was a reasonable bet that no-one would notice three shops suddenly appearing out of nowhere in the centre of town, for Taunton is like that, and it would be up to the Ring-Bearer to decide which one he went into first, and so who should have the first go.

Wellgunde frowned. She was going to have to make an effort.

"Are you looking for anything in particular?" she said sweetly.

There was another potential customer outside, looking through the window at a selection of herbal teas. She turned quickly and smiled at the door. The card obligingly flipped round to read "Closed." Things generally did what she wanted them to when she smiled at them.

"A present for my mother," Malcolm replied, amazing himself with his own inventiveness.

"Does she like cats?" Wellgunde suggested. "Most mothers do."

"Yes, she does."

"Then how about a spaghetti-jar with a cat on the front, or a tea-cosy in the shape of a cat, or a little china cat you can keep paperclips in, or a cat-shaped candle, or a Cotswold cat breadboard? We haven't got any framed cat woodcuts at the moment, but we're expecting a delivery this afternoon if you're not in a huny."

"That's a lot of cats," said Malcolm startled.

"Cats and Cotswolds," said the Rhinedaughter, brightly. "You can sell anything with a cat or a Cotswold on it, although some people prefer rabbits."

She smiled again, so brightly that Malcolm could feel the skin on his face turning brown. He began to feel distinctly uncomfortable.

"I'd better have one of those oven-gloves," he mumbled.

"With a cat on it?"

"Yes, please."

The girl seemed rather hurt as she took Malcolm's money, and he wondered what he had said.

"If she doesn't like it, I can change it for you," said the girl. "No trouble, really."

"I'm sure she'll like it. She's very fond of cats. And cooking."

"Goodbye, then."

"Goodbye."

Wellgunde watched him go, and frowned. "Oh well," she said to herself, "bother him, then."

She smiled at the shop, and just to please her it vanished into thin air. Then she walked down to the banks of the Tone and dived grace-fully into its khaki waters.

"Well," said one old lady to another as a chain of silver bubbles rose to the surface, "you don't see so much of that sort of thing nowadays."

Confused, Malcolm turned up Hammet Street. It was not surprising, he said to himself, that a girl, even a pretty one, should want to smile at someone looking exactly like Siegfried the Dragon-Slayer. And it was Siegfried's appearance, not his, that she had been smiling at, so really the smile was nothing to do with him. Besides, it was probably just a smile designed to sell cat-icons, in which it had succeeded admirably. He felt in his pocket for the oven-glove, but it didn't seem to be there any more. He must have dropped it. What a pity, never mind.

At the junction of Hammet Street and Magdalene Street, there was a health-food shop which had not been there yesterday. Of that Malcolm was absolutely certain, because he had parked his car beside the kerb on which the shop was now standing. He stood very still and frowned.

"Did I do that?" he said aloud. "And if so, how?"

He knew the song about the girl who left trees and flowers lying about wherever she had gone; but trees and flowers are one thing, health-food shops are another. Either it had been built very, very quickly (after his recent experiences with builders at the Hall, Malcolm doubted this) or else it had appeared out of nowhere, or else he was hallucinating. He crossed the road and went in.

"Hello there," said the bewilderingly pretty girl behind the counter. "Can I help you?"

It was probably the dazzling smile that made Malcolm realise what was going on. "Hang on a moment, please," he said, and walked out again. Next door was a furniture shop with a big plate-glass window. Fortunately, the street was deserted, and Malcolm was able to turn himself into the three Rhinedaughters without being observed. He found that he recognised two of them immediately. As an experiment, he smiled a Rhinedaughter smile at a chest of drawers in the shop window. It seemed to glow for a moment, and then its polyurethane finish was changed into a deep French polish shine.

"That explains it," he said to himself, and did not allow himself to think that although that explained the smiles he had been getting, it did not explain the shops that had appeared from nowhere. Take care of the smiles, after all, and the shops will take care of themselves. He understood that the Rhinedaughters, the original owners of the gold from which the Ring was made, were after him, and their smiles were baits to draw him to his doom. Not that there weren't worse dooms, he reflected, but he had the world to consider.

Instead of walking away, however, he turned and went back into the health-food shop. Now that he knew that the smiles were only another aspect of this rather horrible game that Life was playing with him, and not genuine expressions of interest by pretty girls, he felt that he could deal with the situation, for he had a supreme advantage over the previous owners of the Nibelung's Ring. He had no vanity, no high opinion of himself which these creatures could use as the basis for their attack. All that remained was for him to deal with them before they did anything more troublesome than smiling.

"Hello again," said Woglinde.

"Which one are you, then?" he replied, smiling back. Woglinde looked at him for a moment, and then burst into tears, burying her face in her small pink hands. Instinctively, Malcolm was horrified; then he remembered Hagen, Alberich's son, whom the three Rhinedaughters had drowned in the flood, singing sweetly all the while.

"Thought so," he said, trying to sound unpleasant (but he had lost the knack). "So which one are you?"

"Woglinde," sobbed the girl. "And now you're all cross."

The Rhinedaughter sniffed, looked up angrily, and smiled like a searchlight. A carnation appeared in Malcolm's buttonhole, but his resolve was unaffected.

"You can cut that out," he said.

"Oh, well," said Woglinde, and Malcolm could see no tears in her deep blue eyes. He could see many other things, but no tears, and the other things were rather hazardous, so he ignored them.

"Where did the shop come from?" he asked.

"Shan't tell you," said Woglinde, coyly frowning. "You're beastly and I hate you."

"Girls don't talk like that any more," said Malcolm. "A thousand years ago perhaps, but not in the nineteen-eighties."

"This girl does," replied Woglinde. "It's part of her charm. You've been looking for a nice old-fashioned girl all your life and now you've found one."

Put like that, the proposition (accompanied by the brightest smile yet) was somewhat startling, and Malcolm turned away and looked at a display of organic pulses.

"You've been to a lot of trouble," he said.

"I spent ages making it all nice for you," said Woglinde.

"I don't like health food. Especially organic rice."

"Oh, I'm *sorry,*" said Woglinde, petulantly. "If I'd known, I'd have built you a chip-shop instead." She checked herself; she was letting her temper interfere with business. "I still can, if you'd rather."

"I wouldn't bother, if I were you," said Malcolm. "I expect you're sick of the sight of fish."

"If you asked me to I would."

"Forget it, please. I know what you want, and you can't have it."

"Usually that's our line," said the Rhinedaughter casually. Malcolm blushed. "Oh go on," she continued, "it's our Ring, really."

Perhaps the smiles had a cumulative effect. Malcolm suddenly felt a terrible urge to give her the Ring. He had already taken it off his finger before he knew what he was doing, and it was only when he caught sight of her face, like a kitten watching a beetle it intends to eat, that he felt the sense of danger. He thrust the Ring back on, so fiercely that he cut the skin between his fingers.

"I can't," he said, sadly. "I'd love to, but I can't. You wouldn't want it, really."

Woglinde suddenly laughed, and Malcolm felt as if he was being smothered in gossamer, like a fly trapped by a spider. "Don't be silly," she cooed, "I'd like it more than anything in the whole wide world. I think you're *mean.*"

Again there was a hideous temptation to give in, so strong that the Ring seemed to burn his skin. Malcolm could stand it no longer, and tried to command the Tarnhelm to take him away. But his mind could not issue the order; the smiles had got into it, as light gets into photographic film, and blurred all the edges. "Stop that!" he shouted, and Woglinde winced as if he had slapped her. He tightened his hand round the Ring, and her face seemed to collapse. Suddenly, she was not pretty at all; she looked like a thousand-year-old teenager who wanted something she knew she couldn't have. Then, just as suddenly, she was lovelier than ever, and Malcolm knew that she had given up.

"Sorry," he said, "but there it is."

He turned and walked out of the shop, trying not to look back, but the urge was too strong. When he did look back, however, the shop was gone. He had won this bout, then; but was that all? It would probably be unwise to go swimming for a week or so...

After the fight, Malcolm needed a drink. He walked swiftly up Canon Street, heading for his favourite pub. But it wasn't there any more; instead, there was one of those very chic little wine-bars that come like shadows and so depart all over England. He had a horrible idea that he knew where this one had come from.

The wine-bar ("Le Cochonnet") was empty except for a quite unutterably pretty girl behind the bar, tenderly polishing a glass.

"You can put it all back exactly as it was," said Malcolm, sternly.

The girl stared at him in amazement, and for a moment Malcolm wondered if he had made a mistake. But he looked at the girl again, and recognised the third Rhinedaughter. There couldn't be two girls like that in the world, unless he was very lucky.

"So which are you," he said, "Wellgunde or Flosshilde?"

"Flosshilde," said the girl, carelessly. "You've met the other two?"

"That's right." He held up his right hand, letting the light play on the ring, "And I'm not going to give it to you, either. It's not a toy, you know."

Flosshilde studied the glass in her hand for a moment. "All right," she said. "If you insist. Would you like a drink?"

Flosshilde had been rather proud of her wine-bar, and it was with great reluctance that she had agreed to change it back into the French Horn. But she did so with a smile.

"Won't the landlord and the customers be a bit disorientated?" Malcolm asked.

"Not really," said Flosshilde. "All I did was change them into chairs and tables, and they won't have felt anything. For some reason, when I smile at people and change them, they don't seem to mind."

"I can understand that," said Malcolm. "Let me buy you a drink."

"I'll have a Babycham," said Flosshilde. "No ice."

When he returned with the drinks, Flosshilde leaned forward and whispered, "Your Liz is over there in the corner with her boyfriend. The one you threw in the water."

"So what?" said Malcolm coldly. "She's not my Liz."

"I could turn him into a frog for you, if you like," whispered Flosshilde. "Or I could smile at him without turning him into a frog. Your Liz wouldn't like that at all."

"I'd rather you didn't," said Malcolm. "I'm not allowed to be malicious any more."

"That sounds awful." Flosshilde seemed genuinely sorry for him. "Would it count if I did it?"

"Probably. But it's kind of you to offer."

"Any time. I might just do it anyway. I don't like him, he's stuffy. I don't like stuffy people."

"I'd better be careful, then," said Malcolm. "I've become very stuffy since..."

"That's not your fault," said the Rhinedaughter.

"I shouldn't be doing this," said Malcolm. "Fraternising with the enemy."

"I'm not really the enemy, am I?" Flosshilde smiled, but it wasn't a serious smile, just a movement of the lips intended to convey friendliness. Malcolm was intrigued.

"I mean, you're not going to give me the Ring, and why should you? That doesn't mean I hate you."

"Doesn't it?"

"Course not."

"Woglinde burst out crying."

"She does that," said Flosshilde. "She's very bad-tempered. I'll tell her to leave you alone."

"Would you?" Malcolm felt a strange sensation at the back of his head, a sort of numbness. He hadn't chatted like this to anyone for a long time.

"Are you staying in England long?" he asked, trying to sound uninterested.

Flosshilde grinned. "If you like. It's the same for us, you know. We're all in the same boat. Of course, I've got the other two for company, but you know what it's like with sisters. They get on your nerves."

"I know, I've got a sister."

"Then we'll be company for each other," Flosshilde said. "I mean, we can go for drives in the country, or maybe take a boat up the river."

Malcolm remembered Hagen, and said he didn't like boats.

"Won't your sisters mind?" he added nervously.

"Oh bother them," said Flosshilde. "Besides, I can tell them I'm working on you."

"Will you be?"

"You'll have to wait and see," said Flosshilde, carefully not smiling. "Now, why don't you buy me lunch? I'm starving."

Malcolm drove back to Combe Hall in a rather bewildered frame of mind, and nearly rammed a flock of sheep outside Bagborough. Over lunch, Flosshilde hadn't mentioned the Ring once, except in passing (she knew some very funny stories about the Gods, especially Wotan) and seemed to be making no effort at all to lead him to his doom. That, of course, might simply mean that she was being subtle; but Malcolm had taken the precaution of reading her thoughts, and although he knew that one shouldn't believe everything you read in people's minds, he had been rather taken aback by what he had found. Of course, it was possible that she had deliberately planted those thoughts there for him to read, but somehow he didn't think so.

It seemed that Flosshilde had reconciled herself to the fact that the Ring wasn't going to be given to her, and she didn't really mind. Instead, she rather liked the Ring-Bearer. Nothing more than that, but never mind. Nor was it simply his assumed shape that she liked; she had seen that shape before when it had had the original Siegfried inside it, and besides, she didn't judge by appearances. That, it seemed, was not the way these curious other-worldly types went about things, for in the world they inhabited, so many people could change shape as easily as human beings changed clothes, and so you could never be sure whether a person was really handsome or simply smartly dressed. Flosshilde, however, thought that she and the Ring-Bearer might have something in common, and she wanted someone nice to talk to and go out with. There had been more than this, but Malcolm hadn't read it. He was saving it up, to read over lunch tomorrow...

"Well?" said Woglinde. "And where have you been?"

"Having lunch," said Flosshilde, "at Carey's."

"But you haven't got it?" said Wellgunde abruptly.

"True." Flosshilde lay back on the bed of the Tone and blew bubbles. "But who cares?"

Wellgunde stared at her sister, who closed her eyes and let out a rather exaggerated sigh. "I think I'm in love," said Flosshilde.

"Don't be ridiculous," snapped Wellgunde. "You can't be. You aren't allowed to be."

"Oh, all right then, I'm not. But the next best thing. Or the next best thing to that. He's nice, in a quiet sort of way."

"You should be ashamed of yourself," said Woglinde, fiercely; but Wellgunde smiled, confusing a shoal of minnows who happened to get in the way. "If it makes it easier for you to get the Ring," she said softly, "then you go ahead."

"I'm not interested in the silly old Ring," yawned Flosshilde. "It's supremely unimportant."

Wellgunde nodded. "Of course. But it *would* be nicer to have it than not to have it, now wouldn't it?"

"I suppose so."

"And there's no point in your liking him if he doesn't like you."

Flosshilde made a vague grab at a passing roach, which scuttled away. "I don't know. Is there?"

"And if he likes you, he'll be pleased to give you the Ring, now won't he?"

"I don't know and I don't care," replied Flosshilde. "We're just good friends."

"You've only met him once," said Woglinde. "There's no need to get soppy."

"There's every need to get soppy. I like being soppy. What's for dinner?"

"Trout with almonds," said Wellgunde.

"Not fish *again.*"

Wellgunde perched on the edge of a broken wardrobe, one of many that furnished the riverbed. "Nobody says you shouldn't make friends," she said gently. "But what about us? We want our Ring back."

"Once you've got it back, you can be friends with who you like," said Woglinde, inspecting her toenails, "though personally... They need doing again," she added. "There's something nasty in this river that dissolves coral pink."

"Oh, be quiet, both of you," said Flosshilde angrily. "I'm sorry I told you now."

There was silence at the bottom of the Tone for a while, with both Flosshilde and Woglinde sulking. Finally, Woglinde requested Wellgunde to ask her sister Flosshilde if she could borrow her coral pink nail varnish, and Flosshilde asked Wellgunde to tell her sister Woglinde that she couldn't.

"Be like that," said Woglinde. "See if I care."

Flosshilde jumped up and floated to the surface.

"Now look what you've done," hissed Wellgunde. "You've offended her."

"She isn't really in love, is she?" asked Woglinde nervously. "That would be terrible."

"I don't think so. She's just in one of her moods."

"What'll we do?"

"Don't worry," said Wellgunde calmly. "Leave her to me."

8

"Oh, for crying out loud," said Wotan, putting down his fork with a bang, "what do you want now?"

"Sorry," panted Loge, breathless and sopping wet. "I didn't realise you were still having breakfast."

Wotan smiled wanly. "Raining outside, is it?"

"Yes," said Loge. "Very heavily."

"So what was so important it couldn't wait?"

"I think I'm on to something," said Loge, sinking into a chair. The dining room of Valhalla, the castle built by Fasolt and Fafner for the King of the Gods, was furnished in spartan but functional style. It had that air of grim and relentless spotlessness that is described as a woman's touch.

The Lord of Tempests looked at him suspiciously. "If this turns out to be another wild goose chase," he said, "I'll turn you into a reservoir and stock you with rainbow trout."

Loge shuddered. "I'm sure there's something in this," he managed to say. "The ravens have sighted Alberich, and..."

"Aren't you going to offer your guest a cup of coffee?" Schwertleite the Valkyrie had come in with a crumb-brush and was ostentatiously brushing the table. "I do wish you wouldn't bring work home with you."

Wotan turned and glowered at his daughter, who took no notice. "And ask him not to put his briefcase on the table."

The Valkyrie swept out, and Wotan turned the full force of his glare on Loge. "Now look what you've done," he said. "You've started her off."

"But the ravens have seen Alberich and the Rhinedaughters, and they're in this village in England called..."

Schwertleite came back into the room with a bundle of newspapers in her arms. "Ask your friend to sit on these," she said sharply. "I've just had those covers cleaned, although why I bother, I don't know."

"Now you see what I have to put up with," whispered Wotan. "What's this about Alberich and the Rhinedaughters?"

Loge, perched uncomfortably on a pile of back numbers of *die Zeit,* started to explain, but before he could get very far, the Valkyrie Grimgerde stalked into the room with a pot of coffee. She had resented making it, and it would just be left to get cold, but she had made it all the same. "I'm doing you some scrambled eggs," she said accusingly to Loge.

"Please, don't bother."

"I've started now," replied Grimgerde impatiently.

Loge was about to say thank you, but the Valkyrie had gone back into the kitchen. Almost at once, Schwertleite reappeared, with her arms folded.

"There are footmarks all over the kitchen floor," she said icily. "Have you been tracking in and out?"

Before Wotan could reply, she too had gone. Wotan's daughters had a habit of asking leading questions and disappearing before anyone could answer them. They had been doing it for over a thousand years, but it was still profoundly irritating.

"...in a little village called Combe," said Loge, "which is in Somerset. Now why else..."

"What did you say?" Wotan hadn't been listening.

Loge took a deep breath, but could get no further. The Valkyrie Waltraute had come in with a plate of scrambled eggs. "As if I didn't have enough to do," she said, slamming the plate down. "And mind the tablecloth."

"Sorry," said Loge.

"I wouldn't eat that if I were you," Wotan muttered when she had gone. "None of my daughters can cook, although God knows it doesn't stop them. I can cook but I'm not allowed in the kitchen."

Desperately, Loge wondered what to do so as to offend neither the Thunderer nor his daughters. He picked some scrambled egg up on his fork, but did not put it in his mouth.

"I've been putting up with this for eleven centuries," continued Wotan. "Much more of it and I shall go quite mad."

"The ravens," said Loge for the fourth time, "have found Alberich and the Rhinedaughters, hanging around in a little village in..."

"It all started when their mother left me," continued Wotan, "and was I glad to see the back of her. But my dear daughters, all nine of them, decided that I needed looking after. They didn't want to, of course. They all wanted to have careers and lives of their own. I wanted them to have careers and lives of their own, preferably in another hemisphere."

As if to prove his point, the Valkyrie Waltraute came storming in. "You've been eating the bread again, haven't you?" she said bitterly.

"That's what it's there for."

"You've started a new loaf when there was half a loaf left in the breadbin. Now I suppose I'll have to throw it out for the ravens."

"Half a loaf is better than no bread," Wotan roared after her as she stalked out again. A futile gesture. The Father of Battles banged his fist on the table, upsetting a coffee cup. A deep brown patch appeared on the tablecloth and Wotan turned white.

"You did that," he said to Loge. "If they ask, you did that. I've got to live in this house."

Loge, whose titles include the Father of Lies, was not too keen on this particular falsehood, but the alternative was probably metamorphosis into a disused canal. He nodded meekly.

"So we've all been stuck in this wretched great barn of a place, miles from anywhere, driving each other mad for a thousand years," said the King of the Gods. "They hate it as much as I do, but they'll never move."

"At least there are only eight of them now," said Loge. "It must have been far worse when Brunnhilde was..."

Loge fell silent, terrified lest his lack of tact should arouse Wotan's anger. But Wotan only laughed. "You must be joking," he said. "Imagine my delight when I'd finally managed to get one of them off my hands—and no question, Brunnhilde was the worst—and I thought that perhaps they'd all go away and at last I'd be allowed to wear my comfortable shoes in the dining-room. I fixed that miserable child up with Siegfried the Dragon-Slayer, the most marvellous man who ever lived. And look what she did to him."

Loge nodded sympathetically; tact was all that stood between him and a future in fish-farming.

"Mind you," said Wotan, "he was lucky. Imagine what it would have been like being married to her. Give me a spear in the small of the back any day." The Lord of the Ravens shook his head sadly. "They blame me, of course. They blame me for everything. The only people in the world who aren't entitled to."

"About the Rhinedaughters," suggested Loge.

"Ask them to do anything useful, of course, and you get bad temper all day long. No, my family is a great trial to me, and I am a great trial to my family. If I had my time over again..."

"The Hoover's broken," said Waltraute, appearing in the doorway. "I suppose I'll have to do the stairs with a dustpan and brush."

"Yes, I suppose you will." Wotan stood up, his one eye flashing. "You'll enjoy doing that."

He strode through the long corridors of Valhalla with Loge trotting at his heels like a terrified whippet, while all around him there came the calls of the Valkyries, informing him of further domestic disasters, until the vaulted ceiling that the Giants had built re-echoed with the sound.

"England, did you say?" whispered Wotan.

"Yes."

"Oh, good," said Wotan, "Let's go there straight away."

"Mind you," said Wotan, "I don't quite know how we're going to tackle this one."

"Couldn't we just rush him?" Loge suggested. "I'll hold his arms while you get the Ring off him."

They stood and looked up at the electrically-operated gates of the Hall. A gardener in a smart new boiler suit walked up to them, holding a rake.

"You can't park there," he said.

The long, sleek Mercedes limousine was blocking the driveway. Wotan stared at the gardener, who took no notice.

"Move it, or I'll call the police," said the gardener. "I've told you once."

"Certainly, right away," muttered Loge. There was no point in causing unnecessary trouble. "Sorry."

"That's bad," said Wotan, as they walked up from the village green, where they had parked the car. "I tried closing up his lungs to make it hard for him to breathe, but it didn't work. We're too near the Ring-Bearer's seat of power to be able to achieve anything by force. I imagine that idiot was under his protection."

Wotan stopped and studied the gates.

"There's no way through there by violence," he said. "We must be clever."

For some reason or other, Loge had a horrible feeling that by We, Wotan meant him. "What do you have in mind?" he asked.

"There are many things in the world that mortal men fear more than the Gods," said Wotan. airily. "I think it's about time that the Ring-Bearer was brought down to earth. He's a human being, not a God, and he's a citizen of a twentieth-century democracy." Wotan chuckled. "The poor bastard."

Malcolm was feeling happier than he had for some considerable time. He had just had lunch with a remarkably pretty girl, he was going to have lunch with her tomorrow, and, best of all, his secretary had just told him that she was going to take her annual holiday in a week's time. She was, needless to say, going to the Cotswolds. Malcom thought that they would probably make her an honorary member.

So, when the English Rose came knocking on his door at four o'clock, he expected nothing worse than a recital of her holiday plans. He draped a smile over his face and asked her what he could do for her.

"There's a man downstairs," she said, "from the Government."

Given what he had been doing since he acquired the Ring, it was understandable that Malcolm misunderstood this statement. He expected to find a humble messenger imploring him to take over the reins of State, or at least to accept a peerage. What he found was a sharp-faced individual in a dark grey suit with a briefcase.

"Herr Finger," said the intruder, "I'm from Customs and Excise. We're making inquiries about illicit gold dealing."

For a moment, Malcolm forgot who he had become, and his blood froze. Like all respectable people, he knew that he was guilty of something, although what it was he could not say; and the arrival of a representative of the Main Cop only confirmed his suspicions.

"I don't know what you mean," he stammered.

"About a month ago, a considerable sum of money in used currency notes was removed from the vaults of the Bank of England. Similar—withdrawals, shall we say?—were made from state banks all over the world. At the same time, large quantities of gold made an inexplicable appearance in the same vaults. Have you any comment, Herr Finger?"

Malcolm was too frightened to speak, and simply shook his head.

"On close examination, the gold was found to be part of a consignment supplied by a certain..." the man paused, as if choosing the right word "...a certain underground movement," he continued, "to a subversive organisation, based in this country but with international links. This organisation has been secretly undermining the fabric of society for some time, Herr Finger."

"Has it?" Malcolm's throat was dry.

"It most certainly has. And our investigations have led us to the conclusion..."

Malcolm, who for the last twenty-five years had done little in the evenings except watch the television, knew what was coming next. There was no point in running. Faceless men in lounge suits were probably aiming rifles at him at this very moment.

"...that you have some connection with this—this subversive ring."

The word Ring exploded in Malcolm's mind like a bomb. He focused on the intruder's mind, and did not have to read very far.

"*Now* do you have any comment to make, Herr Finger? Or should I say Malcolm Fisher?"

Malcolm leaned back in his chair and smiled serenely.

"If only my mother could see me," he said, and the serene smile became a grin. "Chatting like this with a real God."

"I beg your pardon? Mr. Fisher, this is not a laughing matter."

"You're Loge, aren't you? It's odd. I was frightened of you when I thought you were the taxman, but now you turn out to be a God, I'm not frightened at all."

"Oh, well," said Loge, "I should have known better, I suppose. But Wotan thought it was worth a try."

"It was," said Malcolm. "You had me worried, like I said. What were you going to do?"

"He'll murder me if I go back without it," said Loge. "He's got a horrid temper."

"What can he do to you? You're immortal."

"That's the trouble." Loge was trembling. "If you're mortal, all they can do to you is kill you. But if you're going to live forever, they can really get you."

"Surely not?"

"Don't you believe it. He'll turn me into an aquarium, I know he will."

"I'll get the housekeeper to bring us some tea," said Malcolm soothingly.

Loge calmed down slightly with some tea inside him, but the cup rattled in the saucer as he held it.

"I was meant to put the frighteners on you," he said. "First, I was to be a Customs man, then the VAT inspector, then the Fraud Squad, then MI5. If that didn't work, then I was to be the man from the IPU."

"What's the IPU?"

"Inexplicable Phenomena Unit. Wotan was sure you'd believe in it. It would be something like all those science fiction films about flying saucers invading the earth, and there's always a secret Government agency that knows all about them but keeps them secret so as not to alarm people. They're the ones who come and zap the Martians in the last reel. And I was going to be them, threatening to zap you. Sometimes I think he lives in a world of his own."

"He must be a difficult person to work for," said Malcolm.

"Difficult!" Loge cast his eyes up to the ceiling. "He's impossible."

"But I thought you were the clever one," said Malcolm.

"I used to be, back in the old days when life was much simpler. But progress has left me behind, I'm afraid, and Wotan has got more devious. And he's never forgiven me for the mistake I made in drawing up the contract for Valhalla."

"Mistake?"

Loge nodded glumly. "Oh, yes, it was a mistake all right, and I've never been allowed to forget it. A slip of the pen, and now look at me."

"What sort of a mistake?" asked Malcolm, purely from curiosity.

Loge sighed. "I might as well tell you. You'll find out sooner or later. The contract with the Giants was that they built us the castle in return for trading concessions in Middle Earth, and the German for "free port" is *Freihafen*. But the trouble was," Loge said, and even after a thousand years he blushed, "well, my handwriting has never been marvellous, and what I'd written looked more like *Freia zu haben,* which would mean that they would have the Goddess Freia as their reward for that bloody castle. I don't know what you're laughing at. It was a mistake anyone could have made."

Malcolm, despite his ill-concealed mirth, could sympathise, for his own handwriting was none too good. "But couldn't you explain the mistake?" he said.

"I did, God knows. But they wouldn't listen, and Wotan had just had a quarrel with Freia and was only too glad to get rid of her. He's always quarreling with his relatives."

Again, Malcolm could sympathise. "Well," he said, "at least it explains how that bargain came to be made. I couldn't understand it, the way it is in the books."

"Now you know." Loge was depressed again. "It was only because I suggested this Ring business that he didn't change me into something wet and nasty there and then. And that backfired too—well, you know all about that—and I've been one jump away from metamorphosis ever since."

Malcolm felt a curious sense of authority, and his tone to Loge was pleasantly patronising. "Don't worry," he said, "I won't let him turn you into anything."

"And how exactly will you stop him?"

"I don't know," Malcolm confessed. "But he can't go throwing his weight about like that any more. He'll just have to face facts, he's had his time."

Loge raised an eyebrow. "Don't take this the wrong way," he said, "but for someone who was terrified of the Customs inspector a few minutes ago, you're remarkably confident."

"I know. But that was real life. This is...well, it's real life too, but different somehow." Malcolm was silent for a while, as he tried to work something out in his mind. "You know how some people are good at some things and bad at others," he said. "For instance, some people are marvellous at business or the Stock Exchange or whatever, but they can't change a plug or iron a shirt. Maybe I'm like that. Maybe I'm hopeless at everything except being the master of the Ring, but I'm very good at that. I know how to do it, more or less, and only I can do it, and I'm happy doing it."

"Are you?"

"Well, no. But I'm no more miserable doing it than doing anything else, plus I can do it well, and I can't do anything else. It's like some people are naturally good singers or snooker players or they can compose music, and they've never tried it so they don't know. And then they do try it, just by accident or for fun, never expecting they'll be any good at it, and there they are. I don't know," he said despairingly, "maybe I'm imagining it. Maybe it's so easy any fool can do it. But I'm not afraid any more—not of your lot, anyway."

Loge stared at him in amazement. "You've been drinking," he said at last.

Malcolm shook his head. "No, I mean it. I may be no good at all at real life, but this sort of thing—you can tell your boss to do his worst and see if I care. I've already seen off Alberich and the Rhine-daughters, and I'll deal with him too, if he makes a nuisance of himself. I mean, what can he do to me? I can understand all languages and read people's thoughts, so I'll always know what's really going on. I can change my shape, so anything he tries to attack me with I can either beat or run away from. And I don't think that's all, either. I don't think he's got any power against the Ring. If he wants to do something and I won't let him, then he can't do it. Stands to reason."

"How's that?"

"Simple. Unless I do something wrong or think nasty thoughts, nothing unpleasant can happen in the world. So nothing unpleasant can happen to *me,* can it? I'm just as much a citizen of the world as anyone else, so I'm under my own protection." Malcolm was quite carried away by this train of thought. "What's the bit in the Bible about He saved others, He couldn't save Himself? You won't catch me falling for that one. And that's why I met that girl," he went on, more to himself than to Loge. "Nice things are happening to everyone else, so they're happening to me too." He laughed for pure joy, and Loge tapped the side of his head.

"You're as bad as he is," he said. "Don't say I didn't warn you."

"Don't worry about a thing," said Malcolm, grandly. "Everything will be fine, you'll see."

Loge rose to his feet. "I hope you're right," he said. "If not, come and feed the ducks on me on Sunday afternoons."

Wotan leaned back in the driver's seat of the Mercedes, turning over Loge's story in his cavernous mind.

"He's right, up to a point," said the King of the Gods. "Like I thought, force and violence are no good, and besides, I'm not sure how far I could take them. I still don't think I could actually take the Ring from him against his will without getting into serious trouble."

"Who with?"

"Me, in my role as the God of Justice. If I did take it and I found that I wasn't allowed to, I would have to cease to exist. Damn."

The Sky-God thought hard for a moment, then smiled. He had thought of something. Loge waited impatiently to hear what it was.

"It worked before," said Wotan quietly. "So why shouldn't it work again?"

Loge was mystified. "What?" he asked.

"The Brunnhilde option," said Wotan. "Why not?"

"But it didn't work the first time," Loge said. "It failed miserably."

"Because of the Hagen factor and the Siegfried aspect. And, if we're going to be honest about it, the Brunnhilde aspect, too. But now we're dealing with a different kettle of fish."

The metaphor made Loge squirm. "It's a terrible gamble," he said. "Don't blame me if..."

"As if I would. No, I think I've cracked it. He's just the sort of idiot who'd fall for it."

"That's true." Loge began to feel cautiously optimistic. "Why shouldn't he be his own worst enemy, just like everyone else?"

Malcolm watched the black limousine driving away, and poured himself a small whisky. He was rather worried about what he had said; it was the first time he had ever talked to a God, and perhaps he should have shown more respect. He strolled into the garden, and a blackbird fluttered down and perched in a rose bush beside him.

"Have you seen a white moth with pale blue spots on its wings?" asked the bird.

"No," replied Malcolm, "but I've got some peanuts if you're hungry."

"You can have enough of peanuts," said the bird. "Anyway, I wanted that particular moth. We've got people coming round for dinner to-morrow."

"Good hunting, then," said Malcolm. "Try round by the buddle-ias."

The bird cocked its head on one side. "Thanks," it said. "Good idea. Oh, and by the way."

"Yes?"

"Don't underestimate Wotan, whatever you do. There are more ways of killing a cat, you know."

"What do you mean?"

The bird fluttered its wings. "Don't ask me, I'm only a bird. Be-sides, it's my favourite proverb."

"Hope you find your moth," said Malcolm.

"So do I," said the blackbird. "Good night."

9

Flosshilde was always beautifully dressed. She had been following fashion since the dawn of time, and her wardrobe occupied the space on the bed of the Rhine between Andernach and Koblenz. Not only did she follow fashion, she led it; she had been wearing figure-of-eight brooches when the Iron Age was still in its infancy, and it was her pioneering work that had given the ladies of sixteenth-century Europe the surcingle. In comparison, she thought, the twentieth century was drab, to say the least. Nevertheless, she had looked out a rather clever lemon-coloured pullover and a pair of black and white striped trousers which had, oddly enough, been in vogue at the height of the Hallstadt Culture. If you keep things long enough, she had learnt by experience, they eventually come back into fashion.

To add the finishing touches, she decorated her ears with Snoopy earrings and slipped over her slim wrist a bracelet of amber which had been given to her by the first King of the Langobards and which looked reasonably like tortoiseshell plastic. She would, she concluded, do.

"Sorry I'm late," she said, as she sat down beside Malcolm in Carey's.

"You're not," he replied. "You're exactly on time."

"Am I?" Flosshilde looked most surprised. She had always made a habit of being at least five minutes late for everything, especially dates and assignations. If she had subconsciously decided to be punctual, there was cause for concern...

"I had a visit from Loge yesterday," Malcolm said.

"Loge?" Flosshilde's blue eyes opened wide. "What happened?"

"He tried to frighten me, but I soon got rid of him," Malcolm replied smugly. "He's not too bad when you get to know him."

Flosshilde was going to say something about this, but she somehow decided against it. Instead, she smiled.

"I know a funny story about him," she said.

"Is it the one about the Valhalla contract?"

"Yes," said Flosshilde, slightly annoyed.

99

"Tell me anyway," Malcolm said and, to her surprise, Flosshilde found that she wasn't annoyed any more. She told him the story, and he laughed.

"You tell it better than he does," he said.

"Of course I do," said Flosshilde. "I'm very good at telling stories. Have you heard the one about Hagen and the Steer-Horn?"

The name Hagen made Malcolm feel uncomfortable, and he wondered why she had mentioned it. Perhaps it was a sort of warning. Instinctively, he covered his right hand with his left, so as to hide the Ring.

"Go on," he said nervously.

As she told the story (which was very funny), Malcolm found himself looking at her rather carefully. He had done this before, of course, for she was well worth looking at, and once Malcolm had accepted that there was a future in looking at her it had become one of his favourite occupations. But he was looking for something else now. She was, after all, one of Them, and he would do well not to forget that. To reassure himself, he flicked through her subconscious mind and was delighted to find that there had been developments. It irritated him that he could not read his own inner thoughts, but he had a fair idea of what they were, on this subject at least. In his life to date, he had met very few girls, and most of those had been friends of his sister Bridget. As a result, he had tended to fall in love with all the rest, just to be on the safe side. Since there had been no risk of the love being returned, this was strictly his own business and nothing to do with anyone else. Only since he had met Flosshilde had he become aware that this was a rather foolish thing to do, and he had been relieved to find that the Rhinedaughter had not inspired the usual romantic daze in him that he knew so well. Instead, once he had got over the shock of seeing what was in her mind and wondering if she could really mean him and not some other Malcolm Fisher, he had carefully considered whether or not he liked her. He did, of course, but that was because she was nice, not just simply because she was there.

Tentatively, he lifted his left hand and used it to pick up his fork. The Ring was visible again, but she did not even look at it. Suddenly, a terrible thought struck Malcolm. Bearing in mind the conclusions he had just come to, what was he supposed to do next?

Flosshilde had seemed rather put out when he had told her that he would be busy for the rest of the day, but the statement had been partially true. There had been a letter from a certain L. Walker, of Lime Place, Bristol, that morning, and it seemed that L. Walker was coming to Combe Hall to catalogue the library.

The library, which was huge and contained no funny books, had come with the Hall when Malcolm bought it, and he had left it alone. Books, the estate agent had told him, provide excellent insulation, and since the heating bills would be very considerable in any event, he might as well leave them there even if he had no intention of ever reading them. Ever since he had moved in, however, the English Rose had been nagging him to have the library professionally catalogued, so that Malcolm would be able to know at a glance what he was missing. He had strenuously resisted these attempts, but he supposed that his secretary had booked L. Walker before she left for her holiday and deliberately not told him.

He drove back to Combe and went into the house. The housekeeper had been lying in wait for him, and he was tempted to make himself invisible before she could persuade him to buy a new vacuum-cleaner—she had been demanding one for weeks, although Malcolm knew perfectly well there were at least four in the house already. Perhaps she was starting a collection. But lately he had felt guilty about avoiding people who were, after all, his employees and only doing their jobs, so he stood his ground, like Leonidas at Thermopylae.

"There's someone to see you," said the housekeeper.

"Who is it?"

"About the library," she said. "From Bristol."

She made it sound as if Bristol was somewhere between Saturn and Pluto. But to Malcolm, who had been dealing with strangers from Valhalla and Nibelheim for what seemed like years now, Bristol sounded delightfully homely.

"That'll be L. Walker," he said. "Where did you put her?"

The housekeeper said the lady was in the drawing-room, and Malcolm had walked away before he thought to ask which one. Eventually, he found the stranger in the Blue drawing-room.

L. Walker was about five feet four, roughly twenty-three years old, with long, dark hair and the face of an angel. Malcolm, who knew exactly what an angel looks like, having turned himself into one during an idle moment, felt a very curious sensation, almost like not being able to breathe properly.

"Herr Finger?" said the girl. "I'm Linda Walker. I've come to catalogue the library. Ms. Weinburger..."

"Yes, of course." Malcolm did not want to hear about the English Rose. He wanted to know why his knees had gone weak, as if he had just been running. There was a long silence while Malcolm tried to regain the use of his mind.

"Could I see the library, perhaps?" said the girl.

"Yes," Malcolm replied. "It's through here somewhere."

He found it eventually, which was good work on his part considering that he had just been struck by lightning or something remarkably similar. He opened the door and pointed at the rows of books.

"That's it in there," he said.

"Well," said the girl, "I think I'll start work now, if you don't mind. The sooner I start, the sooner I'll be out from under your feet."

"There's no rush, honestly," said Malcolm quickly. "Please take as long as you like."

The girl looked at him and smiled. Malcolm had come to believe that he was fairly well equipped to deal with smiles, but this was a new sort; not a happy, optimistic smile but a sad, wistful smile. It didn't say, "Wouldn't it be nice if..." like the stock delivery of a Rhinemaiden, but, "It would have been nice if..." which is quite different.

"Thank you," said the girl, "but I'd better get on."

Malcolm began to feel that something he wanted was slipping through his fingers. "Where are you staying?" he asked.

"At the George and Dragon." said the girl. "I hope that's all right. Ms. Weinburger booked me in there."

"You could stay here, if you like. There's masses of room." As soon as he spoke the words, Malcolm wished he hadn't. There was something about this girl that made him feel like a predator, even though such thoughts had not crossed the threshold of his mind. The girl looked at him for about three-quarters of a second (although it seemed much longer). Then she smiled again, an "It's hopeless and we both know that, but..." sort of a smile.

"I'd like that very much," she said. "If you're sure it'd be all right."

As far as Malcolm was concerned, it could go in the Oxford Dictionary as a definition of all right. "I'll get the housekeeper to get a room ready," he said. "How long will it take you, do you think?"

"About a week," said the girl, "if I start today."

"But aren't you very tired, after your journey? How did you get here, by the way?"

"I got the train to Taunton and the bus to Combe," said the girl.

Malcolm was shocked to think of a girl like this having to travel by bus and train. He wanted to offer to buy her a car, but she would probably take it the wrong way.

"Did that take long?" A stupid question, and none of his business.

Why should he care how long it took? Oddly enough, the girl didn't say that. Instead, she answered the question.

"Oh, about three hours. I missed the connection at Taunton, I'm afraid."

Try as he might, Malcolm could think of no way of prolonging the conversation. He had no idea what he should say or do next, which was a pity, since he could imagine nothing in the world more important.

"Well," he said, "I'd better let you get on, then. See you later."

He left the library and walked slowly back to the drawing-room, bumping into several pieces of furniture on the way. This was awful, and he could see that plainly enough. Real life had caught up with him at last; not in the form of a Customs man or the Inexplicable Phenomena Unit, which he could probably have dealt with, but the juvenile delinquent with the golden arrows who had been making a dartboard of his heart since his voice had broken. This was no Rhinedaughter out of the world of his own in which he had been living and where he was master, but a fellow human being, a person, a potential source of great unhappiness.

"Oh *God*," he moaned. "Not again."

He sat down on the stairs and looked across at the library door. If he went away, he might miss her coming out, and that would never do. Then it occurred to him that he could make himself invisible and go and watch her cataloguing books, which must surely be the most wonderful sight in the world. He closed his eyes and was lost to sight.

Beside the unsalubrious waters of the Tone, Flosshilde stood and watched a seagull trying unsuccessfully to catch and eat an abandoned tire. She knew how it felt, in a way, and out of pure sympathy she smiled at the tire, which turned itself helpfully into a fish. The seagull, who had known all along that persistence overcomes all obstacles, devoured it thankfully, which was hard luck on the fish but nice for the seagull. You can't please everybody all the time, Flosshilde reflected, and the relevance of this observation to her own case made her thoughtful.

Not that she had any logical reason to be anything but happy; but in matters of happiness, logic plays but a small part. First, it was annoying that Malcolm had preferred to spend the day with a stuffy old librarian than a gorgeous Rhinedaughter. Second, it was annoying that she should be annoyed. In fact, it was the latter irritation that was the worse, or so she hoped. The first unpleasant thing was merely a matter of her vanity (she told herself). The second unpleasant thing might have serious consequences for her career. An enamoured Rhinedaughter, like a blind chauffeur, is unlikely to progress far in her chosen profession. Try as she might, however, she was unable to feel greatly concerned about the prospect, and that was worse still...

"Bother," she said.

Wellgunde, who had been circling slowly under the surface, jumped up onto the bank. "Get you," she said. "All dressed up and nowhere to go."

Flosshilde put her tongue out, but Wellgunde ignored her. "I thought you'd have been out with your friend," she said, shaking the water out of her hair.

"Well, I'm not," replied Flosshilde.

"Playing hard to get, are you?"

At that particular moment, Flosshilde would have liked to be able to turn her sister into a narrowboat. "Haven't you got anything better to do?" she said wearily.

"I'm keeping you company," replied Wellgunde. "You look as though you could do with cheering up."

"I'm perfectly cheerful, thank you," said Flosshilde coldly.

"It must be wonderful to be in love," cooed Wellgunde. "I'm terribly jealous."

"I'm not in any such thing," snapped her sister. "But I can understand you being jealous."

Wellgunde took out a mirror and examined herself lovingly. "You're only young once, I suppose," she said. "You go ahead and enjoy yourself. Don't you worry about us."

Flosshilde frowned. Sisters can be very annoying at times.

"Don't let it worry you that if you go off with this Ring-Bearer of yours, we'll never get our Ring back ever. Don't let it cross your mind that the Ring is all we've got, since we haven't got dashing boyfriends who have to disguise themselves as other people if they ever want to get anywhere."

"Don't worry, I won't."

"We're your sisters, after all. We don't want to stand in your way for a second. And if you think it's worth it, you go ahead. Well, since you're not going to be busy this afternoon, you might put a duster round the riverbed. It was your turn yesterday, but you were out."

"Oh, go away," said Flosshilde rudely.

"I'm going," said Wellgunde placidly. "I only popped up to tell you that while you've been moping about, we've been working."

"I thought you said you were going to leave him alone."

"We haven't been persecuting your precious darling, if that's what you mean. We've been chatting with Thought and Memory."

"How fascinating."

"Yes, it was rather. Apparently, they've been watching Combe Hall all day, and your friend was having ever such a long chat with an extremely nice-looking girl."

Any doubts Flosshilde might have had about her feelings for Malcolm were dispelled by this news. She went as white as a sheet.

"Of course, they can't read his thoughts because he's the Ring-Bearer, so they can't be sure, but to listen to those two you don't have to be able to read thoughts to see what your friend thinks of his new friend. Written all over his silly face, they said."

"That's nice for him," Flosshilde said, very quietly.

"Well," said Wellgunde, "it's not so nice for us, is it? What if he gives her the Ring? Where would we all be then?"

Flosshilde said something extremely disrespectful about the Ring and dived into the Tone, leaving Wellgunde looking very pleased with herself. Perhaps, mused the eldest of the Rhinedaughters, she hadn't told her sister the whole truth, but then, she had gone off in a huff without giving her a chance. Her conscience was clear...

After spending the whole afternoon lugging heavy books about, Malcolm imagined, she would be sure to want a rest and possibly a drink. He wished he could have helped her, but that would have looked pointed, since one does not buy a dog and bark oneself. Besides, if he had materialised out of thin air and said "Can I carry that for you?" she would probably have had a fit; another of the problems associated with dealing with a real person.

She was certainly conscientious, and Malcolm admired that, but she had carried on with her work for a very long time. When finally she seemed to be about to call it a day, Malcolm transported himself back to the stairs and wondered what on earth he was to do next. It seemed like hours before the library door opened, and still he hadn't thought of anything. He stood up quickly, and tried to look as if he was just passing.

"Finished for the day?" he asked.

"Yes, thanks," she said, and smiled again. This smile, a sort of "If only...but no" smile, wiped Malcolm's mind clean of thoughts and words, and he stood gawping at her as if she was the one who had suddenly appeared out of thin air.

"Are you sure it's no trouble for me to stay here?" she said.

"No, of course not. I told the housekeeper to phone the George and Dragon."

"Thank you, then," she said.

"I took your suitcase up to your room," he went on, as if this act had been comparable to saving her from drowning. "And I've told the cook you'll be having dinner... If that's all right, I mean."

That was not how he had meant to suggest that she should have dinner with him. He had wanted to suggest it casually. He had wanted many things in his life, and got very few of them. But the girl did not seem to mind. She said, "Are you sure that's all right?" and Malcolm felt a tiny flicker of impatience within his raging heart, but it passed very quickly.

"It must be nice having a cook," she said.

Malcolm felt the need to define himself against a charge of hedonism. "I'm afraid I'm a dreadful cook," he said, "and she sort of came with the place."

The girl said nothing, and Malcolm forced some more words into his mouth, grabbing the first ones that came to hand.

"You know how it is," he burbled, "these great big houses."

Utter drivel of course, but she seemed not to notice. "Yes," she said, "we used to live in a huge old house. It was dreadfully difficult to keep it clean and warm."

She seemed unwilling to expand on this point, and they walked on in silence. Malcolm had no idea where they were going, but that did not seem to matter very much.

"Was it as big as this? Your house, I mean." Any more of this, Malcolm thought, and I shall bite my tongue off.

"Yes," said the girl. "It kept me and my sisters very busy."

"You've got sisters, then?" he went on, as if that were the most remarkable thing that he had ever heard.

"Eight," said the girl. "It's a large family. Are you *sure* it's all right me staying to dinner? I mean, you haven't got people coming or anything?"

"No," Malcolm said, "really. Shall we go and sit in the drawing-room?"

The girl was silent, as if thinking this over very carefully. "Yes," she said at last.

It was at this point that it occurred to Malcolm that he hadn't read her thoughts, to see if by any chance they resembled his, no matter how remotely. But he found that he didn't want to. It seemed somehow indecent, for she was not a God or a Rhinedaughter, but a human being. Besides, if she wasn't thinking along the same lines as he was, he really didn't want to know.

"You speak English very well," she said, as Malcolm eventually found the drawing-room.

"Thank you," Malcolm said, deeply touched, and only just managed to stop himself from returning the compliment. "I went to school in England," he said, truthfully. "Can I get you a drink?"

"No, thank you," said the girl, looking down at her feet.

"Are you sure?"

"Well, if you're sure..."

Malcolm was sure, but he felt it would be superfluous to say so. "What can I get you?" he asked.

"A small sherry, please."

Malcolm poured out a small sherry—very small, as it turned out, for he did not want her to think he was trying to get her drunk. "Is that enough?" he asked.

"That's fine." Another smile, this time a "We can't go on like this, you know" smile.

"So how long have you been cataloguing?"

"About two years," said the girl. That seemed to put the seal on that particular subject.

"I suppose it's like being a librarian," Malcolm went on, and he reckoned that digging peat was probably easier work than making conversation under these circumstances. The girl agreed that it was very like being a librarian.

"How long have you lived here?" she asked, and Malcolm found that he could not remember. He had to think hard before he replied. Afterwards, there was a long silence, during which the girl drank a quarter of her small sherry. The temptation to read her thoughts was very strong, but Malcolm resisted it. It wouldn't be fair.

"So how do you set about cataloguing a library?" he asked. The girl told him, and that took up at least three minutes, during which Malcolm was able to collect what remained of his thoughts. Summoning up all his powers of imagination, he compiled a list of questions and topics which might, with a great deal of luck, get them through dinner.

In the event, they nearly did, although Malcolm had to use a great deal of ingenuity. Why did he find it so easy to talk to Flosshilde, who was only a friend, and so difficult to keep a conversation going with the most wonderful person in the world? There was only one topic that he couldn't mention; on the other hand, it was the one topic he did want to discuss with her. Instead, they mostly seemed to talk about libraries, a subject that Malcolm had never given much consideration to in the past. At about half-past nine, even this theme collapsed into silence, and Malcolm resigned himself to yet another disappointment. The girl was obviously nervous and ill at ease; scarcely to be wondered at. She had come here to do a straightforward job of work, the job she had trained to do and at which she was no doubt highly competent, and instead of being allowed to go to a comfortable hotel where she could take her shoes off and read a good book she had been compelled to listen to his inane ramblings. She must think he was mad. Certainly, she wouldn't be there in the morning. At first light, she would unlock her door and make a run for it, or climb out of the window down a rope of sheets. It was all unbearably sad, and as a human being he was a complete and utter failure. He had made the mistake of treating a normal, grown-up woman from the twentieth century as if she was something out of a romantic story, and he deserved all the heartbreak he was undoubtedly going to get.

"I expect you're very tired," he said abruptly, "after the journey and a hard day's work. I'll show you to your room."

They tracked up the stairs in silence. It was still light outside, but she could read a book or something until it was time to go to sleep. At least he wasn't sending her to bed without any supper.

"Good night, then," she said, and she smiled at him for the last time that day. It was a smile you could take a photograph by, and it said, "I like you very much and it's a pity you think I'm so boring, but there we go." The door closed in front of the embers of it, and Malcolm stood in the hall opening and shutting his eyes. To hell with being fair. He located her thoughts and read them. Then he read them again, just to be sure. Then he read them again, because he liked them so much.

"Well I'm damned," he said slowly to himself. "Well I never."

Then he went to bed.

The two ravens floated down and perched on the roof of the Mercedes. Wotan put his head out of the window and said "Well?"

"They've gone to bed," said Thought.

"Separately," said Memory.

"But not to worry," said Thought. "She's doing all right."

Wotan frowned. "But he can read her thoughts," said Wotan. "He'll just look into her mind and then it'll be all over. He'll chuck her out so fast she'll bounce all the way down the drive."

Memory chuckled. "I wouldn't worry on that score," he croaked. "He's dead meat. Head over heels."

"And even if he does," said his partner, "he'll only make things worse for himself. I had a quick look myself."

"Oh." Wotan was baffled. "You can't mean she fancies him?"

"Something rotten," said Thought. "You wouldn't read about it."

"Oh, that's *marvellous,*" Wotan said, disgusted. "Now I'll never get the perishing thing back."

"Relax," said Memory. "You know her. Duty must come first, even if it means betraying the man she truly loves."

"Especially if it means betraying the man she loves," said Thought. "She's a real chip off the old block, that girl."

Wotan was forced to agree. Of all his eight surviving daughters, the Valkyrie Ortlinde most resembled her father in her capacity for self-torture. She would revel in it. Most of all, she would enjoy blaming him afterwards.

"We've cracked it," said Wotan.

10

Alberich loathed travelling by air. This was partly the natural preju-
dice of one who had lived most of his life underground, partly because
the food that they serve you on little plastic trays with hollow mould-
ings to hold the ketchup gave him violent indigestion. But he was a
businessman, and businessmen have to travel on aircraft. Since there
seemed to be no prospect of progress in his quest for the Ring, he had
thought it would be as well if he went back to Germany for a week to
see what sort of a mess his partners were making of his mining consul-
tancy. He had no interest in the work itself, but it provided his bread
and butter; if it did not exactly keep the wolf from the door, it had
enabled him to have a wolf-flap fitted so that the beast could come in
and out without disturbing people.

As luck would have it, he had been given a seat by the window,
and he looked aimlessly out over the world that by rights should have
been his. If he had had any say in its running, there would have been
fewer cities and more forests. He let his attention wander for a moment.

Something was tapping on the window. He looked round, and saw
a slightly bedraggled raven pecking at the thick Perspex with its beak.
A second raven was beating the air furiously with its wings, trying to
hover and fly at the speed of sound at the same time.

"What do you want?" he mouthed through the window.

The raven pecked away vigorously, and Alberich felt slightly nervous. If the stupid bird contrived to break the window, he would be
sucked out into space. "Go away," he mouthed, and made shooing
gestures with his fingers.

"Forget it," Memory shrieked through the rushing wind. "He can't
hear a word you're saying."

But Thought was nothing if not persistent. With his beak, he
pecked a series of little marks onto the Perspex. When he was finished,
Alberich was able to make out the words, "Wotan says stay out of
England," written back to front on the pane. He nodded to the ravens

to acknowledge the message, and they wheeled away exhausted. Alberich pondered this warning for a moment, then looked at his watch.
They were due to land in Frankfurt in half an hour.

At Frankfurt Airport, he telephoned his partner.

"Dietrich?" he said. "It's Hans. Look, I'm at Frankfurt now, but
I've got to go back to England right away. There's a flight in three hours.
Can you bring me some clean shirts and the papers on the Nigerian
project?"

"What have you got to go back for?"

"What's that? Oh, would you believe I left my briefcase behind?
With all the things I need for the Trade Fair?"

"Can't they send it on?"

"It'd take too long. I'm going back."

"Fancy forgetting your briefcase."

"I'm only human," Alberich lied. "Don't forget the shirts."

To his surprise, Malcolm had managed to get some sleep, but he was
awake by six. He went through the events of the previous day in his
mind, trying to reassure himself that it had all happened. Something
inside him told him that this strange happiness was bound to end in
tears, but he put that down to his natural pessimism. Besides, there
was one sure way of knowing whether things were all right or not.

He tuned his mind in to the early morning news and was reassured. No disasters had afflicted the world during the last day, although
there had been one strange occurrence. A farmer from the small village
of Combe in Somerset had been out shooting rabbits at a quarter to
ten last night, and had seen his ten-acre field of wheat change before
his eyes into ten acres of roses, peonies, narcissi, daffodils and tulips.
The farmer, a Mr. William Ayres of Combe Hill Farm, attributed this
extraordinary mutation to a leak from the nearby Hinckley Point nuclear power station, although no such leak had as yet been confirmed
by the CEGB.

Malcolm blinked, and for a moment was concerned. But Mr. Ayres
was bound to be insured, and even if he wasn't, he could pick the flowers
and use them to decorate the church for his daughter's wedding. Malcolm laughed. He bore the Ayres family, both its present and prospec-
tive members, no ill will at all, and that was surely a good thing for
the world.

It occurred to him that he had forgotten to tell the girl when breakfast would be ready. He jumped out of bed, thought up a light blue
shirt and a pair of cream corduroy trousers, and transported himself
across the house. As he passed the library, he heard cataloguing noises.

Although it was only half-past six, the girl was working already. He listened carefully for her thoughts, and a tender smile hitched up the ends of his mouth. She was throwing herself into her work to take her mind off the sad feelings of longing in her heart. A soppy girl, Malcolm could not help thinking, but none the worse for that. He opened the library door and went in.

"You're up early," he said.

"I hope I didn't disturb you," said the girl anxiously.

"Not at all," Malcolm replied. "I'm usually awake by this time. Would you like some breakfast?"

After the inevitable, "If you're sure" ritual, she agreed to have a cup of coffee and a slice of toast, and Malcolm hurried down to the kitchen. The coffee machine seemed to take for ever, as did the toaster, but eventually he got what he wanted out of both of them and carried the tray up to the library. In his mind he tried to re-hearse some way of bringing the conversation round to the issues he wanted to raise, but he had to give up the attempt. He would think of something when the time came, and he did not want to rush something as important as this, even if the result was a fore-gone conclusion.

Let other pens dwell on joy and happiness. It is enough to record that Malcolm hijacked a discussion on card-indexes and used it to con-vey his message. Although he could read the girl's thoughts and so avoid all misunderstandings, he still found it heavy going, and heard him-self using words and phrases that would have seemed excessively sentimental in *True Love* magazine; but everyone has a right to make fools of themselves once in their lives. The main thing was that every-thing was going to be all right now, and he had managed to persuade her of this. She had seemed rather diffident at first, but he had got so used to her saying, "Are you sure you don't mind?" and, "If you're sure it's no trouble," that he took no notice of her words and simply watched her thoughts going round, like the figures on a petrol pump. When the appropriate reading came up, he took her hand and squeezed it gently. Through the snowstorm of emotions that raged around him, he heard a tinkling sound, like a coin dropping on the floor. Suddenly this seemed very important, and he looked down. On the polished wooden floor he saw the Ring, which had somehow slipped off his fin-ger. He felt a sudden urge to give it to her; for what better gift could there be than the whole world?

She was still holding his hand, tightly and trustingly, so that it would be incredibly churlish of him to do anything except sit abso-lutely still and be loved. There was also a particularly fine smile going on, and he let the Ring lie there until it was over. Just to be sure, however, he covered the Ring with his foot.

Everything that needed saying had now been said, and it was obviously the time for action: a kiss, or something of that sort. But Malcolm could not bring himself to initiate such a move, although he could not imagine why. "One thing at a time," whispered a voice in his brain. "Let's not get carried away." So he contented himself with putting his arm tenderly round her shoulders, and suggesting that they go for a walk in the garden. For once, the girl did not ask him if he was sure that would be no bother, and they stood up, still entwined.

"Just a moment," Malcolm said. "Don't go away."

He stooped down swiftly and picked up the Ring. After a moment's hesitation, he pushed it back on his finger. It felt loose and uncomfortable.

"So how did you get her to agree to it?" Loge said. "It must have been difficult."

"Not really," said Wotan. "There was one of those grim silences we know so well in our family, then she said 'If you insist,' and there we were. I was amazed, as you can imagine. I'd thought up all sorts of arguments—you always said you wanted to work in the family business, it'll get you out of the house, a change is as good as a rest, that sort of thing—and I didn't have to use any of them. Women are strange creatures."

"Are you sure she's up to it?"

"Positive. You've only seen her in the domestic mode, nagging and persecuting."

"Which one was it again?"

"Ortlinde. She's the best-looking, and the droopiest. Mind you, with eight of them, I tend to get them mixed up. Maybe I should get them wearing numbers on their backs like footballers. I think Ortlinde's the second from youngest. Fancy another?"

"No, thanks, I'm driving."

"So am I, but who cares? This is something to celebrate." Wotan pulled open the drinks cabinet behind the front seat and took out a bottle of schnapps. "Here's to two birds with one stone. I get control of the Ring and shot of a dopey daughter at the same time."

"I hate to say this..." said Loge.

"I know, I know, it didn't work before and all the rest of it. But that was different."

"Not so different." Loge knew he was pushing his luck, but it had to be said. Besides, if it all went wrong, Wotan would be so furious that he would be lucky to get away with being turned into a trout hatchery. "After all, Siegfried was roughly the same sort of proposition. He'd never had a girl before, either."

"Siegfried wasn't a drip," said Wotan crisply. "This one is. So's she. She's so wet you could grow cress on her."

"She didn't strike me as wet the other morning."

"Ah," said Wotan, "that's different. That's her complicated little psyche belting away, that is. You see, my daughters are all the same. The way they see it, I've ruined their lives for them by making them stay at home in that bloody great house, stunting their emotional growth and all the rest of it, when they should have gone out into the world and had a good time. And you can see their point, I suppose. That house is a liability." Wotan scowled at the very thought of it, and the first drops of rain started to fall. "It's difficult to explain my family to a normal, sane person, but I think it goes something like this. They've been cooped up in Valhalla ever since their mother left, with nothing to do but be resentful and tell themselves how inadequate and unlovable they are, and how nobody could ever be interested in them because of their stunted personalities (stunted by me, it goes without saying). And they take all this out on their poor old dad by making his life almost as miserable as their own, in the tried and tested way you saw the other day."

Loge had been nodding his head and making sympathetic noises until he felt quite dizzy. He didn't want to hear any of this, but Wotan seemed determined to tell him. A combination of schnapps and relief was making him unwind, although whether he would be any safer to be employed by unwound than tensed up remained to be seen. Rattlesnakes, Loge remembered, usually unwind just before they bite.

"So at home they really let fly. Not that we have long, earnest conversations about the state of our tortured personalities, thank God. No, they've decided that they can't talk to me, I'm delighted to say, and so what they do is they sublimate it all—I think that's the right word, isn't it?—into endless domestic trivia, like who had the Sellotape last and how can you expect me to find things if you will insist on moving them. But put them down in the outside world, and they turn into fluffy little bunnies, wouldn't say boo to a goose, you know the sort of thing. I don't know which is worse, actually. At least they keep the place clean. Anyway, no self-confidence is the root of it all, so if our Ring-Bearer can convince Ortlinde that he's serious about her and that somebody really loves her in spite of everything, he'll need a crowbar to get her off him. Serve the idiot right, that would."

"But if she hates you so much, what makes you think she'll get the Ring for you? Won't she just go off with her Redeemer and leave you to get on with it?"

"That was worrying me, I must admit, but when I thought it over, I saw just how clever I'd been," said Wotan smugly. "The fact that she really does love him in her own, unique, screwed-up way means she can't fail. You see, the last thing my daughter wants is to be happy. She'd hate it. No, what she wants is to be finally, definitively unhappy, and for it all to be my fault. It'd finally confirm all her dearest illusions about how her life has been ruined. People like that would far rather be right than happy. No, she'll get that Ring if it kills her."

Loge wiped his forehead with his hand, and wished that he could go away and do something less stressful for a change, such as drive the chariot of the Sun or make the crops grow. But that was out of the question.

"The only thing that could go wrong is if he finds out who she really is," Wotan said, pouring himself another drink. "But my guess is that he won't want to find out, so unless somebody tells him, he won't work it out for himself. I think he's just as bad as she is. In fact, they're perfectly suited to each other. Who knows, they may even stick together after she's got the Ring off him, and I'll never have to see her ever again. Wouldn't that be perfect? Then there would only be seven of them, one for every day of the week. But it's unlikely," he added sadly. "Like I said, she'd go mad if she were happy."

The rain had stopped, and Loge deduced that Wotan was in a good mood for once. That removed the immediate threat of transformation, but he still felt uneasy. Over the last few thousand years, Loge had found that Wotan's good moods always tended to come before periods of universal misery.

"So what do we do now?" he asked.

"Leave her to it," said Wotan, leaning back in his seat. "I always knew she'd come in useful one day."

Love, the songwriter says, is the sweetest thing, and too many sweet things can make you feel slightly sick. But Malcolm had got through the endearments and sweet nothings stage quite safely, and had finally got the girl to tell him all about herself. She had not wanted to, and as he listened to the story that eventually came pouring out, he could quite understand why. Not that he was bored; but an overdose of tragedy can cause roughly the same symptoms as boredom, such as a strong desire to change the subject. That, however, would not be tactful. He only hoped that he would not be called upon to give an equally full account of himself, which might call for more inventiveness than he felt himself capable of.

"You see," said the girl, "none of us could ever really *talk* to my father, and my father could never really *talk* to us, so that in the end I found I couldn't even talk to my sisters. We all just bottled it all up inside ourselves, really, until we wanted to hit out at each other. But we couldn't, because of not being able to talk. Do you see what I'm getting at?"

"Sort of."

"And it was obvious that my father was absolutely heartbroken when my mother left him. He tried to put a brave face on it, of course, but we all knew that she had let him down as well as letting us down, and that somehow we had let him down as well. And, of course, he feels that he's let us down, and so now we can't communicate at all."

"That's dreadful," Malcolm said, wishing he hadn't raised the subject in the first place. It was obviously very painful for her to talk about her problems like this, and he hoped that she would stop and not upset herself further. But no such luck.

"And we could all see how much of a disappointment we were to him. He wanted us to have careers and achieve something in the world, but we knew we couldn't leave him like that after my mother had left him, because he would feel left out and that would be awful."

"But you've got a career," said Malcolm, brightly.

The girl looked startled, as if she had made a mistake. "Well, sort of," she said. "But it's not a proper one."

"But you don't live in the family house any more, do you?"

"Yes. No. Well, sort of. I share this flat, but I go home a lot too."

The girl stopped talking and stared at her shoes. They were sensible shoes and had seen many seasons, like her sensible tweed skirt and her honest cream pullover. Her mother had probably bought them for her, Malcolm thought, just before she left.

"Well," he said, trying to sound cheerful, "you've got me to look after you now."

They sat down on a bench and looked out over the park. It was a beautiful morning, although there had been one brief shower, and as soon as all the tragic stories had been got over with, it would all be perfect.

"What do you like doing?" Malcolm asked.

"Oh, I don't know really." She thought about it for a long time. "Walking, I suppose. And I quite like my work. Well, no, I don't really, but it's better than nothing."

"Let's go for a stroll by the river," Malcolm said firmly.

They walked in silence for a while, and stopped to admire the view of Farmer Ayres' prodigious crop of assorted flowers. In the distance, a

BBC camera crew were unrolling miles of flex, so it would probably all be on the 9 O'Clock News that evening. Malcolm wanted to tell her that he had laid the flowers on for her benefit, to show how much he loved her, but he could not think of a way of explaining it all.

"Who's that girl on the river bank waving at you?"

Malcolm followed her finger and recognised Flosshilde. His heart fell. "That's just a friend of mine," he said. "No-one important."

"I think she wants to say something to you... Oh."

Malcolm could have sworn that she had recognised Flosshilde, but that was obviously impossible, so he did not even bother to check her thoughts. He wanted to walk away and pretend he hadn't seen the Rhinedaughter, for he could not be bothered with her just now. After all, she was a very pretty girl, and Linda might jump to quite the wrong conclusions. Unfortunately, it was too late now. He put his arm around Linda's shoulders rather as a Roman legionary might have raised his shield before facing an enemy, as Flosshilde ran across to join them.

"Hello," said the Rhinedaughter, and there was something very strange about her manner. "Hope you don't mind, but I've been for a swim in your river."

Nervously, Malcolm introduced her to the girl. Flosshilde looked at Malcolm for a moment, then turned and smiled radiantly at the girl, so that for an instant Malcolm was convinced that something terrible was going to happen. But nothing did, and Malcolm reassured himself that he must have been imagining it. For her part, Flosshilde looked very slightly disappointed, although Malcolm could not think why.

"Don't I know you from somewhere?" Flosshilde asked. "Your face is very familiar."

"I don't think so," said the girl, nervously. She was obviously very shy.

"Must be my imagination, then. Well, I must be going. Oh, and I won't be able to make lunch tomorrow. Sorry."

"Some other time, then," said Malcolm. "See you."

"I expect so," said the Rhinedaughter. "Have fun."

She ran lightly down to the river and dived in. For some reason, the girl did not seem surprised by this, and Malcolm was relieved that he would not have to try and find some explanation. He dismissed Flosshilde from his mind.

The Rhinedaughter circled for a few minutes under the surface, then slowly paddled upstream to a deep pool where she knew she could not be seen. It had been pointless trying to turn the woman into a frog;

the daughters of Wotan are not so lightly transformed. At least she had given the Valkyrie notice that she had a fight on her hands.

It was all very well saying that, but Flosshilde had no stomach for a fight. It was inconceivable that Malcolm didn't know who she was or what she was likely to be after, and if he was so much in love that he was prepared to take the risk... After all, he had apparently been prepared to take a similar risk with her before the Valkyrie showed up, and obviously he had not been in love then, just lonely. And any fool could see that Ortlinde was completely smitten, so it seemed likely that she too had given up hope of getting the Ring. After all, Malcolm was in a unique position to know what was going on inside her head. So he could take care of himself.

Vanity, said Flosshilde to herself, and wounded pride, that was all it was. That anyone could prefer a stuffy old Valkyrie to her was naturally hard for her to believe, but Malcolm obviously did, and that was all there was to it.

From the cover of a small boulder, she peered out. The Young Couple were kissing each other rather awkwardly under the shade of an oak tree. Flosshilde shrugged her shoulders and slid back into the water, as graceful as an otter. Beside her, she was aware of her sisters, swimming lazily in the gentle current.

"Told you so," said Wellgunde.

"I couldn't care less," said Flosshilde. "And if you say one word about the Ring, I'll break your silly neck."

"Wouldn't dream of it, would we?" replied Wellgunde smugly.

"I'm bored with England," said Flosshilde suddenly, as they reached the head of the Tone. "Why don't we go back home?"

"What a good idea," said Woglinde. "Let's do that."

11

At Valhalla the Wednesday afternoon General Meeting of the Aesir, or Company of Gods, is presided over by Wotan himself. At these meetings, the lesser divinities—thunder-spirits, river-spirits, cloud-shepherds, Valkyries, Norns, nixies, powers, thrones, ettins and fetches—have an opportunity to bring to Wotan's attention any matters which they feel require action on his part, and receive their instructions for the next seven days. There is also a general discussion on future strategy and a long-range weather forecast.

Loge, as secretary to the Company, had the unenviable task of keeping the minutes of each meeting and presenting the agenda. At the meeting that immediately followed the Ring-Bearer's entrapment by the Valkyrie Ortlinde, he found himself having to reorganise the entire programme to give enough time for a thorough discussion, only to find that the discussion that followed was over much sooner than he had anticipated. There were votes of thanks from the Company to Ortlinde and Wotan, which were duly entered in the records, and Waltraute inquired how long Ortlinde was likely to be away and who was supposed to do her share of the housework while she was absent. Loge was then compelled to proceed to Any Other Business with well over an hour of the scheduled time still to go.

"I would like to bring to the Chairman's attention the fact that the light-bulb on the third-floor landing of the main staircase of Valhalla has gone again, and I would request him to replace it immediately," said Schwertleite, "before someone trips over and breaks their neck."

"That's not nearly as dangerous as the carpet on the back stairs," said Grimgerde. "I've asked you hundreds of times to nail it down properly, but nobody ever listens to a word I say."

Loge was writing furiously. All the minutes of meetings had to be made in runes, which cannot be written quickly.

"May I suggest," said Wotan, grimly attempting to make himself heard, "that this is neither the time nor the place..."

"Next time you stub your toe in the dark because you couldn't be bothered to replace a light-bulb..."

Wotan put his hands in front of his one eye and groaned audibly. "We were discussing the Ring," he muttered.

"And please don't put your elbows on the table," interrupted the Valkyrie Helmwige. "I spent the whole morning trying to get it looking respectable after you spilt coffee all over it."

Wotan made a vague snarling noise at the back of his throat. "This is a meeting of the Aesir," he growled, "and I would ask you to behave in an appropriate manner."

"While we're on the subject," retorted his daughter, the Driver of the Spoil, "you might try dressing in an appropriate manner. Why you insist on wearing the same shirt three days in a row... How am I expected to get the collars clean?"

"Any other business," Wotan said, but his growl was more like a whimper.

"You've got whole drawers full of shirts you never wear," said Grimgerde, with a world of reproach in the deep pools of her blue eyes. She hadn't had a new shirt, or a new anything, for four hundred and twenty years, but she didn't complain. She never went anywhere anyway.

"I shall wear what the hell I like when I like," said Wotan, and what had intended to be authority when the words passed his vocal cords was definitely petulance when the sounds emerged through the gate of his teeth. "Now, can we please..."

A general baying of Valkyries drowned out the voice of the Sky-God, and Loge stopped trying to keep the minutes of the meeting. Over the centuries, he had evolved his own shorthand for the inevitable collapse into chaos that rounded off each Wednesday afternoon in the Great Hall. He sketched in a succession of squiggles under the last intelligible remark he had been able to record and began drawing sea-serpents.

The discussion had moved on to the topic of leaving the tops off jars when a rock-troll, who had been thoroughly enjoying the conflicts of his betters, noticed something out of the corner of one of his eyes. He nudged the middle-aged Norn with mouse-blond hair who was knitting beside him, and they turned and stared at the doorway of the Hall. One by one, the minor deities, then the Vanir, then the High Gods themselves abandoned the debate and gazed in astonishment at the three rather pretty girls who had wandered in through the Gates of Gylfi.

It was at least a thousand years since the Rhinedaughters, who were responsible for the noblest river in Europe, had attended a Wednesday afternoon meeting. No-one except Wotan and Loge could remember exactly why they had stopped coming. Some said that they had been expelled for flirting with the cloud-shepherds at the time of the Great Flood. Others put it down to the girls' natural frivolity and apathy. Wotan and Loge knew that the river-spirits had walked out in tears after the stormy debate that followed the theft of the Ring from Alberich and had not been back since, although both Gods correctly attributed this continued absence to forgetfulness rather than actual principle.

"Well I never!" whispered the Norn to the rock-troll. "Look who it is!"

The rock-troll nodded his head. Since he had been created out of solid granite at the dawn of time, this manoeuvre required considerable effort on his part, but he felt it was worth it. "It's the Girls," he hissed through his adamantine teeth.

It was Wotan himself who broke the silence. "What the hell do you want?" he snapped.

"We just thought we'd pop our heads round and say hello," said Wellgunde sweetly. "It's been simply ages."

The silence gave way to a hubbub of voices, as each immortal greeted the long-lost members of their Company. Most vociferous were a group of cloud-shepherds who, several centuries before, had arranged to meet the Rhinedaughters for a picnic at the place which has since become Manchester, and who had been waiting there ever since. Only the Valkyries and their father seemed less than delighted to see the Rhinedaughters back again. Wotan suspected that he knew the reason for their visit, while his daughters felt sure that the river-spirits hadn't wiped their feet before coming into the Hall.

"So," said Wotan, when the noise had subsided, "what have you been doing all these years?"

"Sunbathing, mostly," said Woglinde truthfully. "Doesn't time fly when you're having fun?"

"It's all right for some," whispered the Norn to the troll. But the troll seemed uneasy. "Something's going to happen," he said, and he sniffed loudly, as if trying to identify some unfamiliar smell.

"Is that all?" laughed Wotan, nervously jovial. "Or have you been doing any work?"

"Depends on what you call work," replied Wellgunde. "The river sort of runs itself really. But we have been looking at other rivers to see if we can pick up any hints."

"Sort of an exchange visit," said Woglinde, helpfully.

"For example," continued Wellgunde, "we visited a river called the

Tone in England. Not very helpful, I'm afraid."

"But guess who we bumped into while we were over there," cooed Woglinde. "Go on, guess."

"I hate guessing," said Wotan irritably, and he picked up a document and began to study it diligently. Since he was to all intents and purposes omnipotent, it was not surprising that he could read a sheet of paper that was palpably the wrong way up.

"Ortlinde, that's who," said Flosshilde, who had not spoken before. Wotan made no reply, being obviously engrossed in his document. Suddenly, Flosshilde smiled at the papers in his hand, which turned into a small dragon. Wotan dropped it with a start, and it crawled away under the table. "Now what on earth was she doing there?"

The Norn had covered her eyes. She was fond of the Rhinedaughters, with whom she had spent many hours exchanging gossip, and Flosshilde's conjuring trick, performed in front of so many witnesses, was as clear a case of treasonable assault on the King of the Gods as one could hope to find. The penalty for this offence was instant metamorphosis, usually into a bush of some kind, and it was common knowledge that Wotan had been desperate for some pretext for getting rid of the Rhinedaughters ever since they had first emerged from the waters of their native river. Slowly, the Norn lowered her hands. The Girls were still there, still in human shape.

"I'll tell you, shall I?" continued Flosshilde. "She was there trying to get the Ring-Bearer to give her our Ring, which you should have given back to us a thousand years ago. So will you please tell her to stop it and go away?"

The Norn covered her eyes again, but she need not have bothered. Wotan simply looked away and threw a piece of cheese to the small dragon, which had curled up on his lap.

"If you don't," said Flosshilde, clear without being shrill, "we'll tell him who she is. Are you listening?"

There was a terrible silence. Never before had anyone, mortal or immortal, dared to threaten the Lord of Tempests in the Hall of his stronghold. Even the rock-troll held his breath, and the beating of his basalt heart was the only audible sound in the whole assembly. Wotan sat motionless for a moment, then rose sharply to his feet, sending the small dragon scampering for the safety of a coffee-table. He looked the Rhinedaughter in the eye, and the Norn held her breath. Then Wotan shook his head in disbelief, and marched out of the Hall.

"*Not* across the floor I've spent all morning polishing," wailed the Valkyrie Gerhilde, but her father took no notice. The meeting broke up in disorder, and the troll and the Norn hurried off to the Mortals' Bar for a much-needed drink.

"I dunno," said the rock-troll. "I've never seen the like."

"He just sat there," said the Norn.

"Who did?"

"Wotan. When Flossie turned that paper into a dragon. It's Kew Gardens for her, I thought, but he just sat there. Didn't do a thing."

"I didn't mean that," said the rock-troll. "I meant the other thing."

The Norn wasn't listening. "What I want to know is," she continued, "who is bluffing who? Is it the Girls bluffing Wotan, or Wotan bluffing the Girls, or are they all at it?"

The troll frowned and scratched his head, producing a sound like two millstones. "What are you on about?" he asked.

"You *are* a slowcoach, aren't you? If the Girls wanted to stop Ortlinde from nobbling the Ring-Bearer, why didn't they just tell him who she was, instead of coming here and making threats to Wotan?"

The troll thought about this for a moment, then nodded his head. He was not so grey as he was granite-looking, and he could see that there was indeed an inconsistency.

"What I think," said the Norn excitedly, "is that the Ring-Bearer already knows who Ortlinde is, and he couldn't care less. They've tried telling him, and he doesn't want to know."

"How do you make that out?" asked the troll.

"Simple," said the Norn, smugly. "They've tried telling him, like I said, and he isn't interested. But they know that Wotan doesn't know that the Ring-Bearer knows who Ortlinde really is. So they threaten to tell the Ring-Bearer, hoping that the threat will make Wotan tell Ortlinde to chuck it and come home."

The troll stared at the bottom of his glass, trying to unravel the Norn's sentence. The Norn took his silence to mean that the troll was not yet convinced, and elaborated her point.

"You see, if Wotan doesn't know that the Ring-Bearer knows, then he'll be afraid in case the Girls tell the Ring-Bearer, and the Girls will try and get him to make some sort of a deal. The Girls can't make the Ring-Bearer chuck Ortlinde, because the Ring-Bearer presumably knows already—I mean he *must* know, mustn't he? But they can get Wotan to tell Ortlinde to chuck it if they can make him think that the Ring-Bearer doesn't know. Do you see what I mean?"

"Did you think all that up for yourself?" said the troll, full of admiration. The Norn blushed.

"That's very clever, that is," said the troll. "But what about the other thing?"

"What other thing?"

"You know." The troll made a vague gesture with his huge paw. "The other thing. I smelt it when the Girls walked in.

"It was the Norn's turn to look puzzled. The troll made a great effort and thought hard.

"Why was it," he said at last, "that old Wotan didn't turn the Girls into something when they gave him all that lip? You answer me that."

"He tried to," said the Norn. "Just before he stomped off."

"Exactly," said the troll. "He tried to, but he couldn't. There was something stopping him."

"What?" cried the Norn, enthralled.

"I dunno, do I? But they brought it in with them. I smelt it. There was something looking after them, or at least it was looking after Miss Flosshilde. Didn't you smell it too?"

"I'm no good at smells," confessed the Norn, who lived on a bleak, wet fell and had a permanent cold as a result. "Was it some sort of Power, do you think?"

The troll had done enough thinking for one day. His mind was made of sandstone and, besides, he had other things on it. He looked at the Norn for a moment and for the first time in his life attempted a smile.

"You're very clever, you are," he said. "Do you come here often?"

The Norn blushed prettily. She noticed that the troll had very nice eyes, and if one of them happened to be in the middle of his forehead, who cared? The conversation veered away from the Ring-Bearer and the strange-smelling Power, which was ironic in a way; for the change of subject and the emotions that had prompted it were largely due to their influence.

The Norn had been right up to a point. Malcolm had discovered who the girl he loved really was, but not from the Rhinedaughters, or even Alberich, who had rushed back from Germany to tell him. He had heard and finally believed the news only when a sparrow had perched on his shoulder in Bond Street and chirped the information into his ear. By that time, of course, Malcolm was engaged to the girl, which made things all the more difficult...

It had only taken thirty-six hours for Malcolm and the girl who had come to catalogue his library to become engaged to be married. Malcolm was not quite sure why he had felt such an urgent need to get official recognition for this strange and unexpected outbreak of love in Middle Somerset. But it seemed the right thing to do, like getting a contract or a receipt. To his utter astonishment, his proposal had been accepted. The girl had simply looked at her shoes for a moment, smiled at him sadly, and said, "If you're sure..." Malcolm had said that he was sure, and the girl had said something along the lines of Yes.

One is meant to do something wildly demonstrative on such occasions, but Malcolm felt too drained to waste energy in running about or shouting. In fact, he realised, he felt rather depressed, although he could not imagine why. For her part, the girl was even more taciturn than usual. The pretty scene had taken place beside the river in the grounds of the Hall, and they had sat in total silence for a while before getting to their feet and walking back to the house. At the door, the girl turned and looked at him for a moment, then muttered something about getting on with the catalogue.

"Catalogue?" Was she thinking about wedding presents already? "What catalogue?"

"Of the library."

"You don't want to bother with that, surely? I mean..."

"Oh, but I must." The girl looked at him again, not as one would expect a girl to look at her future husband. Nor was it an "Oh God what have I gone and done" look; just a look, that was all. Then she went up to the library.

Malcolm sat down on the stairs and put his hands over his ears. He felt confused, and no thoughts would come into his mind. With a tremendous effort, he called up the aspects of the situation that required his immediate attention, and tried to review them in the detail that they seemed to warrant.

Unlikely as it seemed, he had just succeeded in getting himself organised for perhaps the first time in his life. He had fallen in love, and for a change the girl at the other end felt the same way. Instead of letting this chance slip through his fingers, he had got everything sorted out, and that was all there was to it. There was no earthly reason why he shouldn't get married; he had a house and money, which was what a married man was supposed to need, along with a wife. If there had been anything wrong with the idea, then the girl wouldn't have said Yes. She was obviously happy with the arrangement, and it went without saying that it was what he wanted most of all in the whole wide world. Was it? Yes, he concluded, it probably was. Mind you, it did seem a terribly grown-up thing to be doing, but then again, it would be, wouldn't it? So far as he could see, he was Happy. He lacked nothing, and had all sorts of nice things to look forward to,

Malcolm leaned forward, resting his elbows on his knees. It occurred to him that he had only known this girl for about a day and a half, and that he was being a bit hasty. He dismissed this thought, which was simply cowardice. The trouble was, he reckoned, he was probably afraid of being happy, of having what he really wanted. For some reason or other, which he could not be bothered to work out.

He got to his feet and walked slowly to the library. The girl was sitting at a table with a pile of books on it, writing something in what looked like a ledger. She did not hear him come in, and he stood looking at her for a moment. Life, he realised, was a fragile thing, and time and opportunity should not be wasted.

"Blow that," he said, and the girl started. "Let's go and buy a ring."

His words had broken a deep silence, and silence followed them, so that Malcolm had the feeling that he was talking to himself. This would never do.

"Come on," he pleaded. "You don't have to do that now. Everything's going to be all right now."

Oddly enough, the girl seemed to understand what he meant by that, which was more than he did himself. She smiled (why did she always smile and never laugh?) and said Yes, she would like that. So they went downstairs and Malcolm walked out to the garage to get the car.

Alberich was sitting on the bonnet, eating a ham roll.

"This is my lunch, you realise," said the Nibelung. "About the worst thing I could possibly have, barring lobster."

"What are you doing here?" Malcolm asked.

"I came straight back from Germany," continued Alberich. "I saw the two of you together just now, and I knew in a minute what had happened."

"Thank you."

"You know who she is, don't you?"

Malcolm stared at him. "Of course I do," he said. "Do you?"

"Well, of course."

Malcolm frowned. How in God's name did Alberich know who she was? Did he have a library too? Malcolm suddenly felt that he didn't want to know.

"I know all about her," he said. "And we've just got engaged. We're going to London to buy a ring."

"*Buy* a ring?" said Alberich, genuinely surprised. "I'd have thought that was unnecessary."

Malcolm did not understand this remark, so he assumed it must be a joke. Perhaps in the back of his mind he had an idea that Alberich was trying to tell him something very important, but if that was the case he managed to ignore it. He squeezed a polite laugh out of his lungs, and unlocked the car.

"Hang on, though," said Alberich.

"Sorry, I haven't got time," said Malcolm. "1 think we should get it in Bond Street. That's where all the jewellers' shops are, aren't they?"

"Why not Amsterdam? Or Johannesburg?" asked Alberich quietly.

"She wouldn't understand about the Tarnhelm," Malcolm said. "It might frighten her."

"Most unlikely. Are you sure you know..."

Malcolm started the engine and pressed the accelerator hard. Perhaps Alberich was saying something tremendously important; if he was, he couldn't hear a word of it. The Prince of the Nibelungs hopped off the bonnet and banged on the window. Malcolm wound it down and shouted, "I'll see you when we get back. The housekeeper will make you a cup of tea, I expect." Then he let in the clutch and drove furiously out of the garage.

Alberich stood for a moment and scratched his head. Then it occurred to him that he had been wasting his time. He picked up a spanner which was lying on the floor of the garage and hurled it at the wall.

Malcolm deliberately parked on a double yellow line in the middle of Bond Street. It was that sort of a day. If a traffic warden came and wrote him a ticket, he could tell her that he was engaged to be married to the most wonderful girl in the world. He wanted to tell people that, if only to hear himself say it. Anyway, he was feeling much better now, if a trifle hysterical.

The girl seemed to have cheered up, too. Almost for the first time since he had known her, she had laughed properly, and that was a wonderful sound to be anywhere near. In fact, Malcolm was at a loss to know what had got into her, for she behaved very childishly in all the jeweller's shops they went into. She insisted on trying on all the rings they saw, taking them to the window to see what they looked like in the light, and then saying that they wouldn't do. The stones were the wrong colour, or too small, or too big, or the settings were the wrong shape. It almost seemed as if she wasn't taking this business *seriously.*

They had tried six shops, and it was nearly half-past five.

"It's no good," said the girl. "I don't like any of the ones we've seen. And I'm the one who's going to be wearing it. For ever and ever," she added, tenderly. For some reason, this remark struck Malcolm as being rather out of character, but he put it down to excitement.

"We can try that one over there, if we're quick," he suggested.

"No," said the girl, "I know the ring I want." And she told him.

As she did so, it began to rain.

The two sparrows that had been eating crumbs outside the largest of the jeweller's shops looked at each other.

"Did you hear that?" said the first sparrow.

"Don't speak with your beak full," said the other.

"But, Mum," replied the first sparrow, "it's him. And he's going to give her the Big Ring."

"It's none of our business. And you'll catch your death if you don't get under cover this instant."

"But, Mum," insisted the first sparrow, "if he gives her the Big Ring it'd be terrible, wouldn't it?"

"How many times must I tell you not to listen to what other people are saying? It's rude." The second sparrow flapped her wings nervously. It was indeed terrible, and she didn't want to get involved.

"But do you think he knows how terrible it would be? Do you?"

"Quiet! People are staring."

"It's rude to stare," replied the first sparrow, who had been told this many times. "If he doesn't know, shouldn't we tell him? Because if we don't..."

Two ravens had appeared in the sky, wheeling slowly and noiselessly above the street. Nobody noticed them; they had come to see, not to be seen.

"It isn't him at all," said the second sparrow nervously. "It's just your imagination. If you don't come in this minute, I'll tell your father."

Malcolm was standing very still. The girl was smiling at him, saying nothing. He wanted to give her the Ring. He could see no reason why he should not. Almost from the first moment he had met her, he had wanted to give her the Ring, and now he was going to do it. It was the right thing to do. It was the only thing to do.

The young sparrow hopped morosely under a parked van. His mother was scolding him, but he wasn't listening. Surely it couldn't be right that the Ring-Bearer should give the Ring to Wotan's daughter. His mother stopped chirping at him for a moment, and stooped down to peck at a bottle-top. Now was his chance.

"Please," said the girl. "I'd like it very much."

Malcolm took the Ring between the first and third fingers of his left hand and started to pull it off. He was afraid that it might not come away easily, but it slid off effortlessly, and he held it for a moment, The girl was still smiling, not holding out her hand, not making a movement of any sort. He tried to read her thoughts, but he could not. He could feel the rain running through his hair, but he did not know what it was. It was right that the girl should have the Ring. It would be very easy to give it to her. Nothing at all could be easier, and then they would be properly engaged.

The sparrow forced itself through the air like a bullet and landed awkwardly on Malcolm's shoulder. He did not seem to notice. He had other things on his mind.

"Don't do it," shrieked the bird. "She's Wotan's *daughter!*"

For a moment, Malcolm did not know where the voice was coming from. Then he felt feathers brushing the side of his face, which made him jump. As he started, he dropped the Ring, which rolled into the gutter.

"She's Wotan's daughter. She's Wotan's daughter, she's his daughter!" screamed the sparrow. Malcolm swung his left hand furiously through the air and clapped the palm of it onto his right shoulder. He felt something fragile snapping under the fingers, and the voice stopped suddenly. The dead bird rolled down his arm and fell onto the pavement. It looked like a child's toy or a hockey-puck, and it had landed in a puddle.

Then the girl stooped down to pick up the Ring. Without knowing what he was doing, Malcolm covered it with his foot. It was all he was able to do, but apparently it was enough. The girl stepped backwards, and she had a look on her face that Malcolm did not like very much.

"I really do love you," she said.

Without even wanting to, Malcolm found himself reading her thoughts.

"I love you too," he said, and he bent down and picked up the Ring. "If I offered this to you, would you take it?"

"Yes," said the girl.

"And you'd give it to your father?"

"Yes."

Malcolm closed his fist round the Ring. "It's raining," he said, "you'll catch cold."

The girl looked at her shoes and said nothing. He slowly put the Ring back on his finger. He wanted her to have it more than ever, but it felt terribly tight now, and he doubted whether he would be able to get it off again without soap and water. There was some quotation about there being a providence in the fall of a sparrow, but he had never really understood what that meant.

He opened the car door for her. "Are we still engaged, then?" he asked.

"I don't know," she said. "Are we? I mean, is there any point?"

"But we love each other, don't we? Yes, we do," he added, for he knew how indecisive she could be at times. "And there's all the point in the world."

"Everything I told you about my family is true," she, said, fastening her seat-belt. "So I don't think there is any point, really, is there?"

Malcolm could not quite follow that one, but he wasn't bothered about it. He could read her thoughts. This was all so *silly.*

When they were on the motorway, Malcolm broke the silence that had lasted since they had left London.

"Obviously you know who I am," he said. "So you know I can read thoughts. I can read exactly what you're really thinking."

The girl said nothing.

"Which is probably just as well," said Malcolm irritably, "since you never say anything. But I can see what you're thinking, so it's no use pretending. For crying out loud, you love me more than I love you."

"That's for you to say."

"Then be quiet and listen. You don't have to give him the Ring."

"You don't have to keep it."

Malcolm wanted to grab hold of her and shake her, but he was being overtaken by a lorry and needed both hands for the wheel. "Don't you understand anything?" he shouted. The girl stared at the floor and said nothing.

"If I was feeling as bloody miserable as you are, I'd burst into tears," he said savagely. "But you won't let yourself do that, will you?"

He pulled over onto the hard shoulder and stopped the car. Two ravens were circling overhead. Malcolm said a lot of things, some of them very loudly, some of them very quietly, and after a while he started to cry. But the girl said nothing, and there was no point saying any more.

"All right, then," he whispered, "you can have it. But not yet. Not yet."

"I dunno," said Thought, as he watched the car draw up at Combe Hall. "Humans."

The doors opened, and Malcolm and the Valkyrie Ortlinde climbed out.

"Now what?" whispered Memory.

Malcolm put his arm around the Valkyrie, and she rested her head against his face. The sharp eyes of the ravens could easily pick out the Ring, glittering on his finger. Neither the mortal nor the Valkyrie said a word as they went into the house, but the air was full of thoughts, and the ravens felt very frustrated that they could only read

Ortlinde's half of them.

The door of the house closed and the two ravens sat thoughtfully for a while, listening to the wind sighing in the pine trees that surrounded the Hall. They had seen many things in their time. They had seen Alberich screaming with rage and pain when Loge tore the Ring from his chained hands. They had seen Hagen drive his spear between Siegfried's shoulders, and Hagen himself struggling for the last time in the floodwaters of the Rhine. Nothing surprised them any more.

"Thick as two short planks, both of them," said Memory at last.

12

The girl—Malcolm could not bring himself to think of her as Ortlinde —was up at the crack of dawn cataloguing away like a small tornado. She at least had her work to occupy her mind; not that it was her proper work, of course.

Malcolm's own work was not going so well. According to the BBC, a rail disaster in Essex had been narrowly averted, and a nuclear reactor in Kent had been shut down in the nick of time, just before it had a chance to make the English Channel a little bit wider. Needless to say, these unhappy incidents had all taken place at the same time as he had been struggling to keep control of the Ring. It was an added complication, but no more. It wasn't that he couldn't care less; he cared desperately, but what could he do? He was the master of the world, but not of himself.

Alberich had been waiting for him when he returned from London. In fact, he had been pacing up and down in front of the garage all day, which had scarcely helped his digestion, with the result that he lost his temper when he caught sight of Ortlinde and called her some rather crude and unpleasant things. Malcolm had been on the point of hitting him again, but the dwarf had realised the danger he was in and apologised to the Valkyrie, blaming his bad manners on a cucumber sandwich he had been rash enough to eat while he was waiting. Now he had come back and was sitting in the drawing-room, drinking milk.

"I know what you're going to say," Malcolm said.

"Yes," replied Alberich, "you probably do. Whether you understand it or not is another matter. Giant's blood may have made you perceptive, but it hasn't stopped you being plain stupid."

"Thank you," replied Malcolm sullenly, "but I can do without personal abuse."

"Listen," said the Nibelung. "I told you before that you were too nice to be a proper Ring-Bearer. Ring-Bearers can't be like that. Sure, it worked well enough to start off with, but then it went all wrong.

Well, didn't it? A nice but enamoured Ring-Bearer is capable of doing more damage in forty-eight hours than Ingolf managed in a thousand years. You're human; you can't help it. But you aren't qualified to hold the Ring if you're human. Don't you see?"

"No."

Alberich frowned. It was as if someone had said that they could not understand why rain makes you wet. It would take some explaining.

"Take my case," he said. "I'm not human, I'm delighted to say, but even so, the first thing I had to do before I was able to make the Ring in the first place was to forswear Love and all its tedious works. Whoever thought up that particular requirement knew what he was about, believe you me. Not that I was ever romantically inclined myself; my heart has often been burnt but never broken. Anyway, this made me immune from the one single greatest cause of idiocy in the world. Since I took the pledge, I have been smiled at by Rhinedaughters, yearned at by Valkyries, and generally assaulted by beautiful people of every species, all to no effect. And I don't even have the miserable thing any more. I'm just a peripheral character, especially now that you appear to have dismantled the curse I so cleverly put on the Ring. Or perhaps you haven't." Alberich was thoughtful for a while. "Perhaps this Ortlinde nonsense is the curse catching up with you as well. If it is, I'm sorry. Oddly enough I don't feel any real animosity towards you, even if you are as stupid as they come. Curse or no curse, though, you've fallen head over heels into the oldest trap in the book. You really aren't fit to be allowed out on your own, let alone be the master of the universe."

"I never asked for the job," said Malcolm wretchedly.

"That's true, you didn't. But who cares? Shall I tell you about Love?"

"Must you?"

"Yes. The human race—we'll confine our attention to your mob to start with, although what I say is applicable to virtually all mammals—the human race has achieved so much more than any other species in the time it's been on this earth—a couple of million years, which is no time at all; about as long as it takes a sulphur-dwarf to learn to walk—that the imagination is unable to cope with all the things that the human being has done. The human race *created* Things. They built wonderful buildings, invented wonderful machines, brought into being poetry, music and art. To beguile their eighty-odd years they have every conceivable diversion, from the symphonies of Beethoven to the Rubik's Cube. They can rush around in sports cars, they can shoot elephants, they can travel around the world in days, or even hours. In virtually every respect, they have made themselves the equals of the Gods. Most of all, they have all the Things in the world at their disposal to use and entertain themselves with. And what do they like doing best of all? They like taking off all their clothes—clothes over which they have expended so much effort and ingenuity—and doing biologically necessary but profoundly undignified things to other human beings. Any pig or spider can do that, it's the easiest thing in the world. But you bloody humans, who can do so much that no other species could ever do, you can't do *that* efficiently. You agonise over it. You make an incredible fuss over it. You get it all wrong, you make each others' lives miserable, you write dreary letters and take overdoses. You even invent a medicine that deliberately makes the whole process futile. My God, what a species!"

The dwarf fell silent and drank some milk. Malcolm could think of no answer to the case as Alberich had presented it, although he felt sure that there was a flaw in it somewhere. Alberich wiped his moustache and continued.

"And so you give this irregularity in your minds a name of its own. You call it Love, which is meant to make everything all right. Rather than try and sort it out or find a vaccine, you go out of your way to glorify it. I mentioned your art and your poetry just now. What are your favourite themes? Love and War. The two things that any species can do, and which most species do so much more sensibly than you lot—screwing and killing—are the things you humans single out to make a song and dance about. Literally," said Alberich, who above all else detested musicals. "Now be fair," he continued, "can you honestly say that a member of a species with this ancestral fallibility should be allowed to rule the universe?"

"But isn't everybody the same? Don't the Gods and Goddesses ever fall in love? And didn't you once try and chat up the Rhine-daughters?"

Alberich winced. "It is true that the High Gods do occasionally fall in love. You have, as a matter of fact, singled out the one race nuttier than your own. We Elementals have a far better record. The spirits of wood and stone have been known to make idiots of themselves, and I myself did go through a bad patch, I will confess. The spirits of wind and water—the Rhinedaughters, to take an excellent example—have so far proved entirely bulletproof. But even when we do go haywire, we get over it very quickly and very easily. We see how stupid it is, and we pull ourselves together. Look at me. And your lesser Gods, your phenomena and abstractions and so on, have no trouble at all. Seriously, I should consider giving it best and handing the Ring on to a more suitable keeper."

"Such as?"

"Modesty forbids."

Malcolm shook his head sadly. "It's not that I don't accept what you've told me," he said. "You've got a point, I'm sure. But I can't give you the Ring, much as I'd like to. I've promised to give it to her."

"But surely..." Alberich rose to his feet, and then sat down again, a hand pressed to his abdomen. "Don't say I'm getting an ulcer," he moaned, "not on top of everything else."

"You see," Malcolm went on, "the Ring isn't about all that any more. It's the only way I can prove to her that I really do love her. Don't you see how important that makes it?"

At times, Alberich said to himself, there are worse things even than dyspepsia. "You haven't been listening," he said.

"Yes, I have. But she's the most important thing in the world."

"If you weren't bigger than me," said Alberich, "I'd break your silly neck. Make yourself shorter and say that again."

Malcolm wanted to explain, but that would clearly be pointless. The Nibelung, he could see, had no soul. He offered his guest another glass of milk, but the offer was curtly refused, and Alberich left in a huff.

Having filled himself with the conviction that what he was doing was right, Malcolm went down to the library to seek confirmation.

"Hello," said the girl.

"Hello, Ortlinde," he replied. "Funny, isn't it, the way all the people I talk to nowadays have German names?"

"You've got a German name."

"No," he said. "My name's Malcolm."

"They didn't tell me that," said the girl. "I think it's a nice name."

"So is Ortlinde."

"Thank you. It means Place of the Lime Tree."

"I know."

Malcolm remained standing where he was, feeling rather uncomfortable. The girl hadn't moved either, and Malcolm was put in mind of a boxing match he had once seen where both fighters had refused to leave their corners at the start of the first round.

"Are you really cataloguing the library?" he asked.

"Yes," replied the girl, who sounded rather offended.

"Sorry. Did you really train as a librarian, then?"

"No," said the girl, "I never had an opportunity to have a career. But we've got millions of books at home, and my father never puts them back where he got them from. He's very untidy."

"How old are you?" Malcolm asked suddenly.

"One thousand, two hundred and thirty-six."

"I'm twenty-five," said Malcolm, and he made some sort of a joke about having always preferred older women. Ortlinde smiled wanly.

"There's no point, is there?" she said.

"No point in what?"

"In going on like this," she said. "It's not your fault, really. It's my fault."

She was looking down at her sensible shoes again; Malcolm wished that she might learn some sense from them. "I lied to you," she continued. "I was sent to do something and I haven't even managed to do that. It's just that nobody's ever loved me before, and I haven't loved anyone before. But you'll be all right, I know you will. You'll meet someone else and..."

"I don't want to meet anyone else," Malcolm shouted. "Ever again. I'm going to give you the Ring as soon as...as I've sorted everything out," he finished lamely.

"But you can't. If you did, you would know I've let you down, and I would know that too, and you wouldn't be able to communicate with me and I wouldn't be able to communicate with you and this terrible resentment would build up and neither of us would be able to talk to each other..."

She talked, Malcolm thought, in the same way as a rabbit runs; terribly fast for a short burst, then a long, long pause, then another breathless sprint; and every few words, a little nervous smile that made him feel as if someone were crushing his heart like a cider-apple. Unless he found some way of cheering her up, life with her would be intolerable. On the other hand, life without her would be equally intolerable or even worse, so what could he do?

"Of course we'll be able to talk to each other," he said firmly. "All I have to do is give you the Ring, and I'll give it to you because I want to, because it'll show you that I love you more than anyone else or anything else in the whole world."

"No, you don't. You can't. You mustn't."

Malcolm felt as if someone had asked him his name and then contradicted him when he answered. "Why not?" he asked.

"Because I'm not a nice person at all," replied the girl, gazing tragically at her shoelaces. "I'm nasty, really."

"No, you're not."

"Yes, I am."

"No, you're not."

She's probably never been to a pantomime, Malcolm reflected, so she wouldn't know. "Really, you're a wonderful person, and I love you, and you love me, and it's all so bloody simple that any bloody fool could get it right. Don't you understand?"

Malcolm was shouting now, and the girl had gone all brittle, like a rose dipped in liquid oxygen. "Come on," he said, lowering his voice with an effort, "we had it all sorted out a few hours ago. Don't you want to be happy?"

There was a long silence; not a pause for thought, but an unwillingness to communicate. It was like trying to argue with a small child.

"Well, don't you? Look at me when I'm shouting at you."

"I don't know," said the girl, looking even further away.

"Then..." Malcolm did not know what to say. Words were bouncing off her like bullets off a tank. "Then you'll just have to trust me," he said. He had no idea what that remark was supposed to mean, but it sounded marvellous. He put his arm nervously round her shoulder; there was no resistance, but it felt like touching a corpse, which was strange. Up to now, she had been the warmest person he had ever known.

He left the library and wandered out into the drive. A small white Citroën was drawing up; it was the English Rose, back from her holiday. Malcolm groaned, and felt a totally unreasonable surge of resentment towards her. He knew that it had not really been his secretary who had invited the girl down to catalogue the library and so messed up his life. But on another level it had been, and that level suited Malcolm perfectly. He had found someone to blame for all his troubles.

"That bloody librarian you hired," he started.

"Pardon me?" said the Rose. "I engaged no librarian."

"Yes, you bloody did. Linda Walker, Lime Place, Bristol."

The Rose looked mystified. "To catalogue the library? But Herr Finger, you refused categorically to permit me to arrange for any such operation to be performed. I obeyed your instructions on that point to the letter. The person you referred to is unknown to me."

"Oh," said Malcolm. "Then I'm sorry."

The Rose looked at him curiously through her spectacles. "Is there a person of that name—Linda Walker of Lime Place—currently engaged in the work you described?" she asked.

"Yes." Malcolm suddenly realised that he couldn't explain. "Well, now she's here she'd better get on with it, I suppose."

But the Rose seemed intrigued. "Would she by any chance be a young person?"

"Yes, I think so." One thousand, two hundred and thirty-six. Well, you're as young as you feel.

"Excuse me one moment."

Before he could stop her, the Rose scuttled into the house. Malcolm followed, but his secretary proved surprisingly fleet of foot. She had reached the library door before Malcolm caught up with her, and she threw it open.

"For Chrissakes, Lindsy," she wailed, "what are you doing here?"

"Hello, Mother," said the girl.

"Believe me," said the Rose, "it was none of my doing. I came here specifically to prevent any such occurrence."

The three of them were assembled in the drawing-room: Malcolm slumped in an armchair, which threatened to swallow him whole, the Rose perched on the arm of the sofa, and the Valkyrie Ortlinde, the Chooser of the Slain, sitting on a straight-backed chair staring rigidly at a spot on the carpet. The English Rose had sent for tea; it had arrived, and was going cold.

"Who exactly are you, then?" Malcolm forced himself to ask.

"I am Erda," said the Rose, "also known as Mother Earth."

"But you're American."

"That is so; but only by adoption, so to speak. I went to the United States—long before there were any States, united or otherwise—to be as far away as possible from my ex-husband, the God Wotan. Since he refused to allow me access to my daughters, I could see no point in remaining in Europe."

"You're Mother Earth," Malcolm said dumbly. He wanted to argue this point. For a start, she was much too thin to be Mother Earth, but that line of argument would probably cause offence. He could see no reason to disbelieve the claim. Its very improbability made it plausible enough.

"And this," continued the Goddess with a sigh, "is my daughter Ortlinde. I need not ask what she is doing here."

The girl said nothing, which was entirely as Malcolm had expected. "Will someone please explain all this to me?" he asked pitifully. "I'm only human, after all."

"Certainly," said Mother Earth. "When I perceived that you had obtained the so-called Nibelung's Ring, I took it upon myself..."

"How did you find out?"

"I heard it from a nightingale who was present at the scene of the incident. I took it upon myself to place myself in a position where I could take an observer's role, and so masqueraded as your secretary."

"But they said you'd been here for years."

"I am not without influence with the local minor deities," said the Rose loftily. "I am afraid you were misled."

"You mean the auctioneer and the estate agent and all those people were gods of some sort?"

"Certainly not. Only the previous owner, Colonel Booth. He is the spirit of the small trout-stream that runs through the grounds of the house. It was through his co-operation that I was able to secure the use of this house, which I knew you had always wanted to live in."

"And he's a god?"

"Only a very minor one. Many people are, you know; about one person in two thousand is a god or a spirit of some sort. Of course, most of these are mortal and wholly oblivious of their divine status. We prefer to keep it that way. It's like your English system of appointing laymen as Justices of the Peace."

"And where's Colonel Booth living now?" Malcolm asked, expecting the man to appear from the stream at the bottom of the garden.

"I obtained a transfer for him to a tributary of the Indus. His family had served in India for generations, and he was most keen to keep up the tradition."

Malcolm rubbed his forehead with the heel of his hand, but it did no good. The Rose continued.

"I assumed this watching brief with the express intention of making sure that my ex-husband did not try the so-called Brunnhilde option on you. In the past, as you are no doubt aware, it met with some degree of success in the case of your predecessor Siegfried, and I felt sure that if other options failed him Wotan would not hesitate to use it again. I had thought, however, that he had given up for the time being, and so took my annual holiday in Stroud."

"Why Stroud?"

"I am very fond of Stroud. Apparently, as soon as my back was turned, Wotan implemented this strategy." The Rose paused, and looked sternly at her daughter. "Perhaps you would care to leave us, Lindsy." The girl got up and wandered sadly away.

"I must state," continued the Rose, "that I have only the best interests of the world at heart, and so my daughter's personal feelings must not influence my actions at all. Nor must they influence yours."

"You're fired."

"Mr. Fisher, you do not seem to appreciate the gravity of the situation in which you find yourself. The situation as of now is extremely serious, and global security is at stake. To date, you have acted in a highly responsible manner towards the inhabitants of the world, and I felt confident that you could continue with this work without any undue interference from me."

"Hold it," said Malcolm. "You arranged that damned gymkhana thing, didn't you?"

"Correct."

"You must have known I'd have wanted to get my own back on Philip Wilcox. There was nearly an air disaster because of that."

"It was a risk I had to take. Had you continued to remain enamoured of Elizabeth Ayres, serious repercussions would have ensued on an international scale. I had to ensure that such an occurrence would not take place. Similarly it is of the utmost importance that I dissuade you from continuing in a state of love with regard to my daughter Ortlinde. The love syndrome is a condition which no Ring-Bearer should be in for any prolonged period of time."

"I know, I know," Malcolm muttered. "I've heard all that."

"Then," continued the Goddess, "you will be aware that the termination of this unfortunate situation must be expedited. It is as simple as that, Mr. Fisher."

Malcolm laughed loudly for rather longer than the remark justified.

"Your natural reaction, I know, is to protest that the matter is not in your control," said the Rose. "This is self-deception on your part."

"Is it really?" Malcolm turned away and counted to ten. "Why is it," he said at last, "that everyone I meet these days turns out to be a Goddess? You're a Goddess, she's a Goddess, the housekeeper is probably a Goddess."

"Incorrect," said the Rose.

"Oh, good. Look, I don't care, I just want to be left alone."

The Rose continued with the same measured intonation, rather like the Speaking Clock. "Correct me if I am mistaken, but you were primarily attracted to my daughter simply because you believed that she was not a Goddess but a normal, ordinary mortal. A somewhat counter-intuitive reaction for a human being, if I may say so; it seems to be a commonplace of human love that the lover believes his beloved to be in some way divine."

This, Malcolm realised with a shudder, was the Rose's idea of a joke. After a pause for laughter, which was not rewarded by the expected reaction, she continued.

"Now that it transpires that she is not a mortal but merely a Goddess, your affection for her should logically cease. You may argue that she loves you..."

"You noticed that, did you?"

"Indeed. But her feelings towards you are simply the result of un-clear thinking and underlying emotional problems, which I fear have now reached a point where the most competent analyst would be unable to help her. By extending reciprocal affection towards her, you will only cause her emotional situation to deteriorate; so, Mr. Fisher, if I may be counter-factual for a moment, if you care about my daugh-ter, you must stop loving her. It would likewise be in your own inter-est to desist, since you are doing considerable harm to your own emo-tional state which, I hardly need tell you, is by no means satisfactory."

For the first time, Malcolm felt pity for Wotan. This sort of thing all day long would try the patience of any God.

"My husband was a similarly unbalanced person," continued the Rose. "His case should provide you with a most graphic illustration of the dangers of embarking on a serious relationship when the balance of the mind is, so to speak, disturbed. In short, Mr. Fisher, it is im-perative that you abandon your intention of giving the Ring to my daughter. You must set your personal feelings on one side entirely."

"Get knotted," said Malcolm violently. It was no way to talk to a Goddess, but he was past caring.

"Should you fail to do so, I regret to have to inform you that you may well be directly responsible for global cataclysm. If my ex-hus-band were to resume control of the Ring, the consequences for the future of humanity would be at the very least severe, and quite prob-ably grave. You yourself would undoubtedly fail to find the happiness you misguidedly believe would result from a relationship with my daughter; added to which, you would certainly be involved along with the rest of humanity in any potential Armageddon-type scenario that might arise as a result of my ex-husband's ownership of the Ring. In short..."

"Wrong," said Malcolm. "Wrong on every point."

"Pardon me?"

"Where you go wrong is, you think that she'll give the Ring to her father. She won't. Never in a million years. You see, it'll be a present from me, the best present I could possibly give her. She'd never give it to Wotan or anyone else. She loves me, you see. In fact," Malcolm said dreamily, "she'll probably give it straight back again, and then every-thing will be all right."

"I perceive," said the Rose, rising to her feet, "that I have been wasting my time with you, Mr. Fisher. You have failed to grasp the significance of anything I have said to you. I can only implore you to reconsider your decision with the utmost diligence."

"What do you actually do?" said Malcolm. "What's your job?"

"Mostly," said Mother Earth, "I sleep. My sleep is dreaming, my dreaming is thinking, my thinking is understanding. Consequently, my normal role is consultative, not executive. Only in exceptional circumstances, such as a threat of universal oblivion, do I undertake any active part in the day-to-day running of the world."

"Yes, but what do you actually *do?*"

"I advise people," said Mother Earth.

"Like the United Nations does, you mean?"

"There is, I suppose, a degree of similarity."

"You're still fired. Now get out of my house."

"Mr. Fisher," said the Rose, sitting down again, "before I go and attempt to reason with my daughter, on the unlikely chance that she might listen to sense, let me explain to you the nature of what you call love. It is a purely functional system in the human operational matrix. With the lower animals, the urge to reproduce is a purely instinctive thing. The human race, being rational, requires a distinct motivation to reproduce. It has therefore been programmed to process the reproductive urge in a unique way."

"Just out of interest," said Malcolm, "did you design the human race?"

"Correct. As I was saying..."

"Ten out of ten for the Ears and the Eyes," said Malcolm, "the Feet and the waste disposal system not so hot. Friday afternoon job, I always thought."

"You are thinking of the hardware, Mr. Fisher, which is the result of the evolutionary process, and for which I claim no credit or otherwise. My work was entirely concerned with the software, what you would call the feelings and the emotions. As I was saying, the human race needs a reason for everything it does, a reason it can understand within its own terms of reference. Love, companionship, sympathy, affection and understanding are simply the rewards that human beings must receive if they are to be motivated to do something that creatures of their intelligence and sophistication would normally regard as below their dignity. There are so many better things they could be doing. How long does a human being live, Mr. Fisher? Between seventy and ninety years, given optimum conditions. Without some powerful motivating factor, they could not be expected to devote a major proportion of their extremely short lives to the creation and education of other human beings. Therefore, it was necessary to provide them with an incentive, one which they are programmed to accept as worthwhile. Love is nothing, Mr. Fisher. You would do well to ignore it completely."

With that, the English Rose departed, leaving Malcolm alone. His only reaction to these revelations, straight from the horse's mouth, was that it was a dirty trick to play on anybody. But the fact remained that he was human, and he was in love, and that nothing else mattered. If that made him a fool, then so be it; blame the person who invented the state in the first place. But he knew all about love; it was as real as anything else in the world and he could not deny its existence. He resolved to find Ortlinde and give her the Ring at once.

But she wasn't in the library, or anywhere in the house. Perhaps she had gone away. Perhaps her mother had sent her away, or taken her away by force. In his confusion, Malcolm did not use the Tarnhelm to take him to where she was; instead, he ran through the house and grounds calling out her name at the top of his voice. At last he saw someone sitting on the riverbank and ran across. The figure turned and, to his despair, Malcolm saw that it was only Flosshilde.

"Have you seen her?" he panted.

Flosshilde could not read people's thoughts like Malcolm could, but she could guess who he was asking after. "Yes," she said, "I saw her just now down by the little wood, where you get that nice view over the valley. Not that she's looking at the view, she's sitting there looking at her feet again. Size six, at a guess. Mine are size four."

"Thank you." Malcolm turned to go, but the Rhinedaughter called after him.

"Well?" he said. "What is it? I'm in a hurry!"

"I know," said Flosshilde sadly. "I've just got back from Valhalla. I was trying to get Wotan to send her away."

"Not you as well."

"It's for your own good." Malcolm scowled at her, and she felt suddenly angry. "Well, it is. But I failed. Wotan tried to turn me into a hedgehog and it was all for your sake."

"A hedgehog? Why a hedgehog particularly?"

"Fleas and things. But he didn't manage to do it for...for some reason or other." Flosshilde had been wondering what had prevented Wotan from making that transformation. The one plausible theory she had come up with was what had given her hope.

"I'm sorry he failed," Malcolm said, and started to walk away. Flosshilde waited till his back was turned, then deliberately pushed him into the river.

As he hit the water, Malcolm's mind was filled with images of the fate of Hagen, whom the Rhinedaughters drowned, and he instinctively turned himself into a rowing-boat. But the water was only two feet deep at that point, and after a moment he turned himself back again. For all her grief, Flosshilde could not help laughing.

"Shut up," Malcolm snapped.

"I didn't mean it unkindly," giggled Flosshilde. "That was very resourceful of you."

Malcolm had got his shoes and socks wet. He applied to the Tarnhelm for replacements. "You just watch it in future," he said sternly.

"You watch it," said the Rhinedaughter. "And look at me when I'm talking to you."

It was true that Malcolm was looking at his shoes, but only to see what the Tarnhelm had provided him with. "Have you been listening to us?" he said furiously. "When we were talking just now?"

Flosshilde sat down on the bank and combed her long hair with an ivory comb that Eric Bloodaxe had given her many years ago. "No," she said, "I've got better things to do with my time than listen to that sort of rubbish."

Malcolm sat down beside her. "Go on, then," he said. "I'm listening."

"I went to see Wotan," she said, putting the comb away. "I tried to get him to call Ortlinde off. But he said he couldn't. I don't know if he was telling the truth or not, actually. Because if you go off with her, you'll be terribly unhappy, honestly you will. Even if it does work out, and you give her the Ring and she accepts it and all that..."

"How come everyone knows about that?" Malcolm said bitterly. "You must have been listening."

"It's the most important thing in the world right now," said Flosshilde gravely. "What do you expect? Like it or not, you're dealing with the Gods now. I know you don't like us very much, but we're important people. But never mind about the world and things like that. I couldn't care less about the silly old world, or the Ring, or anything. If you go off with her, you'll be utterly wretched. She'll make you miserable, I know she will."

Flosshilde tried to open her mind to make it easier for him to read her thoughts, but apparently he wasn't interested.

"How the hell could you know?"

"Because you're not like that. You think you're in love with her, but you're not. You think that because she's in love with you, you've got to be in love with her. It doesn't work like that."

"You're talking nonsense. It's not like that at all."

"Shut up and listen, will you? You don't understand the meaning of the word Love. It's not that great big romantic thunderbolt you think it is. You saw her, you fell for her, your heart went mushy inside you. That's all totally silly; it doesn't happen that way. You don't

know the first thing about her. How could you, you've hardly got two
sentences out of her since you met. What are the two of you going to
do for the rest of Time, sit around staring at your shoes, trying to
make conversation? You both think you're in love, but you're deceiv-
ing yourselves. She thinks she's in love because she's always been treated
like a piece of old cheese, and then you come along, looking like
Siegfried himself, the most important man in the world, and start
adoring her. And you fell in love with her because she's there and you
thought she was a human being and so she counted. There's me, you
thought; a real live girl, not a Goddess or a water-nymph, is actually
in love with me. Whoopee, I'm not a failure or inadequate or as boring
as hell, let's get married."

"Have you finished?"

"No. You're stupid and silly and romantic, and you deserve to be
miserable all your life. What sort of a world do you think you're living
in? You're only fit to mix with Gods and fairies. You don't stand a chance
in the real world."

"Now have you finished?"

"You think you're strong and marvellous, don't you? But you're as
blind as a bat and they're leading you by the nose. It's them, don't
you see? It's Wotan's grand design, and you've fallen straight into the
trap. I thought there was more to you than that, but I was wrong."

Malcolm did not even bother to unravel this skein of metaphor.
He stood up and walked away. When he was safely out of earshot,
Flosshilde began to cry. As she sat weeping, her sisters put their heads
above the water.

"You're just as bad as he is," said Wellgunde.

"What sort of a world do you think you're living in?" sneered Woglinde. "You're stupid and silly and romantic, and you deserve to be
miserable all your life. Very well put, I thought."

They laughed unkindly and swam away.

"Hello," said Ortlinde.

"Hello," said Malcolm. "What are you doing here?"

"I wanted to be on my own," she replied.

"I love you," said Malcolm. He had grown used to saying that,
and he no longer felt any embarrassment as the words passed his lips.

"You mustn't," said the girl. "Really, I'm not a nice person."

"You said that before," said Malcolm angrily. "Don't try to be
clever with me. I drank Giant's blood, remember? I can read what
you're really feeling."

"I've got no feelings, really. No emotions, no anything. Don't you see? I'm a Valkyrie, I'm Wotan's daughter. I can't be anything else, however hard I try. And if you try and make me be something I never can be, you'll only hurt yourself. I can't be hurt any more, I was born hurt. But I don't want to hurt you. So please leave me alone."

Malcolm could not understand, but that was all right. He didn't want to understand and he didn't need to. He knew that she loved him, and this knowledge was like a gun in his pocket. So long as he was armed with it, no-one could touch him.

"If I give you the Ring, you'll take it?"

"Yes."

"And you love me?"

"Yes."

"What is so bloody fascinating about your bloody shoes? You love me?"

"Yes."

"Oh, *good*. That's settled, then." Malcolm shut his eyes and sat down, exhausted.

"No, it's not." The tone of her voice had not altered, and she was still looking away. Malcolm could only feel frustration and anger, and he wanted to break something. The clouds grew dark, and there was a growl of distant thunder.

"You see?" said Ortlinde, sadly. "That's why it wouldn't be any good."

Malcolm could not understand this at first; then he understood. The storm was gathering fast, and rain was beginning to fall.

"Wotan never did it better himself," she said.

"But I'm not like Wotan. He's a God and he's mad."

"If only you'd seen my mother when she was younger," went on Ortlinde. "But they tell me I'm just like she was at my age."

"One thousand two hundred and thirty-six?"

"More or less. That was before she left my father and went to America, of course. And my father was a nice person then, everyone said so. Do you know what he did to convince her that he loved her? My mother, I mean? You see, there was some sort of difficulty about them, just as there is about us. Anyway, to prove he really loved her, my father deliberately put out his left eye."

"How could that possibly have helped?"

"I don't know, he never told me. We never talk about things like that. Besides, everything was different then, so it probably had some special significance. Anyway, that's how he got like he is now, that and marrying my mother. That's what love does to people like you and me and him, if we let it take over. The best thing to do with all feelings like that is to wait until they go away. They don't mean anything, you know. They hurt, but they're only feelings. They don't draw blood or make it difficult for you to breathe. They're all in the mind. Life is about eating and drinking and sleeping and breathing and working, and not being more unhappy than you absolutely have to."

"For crying out loud," said Malcolm. "It's not like that."

"What's it like, then?"

"I don't know, really." Malcolm was unable to think for a moment. "But isn't it just two people who love each other, and they get married and live happily ever after. I mean, so long as we love each other, what the hell else matters?"

Ortlinde made no reply. It was raining hard, but she didn't seem to mind. She was very, very beautiful, and Malcolm wanted to hold her in his arms, but on reflection he realised that that would not be a good idea. He called upon the Tarnhelm to provide him with a hat and a raincoat, and when they materialised he gave them to her for he did not want her to catch cold. Then he walked away.

A pair of ducks had settled on the surface of the river, and as Malcolm walked back to the house they called out to him.

"Thanks for the weather," they said.

"I'm sorry?"

"Nice weather for ducks," explained one of them. "Get it?"

"Very funny," said Malcolm. He stopped and looked at the two birds, male and female. "Excuse me," he said.

"Yes?"

"Excuse me asking, but are you two married?"

"Well, we nest together," said the female duck, "and I lay his eggs. What about it?"

"Are you happy?" Malcolm asked.

"I dunno," said the female duck. "Are we?"

"I suppose so," said the male duck. "I never thought about it much."

"Really?" said the female duck. "I'll remember you said that."

"You know what I mean," said the male duck, pecking at its wing feathers. "You don't go around saying 'Am I happy?' all the time, unless you're human of course. If you're a duck, you can be perfectly happy without asking yourself questions all the time. I think that's what makes us different from the humans, actually. We just get on with things."

"But you do love each other?" Malcolm asked.

"Of course we do," said the male duck. "Don't we, pet?"

"Then how in God's name do you manage that? It's so difficult."

"Difficult?" said the female duck, mystified. "What's difficult about it?"

"So you love him, and he loves you, and you both just get on with it?"

"Do you mind?" said the male duck. "That's a highly personal question."

"I didn't mean *that,*" said Malcolm. "I meant that because you love each other, it's all right. That's enough to make it all work out."

"What's so unusual about that?"

"Everything," said Malcolm. "That's the way it seems, anyway."

"Humans!" laughed the male duck. "And it's the likes of you run the world. No wonder the rivers are full of cadmium."

At the door of the house, Malcolm stopped. He did not want to go in there, and there was no reason why he should. After all, he had the Tarnhelm, so he could go where he liked. He also had the Ring, so he could do what he liked. This was not his home; it was only a tiny part of it. He owned the world, and everything in it, and it was high time he looked the place over. He closed his eyes and vanished from sight.

13

When sufficiently drunk, Loge will tell you the story of the first theft of the Ring by himself and Wotan from Alberich. According to him, when he realised that the Giants Fasolt and Fafner were determined to exploit his clerical error to the full and claim the Goddess Freia as their reward for building the castle of Valhalla, he decided that the only conceivable way out of his difficulties would be to find an alternative reward which the Giants would prefer.

Finding an alternative to freehold possession of the most definitively beautiful person in the universe, the Goddess of Beauty herself, was no easy matter, and Loge searched the world in vain for anyone or anything who could think of one, starting with human beings, going on to the lower animals, and finally, in desperation, trying the trees and the rocks. The only creature, animate or inanimate, who could think of anything remotely preferable to Freia was the Nibelung Alberich, and when Loge asked him to explain, Alberich rather foolishly told him about the Ring, which first gave him the idea of stealing it.

Malcolm had heard this story from Flosshilde, who did an excellent impression of Loge when drunk, and it was at the back of his mind when he began his world tour. He hoped very much that things had changed since the Dark Ages. Certainly, some things were different now; Freia, for example, had long since fallen in love with a wood-elf, with whom she later discovered that she had nothing in common. Centuries of quiet desperation and comfort eating had taken their toll, and Freia was no longer the most beautiful person in the world. In addition attitudes have altered significantly since the Dark Ages, with the discovery of such concepts as enlightenment, feminism and electricity; Malcolm hoped he would quickly find that he was in a minority in regarding Love as being the Sweetest Thing. A quick survey of the thoughts of the human race would, he felt, help put his troubles in perspective.

With magical speed he crossed the continents, and the further he went the more profoundly depressed he became. Admittedly, the concept of love took on some strange forms (especially in California), but by and large the human race was horribly consistent in its belief in its value.

No matter how confused, oppressed, famished or embattled they were, the inhabitants of the planet tended to regard it as being the most important thing they could think of, and even the most cynical of mortals preferred it to a visit to the dentist. Not that they were all equally prepared to admit it; but Malcolm was able to read thoughts, and could see what was often hidden from the bearers of those thoughts themselves. Furthermore, with very few exceptions, the human race seemed to find its favourite obsession infuriatingly and inexplicably difficult, and considered it to be the greatest single source of misery in existence.

Not that that was an unreasonable view these days. Human beings, as is well known, cannot be really happy unless they are thoroughly miserable, and as a result of Malcolm's work as Ring-Bearer, there was little else for them to be miserable about. Wherever he went, Malcolm saw ordered prosperity, fertility and abundance. Just the right amount of rain was falling at just the right time in exactly the right places, and at precisely the best moment armies of combine harvesters, supplied free to the less developed nations by their guiltily prosperous industrial brothers, rolled through wheat-fields and paddy-fields to scoop up the bounty of the black earth. Even the major armament manufacturers had given up their lawsuits against the United Nations (they had been suing that worthy institution in the American courts for restraint of trade, arguing that World Peace was a conspiracy to send them all out of business) and turned over their entire capacity to the production of agricultural machinery. The whole planet was happily, stupidly content and, in order to rectify this situation, mankind had fallen back on the one source of unhappiness that even the Ring could do very little about.

Despite this lemming-like rush into love, there was a curious sense of elation and optimism which Malcolm could not at first identify. He was sure that he had come across it somewhere before, many years ago, but he could not isolate it until he happened to pass a school breaking up for the holidays. He remembered the feeling of release and freedom, the knowledge that for the foreseeable future—three whole weeks, at least—all one's time would be one's own, with no homework to do and no teachers to hate and fear. It was as if the whole world had broken up for an indefinite summer, and everyone was going to Jersey this year, where there are donkeys you can ride along the beach. All this, Malcolm realised, was his doing, the fruit of his own innocuous nature. He remembered that when he was a child, a princess had chosen to get married on a Wednesday, and all the schools in the country had been emancipated for the day. It had been on Wednesday that his scanty knowledge of mathematics came under severe scrutiny from a bald man with a filthy temper, and he would gladly have given his life for the marvellous lady who had spared him that ordeal for a whole week, allowing him to spend his least favourite day making a model of a jet bomber instead. Malcolm understood that he was now the author of the world's joy, just as the princess had been in his youth.

Actually seeing the results of his work made Malcolm feel unsteady, and at first he did not know what to make of it all. The world was happy, safe and in love, all except a certain M. Fisher who controlled the whole thing, and a small number of supernatural entities, who were out to stop him. There seemed to be an indefinable connection between everyone else's happiness and his own misery, and he began to feel distinctly resentful. This resentment was foolish and wrong, but he could not help it. He had never wanted to take away the sins of the world. Once again, the old pattern was being fulfilled. Everyone else but him was having a thoroughly good time, and he wasn't allowed to join in. His subjects didn't deserve to be happy; what had they done, compared to him, to earn this golden age? Before he realised it, he was muttering something to himself about wiping the silly grins off their faces, and the clouds around the globe began to gather.

The first drop of rain hit the back of his hand as he sat in Central Park, watching the ludicrously happy New Yorkers gambolling by moonlight in what had recently been declared the Safest Place in the USA. A group of street musicians, dressed in frock-coats with their faces painted in black and white squares, were playing the Brandenburg concertos to an appreciative audience of young couples and unarmed policemen, and Malcolm began to feel that enough was enough. He wanted to see these idiots getting rained on, and his wish was granted. As the musicians dived for cover among the trees and rocky outcrops, a tiny Japanese gentleman saw that Malcolm was getting wet and ran across to him with an umbrella. Smiling, he pressed it into Malcolm's hand, said, "Present," and hurried away. Malcolm threw the umbrella from him in disgust.

He sat where he was for many hours, the rain running down his face, and tried to think, but he appeared to have lost the knack. For most of the time he was alone, and the only interruptions to his reverie came from the scores of ex-pushers who had moved out of cocaine into bagels when the bottom fell out of drugs. Just before dawn, however, a pigeon floated down out of a tree and sat beside him.

"Don't I know you from somewhere?" Malcolm asked the pigeon.

"Unlikely," replied his companion. "You were never in these parts before, right?"

"Right," Malcolm said. "Sorry."

"That's okay. Have a nice day, now."

The pigeon busied itself with bagel-crumbs, and Malcolm rubbed his eyes with his fingertips.

"The way I see it," said the pigeon, "you care about people, right? That's good. That's a very positive thing."

"But where's the point?" Malcolm said, and reflected as he said it that he was starting to sound like the bloody girl now. "I mean, look at me. I've never been so wretched in my whole life."

"That's bad," said the pigeon, sympathetically. "By the way, are you British, by any chance?"

"Yes," said Malcolm.

"They had a British week over at Bloomingdales. Scottish shortbread. You get some excellent crumbs off those things."

Already the first joggers were pounding their way across the park, like ghosts caught up in some eternal recurrence of flight and pursuit. Two policemen, who had been discussing the relative merits of their personal diet programmes, paused and watched Malcolm as he chatted with the pigeon.

"There's a guy over there talking to the birds," said one.

"So he's talking to the birds," said the other. "That's cool. I do it all the time."

Malcolm looked round slowly. Only he knew how fragile all this was. The pigeon looked up from its crumbs.

"You seemed depressed about something," it said.

"I've got every right to be bloody depressed," replied Malcolm petulantly. "Everyone's happy except me."

"My, we *are* flaky this morning," said the pigeon. "You should see someone about that, before it turns into a complex."

"Oh, go away."

"You're being very hostile," said the pigeon. "Hostility is a terrible thing. You should try and control it."

"Yes, I suppose I should. Do you know who I am?"

The pigeon looked at him and then returned to his crumbs. "Everybody is somebody," it said. "Don't feel bad about it."

"I thought you birds knew everything," Malcolm said.

"You can get out of touch very quickly," said the pigeon. "Have you been on TV or something?"

"How come," asked Malcolm patiently, "I can understand what you're saying?"

The pigeon acknowledged this. "This makes you something special, I agree. But I'm terribly bad at names."

"It doesn't matter, really."

"I know who you are," said the pigeon, suddenly. "You're that Malcolm Fisher, aren't you? Pleased to meet you. Can you do something about this rain?"

Malcolm did something about the rain. It worked.

"And could you maybe make the evenings a tad longer?" continued the pigeon. "This time of year, the people like to come out and sit by the lake and eat in the evenings, and this is good for crumbs. So if you put say an extra hour, hour and a half on the evenings, there wouldn't be that scramble about half-seven, with all the pigeons coming over from the east. It's getting so that you have to be very assertive to get any crumbs at all, and I don't think being assertive suits me."

Malcolm promised to look into it. "Anything else I can do?" he asked.

"No," said the pigeon, "that's fine. Well, be seeing you."

It fluttered away, and Malcolm shut his eyes. He felt very tired and very lonely, and even the birds were no help any more.

At Combe Hall a small group had gathered in the drawing-room. It was many centuries since they had met like this, and they were very uncomfortable in each other's company, like estranged relatives who have met at a funeral.

Alberich broke the silence first. "He has no right to go off like this," he said. "It's downright irresponsible."

"Why shouldn't he go off if he chooses to?" replied Flosshilde angrily. "He's been under a lot of pressure lately, poor man. And we all know whose fault that is." She looked pointedly at the mother and daughter who were sitting on the sofa.

"Let's not get emotional here," said Mother Earth. "Unfortunately, we are all in his hands, and we can do nothing but wait until he sees fit to return."

"I wasn't talking to you," said Flosshilde. "I was talking to her."

Ortlinde said nothing, but simply sat and stared at the floor. Flosshilde seemed to find this profoundly irritating, and finally jumped up and put a cube of sugar down the Valkyrie's neck. Ortlinde hardly seemed to notice.

"That will do," said Mother Earth firmly. "Lindsy, perhaps it would be best if you went into the library."

"Oh no you don't," said Flosshilde. "I want her here where I can see what she's doing."

"This is what comes of involving a civilian," said Alberich impatiently. "Whose idea was it, anyway?"

"It certainly wasn't mine," said Mother Earth. "The first I knew about it was when I heard the reports."

"That's what I can't understand," said Alberich. "Who is this Malcolm Fisher, anyway? Anyone less suited to being a Ring-Bearer..."

"But he's doing wonderfully," said Flosshilde. "Everything is absolutely marvellous, or at least it was until *she* showed up."

"I'm not denying that," said Alberich. "But the fact remains that he's just not like any other Ring-Bearer there's ever been. Perhaps that's a good thing, I don't know. But if you girls had your way, he could easily turn out to be the worst Ring-Bearer in history."

"Don't look at me," said Flosshilde. "I'm on his side."

"Who chose him in the first place, that's what I want to know," Alberich continued. "That sort of thing doesn't just happen. I mean, look at the facts. He accidentally runs over a badger, who happens to be Ingolf. It doesn't make sense."

"I confess to sharing your perplexity," said Mother Earth. "This is by no means what I had intended..." She stopped, conscious of having disclosed too much.

"Go on, then," said Alberich. "What was meant to happen?"

"I am not at liberty..."

"Since it didn't happen," said Alberich, "it can't be important."

Mother Earth shrugged her bony shoulders. "Very well, then," she said. "The Ring was supposed to pass to the last of the Volsungs."

"There aren't any more Volsungs," said Flosshilde.

"Incorrect. Siegfried and Gutrude did in fact produce a child, a daughter called Sieghilde."

"I never knew that," said Alberich.

"Nobody knew. I saw to that. Sieghilde was brought up at the court of King Etzel of Hungary, where she married a man called Unferth. A most unsuitable match, I may say, of which I did not approve. Unfortunately, I was too late to be able to prevent it."

"And then what happened?"

"I have no idea. Unferth was an itinerant bard by profession, and I lost track of him in his wanderings. By birth he was a Jute, but he never returned to his native Jutland. I can only presume..." Flosshilde ran out of the room.

"What's she up to now?" muttered Alberich. "Why can't people sit still?"

"Anyway," continued Mother Earth, "given the quite remarkable fecundity of the Volsung race, I have little doubt that the family is still extant, and I have spent a great deal of time and effort in trying to trace the survivors of the line. Who could possibly make a better Ring-Bearer than the descendant of Siegfried the Dragon-Slayer? But to date my inquiries have been fruitless."

"So you think there's a Volsung or two wandering about out there just waiting for a chance to snap up the Ring?" said Alberich. "That's all we need."

"On the contrary," said Mother Earth, "I still regard the Volsung option as being the best possible solution. The Fisher episode is surely nothing but a strange and unplanned complication which will undoubtedly resolve itself in time. As soon as the missing Volsung is traced and apprised of his destiny, we can all get back to normal."

"That's not exactly fair on our young friend Malcolm Fisher," said Alberich. "He deserves more consideration than that. I presume that your Volsung would get hold of the Ring in the same way that his ancestor Siegfried obtained it from Fafner."

"That ought not to be necessary," said Mother Earth hurriedly. "No, he has had his part to play as caretaker of the Ring, and to date I must grant you he has played it very creditably. Only this present difficulty has marred an unexpectedly satisfactory period in the Ring's history. Recent events, however, have highlighted the underlying weakness in his emotional composition which makes it obvious that he is not to be trusted with the Ring on a long-term basis. Unfortunately, as we have recently been made to realise, there is very little that any of us can actually do, when the chips are, so to speak, down, to influence matters. Thanks to Wotan, and of course to my daughter here, all may yet be lost."

At this moment, Flosshilde came back into the room, carrying a volume of an encyclopedia.

"Say what you like about old Misery-guts there," she said, "she's made a good job of that library. Here we are."

She laid the book down on the table. "The Jutes," she said, "were part of the Anglo-Saxon alliance that colonised Britain after the Romans went home."

"I seem to remember hearing something about it at the time," said Alberich, "now that you mention it. Go on."

"If your Unferth was a Jute, perhaps he came over to Britain with the rest of them. Have you tried looking here?"

Mother Earth raised an eyebrow. "I must confess that this is a line of inquiry that has not previously occurred to me. These islands have always been so unremarkable, heroically and theologically speaking, that I never for one moment imagined that the Volsung line might be found here. It is of course possible."

Flosshilde seemed excited about something. "Where would the records be?" she asked. "This is worth following up."

"The main archive is at Mimir's Well," replied Mother Earth. "I think it would be in order to check this new lead."

"So what are we waiting for?"

"My dear young woman," said Mother Earth, "you don't expect me to abandon this highly delicate situation at this crucial juncture simply to go chasing through the files. It can certainly wait until Mr. Fisher returns from his holiday and this present difficulty has been satisfactorily resolved."

"Why are you so interested in tracking down this Volsung, anyway?" said Alberich suspiciously. "I thought you were on Fisher's side."

"Don't you see?" said Flosshilde. "If we find the person who ought to have the Ring, Malcolm won't be able to give it to *her*, because it won't be his to give away to anyone. He's got wonderful principles, he'll see at once that he has to give it to this Volsung person, and then everything will be all right."

Alberich shook his head. "You overestimate him," he said. "Besides, what guarantee do we have that this Volsung will be any more suitable than Malcolm Fisher?"

"I can reassure you on that point," said Mother Earth. "I am, after all, the ancestress of the Volsung race. Admittedly, Wotan is their male ancestor, but that cannot be helped now."

"You mean this Volsung would be her cousin?" Flosshilde asked, pointing rather rudely at Ortlinde.

"In strict form, yes."

"Even so," said Flosshilde, "it's worth a try."

"The Volsung race," continued Mother Earth, "was specifically designed from the outset to be Ring-Bearers. They have built into their software all the heroic qualities required to carry out that office in a satisfactory manner. Even after centuries of dilution, the fundamental ingredients ought still to be present. I have no doubts at all in my mind that if a Volsung or Volsungs can be found, our problems will be at an end. But first, it is essential that Mr. Fisher's ridiculous idea of giving the Ring to my daughter..."

"Now there I agree with you," said Flosshilde. "Here, you. Haven't you got anything to say?"

"No," mumbled Ortlinde.

For a moment, Flosshilde felt very sorry for the Valkyrie. Although she would have liked everything to have been Ortlinde's fault, it palpably wasn't, and the girl herself was probably having a rather horrid time. But Flosshilde hardened her heart.

"Why don't you do something useful for a change?" she said. "You nip across to Mimir's Well and look up the records, if you're so good with libraries."

Ortlinde shrugged her shoulders and started to get to her feet.

"Stay where you are," commanded her mother. "I'm not letting you out of my sight until this has been cleared up."

Ortlinde sat down again.

"Well, someone's got to go," said Flosshilde.

"You go, then," said Albench. "You're only getting under our feet here, anyway."

Flosshilde made a face at him. Mother Earth raised her hand for order.

"I shall telephone the Elder Norn," she said. "She is a most competent woman, and I'm sure Mr. Fisher will not begrudge us the cost of the call."

To telephone Valhalla from the Taunton area one has to go through the operator, and the process can take a long time. While Mother Earth was thus engaged, Alberich took Flosshilde on one side.

"You're up to something," he said.

"No, I'm not."

"Yes, you are. You're going to try and nobble this Volsung, aren't you? You failed to nobble Malcolm Fisher, so you want a chance at someone a bit more vulnerable, or at least with better taste."

The Rhinedaughter shook her head sadly. "My nobbling days are over," she said. "I've been nobbled myself."

"Go on!" said Alberich incredulously. "I thought it was all an act."

"I wish it was," sighed Flosshilde. "But it isn't."

"But what on earth do you see in him?"

"I don't know," said Flosshilde. "I suppose he's just different. He's sweet. I really have no idea. But I want to get him out of all this before they do something horrid to him."

Alberich smiled. "This is unusual for you, Flosshilde," he said. "I always thought you were the hardest of the three. Woglinde dries her face with emery paper and Wellgunde cleans her teeth with metal polish, but you were always the really tough cookie. And now look at you."

"All good things must come to an end," said Flosshilde, "and I don't suppose he'll ever be interested in me even if he does get rid of her. Which is funny, really," she said bitterly. "After all, he's nothing special and I am, Heaven knows. But there you are."

"There you are indeed," said Alberich. "Good luck, anyway."

Mother Earth put down the receiver.

"Would you believe," she said, "the Elder Norn is away on her honeymoon. Apparently, she has married a rock-troll she met only recently at a Company meeting. But the Middle Norn has agreed to do the necessary work in the archives, so we can expect results shortly."

"Well, that's something, anyway," said Flosshilde, sitting down and putting her feet up. "Now what shall we do?"

At that moment the door opened and Malcolm walked in. His hair was wet, although it had not been raining in Somerset.

"They told me you were all in here," he said.

"If you've got nothing better to do," said the Valkyrie Grimgerde, "you could fix that dripping tap in the kitchen."

"I'm busy," Wotan said angrily, but the Valkyrie had gone. He leaned back in his chair and poured himself another large schnapps. Despite the schnapps he was profoundly worried; it had been a long time since he had heard anything from Somerset, and surely his daughter should have succeeded in her mission by now. She was not, he was fully prepared to admit, an outstandingly intelligent girl, but intelligence was not really required, only beauty and a certain soppiness. Both of these qualities she had in abundance.

"Must you sit in here?" asked the Valkyrie Siegrune. "I want to hoover this room."

"Go and hoover somewhere else!" thundered the God of Battles. The Valkyrie swept out without a word, leaving Wotan to his thoughts and his schnapps. He bore the human no ill-will, he decided. His handling of the world, he was forced to admit, had been largely adequate. But this state of affairs could not be allowed to continue indefinitely, and if Operation Ortlinde failed, he could not see what else he could reasonably do.

"If that child messes this up," he growled into his glass, "I'll turn her into a bullfrog." He closed his eye, and tried to get some sleep.

When he woke up, he saw that he was surrounded on all sides by daughters. Even allowing for his blurred senses, there seemed to be an awful lot of them. To be precise, eight...

"So you're back at last, are you?" he said. "Well, where is it?"

All the Valkyries were silent, staring sullenly at their shoes, which were identical. When you have eight daughters, you can save a lot by buying in bulk.

"Where is it?" Wotan repeated. "Come on, give it here."

"I haven't got it," Ortlinde said softly. "He doesn't want me."

"You stupid...what do you mean?"

He had spilt schnapps all over the covers of the chair, but none of his daughters said a word. This could only mean that Ortlinde had failed him, and they were all feeling terribly guilty.

"He wouldn't give it to me," said Ortlinde sadly. "He said that he loved me, but he couldn't give it to me. I knew it would happen, sooner or later. So I came home."

"But why not?" screamed Wotan. "You had the sucker in the palm of your hand and you let him get away."

"I know," said the girl. "I've let you down again. I'm sorry."

"Get out of my sight!" Wotan shouted. The girl bowed her head and wandered wretchedly away to clean the bathroom.

After a short battle with his temper, Wotan managed to control himself, and surveyed his seven other daughters with his one good eye.

"Right, then," he said briskly, "who's going to be next?"

There was a long silence. Nobody moved.

"Very well, then," Wotan said. "Grimgerde, go and do something useful for the first time in your life."

Grimgerde shook her head. "There's no point," she said. "He knows all about us."

"He's been talking to Mother," said Waltraute.

"He'd recognise me as soon as I walked through the door," Grimgerde continued. "It wouldn't work. I'm sorry."

For a moment, Wotan was stunned. Then, with a roar like thunder, he leapt to his feet and ran out of the room. All the lights had gone out all over the house.

"We've let him down again," said Grimgerde sadly.

"If only we could *talk* to him," said Waltraute.

"Where's the point?" said Rossweise. "We wouldn't be able to communicate with him."

They went to fetch the Hoover.

14

Malcolm did not know where the others were, nor did he care much. He only knew that Ortlinde had gone. She had packed her suitcase, said goodbye, and walked down the drive, and for all Malcolm knew he would never see her again. Of course, he could not accept this; it seemed incredible that it could all be over, and at the back of his mind he felt sure that it was only a meaningless interruption to an inevitable happy ending. The girl loved him. He loved her. Surely that ought to be enough to be going on with. But she had gone away, and the part of his mind that still dealt with reality told him that it was for ever.

The room in which he had chosen to sit had not been used for many years; there were dust sheets over several pieces of furniture, and he tried to imagine what they looked like under their protective covers. There was half a tune he had heard in New York drumming away in his head; it was not a tune with any emotional or nostalgic significance, but it was there, like a fly trapped behind a windscreen, and he sat and listened to its endless repetitions for a while. In front of him were ten or fifteen sheets of paper on which he had started to write many drafts of the letter that would set everything straight. But the right words somehow eluded him, like a cat that refuses to come in when called. He could concentrate on nothing, and his eyes focused of their own accord on the walls and corners of the room.

"There you are," said a girl's voice behind him. "I've been looking for you everywhere."

He knew even before he looked round that it was only Flosshilde. He said nothing. He did not resent her intrusion; nothing could matter less. He imagined that she would say something or other and then go away again.

Flosshilde sat in the window-seat and put her feet up on a chair. "You don't mind me being here, do you?" she said.

"No," he replied.

"I wanted to get away from the others. They were being awfully stuffy about something."

Malcolm said nothing. He did not believe in the existence of anything outside this room, except of course for Ortlinde, and he wasn't allowed to think about her any more.

"Do you want to talk about it?" Flosshilde asked.

"No," said Malcolm.

"I didn't think you would. She was rather beautiful, wasn't she?"

"She isn't dead, you know," said Malcolm irritably. "She still is rather beautiful for all I know."

"What made you change your mind?"

"I had to do something. That seemed better than the other thing. I don't know. I did what I thought was for the best."

"I think you were right, if that's any help. No, of course it isn't, I'm sorry. I'll be quiet now."

"You can talk if you like," Malcolm said. "It wasn't bothering me."

"Can you play pontoon?"

"No."

"I'll teach you if you like."

"No, thanks."

"I know a game where you take a piece of writing—anything will do—and each letter has a number—A is one, B is two and so on—and you play odds against evens. Each sentence is a new game, and the side that wins gets five points for each sentence. Odds usually win, for some reason. That's what I do when I'm feeling unhappy. It takes your mind off things."

Malcolm wasn't listening, and Flosshilde felt like a castaway on a desert island who sees a ship sailing by without taking any notice of his signals. Perhaps it would be better, she thought, if she went away. But she stayed where she was.

"Shall I tell you the story about the time when the Giants stole Donner's hammer and he had to dress up in drag to get it back?"

"If you like."

She told the story, doing all the voices and putting in some new bits she hadn't thought of before. It was a very funny story, but Malcolm simply sat and looked out of the window. Flosshilde wanted to cry, or at the very least hit him, but she simply sat there too.

"I want your advice," she said.

"I don't think it would be worth much."

"Never mind. One of my sisters is dotty about a man, and he's dotty about a girl, and she doesn't fancy him at all. What should she do?"

"Are you being funny?" Malcolm asked bitterly.

"No, really. What do you think she should do about it?"

"Grow up and get on with something useful."

"I see. Aren't you sorry for her?"

"I suppose so. But I'm not really in the mood just now." He turned away and looked at the wall.

"I'm sorry," said Flosshilde. "I'll shut up now."

She studied her fingernails, which were the best in the world. King Arthur had often complimented her on her fingernails.

"Would you like me to go and talk to her?" Flosshilde said after a long silence.

"Who?"

"Ortlinde, silly. Perhaps there's something I could say..."

"I thought you couldn't stand her. Why is that, by the way?"

"Oh, I don't know," lied Flosshilde. "We quarrelled about something a long time ago."

"Tell me about her. You probably know her a lot better than I do."

"Not really," Flosshilde said. "I've known her on and off for years, of course, but only very generally. I find it pretty hard to tell those sisters apart, to be honest."

"Are they all like her? Her sisters, I mean."

"Very. Ortlinde's probably the nicest-looking, now that Brunnhilde's... And Grimgerde's quite pretty too, in a rather horrid sort of way. Big round eyes, like a cow."

"I'm not really interested in her sisters. She said that the rest of them were all much nicer than she was, but I don't believe her. What did you quarrel about?"

"I honestly can't remember. It can't have been anything important. Is there anything at all I can do?"

"No," said Malcolm. "Perhaps you'd better go. I'm not in a very good mood, I'm afraid."

Flosshilde took her feet daintily off the chair and walked out of the room. Once she had closed the door safely behind her, she shut her eyes and closed her hands tightly. It didn't help at all, and if she screamed somebody would hear her. She went downstairs.

From the landing, she could hear an excited buzz of voices in the drawing-room: Alberich and Erda and someone else, whose voice was vaguely familiar. The newcomer turned out to be the Middle Norn, a round, fairhaired woman in a smart brown tweed suit. She had brought a huge briefcase with her, and the floor was covered with photocopies of ancient parchments. Erda and the Norn were down on their knees going over them with magnifying-glasses, while Alberich was at the desk taking notes.

"...And she married Sintolt the Hegeling," the Norn was saying, "and *their* son was Eormanric..."

"What's going on?" Flosshilde asked.

"There has been a rather singular development," said Erda, looking up from the papers on the floor. She had fluff from the carpet all over her jacket. "We have succeeded in tracing the last of the Volsungs."

"Really?" said Flosshilde. She wasn't in the least fascinated, for it scarcely seemed to matter now. Still, it would be something to do, and if she got bored she could play her word-game.

"I think you will be surprised when you hear it," continued Mother Earth. "Let me just go through the stemma for you."

"Don't bother on my account," said Flosshilde. "I'll take your word for it." She sat down and picked up a magazine. "Just tell me the name."

"There are three living descendants in the direct line," said the Norn, taking off her spectacles. "Mrs. Eileen Fisher, of Sydney, Australia; her daughter Bridget, also of Sydney; and her son Malcolm, of Combe Hall, Somerset."

In an instant, Flosshilde was kneeling beside them. She bullied the Norn into going over every link in the complex genealogical chain, which spanned over a thousand years. The descent was indeed direct, from Siegfried the Volsung, Fafner's Bane, to Bridget and Malcolm Fisher.

"I hurried over as soon as I found out," said the Norn. "Of course, you know what this means."

"No," admitted Flosshilde, breathlessly. "Go on."

"Well," said the Norn, putting back her spectacles. "Siegfried was, at least in theory, a subject of the Gibichung crown when he married Gutrune. Certainly, Sieghilde was a Gibichung subject, and so the Ring, if we accept that it was Siegfried's legitimate property, is subject to Gibichung law in matters of inheritance. Gibichung law is of course very complicated, and on the subject of testament it verges on the arcane, but it so happens that I have made a special study of the subject." The Norn paused, as if expecting some words of praise. None were forthcoming. "Anyway, hereditary as opposed to acquired property cannot, under Gibichung law, pass to the female heirs but is only transmitted through them to the next male heir. That is to say, to the female it is inalienable and she has no right to assign or dispose of it. She can only keep it in trust until the next male heir comes of age at fourteen years."

"What are you going on about?" said Flosshilde.

"Although his mother is still alive and his sister is older than him, Malcolm Fisher is, according to Gibichung law, the rightful heir to the Nibelung's Ring."

"Which ring?"

"My bloody ring," said Alberich impatiently. "Your ring. *The* Ring. Look, if we're going to be all legal about this..."

"Human law," said Mother Earth loftily, "has no bearing on property that is or has been owned or held by a God. Since the Volsung race is descended from Gods and is therefore semi-divine, and since the Ring was, if only for the space of a few hours, once held by the Gods Wotan and Loge, the Ring is subject only to divine law."

"Oh," said the Norn, clearly disappointed. "Never mind, then."

"Under divine law." said Mother Earth, "property descends by primogeniture alone. Mrs. Eileen Fisher, Mr. Fisher's mother—and the eldest surviving Volsung—is therefore the legitimate legal heir to the Nibelung's Ring."

"What about me?" shouted Alberich.

"And me," added Flosshilde. "It was ours to begin with, remember."

"The gold was," said Alberich. "But I *made* the bloody thing."

"I was about to say," said Mother Earth, severely, "that under divine law, right of inheritance is subordinate to right of conquest."

"What?" Flosshilde was now utterly confused.

"It means," said Alberich bitterly, "that if I take something away from you it becomes mine, and if they take something away from me it becomes theirs. That's divine law. Marvellous, isn't it?"

"In other words," said the Norn triumphantly, "it amounts to the same thing as Gibichung law. It belongs to Mr. Fisher."

There was a baffled silence as the four immortals pondered the significance of all this.

"Be that as it may," said Mother Earth at last, "the fact remains that Malcolm Fisher, if not *the* last of the Volsungs, is one of the last of the Volsungs—certainly, he is the most recent of the Volsungs, which is roughly the same thing—and as such is by birth and genetic programming one of the three most suitable people in the world to be the Ring-Bearer. Goddammit," she added.

Flosshilde could hardly contain her excitement. "Just wait till I tell him," she said. "He'll be thrilled."

"I hardly think it would be suitable at this juncture..."

Flosshilde made a rude face and left the room.

"That child is scarcely helping matters," said Mother Earth.

"Guess what," said Flosshilde, bursting into the room. "You're a Volsung."

"I'm sorry?" Malcolm said.

Flosshilde told him everything, putting in explanations where she felt they would be necessary. "So you see," she said, "you're not really human at all. You're one of us. And *she* is your cousin."

Malcolm laughed. "What a coincidence," he said sardonically.

"But don't you care?" said Flosshilde. "You're virtually a God. You're descended from the world's greatest hero. Aren't you pleased?"

"No," said Malcolm truthfully. "I couldn't care less, to be honest with you. Of course, I always knew there was something wrong with me, but now that I know what it is, I don't see that it's going to make a great deal of difference." He continued to stare out of the window.

"Oh, for pity's sake!" Flosshilde was angry now. She had so wanted him to be pleased and excited, and he wasn't. "You're hopeless."

"Very probably. And besides, from what you said, Bridget is the real Volsung, or the eldest, or whatever. That doesn't surprise me in the least. Judging by what I've heard about Siegfried lately, it sounds like she takes after him a whole lot."

Flosshilde knelt down beside him and put her hands on his elbows. "But she hasn't done what you've done. She hasn't made the world a wonderful place or defeated Wotan. You have, all on your own. You're the real hero, much more than Siegfried was, even."

"Really?" Malcolm shook his head. "I don't think so. I've stopped living in a make-believe world, you see. Just finding out that I'm a make-believe person doesn't make any difference. It's not going to change anything."

"But you don't understand..."

"That's the one thing I have got right," he said, looking straight at her. "I *do* understand, and that's the only good thing that's come out of this whole rotten mess. I've been living in a world of my own and..."

"But the world *is* your own," Flosshilde almost shouted. Suddenly Malcolm began to laugh, and Flosshilde lost all patience with him. As long as she lived, she told herself as she walked furiously out of the room, she would never understand humans.

On the landing she met the Norn, who seemed agitated.

"Call him," she said. "Something terrible is happening."

Across the Glittering Plains, which stretch as far as the eye can see from the steep rock on which the castle of Valhalla is built, Wotan had mustered the Army of the Storm. In their squadrons and regiments were assembled the Light and Dark Elves, the spirits of the unquiet dead, the hosts of Hela. At the head of each regiment rode a Valkyrie, dressed in her terrifying armour, the very sight of which is enough to turn the wits of the most fearless of heroes. Around his shoulders, Wotan cast the Mantle of Terror, and on his head he fastened the helmet that the dwarves had made him from the fingernails of dead champions in the gloomy caverns of Nibelheim. He nodded his head, and Loge brought him the great spear Gungnir, the symbol and the source of all his power. When he had first come to rule the earth, he had cut its shaft from the branches of Yggdrasil, the great ash tree that stands between the worlds, causing the tree to wither and die and making inevitable the final downfall of the Gods. Onto this spearshaft, Loge had marked the runes of the Great Covenant between the God and his subjects.

Wotan raised his right hand, and the Valkyrie Waltraute, who closes the eyes of men slain in battle, led forward his eight-legged horse, the cloud-trampling Sleipnir. Above his head hovered two black ravens.

"If you get mud on that saddle," said Waltraute, "you can clean it off yourself."

Without a word, Wotan vaulted onto the back of his charger. As the first bolt of lightning ripped the black clouds he brandished the great spear as a sign of his army, the *Wutende Heer*.

It was over a thousand years since the hosts of Valhalla had ridden to war on the wings of the storm, and the world had forgotten how to be afraid. Like a vast cloud of locusts or a shower of arrows they flew, blotting out the light from the earth. At the head of the wild procession galloped Wotan; behind him Donner, Tyr, Froh, Heimdall, Njord and Loge, who carried the banner of darkness. Close on their heels came the eight Valkyries: Grimgerde, Waltraute, Siegrune, Helmwige, Ortlinde, Schwertleite, Gerhilde and Rossweise, baying like wolves to spur on the grim company that followed them, the terrible spirits of fear and discord. Each of the eight companies bore its own hideous banner—Hunger, War, Disease, Intolerance, Ignorance, Greed, Hatred and Despair; these were the badges of Wotan's army. Behind the army like a pack of hounds intoxicated by the chase followed the wind and the rain, lashing indiscriminately at friend and foe. Below them, forests were flattened, towns and villages were swept away, even the mountains seemed to tremble and cower at the fury of their passing. With a rush, they swept over the Norn Fells and past the dead branches of the World Ash. As they passed it, lightning fell among its withered leaves, setting it alight. Soon the whole fell was burning, and the flames hissed and swayed at the foot of Valhalla Rock. As the army of the God of Battles passed between the worlds, the castle itself caught fire and began to burn furiously, lighting up the whole world with a bright red glow.

The army passed high over the frozen desert of the Arctic, convulsing the ice-covered waters with the shock of their motion, and flitted over Scandinavia like an enormous bird of prey, whose very shadow paralyses the helpless victim. As they wheeled and banked over Germany, the Rhine rose up as if to meet them, bursting its banks and flooding the flat plains between Essen and Nijmegen. Wotan, his whole form framed with the lightning, laughed when he saw it, and his laughter brought towers and cathedrals crashing to the ground. And as the army followed its dreadful course, black clouds of squeaking, gibbering spirits leapt up to swell its numbers, as all the dark, tormented forces of the earth were drawn as if by capillary action into the fold of the Lord of Tempests. The very noise of their wings was deafening, and when they swept low the earth split open, as if shrinking back in horror. But however vast and awesome this great force might seem, most terrible of all was Wotan, like a burning arrow at its head. As he flew headlong over the North Sea, the heat of his anger turned the waters to steam, and soon the forests of Scotland were blazing as brightly as Valhalla itself. As the army neared its goal, it seemed to concentrate into a cloud of tangible darkness, forcing its way through the air as it bore down like a meteor on one little village in the West of England.

"What's going on?" shouted Malcolm. The noise was unbearable, and through the splintered windows of the house a gale was blowing that nearly lifted him off his feet.

"It's Wotan," yelled Alberich, his face white with fear. "He's coming with all his army."

"Is he indeed?" Malcolm replied. "I want a word with him."

All the lights had gone out, but the brilliance of the ball of fire that grew ever larger in the northern sky dazzled and stunned the watchers, so that even Mother Earth had to turn away. But Malcolm walked calmly out of the shattered door and stood in the drive. His hair was unruffled and his eyes were unblinking, and on his finger the Ring felt easy and comfortable. Out of the immeasurable darkness that surrounded it the awful light grew ever more fierce, until the very ground seemed to be about to melt. Like a falling sun, it hurtled towards the ruined house, straight at the Ring-Bearer, like a diving falcon.

"All right," said Malcolm sternly. "That will do."

The light went out, and the world was plunged into utter darkness. A hideous scream cut through the air like a spearblade through flesh, and was held for an instant in the hollow of the surrounding hills. Then it died away, and the cloud slowly began to fall apart. Like a swarm of angry bees suddenly confounded by a puff of smoke, Wotan's army sank out of the air and disintegrated. The black vapours dissolved, and the gentle light of the sun fell upon the surfaces of the wrecked and mangled planet.

"And before you go," said Malcolm, "you can clear up all this mess."

Like a film being wound back, the world began to reassemble itself. Smoke was dragged out of the air back into the stumps of charred trees. Bricks and stones slipped back into place and once more were houses. Glass reformed itself smoothly into panes, and the cracks faded away. The flooded rivers slid shamefacedly back between their banks, taking their silt with them, and the earth silently closed up its fissures. While this remarkable act of healing was taking place, a pale mist formed and hung in the still air above the surface of the world, and the light of the sun was caught and refracted by it into all the colours of the spectrum. Malcolm had never seen anything so beautiful in his entire life.

"What is it?" he asked a passing dove. The bird looked puzzled for a moment.

"Oh, *that,*" it said at last. "That's just the Test Card." Malcolm shrugged his shoulders and walked back into the house.

The drawing-room seemed to be deserted, and Malcolm had come to the conclusion that everyone must have got bored and gone away when he heard a voice from under the table.

"What happened?" said the voice.

"Nothing," said Malcolm. "It's over now."

Looking rather ashamed of herself, Mother Earth crawled out from her hiding-place. "I dropped my goddamned glasses," she mumbled. "I was just looking for them, and..."

"Are you sure they're not in your pocket?" asked Malcolm sympathetically. Mother Earth made a dumb show of looking in her pocket and, not surprisingly, there they were. "Thank you," she said humbly.

"You're welcome," said Malcolm.

Alberich and the Middle Norn emerged from behind the sofa. To his amusement, Malcolm saw that Alberich was holding the Norn's hand in a comforting manner.

"There now," said the dwarf, "I told you it would be all right, didn't I?"

The Norn beamed at him, her round face illuminated by some warm emotion. "I don't know what came over me," she said.

"That was very clever," Alberich said to Malcolm, forgetting to let go of the Norn's hand even though the danger was past. "How did you manage it?"

"What, that?" said Malcolm diffidently. "Oh, it was nothing, really."

Alberich and his new friend walked to the window. In the sky there was a deep red glow, which could have been the sunset were it not for the fact that it was due North. Alberich looked at it for a long time.

"I never did like them," he said at last.

"Who?" Malcolm asked.

"The Gods," said Alberich. Then he turned to the Norn. "You look like you could do with some fresh air," he said. "Do you fancy a stroll in the garden?"

It seemed very probable that she did, and they walked away arm in arm. Malcolm shook his head sadly.

"Who was that, by the way?" he asked Mother Earth, who was busily brushing the fluff off her jacket.

"The Middle Norn," said Mother Earth.

"Doesn't she have a name?"

"I don't know. Probably."

"What's that light in the sky? I thought I'd put everything right."

"That is the castle of Valhalla in flames," replied Mother Earth quietly. "The High Gods have all gone down. They no longer exist."

Malcolm stared at her for a moment. "All of them?"

"All of them. Wotan, Donner, Tyr, Froh..."

"*All* of them?"

"They went against the power of the Ring," said Mother Earth with a shrug, "and were proved to be weaker."

"And what about the Valkyries?" Malcolm's throat was suddenly dry.

"They were only manifestations of Wotan's mind," said Mother Earth. "Figments of his imagination, I suppose you could say."

"But they were your daughters."

"In a sense." Mother Earth polished her spectacles and put them precisely on her nose. "But what the hell, I never really got on with them. Not as *people*. They were too like their father, I guess, and boy, am I glad to see the back of him."

"And they're all dead?"

"Not dead," said Mother Earth firmly. "They just don't exist any more. I wouldn't upset yourself over it. In fact, you should be pretty pleased with yourself. By the way, did Flosshilde tell you about..."

"Yes," said Malcolm, "yes, she did." He was trying to remember what Ortlinde had looked like, but strangely enough he couldn't. He felt as if he had been woken up in the middle of a strange and wonderful dream, and that all the immensely real images that had filled his mind only a moment ago were slipping away from him, like water that you try and hold in your hand.

"Let me assure you," said Mother Earth, "that you have in no sense *killed* anybody."

"I don't believe I have," said Malcolm slowly. "I think I'm beginning to understand all this business after all. By the way, what happens now?"

Mother Earth came as close as she had ever done to a smile. "You tell me," she said. "You're in charge now."

Malcolm looked at the Ring on his finger. "Right," he said, "let's get this show on the road."

Mother Earth yawned. "I'm feeling awful sleepy," she said. "I guess I'll go to bed now, if you don't mind. If I don't get my thousand years every age I'm no use to anybody."

"Go ahead," said Malcolm. "And thanks for all your help."

"You're welcome," said Mother Earth. She was beginning to glow with a pale blue light. "I didn't do anything, really. It was all your work."

Malcolm smiled, and nodded.

"Remember," she said, "whatever you feel like doing is probably right." She was indistinct now, and Malcolm could see a coffee-table through her.

"Sorry?" he asked, but she had melted away, leaving only a few sparkles behind her in the air. Malcolm shrugged his shoulders.

"Never mind," he said aloud. "She's probably on the phone."

Two very bedraggled ravens floated down out of the evening sky and pecked at the window-pane. Their feathers were slightly singed. Malcolm opened the window and they hopped painfully into the room.

"Hello," said Malcolm. "What can I do for you?"

The first raven nudged his companion, who nudged him back.

"We were thinking," said the first raven. "You might be wanting a messenger service."

"Now you've taken over," said the second raven.

"You see," said the first raven, "we used to work for the old management, and now they've been wound up..."

"What do you do, exactly?" Malcolm asked.

"We fly around the world and see what's going on," said the raven, "and then we come and tell you."

"That sounds fine," said Malcolm. "You're on."

The second raven dipped its beak gratefully. "I was thinking of packing it in," he said. "But now the old boss has gone..."

"What are you called?" Malcolm asked.

"I'm Thought," said the first raven, "and this is Memory."

"When can you start?"

Thought seemed to hesitate, but Memory said, "Straight away." When Malcolm wasn't looking, Thought pecked his colleague hard on the shoulder.

"Fine," said Malcolm. "First, go and make sure that all the damage has been put right. Then check to see if any of the old Gods are still left over."

The two ravens nodded and fluttered away. When they were (as they thought) out of earshot, Thought turned to Memory and said, "What did you tell him that for?"

"What?" said Memory.

"About us starting straight away. I wanted a holiday."

"Don't you ever think?" replied Memory. "This is the twentieth century. They've got telephones, they've got computers, they've got Fax machines. They don't need birds any more. Nobody's indispensable, chum. You've got to show you're willing to work."

"Oh, well," said Thought. "Here we go again, then."

After a while, it occurred to Malcolm that he hadn't seen Flosshilde since the storm had died away. At the back of his mind something told him that now that Ortlinde no longer existed, it was time to move on to the next available option, but he recognised that instinct and deliberately cut it out of his mind. It was the old Malcolm Fisher instinct, the one that made him fall in love and be unhappy. He was finished with all that now. He knew of course that there was such a thing as love, and that if you happen to come across it, as most people seem to do, it is not a thing that you can avoid, or that you should want to avoid. But you cannot go out and find it, because it is not that sort of creature. The phrase "to fall in love," he realised, is a singularly apt one; it is something you blunder into, like a pothole. Very like a pothole. In his case, however, he had had the fortune, good or bad, to blunder into a badger, not love, and since he was not accident-prone, that was probably all the accidental good fortune he was likely to get. As for Flosshilde—well, since the passing of the Valkyries, she was officially one of the three prettiest girls in the universe, but only superficial people judge by appearances. Malcolm himself could be a prettier girl than Flosshilde just by giving an order to the Tarnhelm, although it was unlikely that he should ever want to do that. The fact that she was a water-spirit was neither here nor there; he himself was a hero, descended from Mother Earth and a now non-existent God, but he doubted whether that had any influence on his character or behaviour. He suddenly realised that Wotan and Erda and all the rest of them had been his relatives. That at least explained why he had been frightened of them and why he had found them so difficult to cope with.

He smiled at this thought. Family is family, after all, and he had just blotted most of his out. But now he was on his own, which, bearing in mind the case of his unhappy predecessor, was probably no bad thing. It would be foolish to go looking for a consort now that the world depended on him and him alone. A trouble shared, after all, is a trouble doubled.

Nevertheless, he wondered where Flosshilde had got to. Everyone seemed to have drifted away, and for a moment he felt a slight panic. He sat down on the stairs and tried to think calmly. To his relief, he found this perfectly possible to do.

Wotan, he reflected, had gone to one extreme, but Ingolf had gone to the other. One had been caught up in a noisy and infuriating household which had driven him quietly mad. The other had curled up in a hole and allowed his dark subconscious to permit the world to drift into the twentieth century, with all its unpleasant consequences. He sought a happy medium between these two extremes, and in particular considered carefully all that Mother Earth had told him. Then he got up and whistled loudly. To his surprise, nothing happened. Then he realised his mistake and went through to the drawing-room. There were the two ravens, huddled upon the window-sill.

"Everything's fine," said Thought, as soon as Malcolm had let them in. "All the Gods have cleared off."

"Except Loge," said Memory. "He offered us all the dead sheep we could eat if we didn't tell you he was still around, but we thought..."

"I've got nothing against Loge," said Malcolm. "But how come he didn't go down with all the others?"

"He was a bit puzzled by that," said Memory. "Apparently, there he was, surrounded by Gods one minute, all on his own feeling a right prat the next. He thinks it's down to him being a fire-spirit and not a real God."

"Tell him he can have his old job back if he wants it," said Malcolm.

"I'll tell him," said Thought, "but I think he's got other plans. He was talking about going into the wet fish business. Muttered something about he might as well do it himself before somebody did it to him. Gloomy bloke, I always thought."

"Anyway," said Malcolm, "did either of you see Flosshilde?"

"Flosshilde," said Memory thoughtfully. "Can't say I did. In fact, I haven't seen any of the girls since before the Big Bang."

Malcolm suddenly felt very ill. "But they weren't High Gods, were they?" he said. "I mean, they couldn't have..."

"Wouldn't have thought so," said Memory, "but you never know with those three. Very deep they were, though you wouldn't think it to look at them. But they were always mixed up with some pretty heavy things, like the Rhinegold and the Ring. Could be that they had to go along with the rest."

Malcolm sat down heavily, appalled at the thought. He couldn't understand why he was so horrified, but the idea of never seeing Flosshilde again suddenly seemed very terrible. Not that he was in love with her; but he knew now that he needed her very urgently.

"Find her," he snapped. "Go on, move. If you're not back by dawn, I'll turn you both into clay pigeons."

The ravens flapped hurriedly away into the night, and Malcolm closed his eyes and groaned. He had just bumped into something, and it felt horribly disconcerting.

"Oh, God," he said aloud. "Now look what I've done."

Alberich and the Middle Norn looked in to say goodbye, and found Malcolm in a strange mood. He seemed upset about something but would not say what it was, and his manner seemed cold and hostile. The Norn felt sorry for him, but Alberich seemed in a hurry to get away.

"I don't like it," he said. "Something's gone wrong."

"What could possibly go wrong now?" said the Norn coyly.

"I don't know," said Alberich, "but when it does, I want to be safely underground, where it won't matter so much."

They walked in silence for a while, as the Norn nerved herself to ask the question that had been worrying her.

"Alberich," she said.

"Yes?"

"Don't take this the wrong way, but weren't you supposed to have forsworn Love?"

"Yes," said Alberich, "but I'm allowed to change my mind, aren't I?"

"But I didn't think you could. Not once you'd sworn."

"That was conditional on my still wanting the Ring. And now that I couldn't care less about it..."

"Couldn't you?"

"No." He felt rather foolish, but for some reason that was all that seemed to be wrong with him. An unwonted harmony seemed to have overtaken his digestive system.

"To celebrate," he said daringly, "let's go and treat ourselves to the best lunch money can buy in this godforsaken country. I've heard about this place where you can get very palatable lobster."

The Norn stared at him. "Are you sure?" she said.

Alberich smiled at her fondly. "Don't you start," he said.

It was nearly dawn by the time the ravens came back. They perched on the window-sill exhausted, for they had been flying hard all night. Through the open window, they could see the new Lord of Tempests sitting where he had been when they had left him several hours before. He was staring at the ground, and he looked distinctly irritable.

"He's not going to like it," whispered Memory.

"You tell him," replied Thought. "You're the one with the words."

"Why's it always got to be me?" said Memory angrily. "You're the eldest, you tell him."

"How do you make that out?"

"Stands to reason, dunnit? You can't have memory before thought, or you wouldn't have anything to remember. Well, would you?"

Memory clearly had right on his side, and so it was Thought who tapped gingerly on the pane and hopped into the room first. Malcolm looked up, and there was something in his eyes that both ravens recognised.

"Well?"

"Nothing, boss," said Thought. "We did all the rivers, oceans, seas, lakes, lochs, lagoons, burns and wadis in the world. Even did the reservoirs and the sewers. Nothing. Looks like they've just..."

Malcolm let out a long, low moan, and Thought stepped back nervously, expecting every moment to be turned into a small flat disc made of pitch, earmarked for certain destruction. But Malcolm simply nodded, and the two birds flew thankfully away.

"Now look what you've gone and done," said Thought bitterly as they collapsed onto a fallen tree beside the troutstream. "You've gone and got us saddled with another bloody nutter. The last one was bad enough…"

"How was I to know he'd go off his rocker?" said Memory. "He looked all right to me."

"You never learn, do you?" continued Thought. "We could be well away by now, but no, you've got to go and *volunteer* us. If we ever get out of this in one piece…"

In view of the threat recently uttered by the new Lord of the Ravens, that seemed improbable. Dawn was breaking in the East, and Thought regarded it sourly.

"Look at that," he said. "No imagination, this new bloke."

"Come on," said Memory. "We might as well have another go."

They lifted themselves wearily into a thermal and floated away.

15

For about a week after the going-down of the old Gods, Malcolm was kept rather busy. Minor spirits and divine functionaries called at all hours of the day and night with papers for him to read and documents to sign, most of which were concerned with trivial matters. The remaining Gods had been stripped of the last few vestiges of authority by the destruction of Wotan and, try as they might, they could not persuade the Ring-Bearer to transfer any of his duties or powers to them. In the end the majority of them accepted the new order of things, and the few recalcitrant deities who continued to protest found themselves posted to remote and uninhabited regions where their ineffectual energies could be expended without causing any real disturbance.

In an effort to appear positive, Malcolm created a new class of tutelary deities. The rivers and oceans had long had their own guardian spirits, originally installed when shipping was the main form of transport in the world. In the last few centuries, however, this role had diminished, whereas the roads and railways had gone without any form of heavenly representation. Malcolm therefore assigned most of the redundant spirits to the railway networks and motorways, a system which seemed to satisfy most requirements. He commissioned the Norns to set up a system of appointments: all gods wishing to be assigned a road or a railway had to take a written exam, and were posted according to the results they obtained. Since their duties were strictly honorary, it made little difference to the world at large, but it seemed to please the divine community. It gave them a purpose in life, and when one is dealing with immortals, that is no mean achievement.

There were also vacancies in existing posts to be filled, for many river-spirits and cloud-shepherds had perished with their master in the attack on Combe Hall. Again, the Norns were given the task of drawing up a list of unfilled posts, with a parallel list of suitable candidates. Malcolm, who was unfamiliar with divine prosopography, had to rely heavily on the judgment of his advisers, but for some reason virtually all the supernatural beings he met were patently terrified of him, and this terror, combined with his ability to read thoughts, made corruption or favouritism seem unlikely.

He found the terror he inspired in his subordinates extremely hard to understand. Admittedly, his patience was sorely tried at times, for all the gods and spirits took themselves extremely seriously even though their power was non-existent; and he had to admit that he did sometimes lose his temper with them, causing the occasional shower of unplanned rain. But the world continued to thrive and prosper, with only the epidemic of love and romance spoiling an otherwise perfect situation. One thing did worry him, however: the Tarnhelm seemed to have developed a slight fault. Occasionally, after a particularly trying meeting or a long night of paperwork, he found to his disgust that he had changed his shape without wanting to, and for some reason the shape the Tarnhelm selected for him was invariably that of Wotan. This and a curious craving for schnapps gave Malcolm pause for thought, but he dismissed his fears as paranoia, and carried on with the work of reorganisation.

But he was not happy. Although he could not remember what she had looked like, he knew that Ortlinde was very much on his mind, and he could not help feeling horribly guilty about having caused her to cease to exist. He closed up the library at Combe Hall, but the house itself seemed to be haunted by her, and eventually he decided that the time had come to leave it for good. He sent for Colonel Booth (whose real name, he discovered, was Guttorm), thanked him for the loan of his house, and started to look for a new place to live. Somehow, he felt no enthusiasm for the task, and although the Norns, whom he found invaluable, continually sent him details of highly attractive properties all over the world, he found it difficult to summon up the energy to go and view them. Then one day the Younger Norn remarked that there was always Valhalla itself...

"But I thought it had been burnt down," Malcolm said.

"Burnt, yes," said the Norn. "Down, no. The shell is still intact. I've had the architects out there, and they say it could easily be made habitable again. Of course, the best builders in the world were the Giants, and they're all dead now, but they were always expensive and difficult to work with..."

That, Malcolm felt, was something of an understatement. Nevertheless, the idea seemed curiously attractive, and he went out with the Younger Norn to look at the place.

"You could have tennis-courts here, and maybe a swimming-pool," said the Norn, pointing with her umbrella to what had once been the Crack of Doom. "Or if you don't like the idea of that, how about a rock garden? Or an ornamental lake? With real gnomes," she said dreamily.

"I think I'd rather just have a lawn," Malcolm replied. "And some rosebeds."

The Norn shrugged, and they moved on to inspect the Steps of Unknowing. "How about a maze?" suggested the Norn. "Appropriate, really."

"No," said Malcolm. "I think a garage might be rather more use."

"Please yourself. Anyway, you like the place?"

"Well, it's quiet, and the neighbours aren't too bad. I lived most of my life in Derby," Malcolm said. "It's certainly different from there. But it's rather a long way from the shops."

"I wouldn't have thought that would have worried you, having the Tarnhelm and so on."

"True," said Malcolm, "but sometimes I like to walk or drive, just for a change."

"No problem," said the Norn, "we'll build you a replica of your favourite city. Valhalla New Town, we could call it."

The thought of a heavenly version of Milton Keynes was almost enough to put Malcolm off the whole idea, but he asked the Norn to get some plans drawn up and hire an architect. The work would be done by the Nibelungs, who would do a perfectly good job without making unreasonable demands, as the Giants had done.

On the way back, they passed the charred stump of a tree, which had once been the World Ash. To their amazement, they saw a couple of green shoots emerging from the dead and blackened wood.

"That tree's been dead ever since Wotan first came on the scene," said the Norn. "It represents the Life Force, apparently."

"Get someone to put one of those little wire cages round it," said Malcolm. "We don't want the squirrels getting at it."

Malcolm returned from his trip to Valhalla feeling rather tired, not by the journey but by the company of the Younger Nom. He sat down in the drawing-room and took his shoes off; he wanted a quick glass of schnapps and ten minutes with the paper before going to bed. He was getting middle-aged, he realised; but such considerations did not really worry him. Youth, he had decided, was not such a big deal after all.

He looked out over the troutstream and suddenly found himself in tears. For a moment he could not understand why; but then he realised what had caused what was, generally speaking, an unusual display of emotion. The trout-stream had reminded him of Flosshilde, whom he missed even more than the shoe-inspecting Valkyrie. He had treated Flosshilde very badly... No, it wasn't guilt that was making him cry. He had shut it out of his mind for so long that he imagined that it had gone away, but now he knew what his real problem was.

He had heard a story about a man who had gone through life thinking that the word Lunch meant the sun, and it occurred to him that he had been in roughly the same situation himself. Until very recently, he had not known what the word Love really meant; he had thought it referred to the self-deceptive and futile emotion that had plagued him since he first had enough hair on his chin to justify buying a razor of his own. On the night of the confrontation with Wotan, he had suddenly realised his mistake; he had loved Flosshilde then, just at the very moment when she had ceased to exist. So horrible had that thought been that he had excluded it from his brain; but now it had come back and taken him by surprise, and he could see no way of ever getting rid of it. The sorrow he had felt for Ortlinde was little more than sympathy, but he needed the Rhinedaughter. The thought of going to live in Valhalla or being the ruler of the Universe without having her there was unbearable; the thought of being alive without having her there was bad enough.

He shook his head and poured out some more schnapps. Many momentous and terrible things had happened and the Gods had all gone down, just to teach Malcolm Fisher the meaning of the word Love. Had he paid more attention to his English teacher at school, he reflected, the whole world might have been saved a great deal of trouble. He picked up the local paper, and saw a photograph of a tall girl and a man with large ears standing outside a church. Liz Ayres had married Philip Wilcox. He smiled, for this fact meant nothing to him at all. The sooner he got out of this house, the better.

Someone had left the French windows open. He got up and closed them, for the night was cold; summer had passed, and it would be unethical of him to extend it for his own convenience. It had been a strange season, he reflected, and it was just as well that it was over now. The world could cool down again, and he could allow it to rain with a clear conscience.

"Why am I doing all this?" he said aloud.

Now at last he understood. It was blindingly obvious, but because he was so stupid he hadn't seen it before. The world, now God-free and generally purified, was no longer his to hold on to. He must give the Ring to his sister Bridget. She, after all, was older than him, and much cleverer, and generally better equipped to handle difficult problems. He was only the intermediary. Everything fell into place, and he felt as if a great burden had fallen from his shoulders. If only he had done it before, Flosshilde would not have gone down and he might even have had a happy ending of his own; but he had been foolish and willful, just as his mother would have expected. He had suffered his punishment, and now there was no time to lose. As he had said himself, Bridget was the member of the Fisher family who most resembled the glorious Siegfried. It explained why Ingolf had been so surprised when he had heard his name; he had been expecting *Bridget* Fisher on that fateful night.

He looked at his watch, trying to calculate what time it would be in Sydney. Hadn't Mother Earth herself said something about the Ring rightfully being Bridget's property, because she was the eldest? It would, of course, be difficult to explain it all, for his word carried little credibility with his immediate family; if he said something, they naturally assumed the reverse to be true. But Bridget was wise and would immediately understand, even if his mother didn't. With luck, they would let him keep the Tarnhelm, but if Bridget needed it of course she must have it. He swallowed the rest of his drink and called for an overcoat.

He looked quickly in the mirror to make sure that his hair was neat and tidy (his mother was most particular about such things) and saw to his astonishment that he didn't look like Malcolm Fisher at all. Then he remembered that he was still wearing the Tarnhelm. He would need that to get to Australia, but he might as well stop pretending to be somebody he wasn't.

"Right," he commanded, "back to normal."

The image in the mirror didn't change. It was still the Siegfried face he had been wearing for so long.

"Back to Malcolm Fisher," he said irritably. "Come on, jump to it."

No change. Angrily, he felt for the little buckle under his chin, which he hadn't even noticed for so long now. It came away easily, and he pulled the chainmail cap off and tossed it onto the sofa.

No change. The face that stared stupidly at him out of the mirror was the face of Fafner's Bane, Siegfried the Volsung. He groaned, and knelt down on the floor. Once again, his mother had been proved right. He had stuck like it. From now until the day he died, he was going to have to go around with the evidence of his deceit literally written all over his face.

Worse, he could not even remember what he really looked like. If he knew that, he might be able to get some sort of clever mask made. But the picture had completely vanished from his mind. He picked up the Tarnhelm and gazed at it hopelessly, feeling as he had done when, as a child, he had broken a window or scratched the paint. He had done something awful which he could not put right, and it was all his fault.

The next morning was bright and cold, and Malcolm woke early with a headache, which he prosaically blamed on the schnapps. To clear his head, he strolled down by the troutstream and stood for a while kicking stones in the water.

"Do you mind?" said a girl's voice.

He knew that voice. He tried hard not to recognise it, because the girl it had belonged to had gone up in a cloud of theology, along with the rest of the High Gods. He had sent his two ravens out looking for the owner of that voice, and they had searched the earth for many days without finding her. She no longer existed, except in the memories of a few unusual people. So what was she doing in his troutstream?

"Is that you?" he said stupidly.

"Of course it's me," said the voice irritably. "Who do you think it was, the *Bismarck?*"

He scrambled down the bank, slipped, and fell in the water. As he did so, it occurred to him that he couldn't swim, and he had forgotten that the trout-stream was only two feet deep. In his panic, he also forgot about the Tarnhelm, and had already resigned himself to the prospect of death by drowning when Flosshilde fished him out.

"Sorry," she said. "Did I startle you?"

That was one hell of a leading question, and rather than try and phrase an answer that might not be held against him in future, he replied by throwing his arms around her and kissing her, clumsily but effectively. It had not entered his mind that she might object to this; luckily, she seemed to like it.

"Where the hell have you been?" he said at last.

Flosshilde grinned. "Did you miss me?" she asked superfluously.

"I thought you'd been zapped," he said.

"Oh. So you have missed me."

"Of course I've bloody missed you. Where have you been?"

"On holiday."

"On *holiday.*"

"Yes," said Flosshilde, and she could not understand why Malcolm found this so strange. "We'd planned to go to the Nile Delta again this year, but then that Ortlinde business blew up and by the time it was all over everywhere was full. So we went and stayed with our cousins on the seabed. It was rather boring actually. They're terribly stuffy people, and they've got a pipeline running right through the middle of their sitting-room."

"So that's why Thought and Memory couldn't find you."

"Were they looking?"

"They've been doing little else since you vanished. You might have let me know."

Flosshilde grinned again. "I didn't know you cared. Honestly, I didn't. I only came back to look for a comb I'd left behind."

That was not strictly true, except for the bit about the comb, but she hoped he wouldn't notice. It had been no fun at all on the seabed and she hadn't been able to get him out of her mind. His reaction to her last remark was therefore likely to be rather important.

"Well, I do care. I care a whole lot."

"Yes," said Flosshilde, remembering the scramble down the bank and the kiss, "I think you probably do. Snap. By the way, you're all wet."

"Am I?"

"Yes. Perhaps it would be a good idea if we got out of the water."

Malcolm could see no reason for this, for he was happier standing in two feet of water with the girl he loved and needed than he had ever been on dry land. But if she thought it would be a good idea, he was willing to give it a try. They climbed out and sat down under a tree. It so happened that it was the same tree that Ortlinde had been standing under when he had first kissed her, but he couldn't be expected to remember everything.

"Let's not talk about it," Flosshilde said. "You know what that leads to. Let's just have a nice time for the rest of our lives."

Put like that, it seemed perfectly simple. Malcolm leaned back against the oak tree and thought about it for a moment. Whatever he felt like doing was probably right. He had that on the very best authority.

"Fair enough," he said. "But first I must give the Ring to my sister Bridget."

"Don't be silly."

"But I've got to. You see..."

"Don't be *silly.*"

"All right, then," Malcolm said. "I'll give it to you."

He took off the Ring, looked at it for a moment, tossed it up in

the air, caught it again, and slipped it onto the fourth finger of her left
hand. Then he waited for a second. Nothing happened. Flosshilde
stared at him with her mouth wide open.

"It suits you," he said.

"What did you do that for?"

"First," said Malcolm, "because it was originally yours. Second,
because you're much older and cleverer than I am. Third, because I
love you. Fourth, because it's worth it just to see the look on your face."

Flosshilde could think of nothing to say, and Malcolm savoured
the moment. It was probably the last moment of silence he could
expect from her for many, many years.

"Are you sure?" said Flosshilde.

Malcolm started to laugh, for it had been Ortlinde's favourite
phrase, and soon Flosshilde was giggling too. "No, but honestly," she
said, "it's the Ring. Be serious for a moment."

"Serious?" Malcolm grabbed her arm and pulled her close. "Don't
you see? That's the last thing in the world I can afford to be. Ever since
you went away, something terrible has been happening to me. I couldn't
think what it was, even though everyone was trying to tell me. Even
the Tarnhelm. I was turning into Wotan. I was starting to become just
like him."

"Never," said Flosshilde. "You couldn't be. For a start, he was taller than you."

"I could, and I nearly did. When I realised it, my first reaction
was to give the Ring to my sister Bridget, because everyone always
said she was so much more responsible than me. But you were right,
that would have been the worst possible thing I could have done.
Then you came back, and I suddenly understood. The only person in
the world that that thing is safe with is you."

"Me? But that's impossible. I'm not a nice person at all."

"Not you as well."

"No, I mean it. I'm probably not cruel or malicious, but I'm
thoughtless and frivolous. I wouldn't take the job seriously, and the
world would get into an awful mess. I'd forget to make it rain at the
right time, because I'd always want it to be fine for sunbathing, and if
I was bored with it being January, I'd make it July again, and then
everything would get out of gear. I'd be hopeless at it, really."

"That's what I thought when I started. And it hasn't turned out
too badly, has it?"

Flosshilde frowned and bit her lip, a manoeuvre she had often
practised in front of the mirror. "Oh, go on, then," she said, "just to

please you I will."

"That," said Malcolm triumphantly, "is the best possible reason. You've passed. Congratulations."

"I still think," said Flosshilde, holding up the Ring to the light to admire it, "that you're being a bit hasty..." She tailed off. "You're right," she said. "It does suit me. It'll go very nicely with that gold evening dress I got in Strasbourg."

She took one more look at the Ring and promptly dismissed it from her mind, for she had more important things to think about. "Why the sudden change of heart?" she asked. "I mean, when I left for the seabed, you were still madly in love with that stuffy old Valkyrie with the interesting shoes. You aren't going to change your mind about me, are you?"

"I hope not," said Malcolm. "We'll have to see, won't we?"

"Did I ever tell you the story...?"

"Later."

"It's a very funny story."

"Did I ever tell *you* the story of the idiot who ran over a badger?"

"I know that one."

"But I tell it very well, and it's the only really funny story I know."

"Go on, then."

He told her the story and she laughed, although she knew that she could have told it rather better herself. In fact, she could have done his voice rather better than he could. But it didn't matter. This was happiness, she realised, even more than sunbathing or the parties they used to have at Camelot. She was slightly disappointed with herself for being made happy so easily, for she had always thought of herself as a rather glamourous, sophisticated person. Nevertheless, it would do very nicely to be going on with.

Malcolm listened to her laughter, and for the first time in his life he knew that everything was going to be all right. Niceness, he realised, was not enough, and Love was only part of the rest. You had to have laughter, too. Laughter would make everything come out right in the end, or if it didn't nobody would notice. He started to tell her about his plans for the new Valhalla. She liked the idea, and started making suggestions about how the place should be redecorated. These mostly seemed to consist of swimming-pools, flumes and ornamental lakes, and he realised that sooner or later he was going to have to learn how to swim. The thought made him shudder, but he put it on one side.

"By the way," he said. "I suppose you're immortal."

"I think so. Why?"

"Isn't that going to make it rather difficult for me? You see, I'm not."

Flosshilde shook her head. "I solved that one some time ago," she said.

"Did you now? That was thoughtful of you." Flosshilde blushed, spontaneously for once, and realised that she hadn't quite timed it right, which was unusual for her, since she was unquestionably one of the three best blushers in the world. But Malcolm didn't seem to have noticed, and it was nice to be with somebody who didn't criticise when you got things wrong.

"I looked it up in all the books," she went on, "and there's no problem. Every time you feel yourself getting old, you just turn yourself into someone younger."

Malcolm shook his head. "I don't think the Tarnhelm works any more," he said sadly, and he told her about his attempts to go back to being Malcolm Fisher. She laughed, and told him not to be so silly.

"Haven't you learnt anything?" she said. "You tried to turn yourself into Malcolm Fisher. You *are* Malcolm Fisher. Of course it didn't work."

Malcolm didn't quite follow that, but he was reassured. There didn't seem to be anything else to worry about now, so he suggested that they went in and had some breakfast instead.

"Just a moment," said Flosshilde.

She looked hard at the Ring, held her breath and pointed at the sky. A small pink cloud appeared out of nowhere, rushing across the sky until it was directly overhead. There was a blinding flash of pink lightning, and the cloud had vanished. The air was filled with pink rose petals, and a flight of flamingos climbed gracefully into the air.

"No," said Flosshilde, "maybe not. It seemed like a good idea at the time."

"It's the thought that counts," Malcolm said. "Come on, I'm hungry."

They walked into the house, and the two ravens who had been eavesdropping from the branches of the oak tree looked at each other.

"I think that's nice," said Memory.

"Idiot," said Thought. "Is that a dead rabbit I can see over there?"

"Where?"

"Just by that patch of nettles."

"Now you're talking," said Memory.

They glided down and started to peck. It was a good, meaty rabbit, and they were both hungry. When he had finished, Memory wiped his beak neatly on his leg and stood thoughtfully for a while.

"Did you ever see that film?" he said.

"What film?"

"Can't remember. Anyway, it reminds me a bit of that. Happy ending and all."

Thought shook his head. "Don't like happy endings," he said. "They're a cop-out. Life's not like that."

"I dunno," said Memory. "Sometimes it is."

"You're so soft, you are," said Thought scornfully. "Come on, time we were on our way."

They sailed up into the sky, and began their day's patrol. Wherever life was stirring and brains were working they flew, their bright round eyes missing nothing, their ears constantly alert. But today was going to be another quiet day in the best of all possible worlds. After a while they grew bored, and turned back. As they flew over the little village of Ralegh's Cross, they saw three workmen with pickaxes trying to break up a strange outcrop of rock which had appeared in the middle of the road some months earlier. But their tools would not bite on the hard stone, and they had given it up for a while.

"What I want to know is," said one of the men, "how did it get there in the first place?"

Memory dived down and perched on the rock which had once been the Giant Ingolf. "It's a long story," he said.

But the man wasn't listening.

Who's Afraid

BILL
NEVILLE

# of Beowulf?

1

Someone had written "godforsaken" between "Welcome to" and "Caithness" on the road sign. When he saw the emendation, the surveyor almost smiled.

"Tourists, I expect," said the archaeologist disapprovingly. She had decided that the Highlands were authentic and good; therefore, any malice towards them must have proceeded from uncomprehending outsiders.

"I hope not," yawned the surveyor, lighting a cigarette and changing gear. "I was taking it as evidence that there's one native of these parts who can read and write." He paused, waiting for a laugh or an "I know what you mean." Neither was forthcoming. "Though there's no reason why any of them should. After all, you don't need to be able to read if you make your living robbing and killing passing travellers, which has always been the staple industry around here."

The archaeologist looked away. He was off again. An irritating man, she felt.

"Which explains the ingrained poverty of the region," the surveyor went on remorselessly, "because only a few bloody fools ever used to come travelling up here. Until recently, of course. Recently, you've had your coachloads of tourists. Theme holidays for heavy sleepers. Anyway, these days the locals don't even bother killing the travellers; they just sell them tartan key-fobs. And they all take the *FT*, to keep track of currency fluctuations."

The archaeologist had had enough of her companion's diatribe, which had started before the car had got clear of Lairg. Rather ostentatiously she fanned away the cigarette smoke and expressed the opinion that it was all lovely. "I think it's got a sort of—"

The surveyor made a peculiar noise. "Listen," he said, "I was born and bred in bonnie bloody Caithness, and the only thing it's produced in a thousand years is starving people." He'd read that in a Scottish Nationalist manifesto, but it sounded clever. "Five years ago, the inhabitants of Rolfsness pleaded with the Water Authority to turn the wretched place into a reservoir so that they could be compensated and move to Glasgow. But it's too remote even for that. The Army won't have it for a firing range, and the CEGB got lost trying to find it."

He was getting nicely into his stride now, despite the lukewarm response. The archaeologist managed to interrupt him just in time.

"That reminds me," she said, tearing her eyes away from a breathtakingly lovely prospect of cloud-topped mountains, "I wanted to ask you, since you were born here. Are there any old traditions or folktales about Rolfsness?"

"Folk-tales." The surveyor frowned, as if deep in thought. "Well, there's an old superstition among the shepherds and crofters—but you know what they're like."

"Go on." The archaeologist felt a tremor of excitement.

"Well, they *say* that every year on the anniversary of the battle of Culloden—you know about the battle of Culloden?"

"Yes, yes, of course."

"They *say* that every year, at about noon, the bus from Wick to Melvich stops here for three minutes where the old gibbet used to be. But nobody's ever claimed to have seen it for themselves."

Dead silence. The surveyor shook his head sadly. Americans, he reflected, have no sense of humour.

"Otherwise, apart from Bonnie Prince Charlie hiding from Butcher Cumberland's men in what is now the bus shelter, where Montrose had been betrayed to the Covenanters, no. Totally unremarkable place. Now, if there was a story that Montrose *wasn't* betrayed to the Covenanters here, that would be a bit out of the ordinary."

"I see." The archaeologist sniffed. She should have known better than to ask. "So nothing about giants or fairies or the Wee Folk?"

"Round here," said the surveyor grimly, "the Wee Folk means Japanese businessmen looking for sites for computer factories. Not that they ever build any, of course. Have you ever tasted Japanese whisky? All the hotels up here sell it now. Personally, I prefer it to the local stuff."

The archaeologist gave up in despair, and they drove on in silence for a while. Then, as they turned a sharp corner on the side of a towering hill, the archaeologist suddenly asked the surveyor to stop the car.

"What is it?" said the surveyor, glancing anxiously in his rear-view mirror, but the archaeologist said nothing. She had no words to spare for such an insensitive person at the moment when she caught her first glimpse of the sea that washes the flat top of the British mainland, and, grey and soft-edged as any dream-kingdom should be, the faint outline of Orkney. On an impulse, she opened the car door and scrambled up to the top of a rocky outcrop.

Here, then, was the earldom of her mind, her true habitation. She felt as Orestes must have done when, coming secretly out of exile, he looked for the first time upon Argos, the land he had been born to rule. That was the sea of her Cambridge dreams, those were the islands she had first pictured for herself sitting on the front porch in Setauket, Long Island, with her treasured copy of the *Orkney-men's Saga* open on her knee. As a promised land it had been to her as she trod the weary road of professional scholarship, laying down her harp beside the waters of Cam, marching more than seven times round the bookshops of St Andrews. As she gazed out over the sea, called "whale-road" and "world-serpent," she could almost see the blue sails of the Orkney Vikings, the dragon-prows of Ragnar Lothbrok and Erik Blood-axe, sweeping across their great grey highway to give battle to Bothvar Bjarki or Arvarodd in the *vik* at Tongue.

"On a clear day," said the surveyor behind her, "you can just make out the Old Man of Hoy from here. Why you should want to is beyond me entirely."

"I think it's wonderful," said the archaeologist softly.

"I think it's perishing cold. Can we get on now?"

They got back into the van.

"Tell me again what it is you've found," said the archaeologist briskly.

"Well," said the surveyor, leaning back with one hand on the bottom of the steering-wheel, "we were taking readings, and I'd just sent the Land-Rover up ahead when it fell clean through this small mound. Right up to its axles, useless bloody thing, we had to use the Transit to pull it out again. Anyway, we got it out and when we looked down the hole it had made we saw this chamber underground, all shored up with pit props. I thought it was an Anderson shelter or something left over from the war, but the lads all said no, ten to one it was a Viking ship-burial."

"*They* said that?"

"They all work for the Tourist Board over the summer. So we put a tarpaulin over it and sent for your mob."

"Didn't you want to look for yourselves?"

The surveyor laughed. "You must be kidding. Roof might collapse or something. Besides, you aren't supposed to touch anything, are you, until the experts arrive. Or is that murders?"

The archaeologist smiled. "You did right," she said.

"The lads get paid by the hour," said the surveyor, "and I'm on bonus for being in this wilderness. Besides, if it does turn out to be an ancient monument, the project will be cancelled, and we can all go home with money in lieu. Look, there it is."

He pulled over on to the verge, and they picked their way over the uneven ground to the site. The archaeologist found that she was faced with a long leaf-shaped mound about fifty to sixty yards long, pointing due north. Under her woolly hat her hairs were beginning to rise, and she broke into a trot, her moon-boots squelching in the saturated peat. The sheer size of it made her heart beat faster. If there really was a ship down there, and if anything at all was left of it, this was going to make the *Mary Rose* look like a pedalo.

The survey team were staring at her over their cans of lager, but she took no notice. As she struggled with the obdurate ropes that held the tarpaulin in place, an old man in a raincoat apparently moulded on to his body got up hurriedly and started to wave his arms at her. To her joy, the archaeologist realised that he was a Highlander, and that the gist of his broken English was that she was on no account to open up the mound. She beamed at him (for surely this was some survival of the ancestral terror of waking up the sleepers under the howe) and said, "Pardon me?" Her pleasure was somewhat diminished when the surveyor explained to her that what the old fool meant was that he'd spent half the morning nailing the tarpaulin down in the teeth of a gale, and that if she insisted on taking it off she could bloody well put it back herself.

The tarpaulin was thrown back, and the archaeologist nerved herself to look inside and seek her destiny. She had always felt that one day she would make a great discovery, something which would join her with Carnavon, Carter, Evans and Schliemann in the gallery of immortals. On the rare occasions when archaeology had lost its grip on her imagination—seemingly endless afternoons spent up to her knees in mud in some miserable Dartmoor hut-circle—she had consoled herself by trying to compose a deathless line, something which would be remembered beside "I have looked upon the face of Agamemnon." Although so far in her career she had found, apart from enough potsherds to line the bottom of every flowerpot in the world, nothing more prestigious than a Tudor belt-buckle, she knew that one day she, Hildy Frederiksen, would join that select band of immortals who have been fortunate enough to be the first men and women of the modern age to set eyes upon the heirlooms of the human race. She knelt down and with trembling fingers checked the contents of her organiser bag: camera (with film in it), notebook, pencil, small brush, flashlight (free with ten Esso tokens) and small plastic bags for samples.

In the event, what she actually said when the beam of her flashlight licked over the contents of the mound was "Jesus!" but in the circumstances nobody could have blamed her for that. What she saw was the prow of a ship—a long clinker-built ship of a unique and unmistakable kind. The timbers were coal-black and glistening with moisture, but the thing actually seemed to be intact. As the blood pounded in her ears she thanked God for the preservative powers of peat-bog tannin, took a deep breath, and plunged into the hole like a small, learned terrier.

The chamber *was* intact; so much so, in fact, that the possibility of its collapsing never entered into her mind. The sides were propped with massive beams—oak, at a guess—which vaulted high overhead, while the chamber had been dug a considerable depth into the ground. Under her feet the earth was hard, as if it had been stamped flat into a floor. The ship itself reclined at ease on a stout trestle, as if it was already taking its rightful place in a purpose-built gallery at the maritime museum at Greenwich. It was an indescribably beautiful thing, with the perfection of line and form that only something designed to be functional can have, lean and graceful and infinitely menacing, like a man-eating swan. Every feature she could have hoped to find in an archetypal Viking longship was present—this in itself was remarkable, since none of the ships so far discovered looked anything like the authoritative reconstructions in the *Journal of Scandinavian Studies*— from the painted shields beside each of the thirty oar-holes on either side of the ship to the great dragon figurehead, carved with a deep confident design of gripping beasts and interwoven snakes. Although it was strictly against the rules, she could not help reaching out, almost but not quite like Adam in the painting, and tracing with the tip of her left forefinger the line of the surrealistic pattern.

Like a child who has woken to find itself inexplicably inside a confectioner's warehouse, she walked slowly round the great ship, noting the various features of it as if with an inventory. Suddenly the light of her flashlight was thrown back by a sparkle of gold: inlaid runes running back from the prow, glowing bright as neon. She spelt them out, like a child learning its alphabet; Naglfar, the ship of nails, the ferry of the dead. It was so utterly perfect that for a moment she could not bear to look, in case her light fell on an outboard motor bolted to the stern, or a slogan draped across the mast advertising Carlsberg lager.

She touched it again, and the damp sticky feel of the tannin reassured her. Turn the Circus Maximus into a carpark, she said to herself, and wrap fish in the First Folio; preserve only this. As if in a dream, she put her foot on the first rung of a richly carved ladder that rested against the side of the ship.

At the top of the ladder was a small platform, with steps leading down into the hold. She stood for a moment unable to move, for the belly of the ship was piled high with the most extraordinary things, jumbled up together as if History was holding a garage sale. Gold and silver, fabrics, armour and weapons, like the aftermath of an earthquake at a museum. She rubbed her eyes and stared. Under the truncated mast, she could see twelve full sets of armour lying wrapped in fur cloaks, perfectly preserved. No, she was wrong. They were human bodies.

Then the flashlight went out.

The human heart is a volatile thing. A second or so before, Hildy I-Have-Looked-Upon-The-Face-Of Frederiksen had been thanking Providence that she alone had been granted the privilege of being the first living person in twelve hundred years to set foot on the planks of the longship Naglfar. Now, however, it occurred to her as she stood motionless in the complete silence and utter darkness that it would have been quite nice to have had someone there to share the moment with her, preferably someone with a reliable flashlight. She reminded herself sternly that archaeology is a science, that scientists are creatures of logic and reason, that she was a scientist, therefore she was not in the least afraid of the dark. However, being afraid seemed at that particular moment the most logical thing in the world, the reason why fear circuits had been planted in the human brain in the first place. So deathly was the silence that for a moment she took the sound of her own breathing for the snoring of the twelve dead Vikings lying just a few yards away from her under the mast. She tried to move, but could not; her muscles received the command from her brain and replied that they had never heard anything so absurd in their lives. She reflected that burglars must feel like this all the time, but the thought was little consolation.

As suddenly as it had gone out, the flashlight came back on again—the ways of petrol-station flashlights pass all understanding—and Hildy decided that, although it was really nice inside the chamber, it was probably even nicer outside it. As she turned away towards the ladder, she felt something under her foot and without thinking stooped and picked it up. It felt very cold in her hand, and was heavy, like a pistol. She stopped for a moment and looked at it. In her hand was a golden brooch inlaid with enamel and garnets, in the shape of a flying dragon. She half-expected it to move suddenly, like an injured bird picked up in the garden. The beam of the flashlight danced on interlocking patterns and spirals, and she felt dizzy. She knew perfectly well that she ought not to touch this thing, let alone thrust it deep into her pocket, and equally well that no power on earth could stop her doing it. Then she imagined another noise in the chamber and, with the brooch in her pocket, she scurried down the ladder and out of the mound like a rabbit with a ferret the size of a Tube train after it.

As the top of her hat emerged into the light, the surveyor put his copy of *Custom Car* back in his pocket and asked:

"Are you all right, then?"

"Of course I am," Hildy stammered. She was shaking, and sweat had turned her fringe into little black spikes, like the horns of a stag-beetle. "Why shouldn't I be?"

"You were down there an awful long time," said the surveyor. It had just occurred to him that more portable things than ships are sometimes found in ancient mounds.

"Very interesting," Hildy said. "I wish I could be sure it was authentic."

The surveyor was staring at something sticking out of the pocket of her paddock jacket. She put her hand over it and hitched her lips into a smile.

"So there's nothing like—well, artefacts or anything down there?" asked the surveyor, rather too casually. Hildy tightened her grip round the neck of the brooch.

"Could be," she mumbled. "If I'd been brave enough to look. But the roof looks like it might collapse at any minute, so I came out again."

"The roof?"

"Perilous, if you ask me. I think I heard it moving."

The surveyor's face seemed to fall. "Perhaps we should try to shore it up," he suggested. "I could go in and have a look. Of course, you needn't go in."

Hildy nodded vigorously. "Go ahead," she said. "Where's the nearest phone, by the way, in case we have to call for help?"

As she expected, the surveyor didn't like the sound of that. "On the other hand," he said, "it's a job for the experts."

"True."

"Best leave well alone."

Hildy nodded.

It had started to rain, and the survey team were making chorus noises. "What I'd better do," the surveyor said, "since we can't do anything more for the present, is send the lads home and take you back to Lairg. You lot," he shouted to the survey team, "get that hole covered up."

The old man in the raincoat said something authentic, but they ignored him and set about replacing the tarpaulin. "We'd better wait till they're on their way," whispered the surveyor. "Otherwise—well, they might be tempted to see if there was anything of value down there."

"Surely not?"

Neither Hildy nor the surveyor had much to say on the way back to Lairg. Hildy was thinking of a passage from *Beowulf* which she had had to do as a prepared translation during her first year at New York State, all about a man who stole a rich treasure from a hoard he found in a burial-mound, and woke a sleeping fire-drake in the process. She could remember it vividly, almost word for word, and it had had a decidedly unhappy ending.

The surveyor bundled her out of the car at Lairg and drove away rather quickly, which made Hildy feel somewhat suspicious. So she telephoned the police at Melvich and explained the situation to them slowly and lucidly. Once they had been made to understand that she was not mad or drunk they sounded very enthusiastic about the prospect of guarding buried treasure and promised to send the patrol car out as soon as it came back from finding Annie Erskine's cat. Feeling easier in her mind, Hildy went into the hotel bar and ordered a double orange juice with ice. As she drank it, she drew out the brooch and looked round to see if anyone was watching. But the barman had gone back to the Australian soaps in the television room, and she was alone.

The brooch was an exquisite example of its kind, the finest that Hildy had ever seen. The form was as simple as the decoration was complex, and it reminded her of something she had seen recently in quite another context. Slowly, the magnitude of her discovery and its attendant excitement began to return to her, and as soon as she had finished her drink she left the bar, reversed the charges to the Department of Archaeology, and demanded to speak to the Director *personally.*

"George?" she said calmly (he had always been Professor Wood to anyone under the rank of senior lecturer, but *he* had never found so much as a row-boat, "It's Hildy Frederiksen here—yes, that's right—and I'm calling from Lairg. L-A-I-R-G." He was being vague again, she noticed, an affectation he was much given to, especially after lunch. "I'm just back from a first inspection of that mound site at Rolfsness. George, you're not going to believe this, but...."

As she spoke, her hand crept of its own accord into her pocket and closed around the flying dragon. Something seemed to tell her that on no account ought she to keep this extraordinarily beautiful and dangerous thing for herself, but that nevertheless that was what she was going to do, fire-drake or no fire-drake.

In the mound, it was dark and silent once again. For the past twelve hundred years, ever since the last turf had been laid over the trellis of oak-trunks and the horsemen had ridden away to the waiting ships, nothing had moved in the chamber, not so much as a mole or a worm. But now there was something missing that should have been there, and just as one tiny stone removed from an arch makes the whole structure unsound, so the peace of the chamber had been disturbed. Something moved in the darkness, and moved again, with the restlessness that attends on the last few moments before waking.

"For crying out loud," said a voice, faint and drowsy in the darkness, "there's some of us trying to sleep."

The silence had been broken, irrecoverably, like a pane of glass. "You what?" said another voice.

"I said there's people trying to sleep," said the first voice. "Shut up, will you?"

"You shut up," replied the second voice. "You're the one making all the noise."

"Do you two mind?" A third voice, deep and powerful, and the structure of beams seemed to vibrate to its resonance. "'Quiet as the grave,' they say. Some hope."

"Sorry," said the first two voices. The silence tried to return, as the retreating tide tries to claw its way back up the beach.

"I told you, didn't I?" continued the third voice after a while. "I warned you not to eat that cheese, but would you listen? If you can't sleep, then be quiet."

There was a sound of movement, metal scraping on metal, as if men in armour were turning in their sleep and groaning. "It's no good," said the third voice, "you've done it now."

Somewhere in the gloom there was a high-pitched squeaking sound, like a bat high up in the rafters of a barn. It might conceivably have been a human voice, if a man could ever grow so incredibly old. After the sound had died away, like water draining into sand, there was absolute quiet; but an uneasy, tense quiet. The mound was awake.

"The wizard says try counting sheep," said the second voice.

"I heard him myself," said the third voice. "Bugger counting sheep. I've counted enough sheep since I've been down here to clothe the Frankish Empire. Oh, the Hel with it. Somebody open a window."

There was a grating sound, and a creaking of long-relaxed timber. "Sod it," said the first voice, "some clown's moved the ladder."

The old man grinned, displaying both his yellow teeth, and cut the final cord of the tarpaulin. Two of his fellows pulled the cover free, while the other members of the survey team, who had come back in the expectation of wealth, stood by with dustbin liners. In about fifteen minutes, they were all going to be rich.

"Can you see anything, Dougal?" someone asked. The old man grunted and wormed his way into the hole. A moment later, he slid out backwards and started to run like a hare. The survey team watched him in amazement, then turned round and stared at the mouth of the hole. A helmeted head had appeared out of the darkness, with a gauntleted hand in front of its eyes to protect them from the light.

"All right," it said irritably, "which one of you jokers moved our ladder?"

Hildy waited and waited, but no one came. She tried to pass the time by rereading her favourite sagas, but even their familiar glories failed to hold her attention. For in her mind's eye, as she read, the old images and mental pictures, which had been developed in the distant and unheroic town of Setauket, were all displaced and usurped by new, rather more accurate visions. For example, she had always pictured the lonely hall on the fells where Gunnar of Hlidarend, the archetypal hero of saga literature, had made his last stand as being the disused shed on the vacant lot down by the tracks, so that by implication Mord Valgardsson had led the murderers out of the drugstore on the corner of Constitution Street, where presumably they had stiffened their resolve for their bloody deed with a last ice-cream soda. Sigmund and Sinfjotli had been chained to the log that was the felled apple tree in her own back yard, and there the wolf who was really the shape-changer king had come in the blue night and bitten off Sigmund's hand. Thus was maintained the link between the Elder Days and her own childhood; but the sight of the ship and the heaped gold had broken the link. She had seen with her own eyes a real live dead Viking, who had never been anywhere near Setauket and was therefore rather more exciting and rather less safe. Long Island Vikings were different; they had stopped at the front door, and never dared go into the house. But the Caithness variety seemed rather more pervasive. They were all around her, even under the bed—in the shape of the brooch in her suitcase.

Hildy tried her best not to unpack it from under the shirts and sweatshirts and hold it up to the light, but she was only flesh and blood. It seemed to glow in her hands, to move not with the beatings of her pounding heart but with a movement of its own, as if it were some thing of power. She made an attempt to study it professionally, to see if that would dispel its glamour; undoubted Swedish influences, garnets probably from India but cut in Denmark, yet the main work was in the classical Norwegian style and the runes were those of the futharc of Orkney. She stopped, and frowned. She had not noticed the runes before; but the keen light of the reading-lamp seemed to flow into them, like water into a channel when a dam is opened, so that they stood out tiny but unmistakable on the main curve of the central spiral of the decoration.

Runes. For some reason her heart had stopped beating. Perhaps it was some magic in those extraordinary letters, first created at a time when any writing was by definition magical, a secret mark on silent metal that could communicate without speech to the eyes of a wise lore-master. Runes cannot help being magical, even if what they spell out is commonplace; a rune cut on the lintel will keep the sleepless ghosts from riding on the roof, or put a curse on the house that curdles milk and makes all the fires suddenly go out. Runes were also spells of attraction; to learn the runes, the god Odin had made himself a human sacrifice at his own altar, and ever since they had had a power to command. For all she knew, it was their command that had drawn her, by way of New York State and Cambridge, across the grey sea all the way from Setauket to be the improbable heroine of some last quest.

The strange wonder of the thing did not altogether fade or wither as it lay in her hands: the runes were still runes, and the brooch was still incredible. A Viking brooch in a museum or under the fluorescent tubes of the laboratory of the Department of Archaeology was resentfully tame, like a caged lion, and its voice was silent. Outside on the cold hill the wild lion roared, fascinating and dangerous, while in the incongruous setting of a hotel bedroom it was like—well, like a wild lion in a hotel bedroom, where no pets or animals of any description are in any circumstances permitted.

Rationalised, what that meant was that she was feeling guilty about having stolen it, which was effectively what she had done, something which no archaeologist, however debased, would ever conceive of doing. So why, she asked her suitcase, had she done it?

"I must put it back," she said aloud.

The only vehicle for hire in Lairg was a large minibus, by all appearances coeval with the longship Naglfar and about as practical for winding Scottish roads. But Hildy was in no position to be choosy, and she set off with an Ordnance Survey map open on the seat beside her, to drive to Rolfsness and put the brooch back in the mound before the team from St Andrews got there. As the deliberately obstructive road meandered its way through the grey hills, she could feel her resolve crumbling like an ancient parchment; the wild animal commanded her to return it to its natural habitat, not to put it back where middle-aged men with careers would come to find it and make it turn the treadmill of some thesis or scholarly paper.

She stopped the van and took it out once more. The dragon's expression had not changed; his garnet eyes were still red and hot as iron on the anvil; his lips still curved, in accordance with the demands of symmetry and form, in the same half-smile of intolerant mockery. She was suddenly aware that blood had been spilt over the possession of this extraordinary thing, and convinced that blood might well be shed for it again.

A loud hooting behind her, and plainly audible oaths, not in Old High Norse but modern Scots, woke her from her self-induced hypnosis. She rammed the van into first gear and drove on to the verge, letting the council lorry pass. Now she felt extremely foolish, and the voice in the runes fell silent, leaving her to her embarrassment. Listening to dragon brooches, said another, rather more familiar voice in her head, is only one step away from talking to dragons, for which they take you to a place where people are very kind and understanding, and where eventually the dragons start talking back. She bundled the brooch back into her pocket and took off the handbrake.

It was nearly dark when she reached Rolfsness, but the new, sensible Hildy Frederiksen defied nightfall as she defied all the other works of sorcery. She parked the bus under a lonely rowan tree and trotted swiftly over to the mound. There was no tarpaulin over the hole and no sign of the police, and her archaeologist's instinct returned, all the stronger for having been challenged. A terrible fear that the mound had been plundered while her attention was distracted struck her, and she started to blame herself. Why, for a start, had she left the mound in the first place, like a lamb among wolves, unguarded against the return of those unsavoury contractors' men? She fumbled for her flash-light and dropped it; the back came off and all the batteries were spilt into the short wiry grass. Her fingers were unruly as she tried to reassemble it, for clearly everything she tried to do today was fated to come to no good. When the wretched thing was mended, she advanced like an apprentice lion-tamer on the hole in the side of the mound, afraid now not of what she might see but of what she might not. With a deep breath that seemed to fill not only her lungs but also her pockets and the very lining of her jacket she poked one toe into the mouth of the hole, as if it were a hot bath she was testing. Something seemed to move inside.

"Now what is it?" demanded a voice from under the earth.

So she had disturbed the plunderers at their work! Suddenly her small familiar body was filled with cold and unreasonable courage, for here was a chance to redeem herself in the eyes of Archaeology by falling in battle with tomb-robbers and unlicensed dealers in antiquities.

"OK," she said between clenched teeth, "you'd better come out now. We have this whole area surrounded."

There was a clanking noise, as of something very heavy moving, and somebody said: "Why don't you look where you're putting your great feet?" Then a ray of the setting sun fell suddenly on red gold and blue steel, and a man stood silhouetted against the sky on the edge of the mound.

He was a little over six feet tall, clad in gilded chainmail armour. His face was half-covered by the grotesque mask that formed the visor of his shining helmet, while around his bear-like shoulders was a thick grey fur cloak, fastened at the neck by a brooch in the shape of two gripping beasts. In his right hand was a hand-and-a-half sword whose pommel blazed with garnets, like the lights of distant watch-fires.

"Who the hell are you?" said the man from the mound.

Hildy did not answer, for she could not remember. The man clapped his gauntleted hands, whereupon a procession of twelve men emerged from the mound. Nine of them were similarly armed and masked, and on their arms they carried kite-shaped shields that seemed to burn in the setting sun. Of the other three, one was small and stooping, dressed in a long white robe that blurred the outlines of his body like low cloud over a hillside, but his face was covered by a hood of cat skins and he leant on a staff cut from a single walrus tusk, carved into the shape of a serpent. The second of the three was a huge man, bigger than any human being Hildy had ever seen before, and he was dressed in the pelt of a long-haired bear. On his shoulder he carried a great halberd, whose blade was as long as its tree-like shaft. The third was shorter than the rest of the armed men but still tall, slim and quick-moving like a dancer. He wore no armour, but only a doublet of purple and dark blue hose. Tucked under his arm was a gilded harp, while over his right shoulder was a longbow of ash-wood and a quiver of green-flighted arrows.

They looked around them, shading their eyes even against the red warmth of the setting sun, as if any light was unbearable to them. One of the armed men, who was carrying a spear with a banner of cloth bound to its shaft, turned to the others and pushed his helmet back, revealing a face at once young and old, with soft brown eyes under stern brows.

"Well," he said. "Here we are again. So how long do you reckon we've been down there?"

"No idea," said the man next to him, who carried a silver horn on a woven baldrick. "Ask the wizard. He'll know."

The standard-bearer repeated his question, slowly and loudly, to the small stooping man, who made a noise through the cat skins like a rusty hinge.

"He says twelve hundred years, give or take," said the standard-bearer. No one seemed in the least surprised (except Hildy, of course, and she was not as surprised as she would have expected to be). The horn-bearer cast his eyes slowly round the encircling hills, inexpressibly majestic in the light glow of the sunset.

"Twelve hundred years," he said thoughtfully. "Well, if that's true, it hasn't changed a bit, not in the slightest." He looked round again. "Pity, really," he added. "Miserable place, Caithness."

Hildy suddenly remembered that she had to breathe sooner or later or else she would die, and it would be a shame to die before she had found out whether the unbelievable explanation for this spectacle, which was nevertheless the only possible explanation, was correct.

"Excuse me," she said in a tiny voice, "but are you people for real?" The words seemed to flop out of her mouth, like exhausted salmon who have finally given up on a waterfall.

"Good question," replied the leader of the men. "What about you?"

Hildy wanted to say "I'm not sure," but she realised that the man was being sarcastic, which was the last thing she expected. "I'm Hildy Frederiksen," she mumbled, aware that in all this vastness and mystery that one small fact could have little significance. Still, she wanted it put on record before it was wiped out of her mind.

"Well, now," said the leader, still sarcastic but with a hint of sympathy in his voice, "you shouldn't have told me that, should you? After all, when strangers meet by night on the fells, they should not disclose their names, nor the names of their fathers, until they have tested each other's heart with shrewd enquiry." Then his face seemed to relax a little behind the fixed scowl of his visor. "Don't ask me why, mind. It's just the rule."

But Hildy said nothing. The other men from the mound were staring at her, and for the first time she felt afraid.

"Damned silly rule if you ask me," said the leader, as if he sensed her fear. "The hours I've wasted asking gnomic questions when I could have been doing something else. Is this place still called Rolfsness?"

Hildy nodded.

"Then, allow me to introduce myself. I am Rolf. My name is King Hrolf Ketilsson, called the Earthstar, the son of Ketil Trout, the son of Eyjolf Kjartan's Bane, the son of Killer-Hrapp of Hedeby, the son of the god Odin. I have been asleep in the howe for—how long have I been asleep in the howe, somebody?"

"Twelve hundred years," said the horn-bearer.

"Thank you. Twelve hundred years, waiting for the day when I must return to save my kingdom of Caithness from danger, from the greatest danger that has ever or will ever threaten it or its people, according to the vow that I made before the great battle of Melvich, when I slew the host of Geirrodsgarth and cast down the power of Nithspél. These are my thanes and housecarls."

With a sweeping movement of his hand, he lifted his helmet over his head, revealing a magnificent mane of jet-black hair and two startlingly blue eyes. Hildy felt her knees give way, as if someone had kicked them from behind, and she knelt before him, bowing her head to the ground. When she dared to look up, she saw the last ray of the setting sun sparkling triumphantly on the hilt of the King's great sword as, apparently from nowhere, a fully grown golden eagle swooped down out of the sky and perched on his gloved fist, flapping its enormous wings.

2

"Will someone," said the King, "get this bird off me?"

The last ray of the sun faded as the standard-bearer made nervous shooing gestures with his hands. The bird shifted from one claw to the other, but made no sign of being prepared to leave. The man in the bear-skin tried prodding it gently with a huge forefinger, but it bit him and he backed away. In a sudden access of daring, Hildy rose to her feet and clapped her hands. At once the eagle flapped its wings, making a sound like a whole theatre full of people applauding at once, and soared off into the sky. It circled slowly three times and disappeared.

"They do that," said the King, rubbing his wrist vigorously to restore the circulation. "Comes of me being a king, I suppose."

"I'm starving," said the horn-bearer. Several voices told him to be quiet. "But I am. I haven't had anything to eat for twelve hundred years."

A babble of voices broke out, and rose quickly in a sustained crescendo. "Ignore them," said the King softly to Hildy. "Sometimes they're like a lot of old women."

Laying aside his helmet on the grass, he took Hildy's arm, and much to her own surprise she neither winced nor shrank back. He led her aside for a few paces and settled himself comfortably on a small boulder.

"Well, now," he said, fixing her with his bright eyes. "So what's been happening in the world while we've been asleep?"

Hildy looked back at the champions. They seemed to be discussing something of extreme importance, and from what she could make out it was mainly to do with whose job it should have been to pack the food. She sat down beside the King.

"It's a long story," she said.

"It would be, wouldn't it?" he replied, smiling. There was something about his smile that made her feel safe, as if she was under the protection of some great but homely power. She sat in silence for a while, gathering her thoughts. Then she told him.

When she had finished, she looked up. The men were still arguing; they seemed to have narrowed the responsibility down to either the standard-bearer or the horn-bearer, both of whom were protesting their innocence loudly and simultaneously.

"That's it, basically," Hildy said.

"That's it, is it? Twelve hundred years of history? The achievements of men? Men die, cattle die, only glorious deeds live for ever?"

"That's it, yes."

The King shrugged his shoulders, and twelve hundred years of history seemed to slide down his arms and melt into the peat. "But you're sure you haven't left anything out?"

Hildy shuddered slightly. "Lots," she said.

The King nodded. "Yes, of course," he said, "but I mean something really important."

"Like what?"

"I don't know, do I?" He frowned. "No, the hell with that. If it was there, you couldn't have left it out." He stopped frowning, and looked over his shoulder at the bickering champions. "Among the Viking nations," he said wistfully, "the model hero is regarded as being brave, loyal, cheerful and laconic. Three out of four isn't bad, I suppose. So who are you, Hildy Frederik's-daughter?"

"Frederik*sen*," said Hildy automatically. "Oh, I forgot. We did away with *-son* and *-daughter* centuries ago."

"Quite right, too," said the King. "Go on."

"I'm an archaeologist," said Hildy. "I dig up the past."

The King raised an eyebrow. "You mean you refresh old quarrels and keep alive old grievances? Surely not."

"No, no," said Hildy, "I dig up ancient things buried in the earth. Things that belonged to people who lived hundreds of years ago." As she said this, she began to feel uncomfortable. She had forgotten about the brooch.

"Do you really?" said the King. "We used to call that grave-robbing."

Hildy wriggled nervously, and as she did so the brooch slipped out of her pocket and fell on to the ground. "Oh, I see," said the King softly. "Archaeologist. I must remember that one."

Hildy picked the brooch up, trying unsuccessfully to avoid the King's eye. "I was going to give it back, honestly," she said. "That's why I came back again. I'm sorry."

The King sighed and took the brooch. It seemed to kick out of her hand, as if it was pleased to be leaving her.

"I was wondering where that had got to," said the King coldly. "I went to a lot of trouble.... Never mind."

"What is it?" Hildy asked, but the King only smiled rather scornfully and pinned the brooch on to his cloak. Hildy looked away, feeling utterly miserable, like a child who has done something very wrong
and been forgiven.

"You were saying," said the King.

"I came here to explore the mound," said Hildy. "The people
laying the pipeline—"

"You, of course, know what a pipeline is," said the King.

"It's a sort of tube, really. It goes under the sea, and—"

The King frowned again. "Sorry," he said, "I shouldn't have interrupted you. Some men were building a tube, and they broke open the
mound. Was it an accident, or done on purpose?"

"Oh, purely accident," said Hildy. "Then they sent for the archaeologists, in case it was an ancient burial. And I came and—"

"Yes." The King smiled again, this time quite kindly. "You're *sure*
it was an accident? It's rather important."

"Absolutely sure."

Then the King started to laugh, loudly and almost nervously, as
if a great fear had been rolled away from his mind. "That's good," he
said. "Now, then, a pipeline is a sort of tube, is it? A tube for what?"

So Hildy told him all about oil, and natural gas, and electricity,
and even nuclear power and Three-Mile Island, and by the time she
had finished the champions had finished quarrelling and come across
to listen. But Hildy didn't notice; the King's eye was on her, and she
felt absurdly proud that she was the one chosen to tell him, like a
child showing off an expensive new toy to a patient uncle. When she
had finished with power, she went on with technology; motor-cars
and computers and telephones and television. As she did so, she felt
that the King's reaction was all wrong; he didn't seem in the least
surprised. In fact he appeared to understand everything she was telling him, even about fax machines and the way word-processors swallow whole chapters and refuse to give them back. She tailed off and
stared at him.

"I knew you'd left something out," said the King.

"But how could you have known?" Hildy said. "I mean, it must
all be so strange to you."

The King raised his eyebrow again. "What's so strange about
magic?" he said. "Or don't you know anything about the world I lived
in?"

"Yes, I do," said Hildy proudly. "I've read all the sagas, and the
Eddas, and everything."

The King nodded. "A wise-woman, evidently," he said with mock approval. "A lore-mistress, even. So you should know all about magic, then, shouldn't you?"

"But that's not magic," Hildy said. "That's science."

"And you're not a grave-robber, you're an archaeologist." The King laughed again, and Hildy blushed, something she had not done for twenty years. "That is plain ordinary magic, Hildy Frederik's-daughter, only it sounds rather more mundane and there seems to be more of it about than there used to be." As he said the words, something seemed to trouble him and he fell silent.

"When you've quite finished," said a voice behind him, "there's some of us starving and freezing to death over here."

The King closed his eyes and asked some nameless power to give him strength. In the distance Hildy heard the sound of an approaching car. She looked quickly over her shoulder towards the road, and saw headlights. The champions looked round as well; the lights were getting closer but slowing down, and Hildy realised that the car was going to stop. One of the champions had drawn his sword, and the others were muttering something about whose turn it was to fight the dragon, and who had done it the last time, and it wasn't fair that the same person always had to do the lousy jobs. But Hildy suddenly felt that on no account should the King and his men be seen by anybody else; whether it was just a desire to keep them all to herself, for a little longer at least, or whether she had a genuine premonition of danger, she could not tell.

"Please," she said urgently to the King, "you mustn't be seen. Come with me."

The King looked at her, then nodded. The men fell silent and sheathed their swords. "This way," Hildy said, and she made for the minibus, with the King and his champions following her.

"I'm not getting in that," said the standard-bearer. "For one thing, it's got no oars."

"Shut up and get inside," snapped the King. The standard-bearer climbed in and sat heavily down. His companions followed swiftly, treading on each other's feet in the process.

"Get in here beside me," Hildy whispered to the King. "We must be quick."

She released the handbrake, and without starting the engine or putting on the lights she coasted the van over the bumpy ground down the slope to the road. The police car had pulled up, and she could see the light of the policemen's torches as they climbed up towards the mound. She coasted on down the road until she reckoned that she was out of earshot, then started the engine and drove away.

In the deserted mound, nothing stirred and the darkness was absolute. A golden cup, which had been disturbed by a passing foot as the Vikings had climbed out of the ship, finally toppled and slid down into the hold with a bump. But someone with quite exceptional hearing might possibly have made out a slight sound, and then dismissed it as his imagination playing tricks on him; a sound like two voices whispering.

"That's thirty-two above the line, doubled, and six left makes thirty-eight, and two for his nob makes forty, which means another free go, and I'm going to go north this time, so if I make more than sixteen I can pass and make another block."

"Nuts to you," said the other voice disagreeably.

There was a tiny tinkling noise. "Six." said the first voice, with ill-concealed pleasure. "Up six, clickety-click, and buckets of blood, down the ruddy snake."

"Serves you right."

Then there was silence—real silence, unless you could hear the sound of grass forcing its roots deeper into the earth. But by now, of course, your eyes would have picked out four tiny points of soft white light, deep in the gloom under the keel of the ship.

"This is a rotten game," said the first voice. "Why don't we play something else?"

"Just because you're losing."

"We've been playing this game for twelve hundred years," said the first voice peevishly. "I'm bored with it."

The tinkling sound again. "Four," said the second voice. "Double Rune Score. I think I'll have another longhouse on Uppsala."

"I've got Uppsala, haven't I?"

"You sold it to me in exchange for a dragon and three hundred below the line."

"Oh, for pity's sake." Deep silence again. "What was all that moving about earlier?"

"What moving about?" said the second voice. "I didn't notice any moving about."

"There was a lot of coming and going, and voices," said the first voice. "Clanking metal, and people swearing, and even a bit of light."

"Light," repeated the second voice thoughtfully. "That's that stuff that comes out of the sky, isn't it?"

"That or rain. Is that your move, then?"

"Just about."

"Right, then, I'm taking your castle, and I think that's check.... Oh, damn."

"No, you don't. You took your hand off."

"Didn't."

"Did."

Complete and utter silence. Even the worms seemed to have stopped snuffling in the turf overhead.

"Shall we go and have a look, then?"

"What at?"

"The noise. I'm sure there was something moving about."

"You're imagining things."

"No, I'm not. I think it was somebody going out. Or coming in. Anyway, there was something."

"Look, are we playing this game or aren't we?"

"I'm going to have a look." Two of the pale lights seemed to move, round the keel of the ship and up the ladder, then down again, and round the inside of the mound. "Here, come and look at this," said the first voice excitedly. "There's a hole here."

"What sort of hole?"

"Any old hole. I don't know. A hole going out."

The second pair of lights scrambled up and joined the first pair.

"You're right," said the second voice. "It's a hole."

"So what are we going to do about it?"

"Push."

A moment or so later, two small forms were lying on the grass outside the mound, dazzled and stupefied by the dim starlight.

"If this is light," said one to the other, "you can keep it."

But the other was cautiously lifting his head and sniffing. "It smells like light," he said tentatively. "Tastes like light. Do you know what this means, Zxerp?"

"It means that by and large I prefer the other one. Rain, wasn't it?"

"It means we're free, Zxerp. After one thousand two hundred and forty-six years, three months and eleven days in that stinking hole we're actually free."

They were both silent for a moment. "Bit of an anti-climax, really," said Zxerp sadly.

"Oh, the hell with you," said Prexz. Unusually for a chthonic spirit, he was cheerful and optimistic by nature, and ever since he and his brother had got themselves trapped in King Hrolf's mound he had never entirely given up hope of getting out.

"Now what?" said Zxerp. "You realise, of course, that things will have changed rather since we got stuck in there."

"And whose fault was that?" asked Prexz automatically—the issue had not been resolved in over twelve hundred years of eager discussion, and minor disagreements over the precise rules of the game of Goblin's Teeth had not helped them to find a solution to it. But Zxerp refused to be drawn.

"I mean," Zxerp continued, "things are bound to have changed. Twelve hundred years is a long time."

"No, it's not," replied Prexz accurately. Chthonic spirits, like the sources of energy from which they were formed at the beginning of the world, are practically immortal. Like light and electricity, they go on for ever unless they meet some insuperable resistance or negative force; but, having by some freak of nature the same level of consciousness as mortal creatures, they can fall prey to boredom, and Zxerp and Prexz, imprisoned by the staying spell that had frozen the King's company in time, were no exception. It is in the nature of a chthonic spirit to flow imperceptibly through the veins of the earth in search of magnetic fields or feed parasitically on the currents of an electric storm; confinement gnaws at them.

"It is when you're stuck in a mound with nothing to do but play Goblin's Teeth," said Zxerp. "I rather think you'll find..."

But Prexz wasn't listening. "Well," he said, "only one way to find out."

The two spirits sat in silence for a while, as if preparing themselves for a great adventure.

"Right," sighed Zxerp. "If we're going, we're going. Where *are* we going, by the way?"

"Dunno. The world is our oyster, really."

"Terrific. Oh, hang on."

"What?"

"Shall I bring the game, then?"

Prexz scratched his head. On the one hand, the world was full of new, exciting things for a chthonic spirit to do: elements to explore, currents of power coursing through the magma layer to revel in, static to drink and ultrasound to eat. On the other hand, he was winning.

"Go on, then," he said. "Might as well."

"If anybody asks," Hildy whispered, "you're the chorus of the Scottish National Opera off to a rehearsal of *Tannhäuser* in Inverness. I'm going to get some food."

She had parked the van in a backstreet in Thurso, just round the corner from a fish and chip shop. She hated leaving them like this, but the clamour of the King's champions for food was becoming intolerable, and nothing else was open at this time of night, except the off-licence. "Cod and chips for fourteen and fourteen cans of lager," she muttered to herself as she trudged up the darkling street. She only hoped she had enough money to pay for all that. And how long was all this going to last, at three meals a day, not to mention finding them all somewhere to sleep?

Back in the van, the standard-bearer was being difficult, as usual.

"But how do we know we can trust her?" he said. "I mean, you don't know her from Freyja. She's obviously some sort of a witch, or how come this thing moves about without oars."

The King shook his head. "We can trust her," he said. "But she doesn't seem to know very much. Whether that's good or bad, I don't know."

"So you think there's still danger?" said the huge man, who was bent nearly double at the back of the van.

"There's danger all right, Starkad Storvirkson," replied the King thoughtfully. "That much we can be sure of. I can feel it all around me. And I think the woman Hildy Frederik's-daughter is right that we should not reveal ourselves until we have found out exactly what is going on. I do not doubt that the power of the enemy has grown while we have slept."

When Hildy returned, exhausted and laden down with two carrier-bags, the King ordered his men to be quiet. "We had better not stay in this town," he said. "Can you take us back into open country?"

Hildy nodded, too tired to speak, and they drove out of Thurso for about half an hour to a bleak and deserted fell under a grey mountain. There the company got out and lit a fire in a small hollow hidden from the road. Hildy handed out paper packages of cod and chips and cans of lager, which the champions eyed with the greatest suspicion.

"I'm afraid it may have got cold," Hildy said, "but it's better than nothing."

"What is it?" asked the horn-bearer. "I mean, what do you do with it?"

"Try taking the paper off," said Hildy. The huge man looked up in surprise; he had already eaten the wrapping of his.

"The brown stuff on the outside is called batter," Hildy said. "It's made from eggs and flour and things. Inside there's fish."

"I don't like fish," said a champion with a silver helmet.

"The small brown things are chips," Hildy continued. "They

weren't invented in your time. There's beer in the metal tubes."

The champion in the silver helmet started to ask if there was any mead instead, but the King frowned at him. "Excellent," he said. "We owe you a great debt already, Hildy Frederik's-daughter."

Hildy nodded; they owed her twenty-two pounds and seventy-five pence, and she could see little chance of her ever getting it back. The authors of all the sagas she had read had been notably reticent about the cost of mass catering.

"You're welcome," she said wearily. "My pleasure."

"In return," said the King through a mouthful of cod, "I must explain to you who we are and why we were sleeping in the mound in the first place. But I must ask you to remember that this is a serious business. Wise is he who knows when to speak; wiser still, he who knows when to stay silent."

"Point taken," said Hildy, who recognised that as a quotation from the Elder Edda. "Go on, please."

The King bent his can of lager into the shape of a drinking-horn and pulled off the ring-pull. "My father was Ketil Trout," he said, "and he ruled over the Orkneys and Caithness. He was a wise and strong king, not loved overmuch by his people but feared by his enemies, and when he fell in battle he was buried in his ship."

"Where?" Hildy asked, for she still had the instincts of an archaeologist. But the King ignored her.

"I succeeded him as king," he said. "I was only fourteen at the time, and my uncle Hakon Claw ruled as regent until I reached the age of sixteen. When I came to the throne, I led my people out to war. I was strong then, tall for my age and burning with the desire to win glory. The people worshipped me, and I foresaw a succession of marvellous victories; my sword never sheathed, my banner never furled, my kingdom growing day by day in size and power."

The King stopped speaking, and Hildy could see by the light of the fire that there were tears in his bright quick eyes. She waited patiently, and he continued.

"As you can see, Hildy Frederik's-daughter, I was a wicked fool in my youth, blinded with tales and the long names of heroes. That's what comes of paying attention to the stories of long ago; you wish to emulate them, to bring the Elder Days back into the present. But there never was an age of heroes; when Sigurd Fafnir's Bane was digging dragon-traps in the Teutoberger Wald, they were already singing songs about the great heroes and days that would never come again. But I wasted many lives of farmers' sons who could not wait for the barley to ripen, leading armies into unnecessary battles, killing enemies who did not merit killing. What are these songs that they promised me they would make, and sing when I was cold in the howe? You say you have read all the sagas of our people, and studied the glorious deeds of heroes. Is there still a song about the battle of Melvich, or the fight at Tongue, when I struck down Jarl Bjorn in front of his own mainmast?"

Hildy turned away and said nothing.

"They promised me a song," said the King. "Perhaps they made one; if they did not, it does not matter very much. I found all those songs very dreary; warflame whistled and wolves feasted when Hrolf the Ring-Giver reddened the whale-road. The arrows always blotted out the sun, I remember, and the poet didn't get paid unless blade battered hard on helmet at least once in the first stanza."

The King smiled bitterly, and threw more wood on the fire. It crackled and grew brighter, and he continued.

"Then one day I was wounded, quite seriously. Strangely enough, it wasn't a great hero or an earl who did it; it was just a miserable little infantryman whose ship we had boarded. I expected him to hold still and be killed, because I was a hero and he was only a peasant, but I suppose he didn't know the rules, or was too scared to obey them. Anyway, he hit me across the forehead with an axe—not a battle-axe with runes all over the blade, something run up by the local blacksmith. I think it knocked some sense into my thick head, because that was the end of my career as a sea-raider, even though I made a complete recovery. I went back home and tried to take a serious interest in more mundane matters, such as whether the people had enough to eat and were the roads passable in winter. I'm afraid I was a great disappointment to my loyal subjects; they liked their kings bloodthirsty.

"Just when the world was beginning to make a little sense, and nobody bothered to invade us any more because we refused to fight, something started to happen away up north in Finnmark, in the kingdom of Geirrodsgarth, where the sorcerers lived. I think they stopped fighting among themselves and made an alliance. Whatever it was, there was suddenly an army of invulnerable berserks loose in the northern seas; all the fighting men who were too vicious even to be heroes had apparently been making their way there for years, and the sorcerer-king organised them into an army. And that wasn't all. He had trolls, and creatures made out of the bodies of dead men, which he brought back to life, and the spirits of wolves and bears put into human shape. Suddenly the game became rather serious, and the kings and earls settled their differences very quickly, and started to offer high wages to any competent wizard who specialised in military magic. But most of those had joined up with the enemy, and quite soon there were battles about which nobody made up any songs, as the ships from Geirrodsgarth appeared off the coasts of every kingdom in the north.

"There seemed little point in fighting, because the ordinary hacking and slashing techniques didn't seem to work on the sorcerer's army. But I was lucky, I suppose, or my ancestor Odin came to my aid. In a stone hut in Orkney lived a wizard called Kotkel, and he knew a few tricks that the enemy did not. He came to me and told me that I could withstand the enemy, perhaps even overthrow him, if I found a brooch, called the Luck of Caithness; with that in my possession, I could at least fight on equal terms. At that time, all the fugitives from the great kings' armies were pouring into my kingdom, and so I had the pick of the fighters of the age. I chose the very best: Ohtar and Hring, Brynjolf the Shape-Changer and Starkad Storvirksson, Angantyr and Bothvar Bjarki, Helgi and Hroar and Hjort, Arvarodd, who had been to Permia and killed giants, and Egil Kjartansson, called the Dancer. I sent them to find the brooch, and within a month they had found it. Then we went to fight the sorcerer. And we won, at Rolfsness, after a battle that lasted two days and two nights.

"But something went wrong at the last moment. One of us—I can't remember who, and it doesn't matter—had the sorcerer-king on the point of his spear but let him get away, and he escaped, although all his army, berserks and trolls and ghost-warriors, were utterly destroyed. We had failed, in spite of all our efforts, and we knew it. Of course, we did our best to make up. We raised forces in every kingdom in the north and went to Geirrodsgarth, where we razed the sorcerer-king's stronghold to the ground and killed all his creatures in their nests. We searched for him under every rock and in every barn and hay-loft; but he had escaped. Some said he had ridden away on the wind, leaving his body behind, and others assured me that he had sunk into the sea.

"Then the wizard Kotkel came to me and gave me more advice, and I realised that I would have to take it. I ordered my longship Naglfar to be brought up on to the battlefield at Rolfsness and sunk into a mound. While the wizard cast his spells and cut runes into the joists and beams of the chamber, I gathered together my champions and led them into the ship. Then the wizard sang a sleeping spell, and we all fell asleep, and they closed up the mound. That last spell was a strong one; we should not wake until the day had come when the sorcerer-king was once again at the summit of his power and threatening the world. Then we should do battle with him once more, for the last time. And there we have been ever since, Hildy Frederik's-daughter. Quite a story, isn't it? Or aren't there any songs about it? No? I'm not surprised. I think people rather lost interest in stories about heroes after the sorcerer-king appeared; most of them seemed to be in rather bad taste."

For a while, Hildy sat and stared into the heart of the fire, wondering whether or not she could believe this story, even out on the fells, by night beside a fire. It was not that she suspected the King of lying; and she believed in his existence, and that he had just woken up after twelve hundred years of sleep. But something struggling to stay alive inside her told her that some token show of disbelief was necessary if she was to retain her identity, or at least her sanity. Then it occurred to her, like the obvious solution to some tiresome puzzle, that her belief was not needed, just as the meat need not necessarily consent to being cooked. She had entered the service of a great lord; part of the bargain between lord and subject is that the subject does not have to understand the lord's design; so long as the subject obeys the lord's orders, her part is discharged, and no blame can attach to her.

"So what are you going to do?" she asked.

The King smiled. "I shall find the sorcerer-king and I shall destroy him, if I can," he said. "That sounds simple enough, don't you think? If you keep things simple, and look to the end, not the problems in the way, most things turn out to be possible. That is not in any Edda, but I think it will pass for wisdom."

The King rose slowly to his feet and beckoned to the wizard, who had been sitting outside the circle of the firelight, apparently trying to find a spell that would make a beer-can magically refill itself. They walked a little way into the night, and spoke together softly for a while.

Hildy began to feel cold, and one of the champions noticed her shivering slightly and took off his cloak and offered it to her.

"My name is Angantyr," he said, "son of Asmund son of Geir. My father was earl of—"

"Not you as well," moaned the horn-bearer. "Can't we have a song or something instead?"

Hildy wrapped the cloak round her shoulders. It was heavy and seemed to envelop her, like a fall of warm snow.

"Do you mind?" said Angantyr Asmundarson. "The lady and I—"

"Don't you take any notice of him," said the standard-bearer. "He's not called Angantyr the Creep for nothing."

"Look who's talking," replied Angantyr.

"Excuse me," Hildy said. The heroes looked at her. "Which one of you is Arvarodd?"

"I am," said a gaunt-looking hero in a black cloak.

Hildy was blushing. "Are you the Arvarodd who went to Permia?" she asked shyly. For some reason the heroes burst out laughing, and Arvarodd scowled.

"I read your saga," she said, "all about the giants and the magic shirt of invulnerability. Was it like that?"

"Yes," said Arvarodd.

"Oh." Hildy bit her lip nervously. "Could I have your autograph, please? It's not for me, it's for the Department of Scandinavian Studies at St Andrews University," she added quickly. Then she hid her face in the cloak.

"What's an autograph?" asked Arvarodd.

"Could you write your name on—well, on that beer-can?"

Arvarodd raised a shaggy eyebrow, then scratched a rune on the empty Skol can with the point of his dagger and handed it to her.

"Everyone's always kidding him about his trip to Permia," Angantyr whispered in her ear. "All his great deeds, and the battles and the dragons and so forth—well, you heard the saga, didn't you?—and all anyone ever asks him is "Are you the Arvarodd who went to Permia?" And it was only a trading-voyage, and all he brought back was a few mouldy old furs."

The King and the wizard came back to the fire and sat down.

"The drinks are on the wizard," announced the King, and at once the heroes crowded round the wizened old man, who started to pour beer out of his can into theirs.

"Don't worry," said the King to Hildy, "the wizard and I have thought of something. But we're going to need a little help."

There are many tall office-blocks in the City of London, but the tallest of them all is Gerrards Garth House, the home of the Gerrards Garth group of companies. Someone—perhaps it was the architect—thought it would be a good idea to have a black office-block instead of the usual white, and so the City people in their wine bars refer to it as the Dark Tower.

The very top floor is one enormous office, and few people have ever been there. It is full of screens and desk-top terminals, and the telephones are arrayed in battalions, like the tanks at a march-past. On the wall is a large electronic map of the world, with flashing lights marking the Gerrards Garth operations in every country. On a busy day it almost seems as if the entire world is burning.

The building was entirely dark, except for one light in this top office, and in that office there was only one man: a big burly man with red cheeks and large forearms. He was staring into a bank of screens on which there were many columns of figures, and from time to time he would tap in a few symbols. Then the screens would clear and new figures would come up before him. He did not seem to be tired or impatient, or particularly concerned with what he saw; it looked very much as if everything was nicely under control. Thanks, no doubt, to the new technology.

And then the screens all over the office went out, and came on again. All over them, little green figures raced up and down, like snow-flakes in a blizzard, while every light that could possibly flash began to flash at once. Unfamiliar symbols which were to be found in no manual moved back and forth with great rapidity, forming themselves into intricate spirals and interweaving curves of flickering light, and all the telephones began to ring at once. The man gripped the arms of his chair and stared. Suddenly all the screens stopped flickering, and one picture appeared on all of them, glowing very brightly, while the overhead lights went out, and the terminals began to spit out miles of printout paper covered in words from a hundred forgotten languages.

The man leant forward and looked at the screen closest to him. The picture was of a golden brooch, in the shape of a flying dragon.

3

"Admit it, Zxerp," said a voice, "you've never had it so good." The postman, who had just been about to get on his bicycle for the long ride back to Bettyhill, stopped dead in his tracks and stared at the telegraph wires over his head. He could have sworn that one of them had just spoken. He looked around suspiciously, but nothing stirred in the grey dawn.

"I mean," said the voice, "I haven't the faintest idea what this stuff is, but it beats geothermal energy into a cocked hat."

The postman jumped on his bicycle and pedalled away, very fast.

"It's all right, I suppose," replied Zxerp. "A bit on the sweet side for my taste, but it has a certain something." He wiped his mouth with the back of his hand.

"You're never satisfied, are you?" said Prexz, emerging from the wire and hopping lightly down to the ground. "You want magnetism on it, you do."

"Hang on," said Zxerp. He climbed out of the copper core and dropped rather heavily. "Ouch," he said unconvincingly. "I think I've hurt my ankle."

They strolled for a while down the empty lane, and paused to gaze out over the misty hills. The cloud was low, so that the peaks were blurred and vague; it was possible to imagine that they rose up for ever to the roof of the sky.

"So whose go was it?" asked Zxerp after a while.

"Mine," replied Prexz. "Have you got the dice?"

"I thought you had them."

They searched their pockets and found the dice: two tiny cubes of diamond that glowed with an inner light.

"So what are we going to do, then?" asked Zxerp after each had had a couple of turns. He was in grave danger of being Rubiconned (again) and wanted to distract his companion's attention.

"Do?" Prexz frowned. "What we like, I suppose."

"No, but really. We've had a break; we ought to be getting back to work."

Prexz shook his head vigorously, causing great interference with Breakfast Television reception all over Bettyhill. "I've had it up to here with work. At the beck and call of every wizard and sorcerer in Caithness, never a moment to call your own—what sort of a life do you call that? I reckon that if we keep our heads down and play our runes right..."

He stopped, and put his hands to his head. Zxerp stared at him, then suddenly he felt it, too: words of command, coming from not far away.

"Oh, for pity's sake," muttered Prexz. "It's that bloody wizard again."

"I was just thinking," said Zxerp through gritted teeth, "how nice it would be not to have to see that Kotkel again."

"He was the worst," agreed Prexz. "Definitely the worst." The words of command stopped, and the two spirits relaxed.

"Perhaps if we just hid somewhere," Prexz whispered. "Pretended to be a bit of static or something..."

"Forget it." Zxerp was already packing up the game, putting the Community Hoard cards back into their marcasite box. "I knew it was too good to last."

They started to trudge back the way they had come.

"Do you suppose he did it on purpose?" asked Prexz. "Trapped us in the mound deliberately, or something?"

"I wouldn't be surprised," said Zxerp gloomily. "He's clever, that wizard."

Hildy was not used to sleeping out in the open, but at least it hadn't rained, and she had been so tired that sleep came remarkably easily. She had had a strange dream, in which everything had gone back to normal and which ended with her sitting at a table in the University library leafing through the latest edition of the *Journal of Scandinavian Studies.*

When she opened her eyes, she found that the Vikings were all up and sitting round a fire. They were roasting four rabbits on sticks, which reminded Hildy irresistibly of ice-lollies, and passing round a helmet filled with water.

"Why's it always *my* helmet?" grumbled the horn-bearer.

For a moment, the pure simplicity of the scene filled Hildy with a sort of inner peace: food caught by skill in the early morning, and clean water from a mountain stream. Then she discovered that a spider had crawled inside her boot, and that she had a crick in her neck from sleeping with her head on a tree-root. She evicted the spider nervously and tottered over to the fire.

"Have some rabbit," said Angantyr. "It's a bit burnt, but a little charcoal never killed anyone."

Hildy explained that she never ate breakfast. "Where's the King?" she asked.

"He wandered off with that blasted wizard," said the horn-bearer, drying out the inside of his helmet with the hem of his cloak. "I think it's going to rain any minute now," he added cheerfully.

She found the King sitting beside the bank of a little river that rolled down off the side of the fell just inside the wood. He turned and smiled at her, and put a finger to his lips. On the other side of the stream the wizard was standing on one leg, pointing with his staff to a shallow pool. The King was lighting a small fire with a tinder-box.

"What's he doing?" whispered Hildy.

"Watch," replied the King.

The wizard had started mumbling something under his breath, and almost immediately two large salmon jumped up out of the water and landed in the King's lap.

"Saves all that mucking about with hooks and bits of string," explained the King. "Had any breakfast?"

"No," said Hildy. "But I never—"

"Don't blame you," said the King. "Rabbit again, I expect. And burnt, too, if I know them. No imagination."

The wizard had crossed the stream, and the King set about preparing the salmon, while Hildy looked away.

"Kotkel and I have been thinking," said the King. "Obviously, it's no good our hanging about out here having a good time and waiting for the enemy to come to us. On the other hand, we aren't exactly suited for going out and looking for him, although I don't suppose he'll be all that hard to find."

He threw something into the water, and Hildy winced. As a child, she had had to be taken outside when her mother served up fish with their heads still on.

"So I think we should find somewhere where we can get ourselves organised, don't you? And there are things we're going to need. For example, I was never a great follower of fashion, and far be it from me to make personal comments, but does everyone these days wear extraordinary clothes like those you've got on?"

Hildy glanced at the King, in his steel hauberk and wolfskin leggings. "Yes," she said.

"Well," said the King, "we don't want to appear conspicuous, do we? So we'll need clothes, and somewhere to stay, and probably other things as well. I'm afraid you'll have to see to that for us."

Hildy didn't like the sound of that. To the best of her knowledge she had just over two hundred pounds in the bank, and her next grant cheque wasn't due for three weeks.

"The problem is," continued the King, "what do we have to trade?"

Hildy had a brilliant idea. On the King's tunic was a small brooch of enamelled gold in the shape of a running horse. She pointed to it.

"Could you spare me that?" she asked.

"A present from my aunt, Gudrun Thord's-daughter," replied the King, looking down at it. "I never liked it much. Rich is gold, the gift of earls, but richer still the help of friends. So to speak."

He unpinned the brooch and handed it to her. Hildy looked around at the vast empty hills and the dense wood before her.

"I know a couple of dealers in antiquities down in London.... You remember London?"

"Still going, is it?" asked the King, raising an eyebrow. "You surprise me. I never thought it would last. Go on."

"They'd pay a lot for this, with no questions asked. Enough to be going on with, anyway."

"But London is several weeks' journey away," said the King.

"Not any more," said Hildy. "I'd be away two, at the most three days."

The King nodded. "I imagine we'll be able to take care of ourselves for three days. It'll give us time to think out what we're going to do. But be careful. For all I know, the enemy is aware of us already."

For some reason, Hildy felt rather cold, although the King's little fire was burning brightly. She had no notion what this strange enemy was, but when the King spoke his name she was conscious of an inexplicable discomfort, just as, although she did not believe in ghosts, she could never properly get to sleep after reading a ghost story. The King seemed to understand what she was thinking, for he put his hand on her shoulder and said: "I think you will be able to recognise the enemy when you come across him or his works. I suspect that you know most of them already. It will be like a house or a bend in the road which you have passed many times, until one day someone tells you a story about that place—there was a murder there once, or an old mad woman lived there for many years—and the place is never the same again. Here, in these unchanged mountains, I cannot feel properly afraid of my enemy, even though I fought him here once, and smelt his danger in every fold of the land. But now I think his ships are beached somewhere else, and his army watches other roads. I re-member that he used to have birds for spies and messengers, ravens and crows and eagles, so that as we marched we knew that he could see us and assess our strength at every turn. I think he has other spies now; and now it is most important that he does *not* see us. He will look here first, of course, and we are not an army able to do battle; we cannot fight his armies, we can only fight him, hand-to-hand in his own stronghold—if we can find it and get there before he finds us and squashes us under his thumb."

The King stopped speaking and closed his eyes, but Hildy could not feel afraid, even though fear was all around her, for the King was here with his champions, and he would find a way.

"The salmon's ready," he said suddenly. "Help yourself."

"No, thanks," said Hildy, "I never eat breakfast. I'd better get go-ing."

"Good luck, then," said the King, not looking up from his salmon. "Be careful."

Hildy walked back to the camp, where she had parked the van.

"Going somewhere?" asked Arvarodd, who was sitting by the fire sharpening arrowheads on a stone.

"Yes," said Hildy. "I'll be gone for a day or so. The King needs some things before we start out."

"Going alone?"

"Yes."

"Risky." Arvarodd got up and stretched his arms wide. "Never mind, I expect you'll cope. You know all about everything these days, of course, so I don't suppose you're worried."

"Yes," replied Hildy doubtfully, "I suppose I do."

"Better safe than sorry, though," said Arvarodd. He was looking for something in a goat-skin satchel by his side. "Come over here," he said softly.

"Well?"

He took out a small bundle of linen cloth and laid it on the grass beside him. "When I was in Permia," he whispered, "I did pick up one or two useful things, although I made sure no one ever found out about them, so you won't have heard of them in any of those perishing sagas. Never saw a penny in royalties out of any of them, by the way. These bits and pieces might come in useful. I'll want them back, mind."

He unrolled the cloth and picked out three small pebbles and a splinter of bone, with a rune crudely carved on it.

"Not things of beauty, I'll grant you," he said, "but still. This pebble here is in fact the gallstone of the dragon Fafnir, whom Sigurd Sigmundarsson slew, as you know better than I. Improbable though it may sound, it enables you to understand any language of men. This remarkably similar pebble comes from the shores of Asgard. If you throw it at something, it turns into a boulder and flattens pretty well anything. Then it turns back into a pebble and returns to your hand. This bone is a splinter of the jaw of Ymir the Sky-Father. Ymir could talk the hind legs off a donkey, and this makes whoever bears it irresistibly persuasive. And this," he said, prodding the third pebble with his forefinger, "was picked off the roughcast on the walls of Valhalla. I never found out what it does, but I imagine it brings you good luck or something."

He rolled them back up in the cloth and gave it to her. She tried to find words to thank him, but none came.

"You'd better be going," he said, and she turned to go. "Be careful."

"I will. It's not dangerous, really."

"Did you really read my saga?"

Hildy nodded.

"Like it?"

"Yes."

"Wrote it myself," said Arvarodd gruffly, and he walked away.

Danny Bennett's definition of an optimist was someone who has nothing left except hope, and he felt that the description fitted him well. Ever since he had joined the BBC, straight from university, his career had seemed to drift downhill, albeit in a vaguely upwards direction. True, he had made a reputation for himself with the less intense sort of documentary, the sort that people like to watch rather than the sort that is good for them, but although his work interested the public it was not, he felt sure, in the Public Interest. While all around him his colleagues were exposing scandals in the Health Service and uncovering cover-ups with the enthusiasm of small children unwrapping their Christmas presents, he was traipsing round historic English towns doing series on architecture, or lovingly satirical portraits of charming eccentrics. Better, he thought, to suffer the final indignity of producing "One Man and His Dog" than to be caught in this limbo of unwanted success.

As he sat in the editing suite with visions of the Cotswolds flickering before him, he had in his briefcase the synopsis of his life's work, a startling piece of investigation that would, if carried through with the proper resources, conclusively prove that the Milk Marketing Board had been somehow connected with the assassination of President Kennedy. He had seen its pages become dog-eared with unresponsive reading, and always it had returned, admired but not accepted, along with a command to go forth and film yet another half-baked half-timbered village green. All around him teemed the modern world, sordid and cynical and infinitely corrupt, but he was seemingly trapped in the Forest of Arden.

He wound his way painfully through the material in front of him, and for only the fifteenth time that hour wished a horrible death on his chief cameraman, who seemed to believe that people looked better with trees apparently growing out of the tops of their heads. He picked up the telephone beside him.

"Angie?" he said. "Is Bill still in the building?"

"Yes, Mr. Bennett."

"Find him, and personally confiscate that polarising filter. He's used it five times in the last six shots, and it makes everything look like my daughter's holiday snaps. And tell him he's an incompetent idiot."

"There's been a call for you, Mr. Bennett," said Angie. "I think somebody wants you to do something."

Danny Bennett could guess what. There had been a news report that morning about some fantastic archaeological find up in the north of Scotland, and he had felt the threat of it hanging over him all day, like a bag of flour perched on top of a door he must walk through. Five days on some windswept moor, and all the delights of a hotel bar full of sound-recordists in the evenings. He plodded through the rest of the editing, and went to investigate.

"You want to talk to Professor Wood, Department of Archaeology, St Andrews," he was told. "He's on site at the moment with an archaeological team. Apparently, there's gold and a perfectly preserved Viking ship. Sort of like Sutton Hoo only much better."

"And Professor Wood actually found the ship, did he?"

"No, it was one of his students or something. But Professor Wood is the one who's in charge now."

"But I'll have to talk to this student," Danny said wearily. "What was it like to be the first person in two thousand years, and all that. Can you find out who this person is?"

He went to the bar for a drink before going home to pack. One of his colleagues, a rat-faced woman called Moira, grinned at him as he sat down.

"You drew the short straw, then? That Caithness nonsense with the Viking ship?"

"Yes."

"I'm just off to do an in-depth investigation into a corrupt planning inquiry in Sunderland. Nuclear dumping. Wicked alderman.
Rattle the Mayor's chain."

"Good for you."

"It will be, with any luck. Plenty of nice gooey evil in these local-
government stories." She grinned again, but Danny didn't seem to be
in the mood.

"There's a rumour that there's a story in this Scottish thing, actually," she said.

"Don't tell me," said Danny to his drink. "The Vikings didn't get
planning permission for their mound."

"The girl who found the thing," said Moira, "has apparently vanished. Not at her hotel. Hired a van and made herself into air. Can it
be that she has looted the mound and absconded with a vanful of
Heritage? Or are more sinister forces at work up there among the kilts
and heather? You could have fun with that."

Danny shrugged his shoulders. "May be something in it," he said.

"Perhaps"—Moira looked furtively round and whispered,—"perhaps it's the Milk Marketing Board. Again."

"Oh, very funny," said Danny.

It took Hildy some time to get used to the idea that she was still in
Britain in the twentieth century and that, so far as she could tell, no
one was hunting for her or trying to kill her. As she waited for the bus
to Inverness, having dumped the hired van outside Lairg, she had the
feeling that she ought, at the very least, to be using false papers and a
forged driving licence, and in all probability be speaking broken French
as well. But she put this down to having seen too many movies about
the Resistance, and settled back to endure the long and unpleasant
journey.

She made her way uneventfully to the railway station, bought a
copy of *Newsweek,* and read it as the train shuffled through northern
Britain. It was unlikely, of course, that even in that great rendezvous
of conspiracy theories the rising of the sorcerer-king would be reported
in so many words, but at the back of her mind she had an inchoate
idea of where the enemy might be found. Something the King had
said about magic had started her thinking and, although her idea was
scarcely distinguishable from healthy American paranoia, that was not
in itself a reason for discarding it. God, guts and paranoia made America
great.

As she picked her way with difficulty through the various items—
for she had been in England a long time now, and found the language

of her native land rather tiring in long bursts—she began to feel aware of some unifying theme. There happened to be a long article about a group of companies, a household name throughout the world. Then there was another article about advances in satellite communications, and a discussion of the techniques of electoral advertising. There were several letters about commercial funding of universities, and a great deal about nuclear power, apparently cut from the great bolts of similar material that hang in all editorial offices. The whole thing seemed to make some sort of left-handed sense, and she started again from the beginning. The more she read, the more sense it seemed to make, although what the sense was she could not quite grasp. She told herself that she was probably imagining it, and went to the buffet-car for a coffee.

She had a headache now, and tried to get some sleep, but when she dozed a dream came to her, and she thought she stood on the roof of a very high office-block somewhere in Manhattan or Chicago, from which she could see all the kingdoms of the earth below her. That was curious enough but what was odder still was that large areas of the world were apparently dyed or cross-hatched in a colour she had never been aware of before. Then something rolled out of her pocket, and she stooped to retrieve it. It was the third pebble that Arvarodd had lent her, the one whose use was unknown, and it was the same colour as the cross-hatching.

Then the train went over some points, and she woke up. Once she had recovered her wits sufficiently, she took out the roll of cloth and extracted from it the third pebble. It felt warm in her hand, and something prompted her to put it in her mouth and suck it. It tasted rather bitter, but not unpleasantly so, and she picked up the magazine and started to read it a third time.

By the time the train pulled in to Euston, she was sweating and feeling very frightened. She took the pebble out of her mouth and put it away, then walked briskly to a small and not too horrible hotel she had stayed in before. She did not sleep well that night.

The next morning, promptly at nine-thirty, she walked down to Holborn, where the dealers in antiquities have their lairs. There she converted the golden brooch into seven thousand pounds cash money. It seemed strange to be walking about with so much money in her pocket, but she was in no mood to entrust it to a bank.

Next she went to the London University bookshop, where she bought a number of Old Norse and Anglo-Saxon texts, of such great popularity that the prices on the backs were still in shillings, and then to the British Museum, where she spent several hours in the Reading Room. After a cup of coffee and a hamburger, she caught a train for Inverness. It took even longer than the train down, but the journey passed quickly, for she was used to working on trains.

She stayed the night in a hotel in Inverness, and spent the next morning among the secondhand-car dealers, trying to find a fourteen-seater van. Most of those that were within her price range had no engine or less than the conventional number of wheels, but eventually she found something suitable, which she christened Sleipnir, after the eight-legged warhorse of the god Odin. Then she went to Marks & Spencer and bought fourteen suits; she had to guess at the sizes, but she knew that you can always change things from Marks & Spencer if they don't fit. The woman at the cash-desk gave her a suspicious look, and Hildy could not really blame her; but the worst she could be suspected of doing was organising a cell of Jehovah's Witnesses, which was not a crime, even in Scotland. Shoes were more of a problem, but she decided on something large and simple in black; timeless, she thought to herself. They would need to be, after all.

There were other things, notably food and blankets and camping-stoves, and by the time she had got everything there was not much money left and she was exhausted. She filled the van up with petrol—how do you explain petrol to Viking heroes? This wagon has no horses, it moves by burning dead leaves—and started off on the long drive to Caithness.

"Don't talk daft," said the horn-bearer, "that's the Haystack."

"You're the one who's talking daft, Bothvar Bjarki," replied Arva-rodd. "That's Vinndalf's Crown. You find Vinndalf's Crown by going left from the Pole Star until you reach the Thistle, then straight down past the Great Goat."

"If that's all you know about the stars," replied Bothvar Bjarki, "it's no wonder you ended up in bloody Permia. Where were you trying to get to—Oslo?"

Arvarodd gathered up his cloak and moved pointedly to the other side of the fire. There the huge man and another champion were sitting playing chess on a portable chess-set made out of walrus ivory.

"Is that checkmate?" asked the huge man.

"Afraid so," replied his opponent.

"I always lose," said the huge man.

"You can't help it if you're stupid, Starkad," replied his opponent kindly. "A berserk isn't meant to be clever. If he was clever, he wouldn't be a berserk. And you're a very good berserk, isn't he, Arvarodd?"

"Yes," said Arvarodd. The huge man beamed with pleasure, and his smile seemed to light up the camp.

"Thank you, Brynjolf," said Starkad Storvirksson. "And you're a very good shape-changer."

"Thank you, Starkad," said Brynjolf, trying to conceal the fact that he had had this conversation before. "How about another game, then?"

"Don't you want to play, Arvarodd?" Starkad asked, looking at the hero of Permia. Starkad loved chess, even though he invariably lost, although how he managed to do so when everybody cheated to make sure he won was a complete mystery.

"No, not now," Arvarodd said. "I'm going to get some sleep in a minute."

"Can I be black, then?"

"But white always moves first, Starkad," said Brynjolf gently. "Don't you want to move first?"

"No, thank you," said the berserk. "I've noticed that I always seem to lose when I play first."

If Brynjolf closed his eyes, it was only for a moment. They played a couple of moves, and Brynjolf advanced his king straight down the board into a nest of black pieces.

"Tell me something, Brynjolf," said Starkad softly, marching his rook straight past the place Brynjolf had meant it to go, "why do Bothvar and the others call me Honey-Starkad?"

Brynjolf stared at the board and scratched his head. Yet again, it was impossible for him to move without checkmating his opponent. "Because you're sweet and thick, Starkad," he said.

"Oh," said the berserk, as if some great mystery had been revealed to him. "Oh, I *see*. It's your move."

"Checkmate," said Brynjolf.

4

The job description had never said anything about this, thought the young man as he scooped up the armfuls of paper that had spilled out of the printers during the night. The Big Bang, yes. The New Technology, certainly. The waste paper, no.

He paused, exhausted by the unaccustomed effort, and cast his eyes over a sheet at random. It said:

> **ÆO£$¥%{.¬°::}**

And probably meant it, too. It might be BASIC, or it might be FORTRAN, or any other of those computer languages, except that he knew all of them and it wasn't. If he was expected to do a reasoned efficiency breakdown on it and report intelligently in the morning, they were going to be disappointed.

"What are you doing with those?"

The young man jumped, and several yards of continuous stationery fell to the floor and wound themselves round his feet, almost affectionately, like a cat.

"It's last night's printout, Mr...." He never could remember the boss's name. In fact he wasn't sure anyone had ever told him what it was.

"Leave that alone." The old sod was in a worse mood than usual. "Have you looked at it?"

"Well, no, not in any great detail *yet*. I was hoping...."

"Put it down and clear off."

"Yes, Mr...."

No point in even trying to place it tidily on the desk. The young man let it slither from his arms, and fled.

"And find me Mr Olafsen, now."

The young man stopped. One more stride and he would have been out of the door and clear.

"I'm not positive he's in the building, actually, Mr...."

"I didn't ask you if he was in the building. I asked you to find him."

This time the young man made it out of the door. There was something about his employer that he didn't like, a sort of air of menace. It was not just the fear of the sack; more like an atmosphere of physical danger. He asked Mr Olafsen's secretary if she knew where he was.

Apparently he was in Tokyo. Where exactly in Tokyo, however, she refused to speculate. He had been sent there on some terribly urgent business with instructions not to fail. In the event of failure, he should carry the firm's principle of conforming to local business methods to its logical conclusion and commit hara-kiri.

"*He* was in a foul mood that day—worse than usual," went on the secretary. "You might try phoning the Tokyo office. I don't know what time it is over there, and they might all be out running round the roof or kicking sacks or whatever it is they do, but you might be lucky."

A series of calls located Mr Olafsen at a golf-course on the slopes of Mount Fuji, and he was put through to his employer.

"Thorgeir, there's trouble," said the boss. "Get back here as quick as you like."

"Won't it wait? If I can get round in less than fifty-two, we'll have more semiconductors than we know what to do with."

"No, it won't. It's dragon trouble."

"This is a terrible line. I thought you said—"

"I said dragon trouble, Thorgeir."

"I'm on my way."

The boss put down the telephone. The knowledge that he would soon have Thorgeir Storm-shepherd at his side did something to relieve the panic that had afflicted him all day. Thorgeir might not have courage, but he had brains, and his loyalty was beyond question. That at least was certain; any disloyalty, and he knew he would be turned back into the timber-wolf he had originally been, when the sorcerer-king had first found him in the forests of Permia. Timber-wolves cannot wear expensive suits or drive Lagondas with any real enjoyment, and Thorgeir had become rather attached to the good life.

"Why now?" the sorcerer-king asked himself, for the hundredth time that morning. With repetition, the question appeared to be resolving itself. There was the little matter of the Thirteenth Generation, the final coincidence of hardware and software that the sorcerer-king had vaguely dreamt of back at the start of his career under the shade of ancestral fir-trees, when artificial intelligence had been confined to stones with human voices and other party tricks. It had been a long road since then, and he had come a long way along it. No earthly power could prevent him, since no earthly power would for one instant take seriously any accurate description of the threat he posed to the world and its population. But the dragon and the King had never been far from his mind ever since he had abandoned his mortal body on the battlefield at Rolfsness and escaped, rather ignominiously disguised as a Bad Idea.

The sorcerer-king leant his elbows on his desk and tried to picture the Luck of Caithness, that irritatingly elusive piece of Dark Age circuitry. As a work of art, it had never held much attraction for him. As a circuit diagram it had haunted his dreams, and he had racked his memory for the details of its involved twists and curves. For of course the garnets and stones that the unknown craftsman had set in the yellow gold were microchips of unparalleled ingenuity, and in the endless continuum of the interlocking design was vested a system of such strength that no successor could hope to rival or dominate it.

The sorcerer-king shook his head, and struck one broad fist into the other. He had tried everything he knew to avoid this day, and made every possible preparation for it, but now that it had come he felt desperate and hopeless. Yet, if it were to come to the worst, he was still what he had always been, and old ways were probably the best. He rose from his desk and took from his pocket the keys to the heavy oak trunk that seemed so much out of place among the tubular steel of his office. The lock was stiff, but it turned with a little effort, and he pushed up the lid. From inside he lifted a bundle wrapped in purple velvet. He took a deep breath and gently undid the silk threads that held the bundle together, revealing a decorated golden scabbard containing a long beautiful sword. He drew it out and felt the blade with his thumb. Still sharp, after all these years. He made a few slow-motion passes with the blade, and the pull of its weight on the muscles of his forearm reminded him of dangers overcome. With a grunt, he swung the sword round his head and brought it down accurately and with tremendous force on a dark green filing-cabinet, cleaving it from A to J. At that moment, the door opened.

The young man had not wanted to go back into the boss's office. As he turned the handle of the door, he could hear a terrific crash, and he nearly abandoned the mission there and then. But the letters had to be signed.

The sorcerer-king had just lifted his sword clear of the filing-cabinet, feeling rather foolish. He stared at the young man, who stared back. At last the young man, with all the fatuity of youth, found speech.

"Jammed again, did it?"

"Did it?" The sorcerer-king was sweating, despite the air-conditioning.

"The filing-cabinet. I think it's dust getting in the locks."

The sorcerer-king glanced down at the filing-cabinet, and at the sword in his hands. "Come in and shut the door," he said pleasantly.

The young man did as he was told. "If it's about the luncheon vouchers," he said nervously, "I can explain."

"So can I," said the sorcerer-king. Of course, there was no need for him to do so, but suddenly he felt that he wanted to. He had kept this secret for more than a thousand years, and he felt like talking to someone. "Sit down," he said. "What can I get you to drink?"

He laid the sword nonchalantly on his desk and produced a bottle from a drawer. "Try this," he suggested. "Mead. Of course, it's nothing like the real thing...." He poured out two glasses and drank one himself, to show his guest that the drink was not poisoned.

The young man struggled to find something to say. "Nice sword," he ventured. Then he recollected what Mr Olafsen's secretary had been saying about Japanese business methods.

"'Nice' is rather an understatement," said the sorcerer-king, and added something about the cut and thrust of modern commerce. The young man smiled awkwardly. "Tell me, Mr Fortescue," he continued, "do you enjoy working for the company?"

"Er," said Mr Fortescue.

The boss seemed not to have heard him. "It's an old-established company, of course. Very old-established." He leant forward suddenly. "Have you the faintest idea how old-established it is?"

The young man said no, he hadn't. The boss told him. He also told him about the fortress of Geirrodsgarth, the battle of Melvich, and the intervening thousand years. He told him about the dragon-brooch, the King of Caithness, and the wizard Kotkel. He told him about the New Magic and its relationship with the New Technology, and how the Thirteenth Generation would be the culmination of all that had gone before.

"I realised quite early," said the sorcerer-king, "that magic in the sense that I understood it all those centuries ago had a relatively short future. It wasn't the problem of credibility—that was never a major drawback. But it's basically a question of the fundamental problem at the root of all industrial processes." The sorcerer-king poured himself another glass of mead and lit a cigar.

"Look at it this way. In all other industries, the quantum leap from small-scale to large-scale, from workshop to factory, craftsman to mass-production, hand-loom to spinning jenny, is the dividing-line between the ancient and the modern world. Do you follow me?"

"Not really."

"Magic, I felt, fell into the same category. In my day, you had a small, highly skilled workforce—your sorcerers and their apprentices—turning out high-quality low-volume products for a small, largely high-income-group market. Result: the ordinary bloke, the man on the Uppsala carrier's cart, was excluded from participation in the field. Magic was not reaching the bulk of the population. Given my long-term objective—total world dominance—this was plainly unacceptable. What was the use of a lot of kings and heroes being able to zap each other to Kingdom Come when Bjorn Public could take it or leave it alone? Especially since, as my own experience will testify, a little well-applied brute force and ignorance can put an end to the whole enterprise? You appreciate the problem."

"Thank you for the drink. I really ought to be getting back...."

"There had to be a breakthrough," continued the sorcerer-king, "a moment in the history of the world when magic finally had the potential to get its fingers well and truly round the neck of the human race. There were several key steps along the way, of course. The Industrial Revolution, electricity, the motor-car, and of course television—all these were building-blocks. All my own work, incidentally. They may tell you different down at the Patents Office, but who needs all that? He who keeps a low profile keeps his nose clean, as the sagas say.

"And then I came across an old idea of mine I'd jotted down on the back of a goat-skin hood in the old days—the computer. Originally it was just meant to be an alternative to notches in a stick to tell you how much cheese you needed to see you through the winter, and for all I cared it could stay that way. Except, I got to thinking, how'd it be if everyone had one? I mean everyone. A Home Computer. A little friend with a face like a telly, and its little wires leading into the telephone network. All things to all men, and everything put together. You do everything through it—bank through it, vote through it, work through it, be born, copulate and die through it. Good idea, eight out of ten. But the extra two out often is the incredible tolerance the profane masses have towards the evil little monsters. 'Computer error,' they say, and shake their heads indulgently. Three hours programming the perishing thing, and then it goes *bleep* and swallows the lot." The sorcerer-king chuckled loudly over his drink and blew out a great cloud of cigar-smoke, for all the world like a story-book dragon. "Swallows is right. I saw that possibility a mile off. You don't think, do you, that all those malfunctions are genuine? Ever since I got the first rudimentary network established, I've had everything most carefully monitored. Anything I fancy, anything that looks like it might be even remotely useful—*gulp!* and it hums along the fibre-optics to my own personal library."

Up till then, the young man had been profoundly unconvinced by all this. He had never believed in God or any other sort of conspiracy theory, and he could never summon up enough credulity to be entertained by spy thrillers. But even he had sometimes wondered about the teleology of his own particular field of interest. All computer programmers have at some stage come face to face with the one and only metaphysical question of what happens to all the stuff that gets swallowed by the computer. Here at last was the only possible explanation. He sat open-mouthed and stared.

"Now do you see?" said the sorcerer-king.

"Yes," said the young man. "That's clever. That's really clever."

The sorcerer-king smirked. "Thank you. Of course," he continued, "another fundamental cornerstone of modern commerce is diversification of interests. We may not be the world's biggest multinational, but we hold the most key positions. With an unrivalled position in the Media—don't you like that word, by the way? It gives exactly the right impression. I suppose it's because it sounds so like the Mafia. Anyway, with that and a manufacturing base like ours, we have the establishment to support a truly global concern. So it would be pretty nearly perfect. If it wasn't for the setback."

"What setback?"

"The dragon. But never mind about all that." The sorcerer-king was feeling relaxed again. His own narration of his past achievements gave him confidence, for how could such an enterprise, so brilliant in its conception and so long in the preparation, possibly fail? He smiled and offered the young man a cigar. "Fortescue," he said, "I think your face fits around here. I've had my eye on you for some time now, and I think that you could have a future with us after the expansion programme goes through. How would you like to be the Governor of China?"

"What is the point," said Angantyr Asmundarson, "of having the coat and the trousers the same colour?"

There was no answer to that, Hildy reflected. "I'm sorry," she said, "but I thought..."

"I think they're fine," said Arvarodd firmly, as if to say that Hildy was not to be blamed for the follies of her generation. "What are these holes in the side?"

"They're called pockets," Hildy replied. "You can keep things in them."

"That's brilliant," said the hero Ohtar, who had been familiar to generations of saga audiences as an inveterate loser of penknives and bits of string. "Why did we never think of that?"

"Gimmicky, I call it," grumbled Angantyr, but no one paid him any attention. By and large, the heroes seemed pleased with their new clothes—except of course for Brynjolf the Shape-Changer. He had taken one look at his suit and changed himself into an exact facsimile of himself wearing a similar suit, only with slightly narrower lapels and an extra button at the cuffs. The King's suit, of course, fitted perfectly. Even so, like all the others he looked exactly like a Scandinavian hero in a St Michael suit, or a convict who has just been released.

"While you were away," said the King, taking her aside, "Kotkel found two old friends."

"Old friends?" Hildy said with a frown. "Don't you mean...?"

"Kotkel!"

The wizard came out from behind a tree. He had apparently found no difficulty in coming to terms with the concept of pockets; his were already bulging with small bones and bits of rag. He signalled to the King and Hildy to follow him, and led them out of sight behind a small rise in the ground.

"Meet Zxerp and Prexz," said the King.

At first, Hildy could see nothing. Then she made out two faint pools of light hovering above the grass, like the reflection of one's watch-glass, only rather bigger. "His familiar spirits," explained the King. "It seems they got shut in the mound with us. Probably just as well. They are the servants of the Luck of Caithness."

"Do you mind?" said one of the pools of light.

"Kotkel has been telling me how the thing actually works," the King went on, ignoring the interruption, "and these two have a lot to do with it. The brooch itself is a... what was it?" The wizard made a noise like poultry-shears cutting through a carcass. "A jamming device, that's right. It interferes with the other side's magic. But in order to do this it requires a tremendous supply of positive energy, which is what these two represent."

"Glad to know someone appreciates us," said the pool of light.

"Quarrelsome and unco-operative energy," continued the King sternly, "but energy nevertheless. When Kotkel has put together all the right bits and pieces, he can link these two up to the brooch, and all the enemy's magic will be useless. Once that has been achieved, we can get on with the job. He won't be able to use any of his powers to stop us, or even know we're coming, just like the first time. Then it'll just be the straightforward business of knocking him on the head—always supposing that that will be straightforward, of course. But we'll cross that bridge when we come to it."

"That sounds perfectly marvellous," said Hildy a little nervously. There was, she suspected, something to follow.

"The problem, apparently," continued the King, "lies in getting the right bits and pieces. Kotkel isn't absolutely sure what he'll need. He says he won't know what he wants until he sees it." The King shook his head.

"What sort of things does he need?"

"That," said the King, "is a very good question."

Hildy had been to enough academic seminars to know that a very good question is one to which no one knows the answer—counter-intuitive, to her way of thinking; surely that was the definition of a truly awful question—and her face fell. "So what now?"

"I think the best plan would be for us to go somewhere where the wizard would be likely to see the sort of thing he might want, don't you? And that would probably have to be some sort of town or city."

"But wouldn't that be rather dangerous?"

The King smiled. "I hope so," he said mischievously. "I wouldn't like to think that the greatest heroes in the world had been kept hanging around all this time just to do something perfectly safe."

"What I like least about this country," Danny Bennett started to say; and then he realised that he had said the same about virtually everything worthy of mention that he had encountered since the aircraft which had brought him there had landed. "One of the things about this country which really gets up my nose is the way you can rely on all their schedules, timetables and promises."

"Talk a lot, don't you?" said his senior cameraman. It was raining at Lairg, and the van which was supposed to be meeting them to take them up to Rolfsness had entirely failed to appear. All the shops and the hotel were mysteriously but firmly shut; and the only public building still open, the public lavatory, was filled up with camera and sound equipment, placed there to keep it dry. As a result, the entire crew had been compelled to take what shelter it could, which was not much. There was, of course, a fine view of the loch to keep them entertained; but the presence of ground-level as well as air-to-surface water was no real consolation.

"It's a process of elimination, really," Danny continued. He believed in making the most of whatever entertainment was available, and since the only entertainment in all this wretchedness was his own coruscating wit he was determined to enjoy it to the full. "If they say there's rooms booked at such and such or that the van will be there at whenever, you can rely on that. You can be sure that that hotel is definitely closed for renovation, and that that particular time is when all the vans in Scotland are in for their MoT test. Yes," Danny continued remorselessly, "I like certainty. It gives a sort of shape to the world."

The cameraman felt obliged to make some sort of reply. "I was in Uganda, you know, when they had that coup."

"Oh, yes?"

"We were stuck waiting for a bus then, an' all."

"Really."

"Bloody hot it was. Came eventually, of course."

That, it seemed, was that. Danny opened his briefcase and, shielding its contents against the weather with his sleeve, began to read through his notes one last time. Not that there was much point. Without any material from the archaeologists, who were up at Rolfsness in nice dry tents, he couldn't hope to start planning anything. The one thing that might make this into television was an interview with this missing female who had been the first into the mound. There was probably a perfectly good reason why she had gone missing, of course, and he felt that if he was now to be reduced to a curse-of-the-pharaohs angle it was probably not going to work in any event; still, there is such a thing as the Nose for a Story. He reminded himself, for about the hundredth time that afternoon, that a routine break-in at a Washington hotel had led to the full glory of Watergate. As usual when he was totally desperate, he tried to think in children's-story terms, and as he isolated each element he made a note of it in his soggy notebook. Buried treasure. Mysterious disappearance. Remote Scottish hillside. Vikings. A curse on the buried treasure. The fast-breeder reactor twenty miles or so down the coast. Did anyone happen to have a note of the half-life of radioactive gold?

Through the swirling rain, a small man in a cap was approaching. He asked one of the cameramen if Mr Bennett was anywhere.

"I'm Danny Bennett."

"It's about your van, Mr Bennett. The one you were wanting to go up to Rolfsness," the small man said. "I'm afraid there's been a wee mistake."

"Really?"

"Afraid so, yes."

That seemed to be all the man was prepared to say. So far as he was concerned, it seemed, that would do.

"What sort of a mistake?"

"Well," said the man, "I hired my van out on Tuesday, just for the day, and it hasn't been brought back yet. So it isn't here for you."

"Oh, that's bloody marvellous, that is. Look, can't you get another one? It'll take forever to get one sent up from the nearest town."

"There is only the one van."

Danny wiped the rain out of his eyes. "Is there any chance of its being returned within the next couple of hours? Who hired it? Is it anyone you know?"

"Not at all," said the man. "It was a young woman who hired it. The one who came to look at the diggings up at Rolfsness, the same as yourself."

Danny looked at him sharply. "You mean Miss Frederiksen? The American girl?"

"That's right," said the man. "And now I'll be getting back indoors. It's raining out here," he explained. "Sorry not to be able to help."

"Hold it," Danny shouted, but the man had disappeared.

"What was that about our van?" asked the chief sound-recordist.

"It's not coming," Danny answered shortly.

"Thought so," said the sound-recordist. The news seemed almost to please him. "Just like Zaïre."

"What happened in Zaïre, then?"

"Bleeding van didn't come, that's what." The sound-recordist wandered away and joined his assistant under the questionable cover of a sodden copy of the *Observer*. Danny walked swiftly across to the telephone-box, with which he had dealt before. When you admitted that the thing did actually take English money and not groats or cowrie shells, you had said pretty much everything there was to say in its favour. However, after a while he managed to get through to a van-hire firm in Wick and arranged for substitute transport. Then he reversed the charges to London.

So cheerful was he when he came out of the phone-box that he almost failed to notice that the rain had got heavier and perceptibly colder. He had—at last—the bones of a story. Of course, none of the researchers had come up with anything new about the Frederiksen woman. But they had called up her supervisor, a certain Professor Wood. Apparently, when she telephoned him from Lairg (God help her, Danny thought, if she was using this phone-box), her manner had been rather strange. Incoherent? No, not quite. Excited, of course, about the discovery. But not as excited as you would expect a career archaeologist to sound after having just made the most remarkable discovery ever on the British mainland. How, then? Preoccupied, Professor Wood had thought. As if something was up. Something nice or something nasty? Both. Something strange. Strange as in mysterious? Yes. And she had started to say something about a dragon, but then apparently thought better of it.

Danny Bennett sat down and wrote in "Dragon?" in his list of potential ingredients. Then he stared at it for a while, put down "Query Loch N. Monster double-query?" and crossed it out again. He then started to draw out the complicated wheel-diagrams and flow-diagrams from which his best work had originated. He felt suddenly relaxed and happy, and soon he was using the red biro that meant "theme" and the green felt-tip that signified "potential concept." A television programme was about to be born.

"That's settled, then," said the King. "And if we can't find the bits we want in Wick we'll try somewhere else. And so on, until we do find it."

The heroes had taken their briefing in virtual silence, since no one could think of any viable alternative, Angantyr's suggestion of declaring war on England having been dismissed unanimously at the outset. After a formal toast and prayer to Odin, the heroes sat down to polish their weapons and pack for the journey.

Hjort and Arvarodd, who had already packed, and Brynjoif the Shape-Changer (who didn't need to pack) lingered beside the fire, playing fivestones.

"I don't know about all this," grumbled Hjort. "Complicated. All this stealth and subtlety. I mean, we aren't any good at that sort of thing, are we? What we're good at is belting people about."

"True," said Brynjolf wistfully. "But it doesn't look as if there's much to be gained from belting people about these days."

"Isn't there, though?" replied Hjort emphatically. "I reckon there'll be some belting-about to be done before we're finished here. Don't you agree, Hildy Frederik's-daughter?"

Hildy, who was carrying an armful of blankets over to the van, nodded without thinking.

"You see?" said Hjort. "She's clever, she is."

"That's right enough," said Arvarodd briskly. "There's more to that woman than meets the eye."

"Just as well," said Hjort. "I like them a little thinner myself."

Arvarodd scowled at him. "Well, I do," protested Hjort. "I remember one time in Trondheim—before they pulled down the old market to make way for that new potter's quarter—"

"That girl has brains," said Brynjolf hurriedly. "Brains are what count these days, it seems."

"Dunno what we'll do, then," said Hjort. "Never had much use for brains, personally. Messy. Hard to clean off the axe-blade."

"I reckon she's an asset to the team," went on Brynjolf. "As it is, we're strong on muscle and valour, but a bit short on intellect. There's Himself, of course, and that miserable wizard, but another counsellor on the staff is no bad thing. I reckon we should adopt her."

"What, give her a name and everything?" Hjort looked doubtful.

"Why not?" said Arvarodd enthusiastically. "Except that I can't think of one offhand."

"I can."

"Shut up, Hjort. Yes, we must think about that."

Just then, there was a shout from the lookout.

"Hello," said Hjort, suddenly hopeful. "Do you think that might be trouble?"

"Who knows?" said Arvarodd, buckling on his sword-belt over his jacket and reaching for his bow. "Anything's possible, I suppose. Who's moved my helmet?"

The heroes had enthusiastically formed a shield-ring, looking rather curious perhaps in shields, helmets and two-piece grey polyester suits. The King stalked hurriedly past them. "Not now," he said shortly.

"But, Chief..."

"I said not now. Get out of sight, all of you." He crouched down behind a boulder and looked out over the road. Two vans had stopped there. A moment later Hildy and Starkad (who was the lookout) joined him.

"Just drew up, Chief," whispered Starkad. "You said to call you if—"

"Quite right," replied the King. "Who are they, Hildy Frederik's-daughter?"

Hildy peered hard but could make nothing out. "I don't know," she said. "Probably nobody."

Out of the first van climbed a man in a blue anorak with a map in his hand. He walked up to the top of a bank, looked around him, and made a despairing gesture.

"What's he looking for, do you think?" muttered the King. "You stay here. I'm going to have a look."

Before Hildy could say anything, the King slipped over the boulder and crept down towards the road to where he could hear what the people in the vans were saying. The man in the blue anorak had gone back and was shouting at the driver.

"How was I to know?" replied the driver. "One godforsaken hill-side looks pretty much like another to me."

"We'll have to go back to that last crossroads, that's all," said the man in the blue anorak. "Rolfsness is definitely due north of here."

"Why don't we just go back to Lairg and see if the pub's open?" growled the driver. "It's too dark to film anyhow. We're not going to do any good tonight."

"Because I want to get there as soon as possible and talk to those archaeologists. We've wasted enough time as it is. We've got a schedule to meet, remember."

"Please yourself, Danny boy. Since we've stopped, though, I'm just going to take a leak."

"Hurry up, then, will you?"

To the King's horror, the driver jumped out and walked briskly over the rise. The heroes were just over there, hiding. He closed his eyes and waited. A few moments later, he heard a horrified shout, followed by the war-cries of his guard. The driver came scampering back over the rise, pursued by Hjort, Angantyr and Bothvar Bjarki, with the other heroes at their heels and Hildy trotting behind shouting like a small pony following the hunt.

The senior cameraman, who had been about to open a can of lager, dived for his Aaten and started to film through the side-window. The assistant cameraman also kept his head and groped for a light meter, but Danny Bennett was flinging open the van door. "Not now, for Christ's sake; they're gaining on him," shouted the senior cameraman, but Danny jumped out and ran to meet the driver. As he did so, one of the maniacs in the grey suits stopped and fitted an arrow to his bowstring.

"f8," hissed the assistant cameraman to his colleague. "If only there was time to fit the polariser…"

The King jumped up and shouted, and the archer stayed his hand. The heroes stood their ground while the driver leapt into the van, which pulled away with a screech of tyres, closely followed by the second van. A moment later, they were both out of sight. The heroes sheathed their swords and started to trudge back up the rise.

"Who were they?" the King asked Hildy. "Any idea?"

Hildy had seen the cameras. "Yes," she said nervously. "And I think we're in trouble."

When they had made sure they were not being followed, the camera crew pulled in to the side of the road and all started to talk at once. Only Danny Bennett was silent, and on his face was the look of a man who has just seen a vision of the risen Christ. At last, he was saying to himself, I have been attacked while making a documentary. There must be a story in it; and not just a story but *the* story. Who the men in grey suits had been—CIA, MI5, Special Branch, maybe even the Milk Marketing Board—he could not say, but of one thing he was sure. He was standing on the brink of the greatest documentary ever made. Sweat was running down his face, and in front of his eyes danced the tantalising image of a BAFTA award.

5

Kevin Fortescue, Governor of China elect, met Thorgeir Storm-shepherd at the Docklands stolport and drove him back to Gerrards Garth House. On the way, he made it known that he had been let into the secret of the company's history. Thorgeir seemed surprised at this.

"Why?" he said.

"Mr... the boss said he thought I had a lot of potential. In fact, he's offered me China."

"China?"

"I told him I'd give him my decision in the morning, but I'm pretty sure I'm going to take it. I think it would be a good move for me, career-wise. I've got the impression I'm stagnating rather in Accounts."

Thorgeir made a mental note to water down the sorcerer-king's mead with cold tea before leaving the country next time. He had the feeling that the sorcerer-king was due for a change of direction, career-wise. But it would not be prudent to let the feeling develop into an idea.

The sorcerer-king had come down to the lobby to meet him. "How was Japan?" he asked.

"Susceptible," replied Thorgeir, "highly susceptible. And I did get the semiconductors after all. Just time before the helicopter arrived for a birdie on the last hole."

"Good," grunted the sorcerer-king. "No point in letting things slide just because there's a crisis. You've met our new colleague?"

"Yes," said Thorgeir. "What possessed you to do that?"

"Seemed like a good idea at the time."

"You said that about Copernicus, and look where that got us."

"Anyway," the sorcerer-king said, "he'll come in handy. I've had an idea."

Thorgeir knew that tone of voice. Sometimes it led to good things, sometimes not. "Tell me about it."

"It's like this." The sorcerer-king reached for the mead-bottle, and poured out two large glasses. "Our problem is quite simple, when you look at it calmly. Our enemy has reappeared."

"How do you know that, by the way?"

The sorcerer-king explained about the late-night messages. Thorgeir nodded gravely. "So King Hrolf is back, and that dratted brooch. We could do one of two things. We could go and look for him, or we could wait for him to come to us."

"This is meant to be a choice?"

"We could wait for him to come to us." The sorcerer-king leant back in his chair and put the tips of his fingers together. "If he tries that, he will be at a certain disadvantage."

"Namely?"

The sorcerer-king grinned. "One, he's been asleep for over a thousand years, and things have changed. Two, there's no way he can hope to understand the modern world well enough to endanger us without at the very least a three-year course in business studies and a post-graduate diploma in computers. We are talking about a man who had difficulty adding up on his fingers. Three, he has just crawled out of a mound, in clothes that were the height of fashion a thousand years ago but which would now be a trifle conspicuous. He is likely to be arrested, especially if he strolls into the market-square at Inverness and tries to reclaim his ancient throne. Four, just supposing he makes it and turns up in Reception brandishing a sword, his chances of making it as far as the lift are slim. Very slim. I don't know if you've dropped into Vouchers lately, but I didn't hire them for their mathematical ability."

"Fair enough," said Thorgeir patiently. "So?"

"So, since he's not a complete moron, he's not likely to come to us. So we have to go to him. But on whose terms?"

The sorcerer-king leant forward suddenly and fixed Thorgeir with his bright eyes. This had been a disconcerting conversational gambit a thousand years ago, but Thorgeir was used to it by now. After over a millennium of working with the sorcerer-king, he was getting rather tired of some of his more obvious mannerisms.

"Ours, preferably," Thorgeir said calmly. "Explain."

"His best chance," said the sorcerer-king, "is to use the brooch again. He jams up our systems, blacks out our networks, and fuses all the lights across the entire world. Then he sends us a message—probably, knowing him, by carrier-pigeon—to meet him, alone, on the beach at Melvich for a rematch. Personally, I am out of condition for a trial by combat."

Thorgeir nodded. He, too, had grown soft since his timber-wolf days. Apart from retaining a taste for uncooked mutton and having to shave at least three times a day, he had become entirely anthropomorphous. "We can rule that out, then," he said. "I never did like all that running about and shouting."

"Me neither. So we have one course of action left to us. We find him before he's ready, and we kill him. That ought not to be difficult."

"Agreed."

The sorcerer-king poured out more mead. "In that case, where is he likely to be? He's just risen from the grave, right? And he's on foot. All we need to know is where he was buried, and we've got him. Simple."

Thorgeir smiled, and drank some of his mead. Now it was his turn.

"Over the last thousand years," he said, in a slow measured voice, "I, too, have been turning this problem over in my mind, and the big question is this. Given that King Hrolf was the greatest of the Vikings, and his companions the most glorious heroes of the northern world, how come there is no King Hrolf Earthstar's Saga?"

He paused, for greater dramatic effect, and took a cigar from the box on the desk. Having lit it, he resumed.

"And, for that matter, why are the sagas of all the other heroes of northern Europe so reticent about the greatest event of the heroic age, namely our defeat and overthrow? You'd have thought one of them might have seen fit to mention it."

The sorcerer-king frowned. With the exception of the latest Dick Francis or Jeffrey Archer, he rarely opened a book these days, and he had never been a great reader at the best of times.

"There is no record of the final resting-place of King Hrolf Earthstar," said Thorgeir. "If there had been, I'd have bought the place up and built something heavy and substantial over it five hundred years ago. There is no trace or scrap of folk tradition in Caithness about King Hrolf or the Great Battle or anything else; just a lot of drivel about Bonnie Prince Charlie. The only clue is a single placename, Rolfsness, which happens to be the site of a certain battle."

"There you are, then," said the sorcerer-king.

"There you aren't. I've been back hundreds of times. If there had been anything there, I'd have felt it. And there is no record whatsoever of what became of Hrolf Earthstar while we were floating around as disembodied spirits. He just vanished off the face of the earth. For all I know, he could have sailed west and discovered America."

"You think he's in America?"

Thorgeir closed his eyes and counted up to ten. "No, I think he's probably somewhere in Europe. But where in Europe I couldn't begin to say."

The sorcerer-king smiled. "You'd better start looking, then, hadn't you?" he said, and poured himself another drink.

"Those people," said Hildy, "were from television."

"What's that?" asked one of the heroes.

Hildy racked her brains for a concise reply. "Like a saga, only with lights and pictures. By this time tomorrow, everyone in the country will know we're here."

The King frowned. "That could be serious," he said. "We can't have that."

"But how can we stop it?"

"That's easy." The King stood up suddenly. "Where do you think they've gone?"

"Back the way they came, probably to Lairg. They'll want to get the film off to London as quickly as possible. But—"

"We can't make any mistake about this. Kotkel!"

From a small pouch in his pocket, the wizard took a couple of small bones and threw them in the air. As they landed, he stooped down and peered at them intently. Then he pointed towards the south and made a noise like a buzz-saw.

"They went that way," the King translated.

Hildy had never been fond of driving, and at speeds over thirty miles an hour her skill matched her enthusiasm. But somehow the van stayed on or at least close to the road as they pursued the camera crew along the narrow road to Lairg, and caught up with them in a deserted valley beside a river.

"What do we do now?" Hildy asked as the van bumped alarmingly over a cattle-grid.

"Board them," suggested Angantyr. "Or ram them. Who cares?"

"Certainly not," Hildy shouted.

"Stop here," the King said. "Brynjolf!"

"Not again," pleaded the shape-changer. "Last time I sprained my ankle."

No sooner had Danny Bennett realised that the second van had suddenly stopped for no reason than he became aware of a huge eagle, apparently trying to smash the windscreen. The driver swore, and braked fiercely, but the bird merely attacked again, this time cracking the glass. The senior sound-recordist, who had done countless nature programmes in his time, was thoroughly frightened and tried to hide under his seat. The eagle attacked a third time, and the windscreen shattered. The driver put up both his hands to protect his eyes, and the van veered off the road into a ditch.

When Danny had recovered from the shock of impact, he tried to open his door, but a man in a grey suit with a helmet covering his face opened it for him and showed him the blade of a large axe. If this was the Milk Marketing Board, they were probably exceeding their statutory authority.

"Who are you?" Danny said.

"Bothvar Bjarki," said the man with the axe. "Are you going to surrender, or shall we fight for a bit?"

"I'd rather surrender, if it's all the same to you."

"Be like that," said Bothvar Bjarki.

The camera crew were rounded up, while Starkad, apparently without effort, pushed the two vans into a small clump of trees and covered them with branches. The King had found a hollow in the hillside which was out of sight of the road, and the prisoners were led there and tied up securely. Meanwhile, at Hildy's direction, Starkad and Hjort found the cans of film and smashed them to pieces. When Hildy was satisfied that all the film was destroyed, the heroes got back into their vans and drove away.

As the sound of the engine receded in the distance, the assistant cameraman broke the silence in the hollow.

"Reminds me of the time I was in Afghanistan," he said.

Danny Bennett asked what had happened that time in Afghanistan.

"We got tied up," said the assistant cameraman.

"And what happened?"

"Someone came and untied us," replied the assistant cameraman. "Mind you, that time we were doing a report for 'Newsnight.'"

Danny had never worked for "Newsnight," and people had been known to die of exposure on Scottish hillsides. He pulled on the rope around his wrists, but there was no slack in it. A posthumous BAFTA award, he reflected, was probably better than no BAFTA award at all, but awards are not everything.

"If I can raise my wrists," he said to the assistant cameraman, "you could chew through the ropes and I could untie you."

"I've got a better idea," said the cameraman. "You could shut your bloody row and we could get some sleep while we're waiting to be untied...."

"But perhaps," Danny hissed, "nobody's going to come and untie us."

"Listen," said the assistant cameraman fiercely, "I dunno what union you belong to, but my union is going to get me a great deal of money from the Beeb for being tied up like this, and the longer I'm tied up, the more I'll get. So just shut your noise and let's get on with it, all right?"

Danny's head was beginning to hurt. He closed his eyes, leant back against the assistant cameraman (who was starting to snore) and tried to make some sense of what was happening to him.

The men had been partially disguised as Vikings, with helmets and shields and swords; but they had been wearing grey suits, which tended to spoil the illusion. They had, as he had expected, destroyed the film; but that was all. Not even an attempt to warn him off. Only the barest minimum of physical violence. And then there was that girl—Hildy Frederiksen, beyond doubt. Who was she working for, and what lay behind it all? And where in God's name had they got that incredible bird from?

The obvious clues pointed at the CIA. Whatever they do in which-ever part of the world, they always wear grey suits. They buy them by the hundred from J. C. Penney or Man at CIA. That would tie in with the Kennedy connection—at last, after all these years, they were trying to silence him—but the Viking motif was beyond him, unless it was some-thing to do with that tiresome ship. Or perhaps they were in fact wearing protective clothing (the nuclear power station angle) *made to look like* Viking helmets. In which case, why? Unless they were all going on to a fancy-dress party afterwards. The more he thought about it, the more inexplicable it seemed; and the more baffled he became, the more con-vinced he was that something major was going on. All the great conspira-cies of history have been bizarre, usually because of the incompetence of the leading conspirators. As the long hours passed, he traced each convo-luted possibility to its illogical conclusion, but for once no pattern emerged in his mind. At last he fell asleep and began to dream. He seemed to hear voices coming from a small pool of light hovering overhead.

"Seventy-five to me, then," said one voice, "plus the repique on your declaration, doubled. Your throw."

Danny sat up. He wasn't dreaming.

"Six and a four. I take your dragon, and that's forty-five to me. Four, five, six,—oh, sod it, go to gaol."

The rest of the crew were asleep. Danny sat absolutely still. The hair on the back of his neck was beginning to curl, and he found it hard to breathe.

"Trade you Hlidarend for Oslo Fjord and seventy points," said the first voice. "That way you'll have the set."

"No chance," said the second voice. "Up three, down the serpent four five six, and that's check."

"No, it isn't."

"Yes, it is."

The voices were silent for a while, and Danny swallowed hard. Perhaps it was just the bump he had suffered when the van crashed.

"Good idea, that," said the first voice.

"Brilliant," replied the second voice sarcastically. "You don't imagine we're going to get away with it, do you?"

"Why not?"

"Because he'll notice we're not there, that's why. And he's not going to be pleased."

The first voice sniggered. "He'll be miles away by now. And the rest of them. They're going to Inverness. He won't be able to reach us from there."

"Where's Inverness?"

"I haven't the faintest idea. But it sounds a very long way away to me."

The second voice sighed audibly. "You and your ideas," it said.

"Well, what choice did we have?" replied the first voice irritably. "I don't know about you, but I didn't fancy having copper wire twisted round my neck and being linked up to that perishing brooch. Last time, my ears buzzed for a week."

"He'll be back. Just you wait and see."

Another silence, during which Danny thought he could hear a rattling sound, like dice being thrown.

"Well," said the second voice, "we'd better make ourselves scarce anyhow. No good sitting about here."

"Just because I'm winning..."

"Who says you're winning?"

The voices subsided into a muted squabbling, so that Danny could not make out the words. He longed for the voices to stop, and suddenly they did.

The reason for this was that Prexz had just caught the vibrations from an underground cable a mile or so away to the south. He had no idea what it might be, but he was hungry, and it seemed irresistible.

"Put the game away, Zxerp," he said suddenly. "I can feel food."

But Zxerp didn't answer. "I said I can feel food," Prexz repeated, but Zxerp glowed warningly at him.

"There's a man over there listening to us," he whispered.

"Why didn't you say?"

"I've only just noticed him, haven't I?"

Prexz cleared his throat and turned his glow up a little. "Excuse me," he said.

"Yes?" replied Danny.

"Would you happen to know anything about a cable running under the ground about a mile from here and going due north?"

"I would imagine," Danny replied, his heart pounding, "that it has something to do with the nuclear power station on the coast."

"*Nuclear* Power?" Prexz said. "Stone me. Did you hear that, Zxerp? Nouvelle cuisine."

The two pools of light rose up into the air and seemed to dance there for a moment.

"By the way," said Prexz, "if the wizard comes looking for us..."

"The wizard?"

"That's right, the wizard. If he comes looking for us, you haven't seen us."

"Before you go," whispered Danny faintly, "do you think you might possibly untie these ropes?"

"Certainly," said Prexz. As he did so, Danny was aware of a terrible burning sensation in his hands and arms. "Is that all right?"

"That's fine, thank you," Danny gasped. Then he fainted.

"What a strange man," Prexz said. "Right, off we go."

The Dow up three—that won't last—early coffee down, tin's still a shambles, and soon they'll be giving copper away with breakfast cereal. Who needs to buy a newspaper to learn that?

Thorgeir had adapted splendidly to most things in the course of his extremely long life, but the knack of reading the *Financial Times* on a train still eluded him. How one was supposed to control the huge unruly pages was a complete mystery. He was sorely tempted to get the boss to buy up the damned paper, just to make them print it in a smaller format. With a grunt, he retrieved the news headlines. Earthquake in Senegal, elections in New Zealand, massive archaeological find in Scotland...

Massive archaeological find in Scotland. Like a raindrop trickling down a window, his gaze slid down the pink surface and locked on to the small paragraph. At Rolfsness, in Caithness; archaeologists claim to have unearthed a ninth-century Viking royal ship-burial. Unprecedented quantities of artefacts including treasure, armour and weapons. Gold prices, however, are unlikely to be affected.

His fellow-passengers saw the small thin-faced man go suddenly white as he read his *FT*, and assumed that he had failed to get out of cocoa before the automatic doors closed. Thorgeir tossed the paper down on the seat beside him, and fumbled in his briefcase for his radiophone.

"Have you seen it?" he said. "In the paper?"

"What are you going on about, Thorgeir?" said the sorcerer-king, his voice faint and crackly at the other end.

"Front page of the *FT*."

"Hang on, I've got that here." Thorgeir could picture the sorcerer-king retrieving the paper from the early-morning mess on his desk.

"The news section, about a third of the way down."

"You've called me up to tell me about the Chancellor?"

"Stick the Chancellor; it's the bit below that."

When the sorcerer-king panicked, he tended to do so in Old Norse, which is a language admirably suited to the purpose, if you are not in any hurry. Thorgeir listened impatiently for a while, then interrupted.

"Who have we got in archaeology?"

There was silence at the other end of the line. Twelve hundred years he's managed without a Filofax, reflected Thorgeir. The moment he gets one, nobody knows where they are any more. Marvellous.

"In Scotland?"

"Preferably."

"There's a Professor Wood at St Andrews. What do you want an archaeologist for, anyway? I'm going over to Vouchers."

Thorgeir frowned. "No, don't do that," he said quietly. "Get Professor Wood. It says in the paper he's in charge of this dig at Rolfsness. Tell him I'll meet him there."

"I'm still going over to Vouchers."

"You do whatever you like. By the way, where's this train I'm on going to? I've forgotten."

"Manchester."

"Thanks." Thorgeir switched off the phone and consulted his train timetable. He was feeling excited now that the enemy had been contacted, although he still could not imagine how he had overlooked something as obvious as a ship-burial on his many visits to that dreary place. Then it occurred to him that any wizard with Grade III or above would have been able to conceal the traces of life in such a mountainous and isolated spot from any but the most perceptive observer, and King Hrolf's wizard had been a top man. Pity they hadn't headhunted him back in the 870s. What was that wizard's name? Something about the pot and the kettle.

In the age of the supersonic airliner, a man can have breakfast in

London and lunch in New York (if his digestion can stand it); but to get from Manchester to the north coast of Scotland between the waxing and the waning of the moon still requires not only dedication and cunning but also a modicum of good luck, just as it did in the Dark Ages. By the time Thorgeir had worked out an itinerary, the view from the train window had that tell-tale hint of First World War battlefield about it that informs the experienced traveller that he's passing through Stockport. Thorgeir closed his briefcase and leant his head back against the cushions. Kotkel. Hrolf's wizard was called Kotkel, and he had had quite a reputation around Orkney in the seventies. Winner for three years in succession of the Osca (Orkney Sorcerers' Craft Association) for Best Hallucination. No slouch with a rune, either.

"That's all I needed," groaned Thorgeir.

Telephone wires were humming all over Britain, for they had just had to shut down the nuclear reactor on the north coast of Scotland. There was, it had been decided, no need to evacuate the area; there was no danger. It was just that someone had contrived to mislay the entire output of electricity from the plant for just over half an hour. Even the lights had gone out all over the building.

"Has anyone," the controller kept asking, "got a fifty pence for the meter?" The senior engineers led him away and got him an aspirin, while his deputy made another attempt to get through to Downing Street.

No one had yet got around to checking the underground cable that ran due south from the plant, which was where the fault actually lay. It lay on its back, its eyes closed, and it was singing softly to itself.

"For ye defeated," it sang,
"King Hrothgar's army,
And sent them home,
To think again."

The fault's companion was scarcely in a better state. He had never even claimed to be able to hold his electricity, and he had very nearly been sick. It was just as well that he had not, or the entire National Grid would have been thrown into confusion. He gurgled, and went to sleep.

"Prexz," said the fault, "I just thought of something."

Prexz moaned, and rolled on to his face, vowing never to touch another volt so long as he lived.

"How would it be," Zxerp said, "how would it be if..."

"Don't want any more," mumbled Prexz. "Had too much already.

Drunk. Totally drunk. Going to join Electronics Anonymous soon as I feel a little better."

"Don't be like that," whined Zxerp.

"Think they put something in it at the generator," continued Prexz. "Going to sleep it off. Shut up. Go away."

"Wimp," snarled Zxerp. "You're no fun, Prexz. Don't like you any more."

Prexz had started to snore, sending clouds of undecipherable radio signals tojam up the airwaves of Europe.

"I don't like it here," said Zxerp. "I want to go home."

No reply. Zxerp shook his head, which made him feel worse, and he fell heavily against the cable. There was nothing in it, and he was feeling terribly thirsty. He was also feeling guilty.

"Poor old wizard," he said. "Always been good to us. Never a cross word in twelve hundred years. Prexz, shouldn't we go and find the wizard? Shouldn't have run away from the wizard like that. Not right."

Zxerp started to cry, and negative ions trickled down the side of his nose, electrolysing it. At the government listening post in Cheltenham, a codes expert picked up his tears on the short-wave band and rushed off to tell his chief that the Russians had developed a new cipher.

Thorgeir heard about the closedown of the power station over the radio as he drove his hired car past Loch Loyal. The shock made him swerve, and he nearly ended up in the water.

He pulled over and examined an Ordnance Survey map, but that told him nothing he did not already know, and his own personal map, which was traced in blood on soft goat skin and was somewhat out of date. But a call to London on his radiophone told him all he needed to know, and he asked that a helicopter should be laid on to meet him at Tongue. He also enquired whether there was an equivalent to the Vouchers department at the company's Glasgow office.

"Yes? Then, send a couple of them up. Tell them to bring plenty of vouchers."

He pushed down the aerial so violently that he nearly snapped it off, and drove on towards the coast. As he turned a bend in the road beside a small clump of trees, he noticed and just managed to avoid a patch of broken glass in the middle of the carriageway. In doing so he stalled the engine, and while he was persuading it to start again his eye fell on the windscreen of a van among the trees. Someone had apparently been to the trouble of covering this van up with tree-branches. For some reason this seemed terribly significant, and Thorgeir went to investigate.

What he found was two vans with broken windscreens and a good deal of smashed camera gear. As he stood scratching his head, the wind carried back to him what sounded like an argument from the hill on the other side of the road. Something about due north having been over those hills there ten minutes ago, and it reminded someone of that time in Iraq.

Thorgeir looked at his watch. He had plenty of time before he was due to meet the helicopter, and he was starting to get a tingling sensation all down the side of his nose, where his whiskers had once been.

"Told you someone would come and find us," croaked the assistant cameraman. "Just like that time in Cambodia."

"That wasn't Cambodia," said the assistant sound-recordist, "that was Kurdestan."

"We *started* in Iraq," replied the senior cameraman. "That's the bloody point."

"Thank you," gasped Danny Bennett to the stranger. He was hoarse from arguing. For a long time, he had thought that he had imagined the sound of a car engine. "We've been wandering round in circles all day. That fool of a cameraman's got one of those compasses you buy at filling stations, and we'd been walking for hours before we realised that it was being attracted by his solar calculator."

"Are those your vans up there?" said the stranger.

"Yes." Suddenly, Danny seemed to notice something about his rescuer and recoiled violently.

"What's up?" said the stranger.

"Sorry," Danny said. "It's just that suit you're wearing."

"My suit?" The stranger looked affronted.

"It's a very nice suit," Danny said. "It's just that it's grey. But it's not from Marks & Spencer."

"I should think not," said the stranger irritably. "Brooks Brothers, this is. OK, the lapels are a bit on the narrow side, but—"

"It's a long story," Danny said. "And you'd probably think I was mad."

"I already think you're mad," said the stranger, smoothing out the creases on his sleeve, "so what have you got to lose?"

So Danny told him. He explained about the ship-burial, the first attack, the second attack, the eagle and the men in the grey suits. The stranger seemed entirely unsurprised and utterly convinced by it all; in fact he seemed so interested that Danny was on the point of telling him about his President Kennedy theory when the stranger interrupted him.

"Was there an old man with them, by any chance? Very old indeed, with a horrible squeaky voice?"

"Yes," Danny said, "I think so."

"And what about the others?" The stranger described the men in grey suits. Danny nodded feebly.

"Do you know them, then?" he asked.

"Oh, yes. They and I go way back."

Danny dug his fingernails into the palms of his hands. "Who are they, then?"

The stranger grinned in a way that reminded Danny of an Alsatian he had been particularly afraid of as a boy. "I don't really think you want to know," he said. "Not in your present state of mind."

"Yes, I do," Danny said urgently. "And what has Hildy Frederiksen got to do with it?"

The stranger raised an eyebrow. "Who's Hildy Frederiksen?"

"The archaeologist. The one who found the burial. She's with them."

"You don't say." The stranger had stopped grinning. "Listen," he said, taking hold of Danny's sleeve.

"Yes?"

"Who do *you* think those men are?" Danny blinked twice. "Are they from the CIA?"

"In a sense. You're a TV producer, Mr...."

"Bennett, Danny Bennett."

"I envy you, Mr Bennett. You've stumbled on to something big here. Really big."

"Have I?"

The stranger nodded. "This is once-in-a-career stuff. If I were you, I'd forget all about that ship-burial and get after the men in the grey suits."

"Really?" The roof of Danny's mouth felt like sandpaper.

"Just don't quote me, that's all. The road's over there. It was good meeting you." The stranger started to walk away.

"So you don't think I've gone crazy, then?" Danny called after him.

"No," replied the stranger.

"I didn't tell you about the little blue lights, did I?"

The stranger stopped and turned round. Strange-shaped ears that man has, Danny thought. Almost pointed.

"Tell me about the little blue lights," said the stranger.

"If you must hum," said Prexz, "hum quietly."

"I'm not humming," Zxerp replied, "you are."

"No, I'm not. And do you mind not shouting? I feel like I've got a short just above my left eye."

"It must be that cable, then," replied his companion. "Humming."

"Will you shut up about that cable?"

Prexz closed his eyes and resolved to keep perfectly still for at least half an hour. If that didn't work, he could try a brief electric storm.

"Prexz."

"Now what?"

"It's not the cable. It's coming from up there."

Prexz opened his eyes. "You're right," he said. "And it isn't a humming. More like a buzzing, really."

"I don't like it, Prexz. Shouldn't we take a look?"

"Please yourself," grunted Prexz. He lay back against the cable and dozed off. Zxerp tried to follow his example, but the buzzing grew louder. Then it stopped. After a moment, another sound took its place. Prexz sat upright with a jerk.

"It's that perishing wizard," he groaned.

"It's not, you know," whispered Zxerp. "Do you know who I think that is?"

The two chthonic spirits stared at each other in horror as the summons grew louder and louder, until they could resist it no longer. Something seemed to be dragging them up to the surface. As they emerged into the violent light of the sun, they were seized by strong hands and copper wire was twisted around their necks. They were trapped.

6

After breakfasting on barbecued rabbit and lager (from the wizard's now perpetually refilling can) in the ruined broch just south of the Loch of Killimster, King Hrolf Earthstar and his heroes—and heroine—drove into Wick in search of thin copper wire, resistors, crocodile clips and other assorted bits and pieces needed by the wizard for connecting the two chthonic spirits up to the Luck of Caithness. Of course, it had not occurred to any of them to check that the two spirits were still in the small sandalwood box into which the wizard had sealed them with a powerful but imperfectly remembered spell; but even a wizard cannot be expected to think of everything.

The fog and low cloud, which had been hovering over the tops of the mountains for the last few days, had come down thickly during the night, and Hildy, who was not used to driving under such conditions, made slow progress along the road to Wick. The town itself seemed, as usual, deserted, and Hildy felt little trepidation about leading her unlikely looking party through the streets. As it happened, such of the local people as were out and about did stop for a moment and speculate who these curious men in grey suits might be; but after a little subdued discussion they decided that they were a party of Norwegians off one of the rigs, which would account for their uniform dress and long shaggy beards.

There is an electrical-goods shop in Wick, and if you have the determination of a hero used to long and apparently impossible quests you can eventually find it, although it will of course be closed for lunch when you do.

"I remember there used to be a mead-hall just along from here," said Angantyr Asmundarson. His shoes were hurting, and he liked the town even less than he had the last time he had visited it, about twelve hundred years previously. "They used to do those little round shellfish that look like large pink woodlice."

"I thought you hated them," said the King. "You always used to make a fuss when we had them back at the castle."

"I never said I did like them," Angantyr replied. "And, anyway, I don't expect the mead-hall's there any more."

Oddly enough it was, or at least there was a building set aside for roughly the same purpose standing on the site of it. Hildy was most unwilling that the company should go in, but the King overruled her; if Angantyr didn't get something to eat other than rabbit pretty soon, he suggested, he would start to whine, and that he could do without.

"All right, then," Hildy said, "but be careful."

"In what way?" asked the King.

Hildy could not for the moment think of anything that the heroes should or should not do. She tried to imagine a roughly similar situation, but all she could think of was Allied airmen evading the Germans in occupied France, and she had never been keen on war films. "Don't draw attention to yourselves," she said, "and keep your voices down." As she said this, something that had been nagging away at the back of her mind resolved itself into a query.

"By the way," she asked the King, as she brought back a tray laden with twelve pints of Tennants lager and twelve packets of scampi fries, "how is it that I can understand everything you say? It's almost as if you were speaking modern English. You should be talking in Old Norse or something, shouldn't you?"

"We are," said the King, wiping froth from the edges of his moustache. "I thought you were, too. And what's English?"

At this point, the wizard made a sound like a slate-saw. The King raised an eyebrow, then translated for Hildy's benefit.

"He says it's a language-spell he put on us all. He says it would save a great deal of trouble. Unfortunately," the King went on, "he couldn't put one on himself. He tried, using a mirror, but it didn't work. He's now got a mirror that can speak all living and dead languages, but even we can't understand most of what he says because he's got this speech impediment and he mumbles."

Not for the first time, Hildy wondered whether the King was having a joke at her expense, or whether her new friends were just extremely different from anyone she had ever met before. However, the King's explanation seemed to be as good as any, and so she let it go. The thirteen helpings of grilled salmon and chips she had ordered (and paid for; the money wasn't going to last much longer at this rate) arrived and were soon disposed of, despite the heroes' lack of familiarity with the concept of the fork. However, even though they did not know what to use them for, they displayed considerable unwillingness to give them back, and Hildy had to insist. All in all, she was glad to get them all out of the hotel before they made a scene.

"And who do you suppose they were?" asked the waitress as she cleared away the plates.

"English, probably," said the barman.

"Ah," replied the waitress, "that would account for it."

By now the keeper of the electrical shop had returned from lunch, and Hildy, the wizard and the King went in while the heroes waited outside. After a great deal of confusion, they got what they wanted, and Hildy led them back to where the van was parked. She considered stopping and buying some postcards to send to her family back in America, but decided not to; "Having a wonderful time saving the world from a twelve-hundred-year-old sorcerer" would be both baffling and, just for the moment, untrue. She did, however, nip into a camping shop and buy herself a new anorak. Her paddock-jacket was getting decidedly grubby and it smelt rather too much of boiled rabbit for her liking.

"Where to now?" she asked, as they all climbed into the van.

"Home," said the King.

Hildy frowned. "You mean Rolfsness?" she asked. "The ship? I don't think—"

"No, no," said the King, "I said Home."

"Where's that?"

The King, who had already grasped the principle of Ordnance Survey maps, pointed to a spot just to the northeast of Bettyhill. "There," he said.

"Why?" Hildy asked.

"I live there," replied the King simply. "I haven't been home for a long time."

Hildy looked again at the map. It was a long way away, and she was tired of driving. But the King insisted. They filled up with petrol (Hildy now had enough Esso tokens for a new flashlight, but she couldn't be bothered) and set off. Their road lay first through Thurso and then past the now functioning nuclear power station, and the turning for Rolfsness; but the area seemed deserted. Hildy wondered why.

Eventually they crossed the Swordly Burn and took the turning the King had indicated. There were quite a few houses along the narrow road, but Hildy found a small knot of trees where the van could be hidden, and they packed all their goods into the rucksacks she had bought and the heroes wrapped blankets over their shields and weapons. The company looked, Hildy thought, like a cross between an attempt on Everest and a party of racegoers with a picnic lunch.

They had walked about a mile from the road when they came to a small narrow-necked promontory overlooking the Bay of Swordly. Below them the cliffs fell away to the grey and unfriendly sea, and Hildy began to feel distinctly unwell since she suffered from attacks of vertigo. There was only a rudimentary track heading north, over a broad arch of rock, apparently leading nowhere. Hildy hoped that the King knew where he was going.

Suddenly the King scrambled off the path and seemed to disappear into the rock. The heroes and the wizard followed, leaving Hildy all alone on the top of the cliff. She was feeling thoroughly ill and not at all heroic. This was rather like going for walks with her father when she was a child.

"Are you coming, then?" she heard the King's voice shouting, but could not tell where it came from.

"Where are you?" she shouted.

"Down here." The sound seemed to be coming from directly below. She tried to look down, but her legs started to give way under her and she stopped. After what seemed a very long time, the King reappeared and beckoned to her.

"There's a passage just here leading down to the castle," he said. "Mind where you put your feet. I never did get around to having those steps cut."

This time Hildy summoned all her courage and followed him. A door in the rock, like a small porthole, stood open before her, and she dived through it.

"That's the back door," said the King, pulling it shut. It closed with a soft click, and the tunnel was suddenly pitch-dark. The passage was not long, and it came out in a sort of rocky amphitheatre perched on the edge of the cliff. Just below them were the ruins of ancient masonry; but all of a much later period, medieval or perhaps sixteenth-century. The amphitheatre itself, with a deep natural cave behind, was little more than a slight modification of the original rock.

"I see they've mucked up the front door," said the King with a sigh. "Still, that's no great loss." He looked out over the sea, and then turned back to Hildy. "Unless you know what to look for," he said, "this place is invisible except from the sea, and now the front gate's been taken out the only way down here is that door we came through, which is also impossible to find unless you know about it. Someone's been building down there, but this part is exactly as it was. Let's see if the hall's been got at."

He led the way into the cave. The heroes had evidently had the same idea, for another small door had been thrown open, and the sound of voices came out of it. Hildy followed the King into a wide natural chamber.

In the middle of the chamber was a long stone table, on which Starkad and Arvarodd were standing, poking at the ceiling with their spears. "Just getting the windows open," Arvarodd grunted, "only the wretched thing seems to have got stuck," and he pushed open a stone trapdoor, flooding the chamber with light. Hildy looked about her in amazement. The walls were covered in rich figured tapestries, looking as if they had just been made but recognisable as typical products of the ninth century. The table was laid with gold and silver plates and drinking-horns, with places for about a hundred. Beside the table was a hearth running the length of the chamber, and the rest of the floor was covered in dry heather that crackled under Hildy's feet. Against the wall stood a dozen huge chests with massive iron locks, and in the corners of the room were stacks of spears and weapons. Everything appeared to be perfectly preserved, but the air in the chamber was decidedy musty.

"The doors and shutters on the windows are airtight," explained the King. "We knew a thing or two about building in my day."

"What is this place?" Hildy asked.

"This," said the King with a hint of pride in his voice, "is the Castle of Borve, one of my two strongholds. The other is at Tongue, but I never did like it much. The Castle of Borve is totally impregnable, and the view is rather better, if you like seascapes. On a clear day you can see Orkney."

The heroes had got the chests open, and were busily rummaging about in them for long-lost treasures; favourite cloaks and comfortable shoes. Someone came up with a cask of mead on which a preserving spell had been laid, while Arvarodd, who had lit a small fire at one end of the hearth, was roasting the last of the sausages Hildy had bought in Marks & Spencer at Inverness. The heroes had discovered that they liked sausages.

"The Castle of Borve," said the King, "was built for my father, Ketil Trout, by Thorkel the Builder. My father was a bit of a miser, I'm afraid, and, since he was forever going to war with all and sundry, usually very hard up. So when he commissioned the castle from Thorkel, the finest builder of his day, he stipulated that if there was anything wrong with the castle on delivery Thorkel's life should be forfeit and all his property should pass to the King. Actually, that was standard practice in the building industry then."

Hildy, who had had bad experiences with builders in her time, nodded approvingly.

"The trouble was that there was nothing at all wrong with the castle," the King continued, "and Ketil was faced with the horrible prospect of having to pay for the place, which he could not afford to do. So he persuaded the builder to go out into the bay with him by ship, on the pretext of inspecting the front gate. Meanwhile my mother hung a rope over the front ramparts, which, seen from the sea, looked like a crack in the masonry. Ketil pointed this out to Thorkel as a fault in the work, and poor old Thorkel was left with no alternative but to tie the anchor to his leg and jump in the sea. This was really rather fortuitous, since apart from my father he was the only other person to know the secret of the back door, which we came in by. Oddly enough, ever after my father had terrible trouble getting anyone to do any work on the place, which was a profound nuisance in winter when the guttering tended to get blocked."

The heroes had drunk half of the enchanted mead and were beginning to sing. The King frowned. "Anyway," he said briskly, "that's the Castle of Borve for you. Back to business."

He clapped his hands, and the heroes cleared a space on the table. The wizard laid out the various items he had obtained in Wick, and the King laid the dragon-brooch beside them. The wizard set to work with some tools he had retrieved from one of the chests, and soon the brooch was festooned with short lengths of wire, knitted into an intricate pattern. Then he made a sign with his hand, and Ohtar brought over the sandalwood box. The wizard picked it up, shook it and held it to his ear.

"Now what?" demanded the King impatiently. The wizard made a subdued noise, like a very small lathe.

"You haven't!" shouted the King.

The wizard nodded, made a sound like a distant dentist's drill, and hid his face in his hands.

"I don't believe it," said the King in fury. "You stupid... Oh, get out of my sight." The wizard promptly vanished, turning himself into a tiny spider hanging from the ceiling.

"What's the matter?" Hildy asked.

"He's only gone and lost them, that's all," growled the King. "Here, give me that box."

He threw open the lid, but there was nothing inside except the chewed-up remains of a couple of torch-batteries Hildy had put in for the two spirits to eat. For a moment there was total silence in the chamber; then the King threw the box on the ground and jumped on it.

"Now look what you've made me do," he roared at the spider swinging unhappily from the roof.

"But what's happened?" Hildy wailed. She felt that she was in grave danger of being forgotten about.

"I'll tell you what's ruddy well happened," said the King. "This idiotic wizard has let those two spirits escape, that's what. He was supposed to have sealed them in his magic elf-box...." The King stepped out of the smashed fragments of the magic elf-box, which would henceforth be incapable of holding so much as a bad dream. "Now we've got nothing to work the brooch with. Without them it's useless."

The heroes all started to complain at once, and even the spider began cheeping sadly. The King banged his fist on the table and shouted for quiet.

"Let's all stay calm, shall we?" he muttered. "Let's all sit down, like reasonable human beings, and discuss this sensibly." He followed his own suggestion, and the rest of the heroes, still murmuring restlessly like the sea below them, did likewise. The spider scuttled down his gossamer thread and perched on the lip of the King's great drinking-horn.

"All right, Kotkel," snapped the King to the spider, "you've made your point. You can come back now."

The wizard reappeared, hanging his grizzled head in shame, and took his place at the King's left hand. The company that had, a few moments ago, resembled nothing so much as a football team stranded in the middle of nowhere with no beer had become, as if by some subtler magic, the King's Household, his council in peace and war. A shaft of sunlight broke through the stone-framed skylight into the chamber, highlighting the King's face like a spotlight—Thorkel the Builder had planned the effect deliberately, calculating where the sun would be in relation to the surrounding mountains at the time when the Master of Borve would be likely to be seated in his high place. Hildy found herself sitting, by accident or design, in the Counsellor's place at his right hand, so that such of the sunlight as the King could spare fell on her commonplace features. A feeling of profound awe and responsibility came over her, and she resolved, come what may, to acquit herself as well as she could in the King's service.

Arvarodd of Permia, who carried the King's harp, and Angantyr Asmundarson, who was his standard-bearer, rose to their feet and pronounced in unison that Hrolf Ketilsson Earthstar, absolute in Caithness and Sutherland, Lord of the Isles, held court for policy in the fastness of his House; let those who could speak wisely do so. There was total silence, as befitted such an august moment. Then there was more silence, and Hildy realised that this was because nobody could think of anything to say.

"Well, come on, then," said the King. "You were all so damned chatty a moment ago. Let's be having you."

To his feet rose Bothvar Bjarki, and Hildy suddenly remembered that he had been the adviser of the great king Kraki, devising for him stratagems without number, which generations of skalds had kept evergreen in memory.

"We could go back and look for them," suggested Bothvar Bjarki.

"Oh, sit down and shut up," said the King impatiently. "Has anyone got any *sensible* suggestions?"

Bothvar sat down and started to mutter to himself. Angantyr was sniggering, and Bothvar gave him a look. Hildy, thoroughly bewildered, realised that she was on her feet and speaking.

"Perhaps," she stammered, "the wizard can find them. Wasn't there that bit in *Arvarodd's Saga* where someone put a seer-stone to his eye...?"

"Have you got a seer-stone, Kotkel?" demanded the King, turning to the wizard. Arvarodd, sitting opposite Hildy, seemed to be blushing slightly. He leant across the table and whispered: "Actually, I made that bit up. I wanted a sort of mystical scene to counterpoint all the starkly realistic bits. You see, the structure to demand..." Hildy found herself nodding, as she so often had at Cambridge parties.

The wizard was turning out his pockets. From the resulting pile of unsightly junk, he picked out a small blue pebble, heart-shaped, with a hole through the middle. He breathed on it, grunted some obscure spell, and set it in his eye like a watchmaker's lens.

"Well?" said the King impatiently.

There was a sound like a carborundum wheel from the wizard. "Interference," whispered Arvarodd. "Ever since they privatised it—"

But the wizard shook his head and took out the stone. Then he leant across the King and offered it to Hildy.

"Go on," the King said. "It doesn't hurt."

Hildy closed her mouth, which had fallen open, and took the stone from the wizard's hand. It felt strangely warm, like a seat on a train that someone has just left, and Hildy felt very reluctant to touch it. But she held it up to her eye, squinting through the hole. To her amazement, and horror, she found that she could see a picture through it, as if it were a keyhole in a closed door.

She saw a tower of grey stone and glass, completely unfamiliar at first; then she recognised it as an office-block. Pressing the stone hard against her eye, she found that she could see in through one of the windows, and beyond that through the open door of an office. Inside the office was a glass case, like a fish-tank, and inside that were two pools of light. There were wires leading from the tank into the back of a large square box-like trunk, which she could not identify for a moment. Then, with a flash of insight, she realised that the box was a computer, and that whoever it was that had control of the two spirits was using them to cut down on his electricity bills.

She thought she could hear voices; but the voices were very far away—they were coming from the picture behind the stone.

"And two for his nob makes seven, redoubled," said the voice. "Proceed to Valhalla, do not pass Go, do not collect two hundred crowns." The other voice sniggered.

It's them, Hildy thought. She felt utterly exhausted, as if she had been lifting heavy weights with the muscles of her eyes, and her head was splitting.

"I give up," said the first voice. "I never did like this game."

"Let's play something else, then," said the other voice equably.

"I don't want to play anything," retorted the first voice. "I want to get out of here, before they plug us in to something else. I don't mind being kidnapped, but I do resent being used to heat water."

"Impossible," said the second voice. "We're stuck. I suggest we make the most of it." The first light flickered irritably, but the second light ignored it. "My throw. Oh, good, that's an X and a Y. I can make 'oxycephalous,' and it's on a triple rune score—"

"There's no such word as 'oxycephalous,'" said the first voice, "not in Old Norse."

"There is now," replied the second voice cheerfully. "Up the tree, six, and I think I'll see you."

Hildy's eyes were hurting, but she struggled to keep them open, as she had so often struggled at lectures and seminars. With a tremendous effort of will, she forced herself to zoom backwards, widening her angle of view. She saw the office-block again, standing in a familiar landscape, but one which she could not put a name to. Then she made out what could only be a Tube station, stunningly prosaic in the midst of all the magic. With a final spurt of effort she read the name, "St. Paul's." Then the stone fell from her eye, and she slumped forward on to the table.

When she came round, she found the heroes gathered about her. She told them what she had seen, and what she deduced from it. The King sat down again, and put his face in his hands.

"We must take a great risk," he said at last. "I shall have to go to this place and recover the two spirits. Otherwise, there is no hope."

"You mustn't," Hildy protested. "They'll catch you, and then there really won't be any hope." She dug her fingers into the material of her organiser bag until they started to ache. "Let me go instead."

The King suddenly lifted his head and smiled at her. "We'll both go," he said cheerfully, almost lightheartedly. "And you, Kotkel. Only this time you'll do it properly, understand? And you, Brynjolf," he said to the shape-changer, who was trying unsuccessfully to hide behind the massive shoulders of Starkad Storvirksson, "we'll need you as well. And two others. Any volunteers?"

Everyone froze, not daring to move. But after a moment Arvarodd stood up, looked around the table, and nodded. "I'll come," he said quietly. "After all, it can't be worse than Permia." He laughed weakly at his own joke, but all the others were silent. The King looked scornfully about him, and sighed. "Chicken," he said, "the whole lot of you."

Starkad Storvirksson rose to his feet. "Can I come?" he asked mildly. If no one else was prepared to go, he might at last get his chance to do something other than fighting. Fighting was all right in its way, but he was sure there was more to being a hero than just hitting people.

"No, Starkad," said the King kindly. "I know *you're* not afraid. But not this time. I'll explain later."

Starkad sat down, looking dejected, and Brynjolf patted him comfortingly on the shoulder. "It's because you're so stupid, Starkad," he said gently. "You'd only be in the way."

"Oh," said Starkad happily. "If that's the reason, I don't mind."

"I'll go," said Bothvar Bjarki suddenly, and all the heroes turned and stared at him. "What this job needs is brains, not muscle." The King muttered something inaudible under his breath, and said that, on second thoughts, five would be plenty. Bothvar scowled, but the heroes cheered loudly, and raised the toast; first to Odin, giver of victory; then to the six adventurers; then to their Lord, King Hrolf Earthstar. Then Ohtar remembered that there had been another cask of enchanted mead in the back storeroom, and they all went to look for it.

"The others had better not stay here," said the King to Hildy, while they were gone. "They'll have to hunt for food and find water, and I saw too many houses on the road back there. I'll send them up into the mountains." From the back storeroom came sounds of cursing; someone, back in the ninth century, had left the top off the barrel. The King grinned. "It'll give them something else to complain about until we get back."

"Will they be all right?" Hildy asked doubtfully. "They don't seem terribly practical to me."

The King nodded. "I should think so," he said. "Take Angantyr

Asmundarson, for instance. To join the muster at Melvich, he marched all night from Brough Head to Burwick—that's right across the two main islands of Orkney—and since there was no boat available he swam over from Burwick to the mainland, in the middle of a storm. Then he ran all the way from Duncansby Head to Melvich, on the morning before the battle, and still fought in the front rank against the stone-trolls of Finnmark. Complaining bitterly about his wet clothes and how he was going to catch his death of pneumonia, of course, but that's just his way." He paused, and contemplated his fingernails for a moment. "Put like that, I suppose, it rather proves your point. Only a complete idiot would have gone to so much trouble to get involved in a battle. Come on," he said briskly, "it's time we were going."

Thorgeir Storm-shepherd was feeling his age, and since he was nearing his thirteen-hundredth birthday this was no small problem. He could not, he reflected, take the long journeys like he used to, when a flight from Oslo to Thingvellir, perched uncomfortably between the shoulderblades of the huge mutant seagull that his employer had bred specially for him, had just been part of a normal day's work.

He had not been idle. What with dashing about by train, car and helicopter, interviewing Danny Bennett and capturing the two chthonic spirits, then hurrying back to Rolfsness to clear the area of Professor Wood and his archaeologists, he felt he had earned a rest. But now he was back in London, and the sorcerer-king was in the bad mood that usually attended the tricky part of any enterprise.

The two spirits were safely locked up in a spellproof perspex tank, and the Professor had been shunted off to the British Museum to ferret about among the Old Norse manuscripts one more time, just in case anything had been overlooked. Still, the Professor was a useful man. Another practical benefit of commercial sponsorship of archaeology. It had, of course, been fortuitous that a freak and entirely localised storm had threatened to flood the site at Rolfsness, forcing the excavation team to close up the mound and go away, but Thorgeir was not called Storm-Shepherd for nothing. He was glad that he had kept his hand in at that particular field of Old Magic, useful over the past thousand years only for betting on draws in cricket matches and then washing them out. He leant back in his chair and ruffled the papers on his desk. As well as being a Dark Age sorcerer, he was also one of the key executives in the world's largest multinational, and work had been piling up while he was away. As he flicked through a sheaf of "while-you-were-out" notes, he reflected that it was a pity that he had never mastered the art of delegation.

The intercom buzzed, and his secretary told him that his boss was on the scrambler. Thorgeir disliked the machine, but it was better than telepathy, which had until recently been the main method of in-office communication between himself and the sorcerer-king, and which invariably gave him a headache.

"Now what?" said the sorcerer-king.

"That's that," replied Thorgeir, "at least for the moment. Without those two whatsits, the brooch is useless."

"Why can't they just plug it into the mains?"

"Even if they could, they couldn't get enough power from the ordinary mains," Thorgeir explained patiently. "But they can't. They need direct current, and you'd need a transformer the size of Liverpool to convert it. The only power source in the world big enough to power that brooch is sitting in a perspex tank in Vouchers. You have my word on it."

"So now what?"

"With the brooch out of action, they're up the fjord without a paddle." Thorgeir grinned into the receiver. "Lucky, wasn't I?"

"Yes," said the sorcerer-king, "very."

Thorgeir stopped grinning. "So we have all the time in the world to find them and dispose of them. They can't do us any harm."

"You said that the last time, before Melvich."

"That was different."

"So is this different. How do you know they can't modify it?"

"Trust me. Let me rephrase that," Thorgeir added hurriedly, for that was a sore point at all times. "Rely on it. They can't. All they can do is try breaking in here and springing the two gnomes."

"Just let them try."

"Exactly. So relax, won't you? Enjoy yourself. Set up a new newspaper or something. The situation is under control."

"I hope so." The sorcerer-king rang off.

Thorgeir shook his head and returned to his work. The papers from the Japanese deal were starting to come through, and he didn't like the look of them at all. Come the glorious day, he said to himself, I'll turn that whole poxy country into a golf-course, and we'll see how they like that. But before he could settle to it the telephone went again. This time it was Professor Wood, ringing from the call-box outside the British Museum. Thorgeir sat up and reached for a pen and some paper.

After a few minutes, he put the phone down carefully and read back his notes. Things were starting to take shape. In a nineteenth-century collection of Gaelic folktales, the Professor had found a most interesting story, all about a chieftain called Rolf McKettle and his battle with the Fairies. Allowing for the distortions inevitably occurring over a millennium of the oral tradition and home-made whisky, it was a fair and accurate report of the battle of Melvich, and it went on to tell the rest of the story, including where the King had been buried and who was buried with him.

The Professor would be round in about half an hour. Thorgeir dumped a half-hundredweight of unread contracts in his out-tray and went to tell his boss. "Not," he reflected as he got into the lift, "that he'll take kindly to being called a fairy. But there we go."

How long he had been there, or where exactly there was, Danny had no idea, but he was beginning to wonder whether the senior cameraman might not have been right after all. It had been the senior cameraman, armed with the map, who had insisted that the big cloudy thing over to their right was Ben Stumanadh, and that the road was just the other side of it. Danny had been a Boy Scout (although he had taken endless pains to make sure that no one in the Corporation knew about it) and he knew that the assertion was patently ridiculous, and that the cameraman was determined to lead the crew into the bleak and inhospitable interior, where death from exposure was a very real possibility. He had reasoned with him, ordered him, and finally shouted at him; but the fool had taken no notice, and neither had the rest of the crew. Finally, Danny had washed his hands of the lot of them and set out to walk the few miles to the road, which he knew was just over to the left.

Of course the mist hadn't helped, but the further he had gone, the more Danny had become convinced that either the map had been wrong or that someone had moved the road. As exhaustion and hunger, and the loss of both his shoes in a bog, had taken their toll, he had inclined more and more to the latter explanation, especially after his short but illuminating chat with the two brown sheep which had been the only living things he had seen since meeting the strange man who had pointed them all in the wrong direction. Shortly after he had arrived at that conclusion, his eyes started playing tricks on him, and he had spent the night in what appeared at the time to be a fully equipped editing suite, complete with facilities for transposing film on to video-tape. In the cold (very cold) light of morning it had turned out to be a ruined shieling, and he had somehow acquired a rather disconcertingly high fever. But at least it kept him warm, which was something.

Rather optimistically, he tried out his arms and his legs, but of course they wouldn't work, just as his car never used to start when he had a particularly urgent meeting. He felt surprisingly calm, and reflected that that was probably one of the fringe benefits of going completely mad. If he wasn't deeply into the final stage of hallucination that came just before death by exposure, he wouldn't be imagining that the men in the grey suits were coming over the hill towards him.

"Just like old times," one of them was saying. "Out on the fells with no shelter and nothing to eat but rabbit and perishing salmon. If I have to eat any more salmon, I'll start looking like one."

Since over his suit he was wearing a coat of silvery scale armour he already did; but of course, Danny reflected, since the man was not really there he was not to know that. He groaned softly, and slumped a little further behind the stones. If he had to see visions in his madness, he would have preferred something a little less eccentric.

"If you hadn't been so damned fussy," said another of the men, "we could have had one of those sheep."

"He said not to get into any trouble," said the salmon-man. "Stealing sheep counts as trouble. Always did."

"There might be deer in that forest we passed," said a third man.

"Then, again, there might not," replied the salmon-man, who seemed a miserable sort of person. Danny decided he didn't like him much and tried to replace him with a beautiful girl, but apparently the system didn't work like that. "And if you think I'm going to go rushing about some wood in the hope that it's full of deer you can think again," the salmon-man said. The others didn't bother to reply. Danny approved.

"That'll do," said one of them. He was pointing at the shieling, and Danny realised that they intended to make their camp there. That was a pity, since he had wanted to spend his last hours on earth in quiet meditation, not making conversation with a bunch of phantasms from the Milk Marketing Board. In fact, Danny said to himself, I won't have it. An Englishman's fallen-down old shed is his castle, even in Scotland. "Go away," he shouted, and turned his face to the stone wall. The words just managed to clear his lips, but they fell away into the wind and were dispersed.

"There's someone in there," said Starkad Storvirksson.

"So there is," said Ohtar. "I wonder if he wants a fight."

"Better ask him first," said Angantyr. "It's very bad manners to fight people without asking."

"I thought we weren't supposed to fight anyone," Starkad said.

"We can if we have to defend ourselves," said Ohtar, but his heart wasn't in it. The man hardly looked worth fighting anyway. In fact he looked decidedly unwell. Ohtar turned him over gently with his foot.

"Ask him if he's got anything to eat," Angantyr whispered. "Tell him we'll trade him two rabbits and a salmon for anything in the way of cheese."

"Hold it, will you?" said Ohtar. "It's that sorcerer from the van, the one who wouldn't fight with Bothvar." He turned to his companions and smiled. "Things are looking up," he said. "We've got ourselves a prisoner."

7

"Have some more rabbit," said Ohtar kindly. Although Danny had done nothing but eat all night, he felt it would be rude to refuse. Obviously the strange men prided themselves on their hospitality.

"Are you sure you'll have enough for yourselves?" he asked desperately, as Ohtar produced two more burnt drumsticks, still mottled with little flecks of singed fur. The man they called Angantyr made a curious snorting noise.

"Don't you mind him," said Ohtar. "Plenty more where that came from."

"Well, in that case..." Danny sank his teeth into the carbonised flesh and tried not to remember that he had been very fond of his pet rabbit, Dimbleby, when he was a boy. "This is very good," he said, forcing his weary jaws to chew.

"Really?" Ohtar beamed. He had been field-cook to King Hrolf for most of his service, and this was the first time anyone had paid him a compliment. "You wait there," he said and, gathering up his sling and a handful of pebbles, walked away.

"You've made his day," said Angantyr, sitting down beside Danny and absentmindedly picking up the second drumstick. "Personally," he said with his mouth full, "I hate rabbit, but it's a sight better than seagull. You ever had seagull?"

"No," Danny said.

"Very wise," said Angantyr, and he spat out a number of small bones. "Not that you can't make something of it with a white sauce and some fennel. Don't get me wrong," he added, "I'm not obsessive about food, like some I could mention. Five square meals a day is all I ask, and a jug or so of something wet to see it on its way. But I draw the line at seaweed," he asserted firmly. "Except in a mousse, of course."

"Of course," Danny agreed.

Having looked to make sure that there was no more rabbit lying about, Angantyr lay back against the wall of the ruined bothy and pulled his helmet down over his eyes. "Ah, well," he said, "this is better than work. What do you do with yourself, by the way? I know you're a sorcerer of sorts, but that could mean anything, couldn't it?"

"I'm a producer," Danny said.

"Good for you," Angantyr said. "Me, I'm strictly a consumer." The early-morning sun was shining weakly through a window in the cloud, and the hero was in a good mood. "That was always the trouble with this country," he went on. "Too few producers and too many consumers. I admire you people, honestly I do. Out behind the plough in all weathers, or driving the sheep home through the snow. Rotten job, always said so."

"No, no," Danny said, "I'm not a farmer, I'm a producer. A television producer."

Angantyr sat up, a caterpillar-like eyebrow raised. "What's that, then?"

"You know...," Danny said weakly. "I work out the schedules, supervise the crews, that sort of thing."

"You mean a forecastle-man?" Angantyr suspected that his leg was being pulled. "Get out, you're not, are you?"

"Not that sort of crew," Danny said, wishing he had never mentioned it. "Camera crews. Keys, grips, gaffers, that sort of thing. I make television programmes."

"Don't mind me," said Angantyr after a long pause. "I've been asleep for a thousand-odd years."

"No, but really." Danny nerved himself to ask the question that was eating away at the lining of his mind. "Who are you people?"

Angantyr looked at him sternly, remembering that he was a sorcerer. But he looked harmless enough, and they had smashed up all his magical instruments in the Battle of the Vans.

"If I tell you," he said, lowering his voice, "you won't turn into a bird or something and fly away? Give me your word of honour."

"On my word of honour," said Danny. Obviously, he reflected, the man really didn't know what a television producer was, or he would have demanded a different oath.

"We're King Hrolf's men," whispered Angantyr. "We went to sleep in the ship, and now we've been woken up for the final battle."

"You mean the ship at Rolfsness?" Danny asked. Something at the back of his mind was making sense of this, although he wished it wouldn't. By and large, he preferred it when he thought he was going mad.

"That's right," said Angantyr patiently. "We were asleep in the ship for twelve hundred years, and now we've woken up."

Danny closed his eyes. "Then, what about the grey suits?"

"You mean the clothes? That Hildy got them for us. She said we'd be less conspicuous dressed like this."

"Hildy Frederiksen?"

"Hildy Frederik's-*daughter*. Can't be Frederik*sen*, she's a woman. Stands to reason." Angantyr shook his head. "Funny creature. But bright, I'll say that for her. It was lucky we met her, really, what with her knowing the sagas and all. Between you and me," he whispered into Danny's ear, "I think old Arvarodd's gone a bit soft on her. No accounting for taste, I suppose, and there was that time at Hlidarend—"

"Could we go through this one more time?" Danny said. "You were actually *in* the ship when Frederiksen went into the mound?"

"Course we were." It suddenly occurred to Angantyr that the prisoner might find this hard to believe, if he didn't know the story. So he told him the story. Even when he had done this, the prisoner seemed unconvinced.

"I'm sorry," Danny said, when Angantyr put this to him. "I'm not calling you a liar, really. But it's all the magic stuff. You see..."

Angantyr remembered something he had overheard the King saying to Hildy, or it might have been the other way around. "Just a moment," he said. "You call it something else now, don't you? Technology or something."

"No, that's quite different," Danny interrupted. He had a terrible feeling that there was something wrong with his line of argument. "Technology is healing the sick, and doing things automatically. Magic is—"

"Watch this," Angantyr said, and from his pocket he pulled a small doe-skin pouch. "Here's a bit of technology I picked up in Lapland when I went raiding there." He emptied the contents of the pouch on to the ground, and picked up two small bones and a pebble. Then he drew his knife, and with a single blow cut off his left hand just above the wrist. Danny tried to scream, but before the muscles of his larynx had relaxed from the first shock of what he had seen Angantyr picked up his severed left hand with his right hand and put it on Danny's knee.

"Hold that for me, will you?" he said cheerfully. Then he popped the pebble into his mouth, took back the severed hand and drew it back on to his wrist like a glove. Then, with his *left* hand, he took the pebble out of his mouth, wiped it on his trouser-leg and put it back in the pouch. "How's that for technology?" he said. "Or do you want to try it for yourself?"

Danny assured him that he did not.

"It's a bit like grafting apples," said Angantyr, "only quicker. What was the other thing you said? Doing things automatically. Right."

He threw the two small bones up in the air and blew on them as they fell. One started to glow with a bright orange light, and the other burst into a tall roaring flame. Angantyr blew on it again, and it grew smaller, like a gas jet being turned down. Then he whistled, and the flame stopped.

"That's just a portable one," he said, putting the bones and the pouch away. "You can get them bigger for lighting a house and cooking large meals. And they're more controllable than an open fire for gentle simmering and light frying. Cookability, you might say."

Just then, Ohtar came back, throwing down a large sack. Angantyr turned and looked at him cautiously.

"Couldn't find any rabbits," said Ohtar, sitting down beside them and opening the sack. "Will seagull be all right?"

According to the road signs at Melvich, they had finished digging up the A9 at Berriedale, and the main road along the coast was fully open again. Hildy was relieved; she had not been looking forward to going back down the Lairg road, for she felt sure that if their enemy had heard about them he would be watching it, and probably the Helmsdale road as well. The main road would be much safer, as well as quicker.

She still had her doubts about leaving the rest of the heroes to their own devices, even in the wilds of Strathnaver; but she consoled herself with the thought that it would have been even more dangerous to take them to London. not to mention the expense of food, accommodation and Tube tickets for them all. As she turned these questions over in her mind, she realised, with no little pride, that she had become the effective leader of the company, and as she drove she found herself composing the first lines of her own saga. "There was a woman called Hildy Frederiksen...."

"Mind out," said the King suddenly, "you're going out into the middle of the road."

"Sorry," Hildy mumbled. It was like having driving lessons with her father. Even now, seven years after she had passed her test, he still tended to give her helpful advice, such as "Why aren't you in third?" and "For Christ's sake, slow down," when she was doing about thirty-five along the freeway. She hurriedly put *Hildar Saga Frederiksdottur* back on the bookshelf of her mind, and concentrated on keeping closer in to the side of the road.

The King, she felt, was adapting remarkably quickly to the twentieth century, asking perceptive questions and making highly intelligent guesses about the various things he saw as they drove along. Even when they had passed through Inverness, the King's first sight of a major town had not seemed to throw him in any way. When she asked him about this, he simply said that he had seen many stranger things than that in his life, especially in Finnmark, and he expected to see many things stranger still. That, Hildy reckoned, she could personally guarantee. Large container-lorries seemed to intrigue him, but aircraft he regarded as inefficient and somehow rather old-fashioned. The one thing he did find fault with was what he called the "decline of civilisation." Coming from a Viking, Hildy thought, that was a bit much, but the King refused to be drawn on the subject, and Hildy guessed that he meant all that noble-savage stuff that you got in Victorian academic writing.

Rather than risk staying the night in a hotel, they left the motorway at Penrith and found a deserted corner of Martindale Common, near where, disconcertingly enough, the King had fought a battle with the Saxons.

"A race of men I never did take to," the King added, as they roasted the inevitable rabbit. "What became of them, by the way?"

Hildy told him, and he said that he wasn't in the least surprised. "A nation of shopkeepers," he muttered, "bound to do well in the end."

Hildy had written a paper on early Saxon trade, and would have discussed the matter further, but the King seemed not to be in the right mood. In fact, she thought to herself, he's been strange all day. Preoccupied.

The next day, after filling up with petrol at a service station (enough tokens now for a cut-glass decanter, only she didn't want one), they pressed on towards London. In the back, Arvarodd and the wizard were playing the same complicated game of chess that had kept them occupied all the way from Caithness, and the journey seemed not to trouble them at all. It was only when they stopped outside Birmingham for more petrol and a sandwich that Hildy noticed that the shape-changer was nowhere to be seen. "Not again," she muttered to herself, and asked where he'd got to.

"Down here," said one of the chess-pieces.

"We left the black rook behind," Arvarodd explained.

"But don't you mind?" Hildy asked the black rook. The rook shrugged its rigid shoulders.

"It passes the time," he said. "And chess-pieces don't get travel-sick."

"It's just that black always seems to win," Arvarodd said. They had drawn for colours before setting off, and he was playing white. "Not that I mind that much, of course. I generally lose to Kotkel anyway."

"Do chess-pieces get hungry?" Hildy asked. She had only bought enough sandwiches for four.

"This one does," said the rook firmly. Then the wizard grabbed him by the head and used him to take Arvarodd's queen.

They arrived in London late in the evening, and Hildy realised that she had made no plans for their stay there.

"That's all right," said the King absently. "We can sleep in this thing."

Hildy started to explain about yellow lines, traffic wardens and loitering with intent, but the King wasn't listening. He was looking about him and frowning deeply.

"Of course," Hildy said, "this must be all totally strange to you."

"Not at all," said the King. "It's most depressingly familiar."

"It can't be," said Hildy.

"I assure you it is. Isn't it, lads?"

Arvarodd looked up from the chessboard. "Hello," he said, "I've been here before. It's just like—"

"It's just like Geirrodsgarth," explained the King, "where the sorcerer-king had his first stronghold, and which we erased from the face of the earth, so that not even its foundations remained."

Hildy shook her head. "Surely not," she said.

"I started to worry when we went to Wick, but it might just have been coincidence. At Inverness I felt sure. All the other cities we have passed confirmed my suspicions. The enemy has built his new city as a replica of the old one, except that it's much bigger and rather more primitive."

"Primitive?"

"Oh, decidedly so. For a start, the whole of Geirrodsgarth was covered over with a transparent roof. But I suppose it's because he could only influence its design, not order it entirely according to his wishes. All the buildings in Geirrodsgarth were square towers like those over there." He waved his hands at a grove of tower-blocks in the distance. "I suppose he found the Saxons rather more stubborn than the Finns. That's shopkeepers for you."

In the end, Hildy parked in a side-street in Hoxton, beside the Regent's Canal; it would somehow not be safe to go any further. She was aware of some vague but localised menace, and something of the sort was clearly affecting the King and the wizard, who huddled together in the back of the van and talked in low voices. Hildy realised that the wizard had put aside the language-spell, so that she could not understand what was being said. She felt betrayed and rejected. In a strained voice she said something about going and getting some food, and opened the door. The King looked up and said something, but of course she could not understand it. Arvarodd, however, translated for her.

"He says you shouldn't go," he said.

"But I'm hungry," Hildy replied. "And I'm sure it'll be all right."

The King said something else. "He says go if you must, but take the shape-changer with you."

"Don't I get any say in the matter?" asked the black rook. "Two more moves and it'll be check."

Arvarodd picked up the rook and offered it to Hildy. "Just slip him in your pocket," he said.

"No, thanks," said Hildy stiffly. "I don't want to spoil your game."

"Just to please me," said Arvarodd. Startled, Hildy took it and put it in her pocket. Then she opened the door and slipped out.

It took a long time for her to find a chip-shop, and she had a good mind not to buy anything for the King or the wizard. In the end, however, she bought five cod and chips, five chicken and ham pies, and a saveloy for herself, as a treat. She failed to notice that the two youths in leather jackets who had been playing the fruit machine had followed her out.

Halfway back to the van they made their move. One stepped out in front of her, waving a short knife, while the other made a grab for her bag. Hildy froze, clutching the parcels of food to her breast, and made a squeaking noise.

"Come on, lady, give us the bag," said the youth with the knife, "'cos if you don't you'll get cut, right?"

He took a step forward. At that moment, something fell from Hildy's pocket and rolled into the gutter. The knife-man looked round, and suddenly dropped his knife. Apparently from nowhere, a terrifying figure had appeared. At first it looked like a gigantic bear; then it was a wolf, with red eyes and a lolling tongue. Finally, it was a huge grim man brandishing a broad-bladed axe. The two youths stared for a moment, then started to run. For a few moments, they thought that they were being pursued by a vast black eagle. They quickened their pace and disappeared round the corner.

"I knew that stuff you sold me was no good," said one to the other.

"Are you all right?" said Brynjolf, returning and perching on a wing-mirror. He ruffled his feathers with his beak, and then turned back into a chess-piece. "Sorry to be so long," he said. "I couldn't make up my mind what to be. The bear usually does the trick, but the wolf is more comfy."

"That was fine," Hildy mumbled. She was breathing heavily, and there was vinegar all over her new anorak. "Thank you."

"Not at all," said a voice from her pocket. "Who were they, by the way?"

"Just muggers, I think," Hildy replied. "That's sort of thieves."

"I don't know," said her pocket. "Young people nowadays."

"Don't say anything to the King," said Hildy. "He'd only worry."

"Please yourself."

Hildy didn't tell the King when she got back, but she gave Brynjolf the saveloy. It was, she felt, the least she could do.

The next morning, they left the van and set off on foot. They went by Tube from Old Street to Bank, and changed on to the Central Line for St Paul's. The concept of the Underground seemed not to worry the King or the wizard, but Brynjolf and Arvarodd didn't like the look of it at all.

"You know what I reckon this is?" Arvarodd whispered to the shape-changer.

"What?"

"Burial-chambers," replied the hero of Permia, "like those shaft-graves on Orkney only bigger. They must go on for miles."

"And what are we in, then—a coffin?" Brynjolf looked around the compartment. "Can't see any bodies."

"Must be the tombs of kings," replied Arvarodd. "Look, there's a diagram or something up on the side."

Brynjolf leant forward and studied the plan.

"I reckon you may be right," he said, returning to his seat. "I think there are several dynasties down here. Those coloured lines joining up the names must be the family-trees. Funny names they've got, though. Look, there's the House of Kensington all buried together: South Kensington, West Kensington, High Street Kensington—"

"Kensington Olympia," interrupted Arvarodd. "They must have been a powerful dynasty."

"Them and the Parks," agreed Brynjolf. "And the Actons away in the west. Hopelessly interbred, of course," he added, looking at the numerous intersections of the coloured lines at Euston. "No wonder they got delusions of grandeur."

Hildy overheard the end of this conversation but decided not to interrupt. It would be too complicated to explain; and, besides, as a trained archaeologist she felt that their explanation was rather better than the conventional one.

They got off at St Paul's and were faced by the escalator. This Hildy felt she would have to explain, but the heroes seemed to recognise it at once—they must have had them in Geirrodsgarth. At the foot of it, Arvarodd stopped and studied the notice.

"Dogs must be carried on the escalator," he read aloud. "I knew we should have brought a dog. I suppose we'll have to flog up all those stairs now."

"All right," said Brynjolf wearily, "leave it to me." He sighed heavily and turned himself into a small terrier, which Arvarodd picked up and tucked under his arm. "Only, if you've lost your ticket," said the dog, "you're on your own."

Once they reached street-level, the object of their quest was obvious. Before Hildy could point to it and identify it as the building she had seen through the stone, her companions were staring at the soaring black tower that dominated the rest of Cheapside.

"That's him all over," said the King. "No originality."

"Well," said Arvarodd, "do we go in, or what?" His hand was tightening around the grip of the sports-bag in which he was carrying his mail shirt and short sword.

"No," said the King.

"Why not, for crying out loud?" Hildy could see that Arvarodd was sweating heavily; but he was not afraid. There was something uncanny about him, and Hildy edged away.

"Because we wouldn't get past the front gate," replied the King quietly. For his part, he was as cold as ice. He stood motionless, but his eyes were flicking backwards and forwards as he considered every scrap of evidence that the view of the building had to offer. "Or, rather, we would, which would be all the worse for us. I don't think physical force is the answer."

"I don't see that we have that many options," muttered Brynjolf. "Unless you'd like me—"

"Certainly not," snapped the King. "Your magic wouldn't work in there." He turned sharply on his heel and walked away.

"Now what?" Hildy whispered to Arvarodd. "He's not going to give up now, is he?" Arvarodd shook his head.

"He is the King," was all he would say.

The King was talking with the wizard, and they seemed to have agreed on something, for the King turned back and approached Hildy.

"Tell me," he said, "how would the power to work all the machines get into that building?"

Hildy told him about the mains and the underground cables. He nodded, and suddenly smiled.

"And all the houses and buildings in the city are connected to the same source of power?" he asked.

"I think so," Hildy said. "I can't be certain, of course."

"What we need, then," said the King, "is a building."

"Down the tree, four spaces over, and that's check*mate*."

The power-level in the computer wavered suddenly. The grim-faced man got up from his desk and banged on the side of the tank.

"Any more of that," he said savagely, "and I'll take that game off you."

"Sorry," chorused the pale glow inside the tank.

"Well, all right, then," said the grim-faced man, "only let's have less of it." He scowled and returned to his desk.

"For two pins," said Prexz, "I'd run straight up his arm and electrocute him."

"You wouldn't dare," replied Zxerp scornfully. "And, besides, he might have rubber soles on his shoes, and then where would you be?"

"As I was saying," said Prexz through clenched teeth, "checkmate."

"Who cares?" Zxerp stretched out his hand and knocked over his goblin to signify surrender. "What does that make the score?"

Prexz consulted the card. "That's ninety-nine thousand, nine hundred and ninety-nine sets and eight games to me, and four games to you."

"Inclusive?"

"Exclusive," replied Prexz, making a mark on the card. "So I now need only one more game for one match point. You still have some work to do."

"I might as well concede, then," said Zxerp. He pressed his feet against the side of the tank and put his arms behind his head. "Then we can start again from scratch."

"Don't be so damned pessimistic," replied Prexz. "A good match to win, I'll grant you, but it's still wide open."

"We should have brought draughts instead," yawned Zxerp. "I'm hungry."

"You're always hungry. Is there any of that static left, or have you guzzled it all?"

"Help yourself." There was a faint crackling noise and a few blue sparks. "That box of tricks over there fair takes it out of you," Zxerp went on. "I'll need more than static to keep electron and neutron together if I've got to keep that thing going much longer."

Prexz turned and glowered at the computer. It winked a green light at him, and started to print something out. Just then, Prexz felt a vibration in the wire running into his left ear. Zxerp could feel the same thing. He started to protest, but Prexz hissed at him to be quiet.

"It's coming in over the mains," he whispered.

"Tastes all right," said Zxerp. "A bit salty perhaps..."

"Don't eat it, you fool, it's a message."

"The old file-in-a-cake trick, huh?"

"Something like." Prexz closed his eyes and tried to concentrate. "I think it's the wizard."

"Kotkel?" Zxerp leant forward.

"He's talking through the mains running into that machine we're linked up to. Honestly, the things he thinks of."

The two spirits lay absolutely still. "We're going to try to get you out," they heard, "so be ready. But it won't be easy. Don't try to reply or you'll blow the circuit. Bon appétit."

"Very tastefully put," said Zxerp, and he burped loudly.

The proprietor of the hotel gave Hildy a very strange look as she went past, and she could not blame him. After all, she had come in just under an hour ago with four strange-looking men and hired a room; and now they were all going away again. Still, it had been worth the embarrassment, for the wizard had managed to talk to the two captives via the shaver socket—how he had managed it she could not imagine—and they seemed to have received the message. The thing to do now was get away fast, just in case their message had been intercepted and traced.

The van was still where she had left it (why was she surprised by that? It was just an ordinary van parked in an ordinary street) and they all climbed in and drove off, entirely uncertain as to where they were going and why. The King was sitting in the back with the wizard and the shape-changer, and they were all deep in mystical discussion. But Arvarodd sat in the front, and he seemed to be in unusually good spirits.

"Don't you fret," he said, as they drove through Highgate. "We've been in worse fixes than this, believe you me."

"Such as?" Hildy cast her mind back through the heroic legends of Scandinavia in search of some parallel, but the search was in vain. Usually, the old heroes had overcome their improbable trials with brute force or puerile trickery.

"Offhand," said Arvarodd, remorselessly cheerful, "I can't think. But it looks to me like a straightforward impregnable-fortress problem. Let's not worry about it now."

"What's gotten into you?" Hildy asked gloomily. She found the words "straightforward" and "impregnable fortress" hard to reconcile.

"You worry too much," Arvarodd replied, to Hildy's profound irritation. "That's what comes of not having faith in the King. That's what kings are for, so people like you and me don't have to worry."

Hildy, who had been brought up to vote Democrat, objected to this.

"The King doesn't seem to realise—" she started to say.

"The King realises everything," said Arvarodd. "And, even if he doesn't, who wants to know?" The hero of Permia yawned and folded his arms. "If the King says, 'Charge that army over there,' and you say, 'Which one?' and he says, 'The one that outnumbers us twentyfold in that superb natural defensive position just under that hill with the sheep,' then you do it. And if it works you say, 'What a brilliant general the King is,' and if it doesn't you go to Valhalla. Everyone's a winner, really."

"That's what you mean by a straightforward impregnable-fortress problem?"

"Exactly. You have two options. You can work out a subtle stratagem to trick your way in, with an equally subtle stratagem to get you out again afterwards, or you can grab an axe and smash the door down. We call that the certain-death option. On the whole, it's easier and safer than all the fooling about, but you have to go through the motions."

"So you think it'll come to that?" Hildy asked.

"No idea," Arvarodd said. "Not my problem."

After more petrol—if she collected enough tokens, Hildy wondered, could she get a Challenger tank, which really would be useful in the circumstances?—they parked in a side-road on the edge of Hampstead Heath and held a council of war.

"The situation as I see it is this," said the King. "The tower, which would be unassailable even if we were in a position to attack it, which we aren't, is guarded night and day. Our enemy has control of the two spirits, who are essential to us if we are to have any hope of survival, let alone success. Because of the risk of detection, and because detection would mean certain defeat at this stage, we cannot make a more detailed survey of the ground, so to all intents and purposes we know absolutely nothing about the tower, how to get into it or out of it. Again, because of the risk of detection, if we are going to do anything we must do it now. I am in the market for any sensible suggestions."

"Why not attack?" Brynjolf said. "Then we could all go to Valhalla and have a good time."

The wizard made a noise like worn-out disc brakes, and the King nodded. "The wizard says," translated the King, "that the case is not yet hopeless, that courage and wisdom together can break stone and turn steel, and that we have a duty that is not yet discharged. Also, Valhalla is looking pretty run-down these days what with nobody going there any more, the towels in the bathrooms are positively thread-bare, and he's in no hurry. He says he has this on the authority of Odin's ravens, Hugin and Munin, who bring him tidings every morn-ing, and they should know. Anyone else?"

Before anyone could speak, the van was filled with a shrill whis-tling, and Hildy realised that it was coming from her bag. At first she thought it was her personal security alarm, but that went *beep-beep* and, besides, she had left it in St Andrews.

"It's the seer-stone," said Brynjolf, shouting to make himself heard.

"You mean like a sort of bleeper?" Hildy rummaged about and found the small blue pebble. It was warm again, and the noise was definitely coming from it. With great trepidation, she put it to her eye, and saw...

"Really," Danny said, "we'll come quietly."

The police sergeant raised himself painfully on one elbow. "Oh, no, you don't," he groaned. "You said that the last time."

"You shouldn't have tried to handcuff him," Danny said. "He didn't like it."

"I gathered that," said the police sergeant, spitting out a tooth. "If it's all the same to you, I'm going to go and call for reinforcements."

"Are you refusing to accept our surrender?" said Ohtar angrily.

"Yes," said the police sergeant. "I wouldn't take it as a gift."

"Please yourself," Ohtar said, fingering a large stone. "The last person who refused to accept my surrender made a full recovery. Even-tually."

The police sergeant looked round at his battered and bleeding constables, and at the eight grim-faced salmon-poachers standing over them. It seemed that he had very little choice.

"If you're sure," he said.

"We're sure," said Ohtar impatiently. "We've got orders not to get into any trouble."

"It's the others," Hildy said. They've gotten into trouble."

8

It is 520 miles from London to Bettyhill as the crow flies, but if the crow in question is a fully trained shape-changer in a hurry the journey takes just over two and a half hours.

Brynjolf perched on the window-sill of the police station and preened his ruffled feathers. Apart from turbulence over Derby and a nasty moment with a buzzard passing over Dornoch it had been an uneventful flight, and he knew that the tricky part of his mission still lay ahead of him. Cautiously he peered in through the window, and listened.

"No, I don't know who they are," the man in blue was saying, "but they beat the hell out of us. Maybe you should send up some water-cannon or something."

The reply to this request was clearly not the one the man in blue was expecting, for he said, "Oh, very funny," and slammed the phone down. Brynjolf hopped away from the window-sill, spread his wings and floated away to consider what to do next.

Very tricky, he said to himself, and to assist thought he started to sharpen his beak on a flat stone. Shape-transformation is, however, only skin-deep, and he gave it up quickly. Getting the heroes out would be no problem in itself; it was one that they could handle easily by themselves. But getting them out inconspicuously, so as not to cause any further disturbance, would be difficult. He went through his mental library of relevant heroic precedent—heroes rescued by sudden storms, conveniently passing dragons, or divine intervention—but something told him that such effects might be counter-productive. The obvious alternative was the false-messenger routine, but that required a fair amount of local knowledge to be successful. He had no idea who the men in blue took their orders from, what they looked like or what identification would be needed. He had almost decided to turn himself into the key of the cell door and have done with it when he thought of what should have been the obvious solution: the duplex confusion routine or Three-Troll Trick.

First he turned himself into a fly and crawled into the building
through a keyhole in the back door. Once inside, he buzzed tentatively round until he had located the cells where the prisoners were
being held. It was a small cell, and they all looked profoundly uncomfortable. Then he made a second trip and counted up the number of
men in blue. There were only three of them; just the right number.

The Three-Troll Trick, so called because trolls fall for it every time,
is essentially very simple. The shape-changer simply waits until only
one of the gaolers is supervising the prisoners; then he turns himself
into an exact facsimile of one of the other gaolers and, claiming to have
received instructions from a higher authority, releases the prisoners,
who get away as best they can. He then disappears, and leaves the
other gaolers to discover the error and beat the pulp out of the one
they believe has betrayed his trust. In a more robust age, the pre-
sumed traitor would not survive to clarify the misunderstanding; even
if things had changed drastically over the years, Brynjolf reckoned,
the mistake would still be put down to administrative confusion and
quietly covered up. He set to work, and as usual the system worked
flawlessly. The real gaoler lent him his key to the cell, the door swung
open, and the heroes, looking rather sullen, trooped out.

What Brynjolf had overlooked was the fact that nearly three hours'
confinement in a cramped cell, with Angantyr keeping up a constant
stream of funny remarks, had not improved Bothvar Bjarki's temper,
which was at the best of times chronically in need of all the improve-
ment it could get. Also, Brynjolf had inadvertently chosen to imper-
sonate the policeman who had been foolish enough to aim a blow at
Bothvar's head just before the fight started. So when Brynjolf, acting
out his part to the full, shoved Bothvar Bjarki in the back and said,
"Move it, you," in his best gaoler's snarl it was inevitable that Bothvar
should wheel round and thump him very hard on the chin. It was also
inevitable that Brynjolf, who had never really liked Bothvar because of
his habit of paring his toenails with an axe-blade when everyone else
was eating, should forget that he was playing a part, revert to his own
shape, and return the blow with interest. The fact that he rematerialised
with three extra arms was pure reflex.

Brynjolf realised in a moment what he had done, but by then it
was too late. The other two men in blue had come rushing up when
they heard the commotion, and they were standing open-mouthed
and staring.

"That," Bothvar said as he picked himself up from the ground, "is
what comes of trying to be clever."

"I'll deal with you later," Brynjolf replied. The three policemen, guessing who he meant to deal with first, made a run for the door, but the massive bulk of Starkad Storvirksson was in the way. After a one-sided scuffle, the policemen landed in a heap on the ground, and Starkad, remembering his manners, shut the door.

"Here," said a voice from the back of the room, "let me deal with this."

Brynjolf turned and looked for the source. "Is he one of them?" he asked, pointing to Danny Bennett.

"No," said Ohtar, "he's that sorcerer from the van, when you turned into an eagle."

"Him," Brynjolf exclaimed. "What's he doing here?"

"We found him on the fells," said Angantyr, putting a tree-like arm round his new friend's shoulders. "Strange bloke. Eats a lot, very fond of seagull. But he's on our side now. You'll sort it all out for us, won't you?" And he slapped Danny warmly on the back, nearly breaking his spine.

Danny stepped forward and bent over the policemen.

"I'm afraid," he said, "there's been a slight misunderstanding."

"You don't say," said the sergeant.

"You see," Danny continued, "my—my friends here weren't poaching salmon. Like me, I'm sure they're firmly opposed to bloodsports of every sort." The sergeant laughed faintly, but Danny ignored him. "In fact they're part of a team investigating a massive conspiracy to undermine democracy. Really, we need your help."

The sergeant was curiously unmoved by this appeal. He groaned and rolled over on to his face. Danny sighed; he was used to this obstructive attitude from policemen.

"If it's all right by you," he said, "I'll just go through and use your phone." He stepped over them and left the room.

"Is that all sorted out, then?" said Angantyr. "No hard feelings?" One of the policemen raised his head and nodded. "Good," said Angantyr. "We'll just tie you up and then we'll get out from under your feet."

Meanwhile, Danny had got through to his boss in London.

"What the hell are you doing up there?" said his boss. "I've just had a very strange call from a film crew who claim to have been beaten up by lunatics and stranded on a deserted hillside. They also said you'd wandered off and died of exposure. I think they're claiming compensation for bereavement because of it."

"Listen," Danny said, "I haven't much time."

"Oh, no," said his boss. "You're not being followed by the Wet Fish Board again, are you? I thought we'd been through all that."

"It's not the Wet Fish Board, it's—" Danny checked himself. The important thing was to stay calm. "I'm on to something really big this time."

"Whatever you're on," said his boss, "it can't be legal."

"This story's got everything," Danny continued. "Multinationals, nuclear power, spiritualism, ley lines, the lot."

"Animals?"

Danny thought of the eagle that had wrecked his van. "Yes," he said, "there's a definite wildlife angle. Also ecology and police brutality."

The boss was silent for a moment. "This has nothing at all to do with milk?"

"This is bigger than milk," Danny said. "This is global."

Something told Danny that his lord and master wasn't convinced. Desperately, he played his ace.

"You don't want to miss out on this one," he said. "Like when you didn't run the thing about that little girl's pet hamster getting lost inside Porton Down, and the opposition got it. Got her own series in the end, didn't she?"

"All right," said Danny's boss. "Tell me about it."

"What took you so long?"

The crow flopped wearily off the roof of the van, and perched on the King's wrist.

"Lost my way, didn't I?" it muttered, folding its rain-drenched wings. "My own silly fault. Next time I go as a pigeon." The crow disappeared and was replaced by an exhausted shape-changer.

"Well?" said the King, offering him the enchanted lager-can. Brynjolf swallowed a couple of mouthfuls and wiped his mouth with the end of his beard.

"Not so good, I'm afraid," he said. "Everyone safely rescued, but there were complications." He told the King what had happened.

"And," he continued, "there's more. You remember those sorcerers in the vans that Hildy told us we should stop?"

"What about them?"

"One of them, the chief sorcerer, has turned up again. Apparently, the lads captured him wandering about in the hills. Angantyr thinks he's on our side now." He paused to allow the King to draw his own conclusions.

"And is he?"

"Who can tell? After the scuffle, he went off to use one of those telephone things. Could be he really is on our side, but I wouldn't bet on it."

"We'll soon know," Hildy said, and looked at her watch. "We must find somewhere with a TV set."

There was a set in the third pub they tried, but it was showing "Dynasty." There were several protests when Hildy switched the channels, including one from Brynjolf, but when the King stood up and looked around the bar nobody seemed inclined to make too much of it. The nine o'clock news came on. Hildy gripped the stem of her glass and waited.

First there was a Middle East story, then something about the Health Service and an interview with the minister ("I know him from somewhere," Arvarodd said, leaning forward. "Didn't he use to farm outside Brattahlid?"), followed by a long piece on rate-capping and a minor spy scandal. Then there was a beached whale near Plymouth—the Vikings licked their lips instinctively—and the sports news. Hildy started to relax.

"And reports are just coming in," said the presenter, marble-faced, "of a major manhunt in the north of Scotland, which is somehow connected with the recent discovery of a Viking ship-burial and the disappearance of an American archaeologist, Hildegard Frederiksen."

Panoramic shot of an unidentifiable mountain.

"Ten men, believed to be violent, escaped from police custody today at Bettyhill. They have with them a BBC producer, who they are believed to be holding hostage. Police with tracker dogs are searching for the men, who are thought to be armed with swords, axes and spears. Reports that the men are members of an extremist anti-nuclear group opposed to the Caithness fast-breeder reactor project are as yet unconfirmed. The connection with the burial-mound containing a rich hoard of Viking treasure discovered at nearby Rolfsness is also uncertain. A spokesman for the War Graves Commission refused to comment. The man held hostage, Danny Bennett, is best known for his evocative depictions of Cotswold life, including 'The Countryside on Thursday' and 'One Man and His Tractor,' which was nominated for the Golden Iris award for best documentary."

"I didn't know you could disappear, Hildy," said Brynjolf admiringly. "Do you use a talisman, or just runes?"

Back at the van, the King and his company debated what to do for the best.

"I still say we should make an attack and get it over with," said Arvarodd. "Stick to what we know, and don't go getting involved with all these strange people. If we stick around now, and the enemy does come looking for us, we're done for."

"I'm not so sure." The King's eyes were shining, as they had not done since they left the Castle of Borve. "I think our enemy may have got quite the wrong idea from that little exhibition."

"How do you mean?"

"Think," said the King, smiling. "Doesn't it give the impression that we're all still up there, being chased across the hills by those soldiers, or whatever they are? He won't be able to resist the temptation to go up there and see if he can't find us and finish us off. After all, he has nothing to fear from us, so long as he has the spirits safe here."

"He might take them with him," Hildy suggested.

"He wouldn't do that. He wouldn't risk them falling into our hands. But if he thinks we're on the run up there—more important, if he thinks we're so weak that we can be chased around by those idiots Brynjolf was telling us about"—the King grinned disconcertingly—"then he's not going to be too worried about what we can do to him. He'll be concentrating more on what he can do to us. And that'll give us a chance, especially at this end."

If that was the King's definition of a chance, Hildy said to herself, she didn't like the sound of it. "But what about the others?" she said. "What if he catches them?"

"They'll have to look after themselves," said the King shortly, and Hildy could see he was worried. "If the worst comes to the worst, Valhalla. That doesn't really matter at this stage."

"But surely," Hildy started to say; but Arvsrodd trod on her toe meaningfully. The pain, even through her moon-boot, was agonising. "Maybe you're right," she mumbled.

"And meanwhile," said the King suddenly, "we have work to do."

Half-past three in the morning. There were still lights in the windows of Gerrards Garth House; like a crocodile, it slept with its eyes open. Two of the lights, having failed to draw the telex machine into conversation, were playing Goblin's Teeth.

"Are you sure about that?" said Prexz.

Zxerp smiled. "Yes," he said. "Checkmate."

"But what if...?" Prexz lifted the piece warily, then put it back. He was worried.

"Ninety-nine thousand, nine hundred and ninety-nine sets and nine games to you," said Zxerp, "and *five* games to me." Could it be that his luck was about to change?

Prexz knocked over his goblin petulantly. "All right, then," he said, as casually as he could, "I'll accept your resignation."

"Who's resigning?" Zxerp was setting out the pieces.

"You offered to resign after the last game. I'm accepting."

"I've withdrawn," said Zxerp, shuffling the Spell cards.

"Can't do that," replied Prexz. "Rule fifty-seven."

"Yes, I can," said Zxerp. "Rule seventy-two. Mugs away."

Sullenly, Prexz threw the dice and made his opening gambit. ChuChullainn's Leap; defensive, but absolutely safe. There was no known way to break service on ChuChullainn's Leap.

"Checkmate," said Zxerp.

In the street below, a van had drawn up outside the heavy steel doors. The King loosened his short sword in its scabbard and pulled his jacket on over it.

"Remember," he said. "You two wait down here, keep quiet, and do nothing. Just be ready for us when we come out."

Hildy nodded, but Arvarodd made one last effort. "Remember Thruthvangir," he said.

The King stiffened. "That was different," he said. "The lifts weren't working."

"They might not be working now," Arvarodd wheedled, "and then where would you be?"

"For the last time," said the King, "you stay in the van and keep quiet. If we need help, we'll signal."

He opened the back doors and jumped lightly out, followed by the wizard and the shape-changer. They ran silently across to the doors—Hildy was amazed to see how nimbly the wizard moved—and crouched down beside them. The wizard had taken something out of his pocket and was inserting it into the lock.

"Is that an opening spell?" Hildy whispered.

"No," replied Arvarodd, "it's a hairpin."

The great door suddenly opened, and Hildy braced herself for the shrill noise of the alarm. But there was silence, and the door closed behind them.

"Well," said Arvarodd, "they're on their own now." He shrugged his shoulders and ate the last digestive.

"I still don't understand," Hildy said. "Why tonight?"

"Obvious," said Arvarodd with his mouth full. "The Enemy, we hope, has gone off to Scotland. Tomorrow he'll probably be back, having guessed that we aren't there. So now's our only chance."

"But that's not what the King said earlier."

"Him," Arvarodd grunted. "Changes his mind every five minutes, he does."

"The King said," Hildy insisted, "that it was too dangerous to try it now. That's why he was so glad that the others had won us some time."

Arvarodd sighed. "If you must know," he said, "he's worried about the others. He doesn't think they'll be able to cope on their own. Probably right. He knows he ought to leave them to it but, then, he's the King. His first duty is to them. It's going to be Thruthvangir all over again."

"What happened at Thruthvangir?"

"The lifts didn't work." Arvarodd scowled at the steel doors. "That's why he left me out. My orders are, if he doesn't make it, to go back to Scotland and try to save the others. I should be flattered, really."

So that was what they had all been whispering about while she was getting petrol. "Arvarodd," she said quietly, "just how dangerous do you think it is?"

"Very," said Arvarodd, grimly. "Like my mother used to say:

> 'Fear a bear's paw, a prince's children,
> A grassy heath, embers still glowing,
> A man's sword, the smile of a maiden.'

There's a lot more of that," he continued. "Scared me half to death when I was a kid."

Hildy, who had, from force of habit, taken out her notebook, put it away again. The verses suggested several fascinating insights into various textual problems in the Elder Edda, but this was neither the time nor the place. "If it's that dangerous," she said firmly, "we must go and help him."

"But..." Arvarodd waved his hand impatiently.

"He is the King," said Hildy cleverly. "Our duty is to protect him."

"Don't you start," Arvarodd grumbled. He rolled the biscuit-wrapper up into a ball and threw it at the windscreen.

Hildy sat still for a moment, then took the seer-stone from her bag and put it in her eye. She saw the King and his companions crossing a carpeted office. They had not seen the door open behind them, and two men in blue boiler-suits with rifles. Hildy wanted to shout and warn them. The door at the other end of the office opened, and the King shouted and drew his sword. There was a shot and Hildy cried out, but the King was still standing; the man had shot the sword out of his hand. The wizard was shrieking something, some spell or other, but it wasn't working; and Brynjolf was staring in horror at his feet, which hadn't turned into a bear's paws or the wings of an eagle. The guards were laughing. Slowly, the King and his companions raised their hands and put them on their heads.

"Can you see them?" Arvarodd was muttering. There was sweat pouring down his face.

"Yes," Hildy said. "It's no good; they've been captured. Their magic isn't working." She looked round, but Arvarodd wasn't there. He had snatched up his bow and quiver, and was running towards the steel doors. Wailing "Wait for me," Hildy ran after him.

The door was still open. Hildy tried to keep pace with Arvarodd as he bounded up the stairs but she could not. She stopped, panting, at the first landing, and then looked across and saw the lift. Against all her hopes, it was working. She pressed 4—how she knew it would be the fourth floor she had no idea—and leant back to catch her breath. The doors slid open, and she hopped out.

What on earth did she think she was doing?

She turned back, but the lift doors had shut. Down the corridor she could hear the sound of running feet. She opened the door of the nearest office and slipped inside.

It was a small room, and the walls were covered with steel boxes, like gas-meters or fuseboxes. She had a sudden idea. If she could switch off the lights, perhaps the King could escape in the darkness. She pulled out her flashlight and started to read the labels. Down in a corner she saw a little glass box.

"MAGIC SUPPLY," read the label. "DO NOT TOUCH." And underneath, in smaller letters: "In the event of power supply failure, break glass and press button. This will deactivate the mains-fed spell. The emergency spell will automatically take effect within seven minutes."

With the butt of her torch Hildy smashed the glass and leant hard on the button. A moment later, the guards' rifles inexplicably turned into bunches of daffodils.

"Daffodils?" asked the King, as he banged two heads together. The wizard shrugged and made a noise like hotel plumbing.

"Fair enough," said the King. "Let's get out of here."

They sprinted back the way they had come, nearly colliding with Arvarodd, who was coming up the stairs towards them.

"What happened?" he said.

"Our magic failed," replied the King. "Then theirs did. No idea why."

"Have you seen Hildy?" At that moment, Hildy appeared, running towards them. "Quick," she gasped, "we've only got three minutes."

A shot from an ex-daffodil bounced off the tarmac as they drove off.

"Far be it for me to criticise," said Thorgeir, gripping his seat-belt with both hands, "but aren't you driving rather fast?"

The sorcerer-king grinned. "Yes," he said. He drove even faster. Childish, Thorgeir said to himself, but, then, he's like that. Mental age of seventeen. Only a permanent adolescent would devote hours of his valuable time to laying a spell on a Morris Minor so as to enable it to burn off Porsches at traffic lights. "I want to get back to London as quickly as possible," he explained.

"Then, why didn't we fly?" asked Thorgeir.

"We can do that if you like," said the sorcerer-king mischievously. "No problem."

"Stop showing off," Thorgeir said. A land-locked Morris Minor was bad enough. "You don't seem to appreciate the situation we're in."

"On the contrary," said the sorcerer-king, putting his foot down hard. "That's why I'm in such a good mood."

"You seem to have overlooked the fact that they got away," Thorgeir shouted above the scream of the tortured engine. He shut his eyes and muttered an ancient Finnish suspension-improving spell.

"Only by a fluke," replied the King. "Next time they won't be so lucky. Next time we'll be there."

"You think there'll be a next time?"

"Has to be." The sorcerer-king removed the suspension-improving spell and deliberately drove over the cat's eyes. "What else can he do?"

Thorgeir, whose head had just made sharp contact with the roof, did not reply. The sorcerer-king chuckled and changed up into fourth.

"The trouble with you," he said, "is that you can't feel comfortable unless you're worried about something." Thorgeir, who was both worried and profoundly uncomfortable, shook his head, but for once the sorcerer-king had his eyes on the road. "You don't believe in happy endings. Look at it this way," he said, overtaking a blaspheming Ferrari. "If they had anything left in reserve, why did they try to pull that stunt last night? They're finished and they know it. That was pure Gunnar-in-the-snake-pit stuff, a one-way ticket to Valhalla. Not that I begrudge them that, of course," said the sorcerer-king magnanimously. "If they want to go to Valhalla, let them. Nice enough place, I suppose, except that the food all comes out of a microwave these days and the wish-maidens are definitely past their prime. A bit like one of those run-down gentlemen's clubs in Pall Mall, if you ask me."

Thorgeir gave up and diverted his energies to worrying about the traffic police. Last time, he remembered, the sorcerer-king had let them chase him all the way from Coalville to Watford Gap, and then turned them all into horseflies. Turning them back had not been easy, especially the one who'd been eaten by a swallow.

"Now you're sulking," said the sorcerer-king cheerfully.

"I'm not sulking," said Thorgeir, "I'm taking it seriously. Who did you leave in charge, by the way?"

"That young Fortescue," said the sorcerer-king. "Since he's in on the whole thing, we might as well make him useful. Or a frog. Whichever."

Thorgeir shuddered. Much as he deplored unnecessary sorcery, he felt that the frog option would have been safer.

In fact, the Governor of China elect was doing a perfectly adequate job back at Gerrards Garth House. He had seen to the removal and replacement of the anti-magic circuit, debriefed the guards and written a report, all in one morning. At this rate, he felt, he might soon count as indispensable.

After putting his head round the door at Vouchers to make sure that the prisoners were still there, he sent for the Chief Clerk of the department and asked him about the arrangements for tracking the getaway van the burglars had used. All that was needed was a simple tap into the police computer at Hendon, he was told, to get the registered owner's name and address. Then it would be perfectly simple to slip the registration number on to the computer's list of stolen vehicles and monitor the police band until some eagle-eyed copper noticed it.

"But what if they get arrested?" Kevin asked.

"Then we'll know where they are," replied the Chief Clerk. "Easy."

"No, it's not," Kevin objected. "They won't get bail without having plausible identities or anything, and they'll probably resist arrest and be kept in for that. And we can't go bursting into a police station to get them; it'd be too risky."

The Chief Clerk's smile was a horrible sight. "No sweat," he said. "Lots of things can happen to them. In the police cells, on remand, being transferred, on their way to the magistrates' court, anywhere you like. Easiest thing would be to wait till they're convicted and put away. We can get to them inside with no trouble at all. But I don't suppose the Third Floor will want to wait that long. Best thing is if they do resist arrest. Dead meat," he said graphically. "I think our police are wonderful."

Kevin Fortescue was relieved to get back to his office, for the Chief

Clerk gave him the creeps. Still, he reflected, you have to be hard to get on in Business. He dismissed the thought from his mind and took his well-thumbed *Oxford School Atlas* from his desk drawer.

"Winter Palace in Chungking," he said to himself. "Not too cold and a good view of the mountains."

Danny Bennett was being shown round the Castle of Borve.

"Mind you," said Angantyr Asmundarson, as Danny expressed polite admiration, "it's perishing cold in winter and one hell of a way to go to get a pint of milk. Or was," he reflected. "We used to have our own house-cows, of course. Enchanted cows, naturally. But they were enchanted to yield mead, honey and ale, which is all very well but indigestible on porridge. Couple of Jerseys."

Danny ducked his head under a rock lintel. The one thing he wanted was access to a television set, for his story, if it was going to break at all, would be doing so at this very minute, and it was too much to hope that anyone would tape it for him.

"That's the mead-hall through there," said Angantyr, "and the King's table. The main arsenals and the still-room are round the back."

This man would make a good estate agent, Danny reflected. He nodded appreciatively and smiled. Why hadn't he bought one of those portable wrist-watch televisions, like he'd seen them wearing at the Stock Exchange?

"So how long do you think we can stay here for?" he asked.

"Indefinitely," said Angantyr. "You see, this place is totally hidden. Unless you know how to find it...."

"Yes," said Danny, "but you'll have to go out occasionally, to get water and food and things."

"No need," said Angantyr proudly. "There's a natural spring—still there, we checked—and as for food there's any amount of seagulls. You like seagull," Angantyr reminded him. "You're lucky."

Danny repressed a shudder. "Actually—" he started to say.

"Last time we were besieged in here," Angantyr went on, "we stuck it out for nine months, until the enemy got bored out of their minds and went away. We were all right, though," said Angantyr smugly. "We remembered to bring a couple of chess sets."

"I can't play chess."

"I'll teach you. It's pretty easy once you've got it into your head that the knight can go over the top of the other pieces. And there's other things to do, of course. I used to make collages with the seagull feathers. Anyway," Angantyr said, "we probably won't be here too long this time. It'll all be over soon, one way or another. That reminds me." He dashed off, and Danny sat down on a stone seat and took off his shoes. His feet were killing him after the forced march from Bettyhill. The Vikings walked very quickly.

Angantyr came back. He was holding a helmet and a suit of chain armour, and under his arm was tucked a sword and a spear.

"Try these," he said. "They should be small enough. Made for the King when he was twelve."

Danny tried them on. They were much too big, and so heavy he could hardly move in them. "Thanks," he said, as he struggled out of the mail shirt, "but I won't be needing them anyway, will I?"

"Don't be so pessimistic," Angantyr said. "There's always a bit of fighting at a siege. I remember when we were stuck in Tongue for six months—"

"You don't understand," said Danny, "I'm a non-combatant. Press," he explained. "And anyway, if there is any violence, these wouldn't help."

"What do you mean?" said Angantyr, puzzled. Danny explained; he told him about CS gas and stun-grenades, machine-pistols and birdshot.

"You mean Special Effects," said Angantyr. "Don't you worry about that. All our armour is spellproof."

"Spellproof?"

"Guaranteed. All that stuff," he said, dismissing all human endeavour from Barthold Schwartz to napalm with a wave of his hand, "is obsolete now."

"No, it's not."

"Well, it *was*. Don't say you people still believe in the white-hot heat of magic and so on. Very old-fashioned. No, all our gear's totally magic-resistant. Unless, of course, the other side's got counter-spells."

"Counter-spells?" All this reminded Danny of something.

"Counter-spells. Of course, most of those were done away with after the MALT talks. It was only when the Enemy started cheating and using them again after we'd all dumped ours that things got unpleasant and we had to use the Brooch. That was the biggest counter-spell of them all, you see."

"I see." Danny rubbed his head. There was another story here, but one he had no wish to get involved in.

"Of course," went on Angantyr, "the Enemy's probably still got all his, and they don't make you invulnerable against conventional weapons. Still, it does even things up a bit."

"Even so," Danny said, "I'm still a non-combatant. I don't know how to use swords and things."

Angantyr shrugged his shoulders. "Have it your own way," he said. "You'd better have the armour, all the same."

Danny decided it would be easier to agree. "I'll put it on later," he said.

At that moment, Starkad, who had been left on watch, came running down the narrow spiral stairway. He was shouting something about a huge metal seagull with wings that went round and round. A moment later, Danny could hear the sound of rotor-blades passing close overhead and dying away in the distance.

"Dragons?" Angantyr asked. Danny told him about helicopters. "It means they're looking for us," he said. "They might have those infra-red things that can trace you by your body-heat. Unless those count as magic."

But Angantyr hadn't heard of anything like that. Danny felt vaguely proud that the twentieth century had at least one totally original invention to its credit.

"Don't like the sound of that," Angantyr muttered.

"That's what I've been trying to tell you," Danny said. "This castle may have been impregnable once, but—"

Angantyr shook his head. "Still is," he replied. "I don't mean that. It's just the noise that thing makes. It'll frighten off all the seagulls."

"So now what do we do?" said Arvarodd.

"Speaking purely for myself," said the King, "I'll have the pancake with maple syrup. What is maple syrup?" he asked Hildy.

They were sitting in a deserted Little Chef in the middle of Buckinghamshire. How they had got there, Hildy had no idea; she had just kept on driving until the petrol-tank was nearly empty, then pulled in at the first service station for fuel and food. Her heroism of the previous night had thoroughly unnerved her, and she wanted to go home to Long Island.

"It's a sort of sweet sticky stuff you get from a tree," she said absently. "What *are* we going to do?"

"I haven't the faintest idea," said the King. He was taking it all very calmly, Hildy thought. Why, if it hadn't been for her...

"If it hadn't been for you," said the King suddenly, "Odin knows what would have happened back there. That was quick thinking."

"Pure luck," Hildy said.

"Yes," agreed the King, "but quick thinking all the same. Five pancakes, please," he ordered. "All with maple syrup."

"Do you think they'll follow us?" Hildy asked.

"They'll try," said the King, "but not too hard. We must get rid of that van first. Isn't that number written on the back and front some sort of identification mark? They're bound to have seen that. We'll sell the van in the next town we come to and get something else."

Hildy realised that she should have thought of that. She made an effort and pulled herself together. "And after that?" she said.

"After that, we'll do what we should have done in the first place."

"What's that?"

"We'll get hold of that bloody wizard," said the King grimly, "and hold his head underwater until he thinks of something." The wizard made a soft grinding noise, but they ignored him. "After all, he got us into this mess."

They stared aggressively at the wizard, who took a profound interest in his pancake. He seemed to have lost his appetite, however, and put his spoon down.

"Get on with it," said the King. The wizard snarled and draped his paper napkin over his head. There was an anxious silence; then from under the napkin came a noise like a coffee-mill which went on for a very long time.

"Are you sure?" said the King. The coffee-mill noise started up again.

"Positive?"

The napkin nodded.

"What did he say?" Hildy demanded.

"Well," said the King, leaning forward, "he reckons that there's a brooch with a spell-circuit—you know, like the dragon-brooch—that might be able to cut off the magic inside the tower, and it should be possible to run it off a much weaker source of power, like a car battery."

"How does he know about car batteries?" Hildy asked.

"Worked it out from first principles," said the King. "Anyway, if we get hold of this brooch, we might have a chance. According to Kotkel, it was made by Sitrygg Sow, who had the design from Odin himself. But he's only seen it once, and he's never tried it out for himself. It's a very long shot."

"But God knows where it's got to," said Hildy. "Even if it still exists, it's still probably buried somewhere."

"In that case," said the King, "all we'll need is a shovel and a map. You see, it belonged to a king of the Saxons down in East Anglia, and it was buried with him. One of the Wuffing kings, can't remember which one. But he was the only one buried in a ship, that I can tell you. In a minute, I'll remember the name of the place."

"Sutton Hoo," Hildy murmured.

"That's it," said the King. "How did you know that?"

"Is this brooch," Hildy asked, "also in the shape of a dragon?" There was a bright light in her eyes, and her hands were shaking.

"That's right," the King said. "More of a fire-drake, actually. Never had any taste, Sitrygg."

"Gold inlaid with garnets?"

"Yes."

"Then," said Hildy, "I know where it is. It's in London. In fact, it's in the British Museum." She rummaged about in her organiser bag for her copy of the latest *Journal of Scandinavian Studies*. "Is this it?" she said, thrusting the open book under the wizard's nose. The wizard pointed to plate 7*a* and nodded.

"Is that good or bad?" asked the King.

9

"Originally," said the lecturer, "this was believed to have been the king's standard, to which his troops rallied in time of war. It has now been reidentified as a hat-stand."

He looked round his audience. For once, he noticed, there were a couple of intelligent faces among them. One of them, a big man with a beard, was nodding approvingly. He decided to tell them about the quotation from *Beowulf* after all.

"He's wrong, of course," whispered Brynjolf to Hildy, "but he wasn't to know that. Only idiots like the East Saxons would use a hat-stand for a battle-standard."

Hildy sighed. The neatly argued little paper intended for the October edition of *Heimdall* in which she proved conclusively that the Chelmsford Standard was in fact a toast-rack would have to be shelved.

"These," said the lecturer, pointing at a glass case, "are among the earliest finds from the period of Scandinavian settlement in Sutherland and Caithness. The Melvich Arm-Ring..."

Arvarodd was staring. Hildy prodded him in the ribs, but he didn't seem to notice. "That's mine," he whispered.

"Are you sure?" asked Hildy.

"Course I'm sure. Given to me when I killed my first wolf. Sure, it's only bronze, but it has great sentimental value."

"Keep your voice down," Hildy hissed.

"Bergthora said if I didn't chuck it out and get a new one she'd give it to a museum," went on the hero of Permia. "I never thought she'd do it."

"Who was Bergthora?" Hildy asked. Arvarodd blushed. "Although the workmanship is crude and poorly executed," continued the lecturer, "and not at all representative of the high Urnes style that was shortly to..."

"He's getting on my nerves," Arvarodd said. Hildy glowered at him.

The lecturer moved on and started to tell his audience about a set of drinking-horns. The King and his party hung back.

"Remember," he said, "we're just here to have a look, so don't get carried away. We'll come back later when it's not so crowded."

"And here we have the crowning glory of our Early Medieval collection," the lecturer said proudly, "the Sutton Hoo treasure. Until recently, this was the richest find ever made on the British mainland. Now, however, the recently discovered Rolfsness treasure..."

Arvarodd muttered something under his breath, but the wizard was pointing. So was the lecturer.

"The dragon-brooch," he was saying, "is one of the most interesting pieces in the entire hoard."

When the lecture was over, and Hildy had managed to distract Arvarodd's attention when the lecturer asked if there were any questions, the King and his company went for a drink. They felt that they had earned one.

"Simple theft is what I call it," Arvarodd complained. "How would he like it if I took his watch and put it in a glass case and made funny remarks about it?"

"Shut up about your arm-ring," said the King. "They've got all my treasure down in their basement, and I'm not complaining. Well, almost all. That reminds me."

From his finger he drew a heavy gold ring. Hildy had often admired it out of the corner of her eye.

"While we're here," he said, "we'd better sell this. I don't suppose there's much money left by now."

Hildy, as treasurer, nodded sadly. She hated the thought of such a masterpiece going to some unscrupulous collector, but buying the new car had more or less cleaned them out, and even then they'd only been able to afford a horrible old wreck, held together by body putty and, after the wizard had been at it, witchcraft. She took the ring and put it in her purse.

"Back to business," said the King. "After we've got this brooch, we'll have to move quickly. I'm still worried about the others...."

At that moment the television above the bar announced the one o'clock news.

"There have been dramatic new developments," said the newsreader, "in the manhunt in the north of Scotland, in which the police are seeking the eight armed men who are believed to have abducted a female archaeologist and a BBC producer. Helicopters equipped with infra-red sensors..."

Picture of the Castle of Borve.

"Don't worry," said Angantyr Asmundarson.

But Danny was very worried. He'd seen the police marksmen getting into position all morning, and the way Angantyr was testing his bowstring had made him shiver.

"How many do you reckon there are?" asked Hjort over his shoulder, as he plied a whetstone across his axe-blade.

"About ten each," Angantyr replied. "Still, if we wait a bit longer some more may turn up."

"Cheapskate, that's what I call it," Hjort grumbled. "Hardly worth sharpening up for."

"Anyway," said Bothvar Bjarki, "I'm having the one with the trumpet."

"No, you're not."

"We drew lots," Bothvar whined.

"You cheated," said Hjort. "You always cheat."

"I did not," replied Bothvar angrily, surreptitiously slipping his double-headed coin into Danny's jacket pocket. "Anyway, look who's talking."

Danny wasn't listening. He was calculating whether it would be possible to slip out unobserved while the heroes were squabbling. But, if he did, the police might shoot him. And if he were to put on one of the mail shirts the police would take him for one of the heroes and would undoubtedly shoot him.

"This is Superintendent Mackay," came a voice from outside. "We have you completely surrounded by armed police officers. Throw out your weapons and come out."

That, Danny realised, could have been better phrased, given that the heroes were armed with javelins and throwing-hammers. He ducked under the parapet and put his hands over his head.

"You missed!" jeered Bothvar, as Hjort picked up another javelin.

"Of course I missed," said Hjort, standing up to throw again. A bullet sang harmlessly off his helmet and landed at Danny's feet. "There's few enough of them as it is without frittering them away with javelins."

"I don't think they meant it like that," Danny shouted. "I think they want you to surrender." A CS-gas canister whizzed over the parapet, spluttered and went out.

"Surrender?" Hjort's face fell under his jewel-encrusted visor. "Are you sure?"

"Doesn't look like it to me," said Angantyr cheerfully, as he caught a stun-grenade in his left hand. He looked at it, threw himself a catch from left to right, and hurled it back. It exploded. "If they want us to surrender, they shouldn't be shooting at us."

"They've stopped," said Hjort wistfully. "Call this a siege?"

"Here, Danny," Angantyr said, "what's the form these days?"

But Danny wasn't there. As soon as the shooting had stopped, he had slipped away and crawled back into the hall. Frantically he unbuttoned his shirt, which was white enough if you didn't mind the stewed seagull down the front of it, and tied the sleeves to the shaft of a javelin. He looked around, but all the heroes were at the parapet. Very cautiously, he started to climb the spiral stair.

"Reports are just coming in," said the newsreader, "that the police have made an attempt to storm the ruined castle where the ten men have barricaded themselves in. According to the reports, the attempt was unsuccessful. It is not yet known whether there were any casualties. A spokesman for the Historic Buildings Commission..."

The King clenched his right fist and pressed it into the palm of his left hand. His face was expressionless. "I hate this job," he said.

Hildy had taken out the seer-stone, but the King told her to put it away. "I don't want to know," he said. "They'll have to look after themselves."

"If I know them," said Brynjolf, "they'll be having the time of their lives."

"Remember," said the superintendent, "the last thing we want is a bloodbath."

The man in the black pullover grinned at him, his white teeth flashing out from the black greasepaint that covered his face. "Sure," he said, and stuck another grenade in his belt for luck. He hadn't been jolted about in a helicopter all the way from Hereford just to ask a lot of terrorists if they fancied coming quietly. "How many of them are there?"

"Ten, according to our intelligence," said the superintendent.

"One each," said the man in the black pullover. He sounded disappointed.

Just then, there was a rattling of rifle-bolts. A solitary figure with a white flag had appeared on the side of the cliffs "Hell," said the man in the black pullover.

"Put your hands on your head," boomed the megaphone, "and

walk slowly over here." The man dropped the white flag and did as he was told.

"Be careful," said the man in the black pullover, "it could be a trap." But his heart wasn't in it. He started to take the grenades out of his belt.

"It's that perishing sorcerer of yours," muttered Hjort, staring out over the parapet. "He's gone over to the enemy."

"Has he indeed?" said Angantyr grimly. "We'll soon see about that." He bent his great ibex-horn bow and sighted along the arrow.

"Don't do that," said Hjort. "You'll frighten them away. And there's some more just arrived. In black," he added, with approval.

"What's going on?" said Bothvar, dropping down beside them. He had been searching everywhere for the magic halberd of Gunnar, which he'd put away safely before going into the mound at Rolfsness. Eventually he'd found it down behind the back of the treasure-chests. "I do wish people wouldn't move my things."

"We've just been betrayed by a traitor," said Angantyr.

"That's more like it," said Bothvar.

"And we're now going over live to the armed siege in Scotland," said the newsreader. "Our reporter there is Moira Urquhart."

The sorcerer-king leant forward and turned up the volume. "Are you taping this?" he asked.

Thorgeir nodded. "I'm having to use the 'Yes, Minister' tape, but it's worth it."

"They'll repeat it again soon, I expect," said the sorcerer-king. "Look, isn't that Bothvar Bjarki?" The camera had zoomed in on a helmeted head poking out above the parapet. "I'd know that helmet anywhere."

"I've just thought of something," said Thorgeir. "That armour of theirs..."

"One of the terrorists seems to be shouting something," said the reporter's voice over the close-up of the helmeted head. "We're trying to catch what he's saying... Something about a seagull... It could be that they're demanding that food is sent in."

"I never could be doing with seagull," said the sorcerer-king, spearing an olive. "Except maybe in a casserole with plenty of coriander."

"Fried in breadcrumbs, it's not too bad," said Thorgeir. "Isn't that Angantyr Asmundarson beside him?"

"It seems that the terrorists are in fact assuring us that they have plenty of food," said the reporter. "In fact they're telling us that they're capable of withstanding a long siege and inviting us to storm the castle. In fact," said the reporter, "they've started slow hand-clapping."

"Childish," said the sorcerer-king.

"And since not much seems to be happening at the moment," said the reporter, "I'm now going to have a few words with the BBC producer, Danny Bennett, who was held hostage by the terrorists and managed to escape a few minutes ago. Tell me, Danny..."

"Who's he?" asked Thorgeir.

"Search me," said the sorcerer-king.

"They aren't terrorists at all," Danny Bennett was saying. "More like...well, it's a long story. Big, but long." He mopped his brow with the corner of the blanket they had insisted on putting round his shoulders. "And they didn't kidnap me."

"You mean you went with them voluntarily?"

"Sort of," Danny said. "That is, they rescued me when I was wandering about lost in the mountains. I'd got separated from the rest of the crew, you see. And then they told me all about it, and it was such a big story that I decided I'd stay with them. Until the shooting started, of course."

"I see." The reporter was trying to get a good look at the back of Danny's head, to see if there were any signs of a recent sharp blow. Still, she reflected, it was good television.

"I can't say much about the story just now," Danny went on, "because it's all pretty incredible stuff and, anyway, I told Derek all about it over the phone from the police station at Bettyhill...."

"You mean you were in contact with the BBC at the time of the breakout?" The reporter was clearly interested. "Are you trying to say there's been a cover-up?"

"How the hell do I know?" Danny said. "There isn't a telly in that bloody cave."

"What were you saying about their armour?" said the sorcerer-king.

"Oh, yes," said Thorgeir Storm-shepherd. "It'll be enchanted, won't it?"

"Sod it," said the sorcerer-king. "Hang on, something's happening."

"The hell with this," said Bothvar. He was hoarse from shouting. "If they're just going to sit there, when they know about the secret passage and everything..."

"Maybe they don't," said Angantyr. "Maybe he hasn't told them."

Bothvar laughed, but Angantyr wasn't so sure. Danny hadn't seemed the treacherous type to him. "Maybe he went to negotiate," he suggested.

"Without telling us?"

"We wouldn't have let him go if he'd told us," said Angantyr. Bothvar considered this.

"True," said Ohtar, testing the edge of his sword with his thumb. "And he did say he liked my cooking. Can't be all bad."

"And what does that prove?" said Bothvar. "The man's either a liar or an idiot. How are we for javelins, by the way?"

"Running a bit low," said the hero Hring, who was quartermaster. "They don't throw them back, you see."

"That's cheating," said Bothvar. "If they go on like that, we'll have to stop throwing them. Still, there's rocks."

"I think he went out there to try to negotiate," repeated Angantyr Asmundarson. "Otherwise they'd have made an assault on the hidden passage by now."

"Could be," said Hjort. He could see no other possible explanation for the enemy's lack of activity. "After all, they outnumber us at least eight to one." He said this very loudly, in the hope that the enemy might overhear him. They obviously needed to be encouraged.

"And he did try to warn us about the big metal seagulls they used to find us. And about the Special Effects," Angantyr continued. "I think he got frightened and went out to try to negotiate."

"Frightened?" said Bothvar incredulously. "What by?" He picked a spent bullet out of his beard and threw it away.

"In which case," said Hring, "they've detained a herald."

"That's true," said Bothvar. "We must do something about that."

"The King did say we were only to defend ourselves," said the hero Egil Kjartansson, called the Dancer, or more usually the Wet Blanket. "No attacking, those were his orders."

"But this is different," said Angantyr. "Detaining a herald is just like attacking, really. You've got to rescue your heralds, or where would you be?"

There was, of course, no answer to that. "All right then," said Egil Kjartansson, "but don't blame me if we get into trouble."

"Hoo-bloody-ray, we're going to do something at last." Hjort rubbed his hands together and put his left arm through the straps of his shield. "Starkad! Hroar! Come over here, we're going to attack."

The remaining heroes rushed to the parapet, while Hring distributed the javelins. Starkad Storvirksson, who was the King's berserk, lifted his great double-handed sword and began the chant to Odin.

"Can it," Bothvar interrupted him. "We've wasted enough time as it is."

With one movement, like a wolf leaping, Starkad Storvirksson sprang up on to the parapet and brandished his sword. Then he hopped down again.

"Bothvar," he said plaintively, "I've forgotten my battle-cry."

"It's 'Starkad!', Starkad," said Bothvar. "Can we get on, please?"

With a deafening roar of "Starkad!" the berserk vaulted over the parapet and led the charge. After him came Bothvar, wielding the halberd of Gunnar, with Angantyr Asmundsson close behind and Hroar almost treading on his heels. Then came Egil Kjartansson, his shield crashing against his mail shirt as he ran; Hring and Hjort, running like hounds on a tantalising scent, and finally Ohtar, who had finished up the seagull flan because nobody else wanted any more, and had raging indigestion as a result. In their hands their swords flashed, like the foam on the crests of the great waves that pounded the rocks below them, and as they ran the earth shook. A man with a megaphone stood up as they charged, thought better of it, and ducked down; a moment later, Bothvar's javelin transfixed the spot where he had been standing, its blade driven down almost to the shaft in the dense springy peat.

"That'll do me," said the man in the black pullover, as the spearshaft quivered beside him. "Let 'em have it." His men shouldered their automatic rifles and started to fire.

"Don't bother with shooting over their heads," said the man in the black pullover.

"We're not," said one of his men. He looked worried.

"Told you," said Thorgeir, pointing at the screen. The picture was wobbling fearfully, as if the cameraman was running: a close-up of one of the heroes, dribbling an unexploded grenade in front of him as he charged.

"Can't think of everything, can I?" grumbled the sorcerer-king. "Anyway, we can fix that later."

"It's unbelievable," panted the reporter. "All the bullets and bombs and things seem to be having no effect on them at all. They're just charging... And the police are running away... For Christ's sake, will you get me out of here? This is Moira Urquhart, BBC News, Borve Castle."

The picture shook violently and the screen went blank. Someone had dropped the camera.

"Pity," said the sorcerer-king. "I was enjoying that."

Bothvar Bjarki leant on his halberd and tried to get his breath back. "Swizzle," he gasped.

"You're out of condition, you are," said Hjort, mopping his forehead with the hem of his cloak.

Overhead, the helicopters were receding into the distance, their fuselages riddled with javelins and arrows, flying as fast as they could in the general direction of Hereford. "Chicken!" Hjort roared after them. He tied a knot in the barrel of an abandoned rifle and sat down in disgust.

"I nearly got the leader of those men in black," said Starkad Storvirksson. "I thought for a moment he was going to stand, but in the end he jumped on to the metal seagull along with all the others." He dropped the piece of helicopter undercarriage he had been carrying and went off to help Hring pick up the arrows.

"Never mind," said Angantyr. "It was a victory, wasn't it?"

"I suppose so." Bothvar yawned. "Anyway, they might come back." He chopped up a television camera to relieve his feelings. "Oh, look," he said, "there's glass in these things."

Angantyr sheathed his sword. "You know what we haven't done?"

"What?"

"We haven't rescued the herald," Angantyr said. "That's no good, is it?"

"Maybe he wasn't a herald after all, only a traitor," said Ohtar. He had found a lunch-box dropped in the rout and was investigating the contents. "Anyway, we did our best." But Angantyr jumped up and started to search. He did not have to look far. Danny, with a disappointing lack of imagination, had climbed a tree, only discovering when he reached the top that it was a thorn-tree and uninhabitable.

"Hello," Angantyr said, "what are you doing up there?"

"Help!" Danny explained. "I'm stuck."

With a few blows of his sword, Angantyr chopped through the tree and pushed it over. Danny crawled out and collapsed on the ground. "What happened?" he said.

"We came to rescue you," said Angantyr. "You did go to try to negotiate, didn't you?" he asked as an afterthought. Danny assured him that he had. "And you didn't tell them about the secret passage?"

"Of course not," Danny replied. He had tried to, but no one would listen.

"That's all right, then," Angantyr said cheerfully. "You've got thorns sticking in you." Danny followed Angantyr back to where the other heroes were sitting and thanked them for rescuing him. He didn't feel in the least grateful, but having seen the heroes in action he reckoned that tact was probably called for.

"No trouble," said Ohtar. He bit into a chocolate roll he'd found in the lunch-box and spat it out again. "Don't like that," he said.

"You're supposed to take the foil off first," Danny said.

"Gold-plated food," said Ohtar admiringly. "Stylish."

The spokesman from Highlands and Islands Development Board was refusing to comment, and Thorgeir switched the set off. The sorcerer-king was counting on his fingers.

"So that leaves four unaccounted for," be said. "The King, the wizard, Arvarodd of Permia and Brynjolf the Shape-Shifter."

"Plus that lady archaeologist makes five," said Thorgeir. "Trouble is we haven't the faintest idea where they are."

"You're worrying again," said the sorcerer-king. He turned to his desk and tapped a code into his desktop terminal.

"Trying the Hendon computer again?" Thorgeir asked. The sorcerer-king shook his head, and pointed to the screen. On a green background, little Viking figures were rushing backwards and forwards, vainly trying to avoid the two ravening wolves that were chasing them through a stylised maze.

"I had young Fortescue run it up for me this morning," said the sorcerer-king. "He's good with computers, that boy."

Thorgeir shook his head sadly, but said nothing. There had been a word in one of the Old Norse dialects that exactly described the sorcerer-king. "Yuppje," he murmured under his breath, and went away to get on with some work.

The new car, despite being a useless old wreck, had a radio in it, and the King's company were listening to the news.

"The search is continuing," said the newsreader, "for the ten men who routed police and SAS units in a pitched battle in the north of Scotland yesterday. They are believed still to be in the Strathnaver district. Two companies of Royal Marines have reinforced the police, and Harriers from RAF Lossiemouth are on standby. In the House of Commons, the Defence Minister has refused to reply to Opposition questions until the conclusion of the operation."

The King shrugged his shoulders. "Might as well leave them to it," he said. "They seem to be coping."

"You should have told me about the armour," Hildy said.

"You should have told me about the Special Effects," replied the King. "Now you see what I mean about the decline of civilisation. But we can't leave things too long. It depends on what he's doing. If he's gone up there or sent someone to put a counter-spell on the lads, it'll all be over in a matter of minutes. Of course, he'll have to find them first. But with luck..."

Hildy parked the car, praying that it wouldn't be clamped while they were inside the Museum, for that would interfere quite horribly with their well-planned escape. Still, she reflected, so many things could go wrong with this lunatic enterprise that it was pointless to worry about any one of them.

The King, the wizard, Arvarodd and Brynjolf had put their mail shirts on under large raincoats bought that afternoon with part of the proceeds of the King's ring and hung short swords by their sides. For her part, Hildy had been given a small flat pebble with a rune scratched on it which was supposed to have roughly the same effect as an enchanted mail shirt, and she had put it in her pocket wrapped up in two handkerchieves and a scarf, to protect her against the side-effect (incessant sneezing). She had also found the magic charms that Arvarodd had lent her on her first trip to London; she offered to return them, but Arvarodd had smiled and told her to hang on to them for the time being.

Past the guards at the big revolving door without any trouble. Up the main staircase and through the Egyptian galleries, then out along a room full of Greek vases and they were there.

The lecturer was giving the afternoon lecture. This time his audience consisted of five Germans, three schoolboys, a middle-aged woman and her small and disruptive nephew. No point in even considering the *Beowulf* quotation.

"Well," said Brynjolf, as they stood in front of the big glass case that contained the shield, harp and helmet, "what's the plan?"

"Who needs a plan?" replied the King. "But we'll just wait till these people go away again."

"That's all wrong, of course," said Arvarodd, contemplating the helmet, which teams of scholars had pieced together from a handful of twisted and rusty fragments. "You imagine wearing that."

Unfortunately the lecturer, who was just approaching the Sutton Hoo exhibit, took that as a question. After all, it was a comment he had often been faced with, and by now he had worked out a short and well-phrased answer. He gave it. Arvarodd listened impatiently.

"Here," he said when the lecturer had finished, "give me a pencil and a bit of paper." Resting the paper on the side of the glass case, he drew a quick sketch of what the helmet should have looked like. "Try that," he said.

"But that...that's brilliant," said the lecturer, his audience quite forgotten. "So that's what that little bobble thing was for."

"Stands to reason," said Arvarodd.

The lecturer beamed. "Tell me, Mr...."

"Arvarodd," said Arvarodd.

The lecturer stared. Perhaps it was something in the man's eyes, but there was something about him that made the hair on the back of the lecturer's head start to rise. The palms of his clenched hands were wet now, and he found it difficult to breathe. He narrowed his eyebrows.

"Arvarodd?"

"That's right," said Arvarodd.

The lecturer took a deep breath. "Aren't you the Arvarodd who went to Permia?" he asked.

Arvarodd hit him.

"That," he said, "is for stealing my arm-ring." He strode across to the glass case, drew his short sword, and smashed the glass. Alarms went off all over the building.

"Quick," said the King. With his own short sword, he smashed open the case containing the brooch, grabbed it, and stuffed it into his pocket. The middle-aged woman shrieked, and the small nephew kicked him. "Right," said the King, "move!"

But Arvarodd was gazing at his arm-ring, running his fingers over the beloved metal, his mind full only of the image of his first wolf, at bay on the hillside above Crackaig. The lecturer wiped the blood from his nose and staggered to his feet.

"*Your* arm-ring?" he said in wonder.

"Yes," snapped Arvarodd, wheeling round. His hand tightened on his sword-hilt. "Want to make something of it?"

"But it's eighth-century," said the lecturer. "And you're seventh."

"Who are you calling seventh-century?"

"But your saga..." Heedless of personal danger, the lecturer grabbed his sleeve. "Definitely set in seventh-century Norway."

"I know," said Arvarodd sadly. "Bloody editors," he explained.

Suddenly, the gallery was filled with large men in blue uniforms. Before Hildy could warn them, they ran towards the King. Glass cases crashed to the ground.

"Oh, no," Hildy wailed, as a case of silver dishes was crushed beneath a stunned guard, "not here." Suddenly she remembered Arvarodd's magic charms. She fished in her pocket and pulled out the fragment of bone that made you irresistibly persuasive. Quickly she seized hold of the nearest guard.

"Not theft," she said, "fire."

The guard looked at her. She tightened her hand round the fragment of bone. "Fire," she repeated, "It's a fire alarm."

"Oh," said the guard. "Right you are, miss." He hurried off to tell the others. The battle stopped.

"Then, why did he break that glass case?" asked the chief guard.

"You know what it says on the notices," replied Hildy desperately. "In case of fire, break glass."

The guards dashed away to evacuate the galleries.

Just as Hildy had feared, they had clamped the car. But the King was in no mood to be worried by a little thing like that. With a single blow of his sword, he sliced through the yellow metal and flicked away the wreckage. There were several cheers from passing motorists. The King and his company jumped into the car and drove away.

"That was quick thinking," said the King, as Hildy accelerated over Waterloo Bridge.

"What was?"

"The way you got rid of those guards."

"It was nothing," Hildy said quietly. "It was all down to that jawbone thing of Arvarodd's."

"Nevertheless," the King smiled, "I think you've definitely done enough to deserve a Name...."

"A Name?" Hildy gasped. "You mean a proper Heroic Name?" She flushed with pleasure.

"Yes," replied the King. "Like Harald Bluetooth or Sigurd the Fat, or," he added maliciously, "Arvarodd of Permia. Doesn't she, lads?"

From the back seat, the heroes and the wizard expressed their approval. In fact Arvarodd had been addressing himself to the problem of a suitable Name for Hildy for quite some time; but even the best he had come up with, Swan-Hildy, was clearly inappropriate.

"So from now on," said the King, "our sister Hildy Frederik'sdaughter shall be known by the name of Vel-Hilda."

"Vel-Hilda?" Hildy frowned. "I don't get it," she said at last.

The King grinned. "The Norse word *vel*," he said, "as you know better than I, is short and means 'well.' The same, Hildy Frederik'sdaughter, may be said of you. Therefore..."

"Oh," said Hildy. "I see."

10

"Checkmate."

Anyone looking through binoculars at the darkened windows of Gerrards Garth House would have thought that someone was signalling with a torch. In fact the little points of flickering light were Prexz, blinking in disbelief.

"Ninety-nine thousand, nine hundred and ninety-nine sets and nine games to you," said Zxerp, almost beside himself with malicious pleasure, "and *nine* games to me. All the nines," he added, and sniggered.

"You're cheating," Prexz muttered. But Zxerp only smiled.

"Impossible to cheat at Goblin's Teeth," he said benignly. "God knows, I've tried often enough. No, old chum, you've just got to face the fact that I'm on a winning streak. Mugs away."

"Let's play Snapdragon, for a change."

"Your move."

"Or Dungeons and Dragons. You used to like Dungeons and Dragons."

"Or would you rather I moved first?" Zxerp grinned broadly. "For once."

Angrily, Prexz slammed down the dice and moved his knight six spaces.

"'Go directly to Jotunheim,'" Zxerp read aloud. "Hard luck, what a shame, never mind. Six," he noted, as he examined the dice he had thrown. "Getting to be quite a habit. I think I'll take your rook."

"I think it's something to do with that thing over there," grumbled Prexz. He pointed at the computer banks.

"Could be," said Zxerp. "But..." He quoted rule 138. Prexz muttered something about gamesmanship and tried to get his knight out of Jotunheim. He failed.

"And now your other rook," chuckled Zxerp. "That's bad, losing both your rooks. Remember how I always used to do that?"

Suddenly, the room was flooded with light. From somewhere down the corridor came the noise of confused shouting and the ring of metal. Zxerp looked up, and Prexz nudged his queen on to a black square.

"I'll see you," he said.

But Zxerp wasn't listening. "Something's happening," he whispered.

"I know," replied Prexz, "I'm seeing you."

"Shut up a minute," hissed Zxerp. "There's someone coming."

The door to the office flew open. Five men in boiler-suits staggered into the room, beating vainly at an enormous bear with bunches of marigolds and tulips. With a swipe of his huge paw, the bear sent them flying into the computer bank, which was smashed to pieces. The bear stopped, nibbled at the tulips for a moment, then advanced on its terrified assailants, who took cover behind the spirits' tank. At that moment, the King, Hildy and the wizard came running in.

"Here they are," shouted Hildy. The bear vanished, and was replaced by Brynjolf the shape-changer, spitting out tulip petals. "What kept you?" asked Brynjolf.

The King looked down at the front of his coat, to make sure the Sutton Hoo brooch was still there, and drew his short sword. The men in boiler-suits covered their eyes and whimpered as he strode up to the tank, but the King paid no attention to them. With a wristy blow, he shattered the glass.

"Quick," he said to the wizard. In the doorway Arvarodd appeared. He had a boiler-suited guard in each hand, and there was pollen all over his sleeves. "All clear," he said. "The rest of them have bolted, but I don't think they're going to bother us."

The wizard had disconnected the wires around the spirits' throats, and replaced them with wires of his own. Prexz struggled for a moment, but Zxerp was too busy bundling the pieces into their box to offer any resistance. All over the building, sirens were blaring.

"Right," said the King, "that's that done. Time we were on our way."

At the end of the corridor, Thorgeir Storm-shepherd crouched behind a fire-door and listened. He had been working late, trying to catch up on the Japanese deal. He had realised immediately what was happening, and had hurried down to see the King and his bunch of idiots being blasted back into the realms of folk-tale by the automatic weapons of Vouchers. From his hiding-place he had seen the guns turn into bunches of flowers, and Arvarodd and Brynjolf scattering the bemused guards. He had seen the Sutton Hoo brooch on King Hrolf's chest. It had reminded him that he never had tracked down the prototype of the Luck of Caithness.

He should have had two options, he reflected. One would have been to stand and fight, the other to run away. The latter option would have had a great deal to be said for it, but sadly it was no longer available to him. He sighed, and glanced down at his crocodile shoes, his all-wool Savile Row suit, and the backs of his hands, which were now covered in shaggy grey fur. His nails had become claws again, and his dental plate was being forced out of his mouth by the vulpine fangs that were sprouting from his upper jaw. He pricked up his ears, growled softly, and wriggled out of his human clothes. Wolf in sheep's clothing, he thought ruefully. He lifted his head and howled.

"Jesus!" said Hildy. "What was that?"

"Just a wolf, that's all," said Arvarodd, tightening his grip on the two squirming guards. "Hang on, though," he said and frowned. "I knew there was something odd going on, ever since I woke up in the ship, but I couldn't quite put my finger on it. No wolves."

"There aren't any more wolves," said Hildy, shuddering. "They're extinct in the British Isles." She had never actually seen a wolf, not even in a zoo; but she remembered enough biology to know that wolves are related to dogs, and she was terrified of all dogs, especially Airedales.

"No, you're wrong there," said Arvarodd firmly. There was a hopeful light in his eyes, and he was fingering his newly recovered arm-ring. "For a start, there's one just down the corridor. Here, hold these for me." He thrust the two guards at Hildy and ran off down the corridor. Without thinking, Hildy grabbed the guards by the collar. They made no attempt to escape.

"Where's he gone?" asked the King. "We haven't got time to fool about."

"He heard a wolf," said Hildy faintly.

"Him and his dratted wolves," said the King impatiently. "All he thinks about."

"But there aren't any wolves," Hildy insisted, "not any more."

"Oh." The King turned his head sharply. "Aren't there now?" He looked at the wizard, who nodded. "That's awkward," he said.

"Awkward?"

"Awkward. You see, our enemy had a henchman, Thorgeir Storm-Shepherd. Originally, Thorgeir was not a human being but a timber-wolf of immense size and ferocity, whom the enemy transformed into a human being by the power of his magic...." He fell silent.

"And the magic's been cancelled out by the brooch we took from the Museum," said Brynjolf. He was looking decidedly nervous. "So if Thorgeir's anywhere in the building he'll have changed back into a wolf."

"Who is this person?" Hildy asked, but the King made no reply. "Someone ought to go and tell Arvarodd that that isn't an ordinary wolf," he said quietly. "Otherwise he might get a nasty shock."

As it happened, Arvarodd was on the point of finding out for himself. The excitement of the wolf-hunt had chased all other thoughts from his mind: the quest, the need to get out quickly, even his duty to his King. It did not occur to him that office-blocks are not a normal habitat for normal wolves until he rounded a corner and came face to face with his quarry. He drew his short sword and braced himself for the onset of the animal; as he did so, he noticed that this was a particularly large wolf, bigger than any he could recall having seen in all his seasons with the Caithness and Sutherland. The fact that its coat was so dark as almost to be black was not that unusual—melanistic wolves had not been so uncommon, even in his day—but the way that its eyes blazed with unearthly fire and the foam from its slavering jaws burnt holes in the carpet tiles marked it out as distinctly unusual. A collector's item, he muttered to himself, as he tightened his grip on his sword-hilt.

The wolf was in no hurry to attack. It stood and pawed at the carpet, growling menacingly and lashing its tail back and forth. In fact it was trying to remember exactly how a wolf springs, and regretting the second helping of cheesecake it had had with its dinner at the Wine Vaults that evening. It is difficult for a wolf to feel particularly bellicose on a full stomach, unless its whelps are being threatened; and Thorgeir's whelps, to the best of his knowledge, were quite safe in their dormitory at Harrow. He growled again, and showed his enormous fangs. Arvarodd stood still, just like the picture in the coaching manual: weight on the back foot, head steady, left shoulder well forward.

"Get on with it," growled the wolf.

Arvarodd raised an eyebrow. Wolves that talked were a novelty to him, and he didn't think it was strictly ethical. "Did you say something?" he said coldly.

"I said get on with it," replied the wolf. "Or are you scared?"

"If I was scared, I wouldn't be standing here," said Arvarodd indignantly. "I'd be running back down the passage, wouldn't I?"

"Not if you were too terrified to move," said the wolf. "Then you'd just be standing there mesmerised, waiting for me to spring. Rabbits do that."

"But I'm not a rabbit," Arvarodd pointed out. "And I'm not mesmerised. Neither am I stupid. It's your job to attack."

"Says you," retorted the wolf. "So let's have less chat and more action, shall we? Unless," he added, trying to sound unconcerned, "you'd rather scratch the whole fixture."

"You what?"

"I mean," said the wolf, relaxing slightly, "you're not going to attack, and I'm buggered if I am. So we can wait here all night, until the sorcerer-king turns up and zaps you into a cinder, or we can go our separate ways and say no more about it. Up to you, really."

"You're not really a wolf, are you?" said Arvarodd.

"Don't be daft," said the wolf, and growled convincingly. But Arvarodd had remembered something.

"Our enemy had a sidekick called Thorgeir," he said. "Nasty piece of work. Used to be a wolf, by all accounts. Not a pure-bred wolf, of course." The wolf snarled and lashed its tail. Arvarodd pretended not to notice. "I seem to remember there was a story about his mother and a large brindled Alsatian—"

The wolf sprang, but Arvarodd was ready for it. He stepped out of the way and struck two-handed at the beast's neck (plenty of bottom hand and remember to *roll those wrists!*). But the wolf must have sensed that he was about to strike, or perhaps instinct made him twist his shoulders round; Arvarodd's blow overreached, so that his forearms struck on the wolf's back and the sword was jarred out of his hands. The wolf landed, turned and prepared to spring again. Arvarodd shot a glance at the sword, lying on the other side of the corridor, then clenched his fists. As he prepared to meet the animal's onslaught, he thought of what his coach had told him about facing an angry wolf when disarmed. "Stand well forward and brace your feet," he had said. "That way, the wolf might break your neck before he has a chance to get his teeth into you."

"Never believed that story myself," he said. "I hate malicious gossip, don't you?"

"No," snapped the wolf, and leapt at his throat.

"Hell," said the King. "A wire's come loose on the brooch. Look."

When the wolf turned back into a middle-aged stark-naked businessman in mid-air, Arvarodd was surprised but pleased. He made a fine instinctive tackle, and threw his assailant through a plate-glass door. Then he made a grab for the sword. But Thorgeir had the advantage of local knowledge. He picked himself up and ran. After a short chase through a labyrinth of offices, Arvarodd gave up. After all, his enemy might change back into a wolf again at any minute, and he was clearly out of practice. He retraced his steps, and met the King and his company by the lift-shaft.

"Where the hell have you been?" said the King.

"There was this wolf," said Arvarodd, "only he wasn't. I think it was Thorgeir."

The King seemed to regard this as a reasonable explanation. "We've got to go now. This brooch got unconnected from its batteries for a couple of minutes, and I'm not going to take any chances."

"Good idea," said Arvarodd. He was feeling slightly foolish. But not as foolish as Thorgeir. No sooner had he escaped from Arvarodd than he changed back into a wolf; and then, as he had gone bounding down the corridor to see if he could continue the fight where he had left it, he had turned back into a human being again, at the very moment when the King (and the Sutton Hoo brooch) had left the building. He gave the whole thing up as a bad job and went to look for his clothes.

As soon as he saw the smashed tank and the cowering guards, he guessed what had happened. He sat down on a wrecked photocopier and thought hard. He ought to go at once to the sorcerer-king and warn him, to give him time to prepare his defences. But something seemed to tell him that this would be a bad idea. What if the sorcerer-king should lose and be overthrown? Thorgeir bit his lip and forced himself to consider the possible consequences. On the one hand, the boss's magic had preserved him, in human form, for twelve hundred years—without it, he would go back to being a twelve-hundred-year-old wolf, and wolves do not, even in captivity, usually live more than sixteen years. If the sorcerer-king's spell was broken, he would become, in quick succession, an extremely elderly wolf and a dead wolf; and if that had been the pinnacle of his ambition he would never have left the Kola Peninsula. On the other hand, King Hrolf's wizard was presumably competent in all grades of anthropomorphic and life-prolonging magic, and his employer might just be persuaded to do a little deal. On the third hand, if the sorcerer-king won, which was not unlikely, and he found out that his trusty aide had betrayed him, being a dead wolf would be a positive pleasure compared to the penalty the boss would be likely to impose. Tricky, Thorgeir thought. He took a small slice of marrowbone from his pocket and chewed on it to clear his head.

Of course, in order for the sorcerer-king to win or lose, there would have to be a battle; if he could make sure that that battle took place, quickly and on relatively even terms, he could then have a claim on the eventual winner, whoever he turned out to be. Looked at from all sides, that was the safest course, but there was one deadly drawback; he didn't have the faintest idea where King Hrolf was. He sighed, spat out the marrowbone, and put his socks back on. Just then, the telephone rang. He picked it up without thinking.

"Olafsen here," he said. Who could it be at this time of night?

"Mr. Olafsen?" It was the governor-presumptive of China. Thorgeir groaned; he was not in the mood for young Mr Fortescue.

"I thought I should tell someone at once," said young Mr Fortescue. "I've just heard that the car that Our Enemies are using," and he mentioned the type and registration number, "has been traced and seen by a police patrol in Holland Park. I'm there now, in fact. I'm talking to you"—there was a hint of pride in the young man's voice—"over my carphone. What should I do now?"

Thorgeir muttered a quick prayer to Loki, god of villains, and said: "Follow them. For crying out loud, don't lose them. And keep me posted on my personal number, will you?"

"Will do, Mr Olafsen. Do you think," asked Mr Fortescue diffidently, "I could have Korea as well?"

"Of course you can," replied Thorgeir indulgently. "So long as you don't lose that car, you can have Korea and Mongolia as well."

"Thanks, Mr Olafsen."

Thorgeir put the receiver down, and found an unbroken computer terminal. Within a few minutes, he had withdrawn the car from the police computer—the last thing anyone wanted was a cloud of bluebottles getting in the way. Then he sprinted down to the underground carpark and got out his car. Almost before he had closed the door, the phone buzzed.

"They're just moving," said Mr Fortescue. "Going up towards Ladbroke Grove."

"Stay with them," urged Thorgeir. "I'll be with you shortly. And Tibet," he added.

Just as the dial reached £11.65, petrol started to overflow from the tank, and Hildy put the filler nozzle back in its holder and went to pay. Just her luck, she reflected; another thirty-five pence worth of petrol, and she would have got two Esso tokens, which would have been enough for the trailing flex.

Had she been a true Viking, of course, she would have gone on filling, and to hell with the spilt petrol and the fire risk. Reckless courage was the hallmark of the warrior. She looked at her reflection in the plate-glass window of the filling station and, not for the first time, wished that there was rather less of her face and rather more of the rest of her. Short and means well. True. Very true.

As she waited her turn in the queue, it occurred to her that if she bought a couple of Mars bars, she could knock the grand total up over twelve pounds. Shrewdness and cunning are the hallmark of the counsellor, and you don't have to look like one of those creatures on the magazine covers to be clever. The cashier took her money and handed her one token.

"Excuse me," she said assertively, "my purchases were over twelve pounds. I should get two tokens."

"Only applies to petrol," said the cashier. "Can't you read?"

Someone in the queue behind her sniggered. She scooped up her token and fled.

"What's up?" said the King. "You look upset."

For a split second, she toyed with the idea of asking the King to go and split the cashier's skull for her, but she decided against it. That would be over-reacting, and the wise man knows when to do nothing, as the Edda says. "No, I'm not," she replied. "Where to now?"

"Somewhere nice and quiet," said the King, "where we won't be disturbed."

Hildy nodded and started the engine. She drove for nearly an hour in silence, heading for no great reason for the Chilterns. The heroes were asleep, and the wizard was reading a spell from a vellum scroll by the faint light of Zxerp and Prexz.

"This'll do," said the King.

Hildy stopped the car beside a small spinney of beech-trees and switched off the lights. The car which had been behind her all the way from London drove on past and disappeared round a corner. Hildy breathed a faint sigh of relief; she had been slightly worried about that.

"I don't suppose anyone's considered anything so prosaic as food lately," said Brynjolf, stretching his arms and yawning. "I had this marvellous dream about roast venison." Hildy frowned and offered him a Mars bar.

"What's this?" he asked.

"You eat it," Hildy said.

Brynjolf shrugged, and did as she suggested. Then he spat. "No, but really," he said. "A joke's a joke, but—"

"Go turn yourself into a sandwich, then," Hildy snapped. "I'm exhausted, and I can't be doing—"

"All right," said Arvarodd wearily, "leave it to me. Only it'll have to be rabbit again."

"If I have any more rabbit," said Brynjolf, "I'll start to look like one."

"That's a thought," replied Arvarodd. "Decoy," he explained. The two heroes got out of the car and wandered away.

"That, Vel-Hilda," said the King, "is heroic life for you. Rabbit seven times a week, and that's if you're lucky. Just be grateful you're not on a longship. Let's get some air." He opened his door and climbed out, stretching his cramped limbs.

"Will the wizard be all right on his own?" whispered Hildy. "I mean..."

"We won't go far," said the King. "You'll be all right, won't you, Kotkel?"

The wizard looked up from his scroll, nodded absently, and muttered a spell. On the seat beside him a giant hound appeared.

"Just a hallucination," explained the King, "but who's to know?"

Hildy shrugged, and strolled out into the spinney. It was a still night, slightly cold, and the wind was moving the leaves on the tops of the trees. The King spread his cloak over a stump and sat down. Across his knees he laid his broadsword in its jewelled scabbard.

"This sword," he said, "is called Tyrving. You're interested in the old days. Would you like to hear about it?"

Hildy nodded, and sat down beside him.

"One day," said the King, in a practised storyteller's voice, "the gods Odin and Loki were out walking far from home. Why, I cannot tell you. I always thought it was a strange thing for them to be doing, since by all accounts they hated each other like poison. However, they were out walking, and there was a sudden thunderstorm. Again, it seems strange that Thor should inflict a sudden thunderstorm on his liege-lord and best friend Odin for no reason, but perhaps it was his idea of a joke. Odin and Loki sought shelter in a little house, where they were greeted by a little old woman. She did not know that they were gods, so the story goes—and if you believe that, you'll believe anything; but she offered them some broth, although she had little enough for herself, and put the last of the peat on the fire so that they might be warm. All clear so far?"

"Yes," said Hildy. "Go on."

"When the two gods had finished their broth and dried their clothes, they lay down to sleep. The old woman gave them all her blankets, and the pelts of otters for pillows. In the morning the gods woke up and it had stopped raining. 'Old woman,' said Odin, 'you have treated us kindly.' I don't know if Odin was given to understatement, but that's what the story says. 'Learn that the guests you have sheltered are in fact the gods Odin and Loki. In return for your hospitality, I shall give you a great gift.' And he drew from his belt his own sword, which the dwarfs had forged for him in the caverns of Niflheim, and gave it to the old woman, who thanked him politely, no doubt through clenched teeth. Odin then put a blessing on the sword, saying that whoever wielded it in battle should have victory. But Loki, who is a malevolent god, put a curse on it, saying that the first man to draw it in battle should eventually die from a blow from it. The old woman put the sword away safely, and in due course she gave it to her grandson Skjold, who went on to become the greatest of the Joms-vikings. When Skjold was an old man, and had long since given up fighting, he used to laugh at Loki's curse. But one day he was teaching his little son Thjostolf how to fight, and Thjostolf parried a blow rather too vigorously. Skjold's sword flew from his hand and struck him above the eye, killing him instantly. Thjostolf went on to lead the Joms-vikings as his father had done, and when he died his son Yngvar succeeded him, and the sword brought him victory. But one day he lost the sword when out hunting, and in the next battle he fought he was killed, and all his men with him. Eventually, the sword came into the hands of my grandfather, Eyjolf, who was Odin's grandson. That story is supposed to prove something or other, but I forget what."

Hildy sat still and said nothing. The moon, coming out from behind a cloud, cast a shaft of light through the trees which fell on the hilt of the sword, making it sparkle. The King smiled, and with an easy movement of his arm drew the sword from its scabbard. For some reason, Hildy started to shiver. In the moonlight the blade glowed eerily, and the runes engraved on its hilt stood out firm and clear.

"Of the sword itself," continued the King, "this is said. The blade is the true dwarf-steel, but the hilt and furniture was replaced by Yngvar with the hilt of the sword Gram, which Sigurd the Dragon-Slayer bore. The blade of that sword was lost, but the hilt was preserved as an heirloom by the children of Atli of Hungary. In turn, my grandfather Eyjolf had a new quillon added; that came from the sword Helvegr, which once belonged to the Frost-Giants of Permia. My father Ketil added the scabbard, which once housed the sword of the god Frey, and fitted to the pommel the great white jewel called the Earthstar, which fell from the sky on the day I was born, and after which I am named." He smiled, and laid his hand gently on the hilt. "It's not a bad sword, at that. A bit on the light side for me, but nicely balanced. Here." And he passed the sword to Hildy. For a moment she dared not take it; then she grasped it firmly and lifted it up. She was amazed by how light it seemed, like a living thing in her hands.

"It's wonderful," she said. As she gazed at it, blazing coldly in the moonlight, her eyes were suddenly opened, and she saw, as in a dream, the faces of many kings and warriors, and blood red on the blue steel. She saw the dwarfs busy over their forge in a great cave, vivid in the orange light of the forge, and heard the sound of their hammers, the hiss as the hot metal was tempered, and the scrape of whetstones as the edge was laid. She saw a tall dark figure muffled in a cloak, who watched the work and added to the skill of the smiths the power of wind, tide and lightning. She saw him take the blade in his hands, as she was doing now, and look down it to make sure that it was straight and true. Then, suddenly as it had come, the vision departed, leaving only the moonlight, still flickering on the runes cut into the langet of the hilt. As she spelt out the letters one by one, her heart was beating like a blacksmith's hammer.

Product of more than one country.

The moon went back behind its cloud.

"Very nice," she said, and gave it back to the King, who grinned and slid it back into the scabbard.

"For all I know," he said, "the legends are all perfectly true. True but largely unimportant. Like I said, that's heroic life for you. Like all heroes have magnificent bushy beards because it's difficult to shave on a storm-tossed longship without cutting yourself to the bone."

"I see," said Hildy.

"And this particular adventure," said the King, "is all heroic life, too; and you are a heroine just as much as we are heroes. It's incredibly dangerous, but you haven't been thinking about that. Just a game, a little reprise of childhood—or why do you think that in the end all the legends of heroes and warriors end up as children's stories? When I was a little boy, I wanted to be a fisherman."

"When I was a little girl," said Hildy, "I wanted to be a Viking." She laughed suddenly. "It's been fun," she said, "but not in the way I thought it would be. If we do get killed, will we go to Valhalla, across the Rainbow Bridge?"

"The Rainbow Bridge," said the King, "is something to be crossed when you come to it. If we fail, then we leave the world in the hands of its natural enemy. But, for all I know, nobody would notice except a few of the leading statesmen. Still, that's not a risk worth taking. Not only is our enemy very cruel and very evil, he is also very, very stupid. A good magician—the best ever—but I wouldn't trust him with running a dog-show, let alone the world. And I don't think, for all his magic, that he could ever become ruler of the world; if he can't catch us, then he hasn't got the resources, and anyway I think the world has changed too much, though I don't suppose he's realised. But what he would almost certainly do is start enough wars to finish off the human race, one way or another, which would be rather worse. And he's certainly a good enough magician to manage that."

"Don't let's talk about it," said Hildy. "We'd better go see how Kotkel's getting on—"

Just then, Arvarodd came hurrying up. Brynjolf was with him, dragging along a man by the lapels of his jacket.

"Guess who's just turned up," said Arvarodd.

"My liege," said the man, bowing low to the King. "I have come..."

"Hello, Thorgeir," said the King. "I was expecting you."

"Thorgeir?" Hildy stared. "You said he was a wolf or something."

"Only sometimes," said the man. "It's a long story."

"Shaggy-wolf story," muttered Arvarodd. "I found him snooping about in the woods back there. By the way, we couldn't find any rabbits, so it'll have to be squirrel."

"I wasn't snooping," said Thorgeir. "I came here to tell you something that you might like to hear."

"How did you find us?" The King's face was expressionless.

"Oh, that was easy," said Thorgeir. He smoothed out the lapels of his jacket and sat down, his manner suggesting that he wouldn't mind at all if they all did the same. "You don't suppose I haven't known all along, do you?"

"Of course you didn't know," said the King. "Otherwise we'd all be dead."

"You'd have been dead if my lord and master knew where you were," said Thorgeir patronisingly. "I knew all along. He leaves things like that to me, you see, and a lot of trouble I've had keeping it from him."

"And why should you want to do that?" asked the King.

"Guess." Thorgeir smiled.

"For some reason, envy or fear or hatred, you want to betray him to us. Or you wanted to see which of us was more likely to win before you chose sides." The King raised an eyebrow. "Something like that?"

"More or less." Thorgeir scratched his ear, where for some reason a little grey fur still remained. But the King's eyes were on him.

"I was born," said the King, "in the seventh year of the reign of Ketil Trout. In other words, not yesterday. What you meant to say was that owing to your extreme negligence we were able not only to escape the notice of your lord and master, but also to recapture the two earth-spirits we need to overthrow his power. As soon as you realised that we had an even chance of winning, you decided to hedge your bets. By a stroke of good luck—I can't say what, but I expect I'm right—you found us. You decided to come to me and persuade me to attack at a certain time and place. If I win, you claim to have given me victory. If he wins, you can claim to have brought me to him. Correct?"

"Absolutely." Thorgeir widened his smile slightly. "Isn't that what I said?"

"More or less." The King leant back and thought for a moment. "What you will do is this. You will get in touch with your master and tell him that you have found us, that we are weak and unprepared, and that something has gone wrong with our magic. You will do this gladly," said the King, "because for all I know it may very well be true and, if I lose, you can take the credit, as you originally planned. While we are waiting for our enemy to arrive, you will tell me everything you know about his strength and, more important, his weaknesses. You will do this truthfully, firstly because if you do not my champion Arvarodd will cut you in half, secondly because it probably won't have any effect on the outcome, one way or another. Is that clear?"

"As crystal." Thorgeir nodded approvingly. "But what if he won't come?"

"He'll come," said the King. "Sooner or later there must be a fight, and I expect your master is as impatient as I am."

"But he doesn't want to come out to you. He wants you to go to him."

"Then, why," said the King gently, "did you imagine that you could save yourself by tempting him to come and fight on even terms? Be consistent, please."

Thorgeir shrugged his shoulders. "And if I do what you ask," he said, "and if you do win, what will happen to me?"

"I have no idea," said the King. "It'll be interesting finding out, won't it? I could promise to spare you, or even give you a kingdom in Serkland, but you wouldn't trust me, now would you?"

"Of course not," said Thorgeir. "So that's settled, then, is it?"

"Settled." The King clapped him on the shoulder. "And to make sure, Arvarodd will stand one step behind you all the time with his sword drawn. Arvarodd is bigger than you, at least so long as you are in human shape, and I fancy he doesn't like you after your confrontation earlier this evening. Now, tell me all about it."

So Thorgeir told him.

"But why there?" said the sorcerer-king for the fifth time. "I thought we agreed..."

Thorgeir glanced over his shoulder at Arvarodd. "Because it may be your last chance at anything like decent odds," he said. "It's worth the risk, believe me. Listen, Hrolf and his men have got those two spirits back. They broke into the office and rescued them." He held the receiver away from his ear. Judging by the noises that came out of it, this was a wise move. When they had subsided, he said: "I know, I'm sorry, it's not my fault. But I followed them here, and it'll be a couple of hours before they get the brooch wired up. There's still time."

"Hold your water, will you?" Thorgeir waited breathlessly, and behind him Arvarodd patted the flat of his sword on the palm of his hand and made clucking noises. "Even if you're right," said the sorcerer-king, "there won't be time to muster any force. It'd be suicide."

"Balls," said Thorgeir. "I'm looking at them now. There's the King and that female, the wizard, Brynjoif and Arvarodd. You know," he couldn't resist adding, "the one who went to—"

"I know, I know. Shut up a minute. I'm thinking. Look, I could get together a portable set and some Special Effects, and there's the Emergency Kit all charged up, of course, and you could be a wolf. With that and the lads from Vouchers—"

"It'd be a doddle," Thorgeir urged. Arvarodd was pressing his sword-point against the back of his neck. "Get a move on, though, or they'll see me. God knows how I followed them so far without them spotting me."

"If this goes wrong, I'll have your skull for an eggcup," muttered the sorcerer-king. Thorgeir shut his eyes and offered a prayer of thanksgiving to his patron deity. "Don't worry," he said, "it'll be no problem. Promise."

"How long will it take me to get there?"

"The way you drive, forty minutes tops. It's just past the turning to Radnage. You got that?"

"The trouble with you, Thorgeir," said the sorcerer-king, "is that you combine stupidity with fecklessness. Be seeing you."

There was a click and the dialling tone. "Well," said Arvarodd, "is he coming or do I chop you?"

"He's coming," said Thorgeir, straight-faced. "Exactly like you wanted it. And he hasn't got any time to get his forces together; it'll be him and a couple of extras. You'll walk it, you'll see."

Arvarodd shook his head and marched Thorgeir away. As he went, Thorgeir congratulated himself on his rotten memory. He had honestly forgotten all about the Emergency Kit.

11

"I still think this is a bad idea," whispered Danny Bennett. Angantyr nudged him in the ribs, expelling all the air from his body, and told him to be quiet. Utterly wretched, he lay still in the heather and turned the matter over in his mind.

On the credit side, he had persuaded them not to declare war. That had taken some doing, after such a conclusive victory. Hjort had already prepared the Red Arrow, to shoot over the battlements of Edinburgh Castle, and Angantyr was talking glibly of annexing Sunderland as well. It was the thought that they might conceivably win that had spurred Danny on to unimagined heights of eloquence, and in the end he had succeeded. But in order to do so he had had to make certain concessions, the main one being that they should all go to London and help the King. Although they would not admit it, some of the heroes were beginning to worry, and all of them hated the thought of missing the final excitement. So here they all were, lying in wait for the first suitable vehicle, and it was Danny's turn to be seriously anxious, although he had no qualms at all about admitting it. There was bound to be violence. There might well be bloodshed. If they did manage to get a van or a bus, he was going to have to drive it.

Round the bend in the road came a large red thing, with the number 87 displayed in a little glass frame above its nose. Danny closed his eyes and hoped that his companions wouldn't notice it; but they did.

"Here, Danny," hissed Angantyr, "how about that one?"

"Oh, no, I don't really think so," Danny gabbled. "I mean, it's probably too small."

"Doesn't look it," said Hjort on his other side.

"They're much smaller inside than out," said Danny. "Really."

Hjort shook his head. "No harm in trying," he said cheerfully. "What do you think, lads?"

Several heads nodded, the boar-shaped crests of their helmets visible above the heather like a covey of skimming larks. "When you're ready, Starkad," said Hjort.

"Hold it, hold it," snarled Angantyr. "And since when were you in charge of this, Hjort Herjolfsson?"

"Someone's got to do it, haven't they?" Hjort raised his head to glower at Angantyr.

Danny saw a gleam of hope. If he could start them quarrelling... "I'm with you, Angantyr," he said, and looked expectantly at Hjort.

But the hero simply shrugged and said, "See if I care."

"Here," said Starkad, "do I go, or what?"

"Yes," said Hjort and Angantyr simultaneously. They glared at each other.

Starkad was on his feet. He could run like the wind if he didn't trip over something, and soon he had overtaken the bus. With a spring like a wild cat, he leapt at the driver's door, grabbed the handle and, bracing his feet against the frame, wrenched it open. The bus swerved drastically, mowed down a row of snow-poles and stopped dead.

The driver, his head spinning, pushed himself up from the steering-wheel and stared helplessly at the group of maniacs who had come running up out of nowhere. All save one of them were waving antiquated but terrifying weapons: swords, spears and axes. It could conceivably be a group of archaeology students staging a reconstruction of Culloden, but he wasn't hopeful. The one who was unarmed leant forward into the cab and cleared his throat.

"Excuse me," he said, "does this bus go to London?"

The driver dragged breath into the vacuum of his lungs. "If it's the money you're after," he gasped, "there's three pound forty-two pence. Take it all."

"Actually," said the unarmed man, "would you mind if we borrowed your bus? It's just for a day or a week or so."

"Are you hijacking my bus, then?" asked the driver.

"Yes," said the unarmed man unhappily. The driver went white, and Danny felt panic coming on. What if the man tried to resist and defend his passengers? Bothvar Bjarki would like that.

"It's all right, really," he said, as reassuringly as possible, "I'm with the BBC."

"Is that right?" said the driver. He did not look reassured. "Would you be the blokes who beat up all those coppers and soldiers at Farr the other day?"

"Yes," said Angantyr. He stuck out his bearded chin impatiently and tapped his sword-blade with his fingers.

"The Army's looking for you," said an old lady from the second row of seats. "They're all over Strathnaver with armoured cars."

"Really?" Angantyr's eyes lit up. "Hey, lads," he called out, "did you hear that? They've come back." The heroes began to chatter excitedly.

It was, Danny decided, a moment for action, not words. He grabbed the driver by the sleeve and pulled him out of his seat. "Right," he tried to shout (but the words came out as an urgent sort of shriek), "I want everybody off the bus."

"You must be kidding, son," said the old lady. "There's not another bus till Wednesday, and I've the week's shopping to do."

Bothvar Bjarki climbed inside. "You heard him," he growled. "Off you get, now."

"Are we being taken hostage?" asked an old man in the fourth row.

"No," said Danny. "You're free to go."

"Pity," said the old man. "That would have been one in the eye for George Macleod and his pigeons." He shrugged his shoulders wearily and picked up his shopping-bag.

The passengers shuffled off the bus, all of them taking a good look at Danny as they went, and the heroes scrambled in. Danny took a deep breath and sat in the driver's seat. The driver raised an eyebrow.

"Do you know how to drive a bus then, mister?" he asked.

"I haven't the faintest idea," Danny confessed. "Is it difficult?"

"Yes," said the driver. "Very. Are you going far?"

"London," Danny said.

The driver shook his head sadly, and deep inside Danny's soul something snapped. Perhaps he had Viking blood in his veins, or perhaps he was just fed up. "All right," he said quietly, "you drive."

"Me?" The driver stared. "All the way to London?"

"Yes," said Danny.

"Now, look here," said the driver. "The Ministry regulations say—"

"Stuff the Ministry regulations." Danny wished he had accepted Angantyr's offer of a sword. "Drive this bus to London or you'll be sorry." Behind him, Angantyr nodded approvingly and clapped Danny on the shoulder.

"That's right," he said, "you tell him." For some reason which he could never fathom, Danny glowed with pleasure.

"Right," he said, giving the driver a shove. "Let's get this show on the road."

"What show?" asked Hjort, but Danny ignored him, for he had

had a sudden inspiration. He leant forward and pointed to the roller above the driver's seat that changed the number on the front of the bus. "Change that," he ordered.

"What to?" asked the driver.

"'Special,' of course," Danny replied. "Come on, move it."

The driver did as he was told, and then started the engine. Danny stuck his head out of the window and waved to the ex-passengers.

"Never mind," he shouted, "there'll be another one along in a minute."

The bus moved off, and Danny sat down in the front row of seats, feeling very surprised at himself but not at all repentant. He was, he realised, starting to enjoy all this.

"You realise," said the driver over his shoulder, "we'll run out of fuel before we're past Inverness."

"Then, we'll get some more, won't we?" Danny replied. "Now, shut up and drive."

Angantyr came forward and sat down beside him. "Have some cold seagull," he said. "I saved some for you."

"Thanks." Danny bit off a large chunk. It tasted good.

"You did all right back there," said Angantyr Asmundarson. "In fact, you're coming along fine."

"It was nothing," said Danny with his mouth full.

"I know," said Angantyr. "But you handled it pretty well, all the same."

"Thanks." Danny chewed for a moment, then scratched his head. "Angantyr," he said, "I've thought of something."

"What?"

"When we get to London, how will we find them?"

"Don't ask me," said Angantyr. "Is it a big place?"

"Quite big." Danny frowned. "So you don't know where they're likely to be?"

"It was your idea we go," Angantyr replied.

"Was it?"

"Yes," said Angantyr. "Don't you remember?"

Danny leant back in his seat. After all, it was a long way to London. He would have plenty of time to think of a plan.

"So it was," he said, and yawned. "You leave everything to me."

Angantyr grinned. "You've changed your tune a bit, haven't you?" he said. Danny shook his head.

"It just takes some getting used to, that's all," he said. "And you've got to start somewhere, haven't you?"

"That's very true," said Angantyr.

"It was the same when I shot my first feature," Danny went on. Angantyr nodded.

"Did you miss?" he said sympathetically.

Danny remembered the reviews. "Yes," he said.

"Same with me and my first wild boar," said Angantyr. "Nerves, principally. They all laughed."

Danny sighed; he knew the feeling. "The main thing is," he said, "not to let it get to you."

"That's especially true of wild boar," Angantyr agreed. "Tusks like razors, some of them. I remember one time in Radsey—"

He stopped short and stared. A great black cloud had appeared out of nowhere and was covering the sky. In a few moments it was as dark as night. From where the sun should have been there came a piercing cry; but whether it was pain or triumph no one could tell. A great wind rose up all around, and the air was filled with rushing shapes, like bats or small black birds. Then a great bolt of lightning split the sky, and hailstones crashed against the windows of the bus. The driver pulled over and hid under the seat, whimpering.

"Oh, well," said Angantyr, "looks like we're going to miss all the fun."

King Hrolf staggered, tripped, fell and lay still. For a moment he could do nothing except listen to the beating of his own heart and the howling of the storm. Then he became aware of the blaring of the horns and the cries of the huntsmen and forced himself to rise. The savage music was too close. He commanded his knees to bear his weight, leant forward and ran.

Something had gone wrong, many hours ago now. A man whose face was familiar had driven up in a small black car. He had climbed out and walked forward, as if to surrender. Arvarodd had turned to look, and then Thorgeir had broken free from his grip. Before anyone could stop him, he had wrenched away the wires from the brooch, and then the storm had begun. However brave and strong he may be, a man cannot fight against lightning, or waves of air that strike him likes hammer. He had clung on to his sword and ran, and the storm had followed him.

That was all a long time ago, and he had not stopped running. He had passed through towns and villages, frozen and lifeless in the total darkness, across open fields and through woods, whose trees were torn up by the roots as he passed. Lightning had scorched his heels, flying rocks had grazed him, and the hailstones whipped and punched him as he ran. Sometimes his path had been blocked by strange shapes, sometimes human, sometimes animal; sometimes the ground had opened up before him, or burst into flames under his feet; sometimes the hail gave way to boiling rain that scalded his face and hands, or black fog that filled his lungs like mud. All these, and other things, too, he had run through or past, while all the time his pursuers were gaining on him; slowly, a yard or so each hour, but perceptibly closer all the time. So must the hour hand feel when the minute hand pursues it.

He stumbled again, and crashed to the ground. This time, his knees refused to obey, and the earth he lay on shook with the sound of many feet. King Hrolf raised his head and wiped the blood away from his eyes. In front of him the ground had fallen away on all sides. He was on a plateau, with a sheer drop all around him. Suddenly the wind dropped. Absolute silence.

King Hrolf drove his sword into the ground and used it to lever himself up to his feet. He filled his lungs with air and held it there.

"So." The voice was all around him. "This is where it must end."

"This is as good a place as any," said the King. The voice laughed.

"It is indeed. Was it worth it, Hrolf Earthstar?"

The King jerked his sword out of the turf and held it in front of him. "That depends on the outcome," he said.

The voice laughed again, and the skin of the earth vibrated like the surface of a drum. "Well said, Hrolf Ketilson. If you wish, I will let you run a little further."

"I am getting too old to run," replied the King. "I have lived long enough."

"Too long." The voice laughed a third time.

"I have only one favour to ask you," said King Hrolf, raising his head and smiling. "It is a small thing, but it would please me to know your name."

"My name? That is no small thing. But because you have run well, and because when you are dead no one will ever be born again who would dare ask it, I shall tell you. Listen carefully, Earthstar."

King Hrolf lowered his sword and leant on it. "I am listening," he said.

"Well, then," said the voice, "I am called Vindsval and Vasad, Bestla and Beyla, Jalk and Jafnhar. In Finnmark my name is Geirrod, in Gotland Helblindi, in Markland Bolverk, in Permia Skirnir, in Serkland Eikenskjaldi. Among Danes I was called Warfather, among Saxons Master; to the Goths I was Gravemaker, and in Scythia Emperor. The gods called me Hunferth, the elves named me Freki, to the dwarfs my name was Ganglati and to men..."

King Hrolf put his hands over his ears.

Hildy rolled over on to her side and opened her eyes. That meant she was still alive, for what it was worth. Through the gloom she could see Brynjolf lying on his face where the first gust of wind had blown him, and the wizard Kotkel, where Thorgeir had struck him down. Painfully she lifted herself up on one elbow and looked round. There was Arvarodd, or his dead body, and over it stood a great grey wolf. She remembered how they had fought until Arvarodd's sword had shattered into splinters in his hand, and his shield had crumpled like a flower under the impact of the wolf's assault. Then something had flown up into her face, and she had seen no more. Of the King there was no sign.

The wolf turned its head and growled at her, and licked blood off its long jaws. But Hildy was no longer afraid. She had reached the point where fear can no longer help, and anger offers the only hope of survival. She hated that wolf and she was going to kill it. She looked around for a weapon, but could see none, except the hilt of Arvarodd's sword. The wolf was trotting towards her, like a dog who has heard its plate scraping on the kitchen tiles; she watched it for a moment, suddenly fascinated by the delicacy of its movement. Then, inexplicably, her hand was in her pocket. The little roll of cloth that Arvarodd had given her all that time ago had come loose, and her fingers touched and recognised the contents of it; the stone that gave mastery of languages; the splinter of bone that gave eloquence; the pebble that brought understanding, the pebble from the shores of Asgard....

If you throw it at something, it turns into a boulder and flattens pretty well anything. Then it turns back into a pebble and returns to your hand.
She threw it. She missed.

The wolf gave a startled yelp and galloped away. The pebble came whistling back through the air, stinging Hildy's palm as it landed, so that she nearly dropped it. She swore loudly and threw again. A loud crash told her that this time she had hit the car. By the time the pebble was between her fingers once more, the wolf was nowhere to be seen. She started to run after it, but stopped in mid-stride.

"Aren't you forgetting something?" said a voice.

She turned unsteadily on her heel and peered through the darkness. There were two tiny points of light....

"Instead of throwing things at us," said the voice, "you might get this contraption wired up."

"Shine brighter," said Hildy. "I can't see."

The lights flared up, and Hildy could make out the outline of the car.

"You could see well enough to throw that rock at us," said the light. "What harm did we ever do you?"

"I wasn't throwing it at you," said Huldy. "There was this wolf...."

"Pull the other one, it's got bells on it," said the light. "The brooch is just over there."

The light flashed brilliantly on a garnet, and Hildy picked up the brooch. "What do I do?" she said.

"Twist the ends of the wires round our necks," said the light.

"Have you two got necks?" said Hildy doubtfully. All she could see was a pool of light. The pool of light flickered irritably.

"Of course we've got necks," said the pool of light. "You'll find them between our heads and our shoulders."

Hildy grabbed at the light. "Ouch," it said, "do you mind?"

"Sorry." She grabbed again.

"Getting warmer," said the light. "Up a bit. That's it."

With her other hand, Hildy took the end of one of the wires. "Stay still," she begged.

"Difficult," said the light. "It tickles."

Hildy drew a loop in the wire and tied it. There was a spluttering noise and she apologised. She did the same with the other wire.

"Idiot," said the light. "That's my ankle."

"Oh, for Chrissakes." Fumbling desperately, she untied the wire and lunged. "That's right," gasped the light, "throttle me." She tied the second knot.

Suddenly, the sun came out.

The sorcerer-king froze. Something had gone wrong. He stared wildly at the sun, riding high in the clear blue sky, and the ground, inexplicably beneath his feet. He swallowed hard.

"But you," he said, "can call me Eric."

"Right," said the King, "Eric. Shall we get on with it?" He lifted his sword and whirled it around his head.

"I'm in no hurry," said the sorcerer-king, backing away. "As you know, I'm firmly opposed to needless violence."

"What about necessary violence?" asked the King unpleasantly.

"That, too," said the sorcerer-king. "Besides, I seem to have come out without my sword."

"What's that hanging from your belt, then?"

"Oh," said the sorcerer-king, "that." Very unwillingly, he drew the great sword Ifing from its scabbard. The sun flashed on its well-tended blade.

"Ready?"

"No," said the sorcerer-king.

"Tough." Hrolf took a step forward.

"Toss you for it?" suggested the sorcerer-king. "Heads I go away for ever, tails I disappear completely."

"No," said Hrolf. "Ready now?"

"Best of three?"

"No."

"Oh, have at you, then," said the sorcerer-king wretchedly, and launched a mighty blow at the King's head. Hrolf parried, and the two swords rang together like a great bell. Hrolf struck his blow, first feinting to draw his adversary over to the left, then turning his wrist and striking right; but he was wounded and exhausted, and the sorcerer-king, who had always been his match as a swordsman, was fresh and unhurt. The blow went wide as the sorcerer-king sidestepped nimbly, and Hrolf fell forward. Quickly, the sorcerer-king lifted Ifing above his head and brought it down with all his strength, hitting Hrolf on the shoulder. The blade cut through the steel rings of the mail shirt and grazed the flesh, but that was all. The armourers of Castle Borve made good armour. In an instant, Hrolf was on his feet again, breathing hard but with Tyrving firm in both hands.

"Cheat," said the sorcerer-king.

"Cheat yourself," replied Hrolf, and lunged. The sorcerer-king raised his guard and parried the blow with the foible of his blade. Hrolf leant back, and the sorcerer-king swept a powerful blow at his feet. But Hrolf had anticipated that, and jumped over the blade. The sorcerer-king only just managed to avoid his counter-attack.

"Sure you wouldn't rather toss for it?" panted the sorcerer-king. "Use your own coin if you like."

Hrolf shook his head and struck a blow to the neck. His opponent stopped it with the cross-guard, and threw his weight forward, sliding his sword down Hrolf's blade until the hilts locked. For a moment, Hrolf was taken off balance, but just in time he moved his feet and drew his sword away sharply. The sorcerer-king staggered, lost his footing and fell, his sword flying from his hand as he hit the ground. Before he could get up, Hrolf was standing over him, and the point of Tyrving was touching his throat.

"Now we'll toss for it," Hrolf said.

"Why now?" said the sorcerer-king bitterly. "You could have done me an injury."

"Heads," said Hrolf, "I let you have your sword back." The sorcerer-king started to protest violently, but Hrolf smiled. "What's up?" he said. "Lost your sense of humour?" He lifted the sword and rested it against his shoulder.

"All right, Cleverclogs," said the sorcerer-king, struggling to his feet, "you've made your point. Can we call a halt to all this fooling-about now?"

Hrolf grinned and put his foot on the sorcerer-king's sword. "Is your name really Eric?" he asked.

"There's no need to go on about it," muttered the sorcerer-king. "I tried spelling it with a K, but people still laughed."

"I think it's a nice name," said King Hrolf.

"You would."

"Seriously, though," said King Hrolf, leaning on his sword, "I've got to kill you sooner or later, and I'd much rather you defended yourself." He kicked Ifing over to the sorcerer-king, who scowled at it distastefully.

"I'm not really evil, you know," said the sorcerer-king.

"You do a pretty good imitation."

"Where I went wrong was fooling about with magic," the sorcerer-king went on. "Dammit, I don't even enjoy it. I'd far rather slop around in old clothes and play a few games of Goblin's Teeth."

"Goblin's Teeth?"

"It's a sort of a game, with dice and—"

"I know," said the King, with a strange expression on his face. "So you play Goblin's Teeth, do you?"

"Yes," said the sorcerer-king. "Why, do you?"

The King inspected his fingernails. "I used to dabble a bit," he mumbled.

"Really?"

"Actually," the King admitted, "I was Baltic Champion one year. Pure fluke, of course."

"I won the Swedish Open two years running," said the sorcerer-king with immense pride. "I cheated," he admitted.

"You can't cheat at Goblin's Teeth," said the King. "It's impossible."

The sorcerer-king smirked. "No, it's not," he said.

"Go on, then," said King Hrolf, "how's it done?"

"I can't explain just like that," said the sorcerer-king. "I need the board and the pieces." He stopped, and gazed at Hrolf hopefully. "You haven't got a set, by any chance? I lost mine back in the fifteenth century."

"No," said King Hrolf, his eyes shining, "but I know someone who has."

Brynjolf sat up and rubbed his head. It hurt.

"What happened?" he asked.

"No idea." Brynjolf looked up and saw Arvarodd leaning against the car. "But it's not looking too bad at the moment. Is it, Kotkel?" But the wizard shook his head, and made a sound like a worried cement-mixer.

"Pessimist," said Arvarodd. "Me, I always look on the bright side. Even when that perishing wolf was standing over me making snarling noises, I said to myself: Arvarodd, you've been in worse scrapes than this one."

"Where?" muttered Brynjolf. "In Permia?"

"I'll ignore that remark," said Arvarodd coldly. "And, sure enough, I just pretended to be dead and it went away. Saw a rabbit, I think. Then, I grant you, I passed out. But I'm still alive, aren't I?"

"Where's Vel-Hilda?" said Brynjolf.

"Here," said Hildy as she came out from the spinney. "I've been wolf-hunting. Look."

On the end of the piece of rope she held in her hand was a sullen-looking wolf. "Sit," she said. The wolf glared at her, and sat.

"I'm going to call you Spot, aren't I, boy?" she said. The wolf growled, but she took a pebble from her pocket and showed it to him. He wagged his tail furiously and rolled on his back, waving his paws in the air.

"What are you so cheerful about?" said Brynjolf resentfully.

"I've just seen the King through the seer-stone," she said. "He's all right and I think he's captured the Enemy. In fact, they seemed to be getting on fine." She leant forward and tickled the wolf's stomach. "Who's got four *feet* then?" she asked. The wolf scowled at her.

"By the way," said Arvarodd, "in case you were worried, we're all alive."

"I know," said Hildy, apparently oblivious to all irony. "I made sure of that before I went after the wolf. Lucky."

"I dunno," moaned Brynjolf. "Women." He turned himself into a statue of himself. Statues, especially stone ones, do not have headaches. Hildy tied the wolf's lead to his arm and sat down.

"I'm glad it's all worked out so well," she said.

12

"This," Hildy said, "is for you."

"Are you sure?" said the King gravely. Hildy nodded.

"Yes," she said, and handed the decanter to him. She had finally traded in all her Esso tokens. "Think of me when you use it in Valhalla," she said.

"I shall, Vel-Hilda," replied the King. "What's it for?"

"You could put mead in it," she said. "But be careful. It's fragile."

The King nodded, and with scrupulous care wrapped it up in his beaver-fur mantle. "It is a kingly gift," he lied.

The last rays of the setting sun shone in through the skylights of the Castle of Borve. It had not been easy getting there through the cordon of armoured cars, and in the end the wizard had had to make them all invisible. This had caused difficulties; in particular, Arvarodd kept treading on Hildy's feet, which he could not see, and it took the wizard several hours and three or four embarrassingly unsuccessful attempts to make them all visible again. Eventually, however, they had reached the castle, where the other heroes, located by Hildy through the seer-stone and warned by Brynjolf in corvid form to expect them, had prepared a triumphant banquet of barbecued seagull and seaweed mousse.

"Time to switch on the lights," said the King. He nodded to Kotkel, who connected some wires up to the two chthonic spirits, who were sulking. They had just been playing a three-handed game of Goblin's Teeth with the sorcerer-king, and they suspected him of cheating.

"Don't ask me how," whispered Zxerp to his companion. "I just know it, that's all."

Two great golden cauldrons, filled from the enchanted beer-can, were passed round the table, and Danny Bennett replenished his horn. It had been made by Weyland himself from the horns of a prize oryx, and the spell cast on it protected the user from even the faintest ill-effects the next morning. That was probably just as well. Nevertheless, he had reason to celebrate, for his career and his BAFTA award

were now both secure; his interview with King Hrolf, complete with
an utterly convincing display of magical effects by the wizard to lend
credibility to the story, was safely in the can, thanks to a video-camera
he had recovered from the spoils of the Vikings' most recent encoun-
ter with the forces sent to subdue them. Angantyr had been the cameraman; he had shown a remarkable aptitude for the job, which did
not surprise Danny in the least. "You're a born cameraman," Danny
had said to him, as they had played the tape back on the monitor.
Fortunately, Angantyr was ignorant enough to take this as a compliment.

"I'll make sure you get your credit," Danny assured him. "Camera—A. Asmundarson, and the EETPU can go play with themselves."
He drained his horn and refilled it.

"Pity I won't see it," said Angantyr.

"If only you were staying on," Danny said. "I could get you a job,
no trouble at all."

"Wish I were," said Angantyr. "The way you describe it, sounds
like the life would suit me fine. But there it is."

"Tell you what," said Danny, putting his arm round his friend's
shoulders, "why don't you take the camera and the monitor with you
to Valhalla? There's plenty of spare tapes. It'd be something to do if
you got tired of fighting and feasting."

"Good idea," said Angantyr. He filled up his friend's horn. "In
return, I must give you a gift."

"A gift?" Danny beamed.

"A gift," said Angantyr, wishing he hadn't.

"Really?" Danny slapped him on the back, making him spill his
horn. "That's...well, I'm touched, I am really."

"Oh, it's just heroic tradition," said Angantyr, wiping beer off his
mailshirt. He felt slightly ashamed of his previous reluctance, and
considered what Danny might find most useful. An enchanted helmet? An arrow that never missed its mark, in case he ever went fea-
ture- hunting again? Somehow, such a gift seemed meagre. He braced
himself for the ultimate act of generosity.

"I shall give you," he said tight-lipped, "my own recipe for cream
of seagull soup."

"Oh," said Danny. "How nice. Hold on while I find a pencil.
Right."

"First," Angantyr dictated, "catch your seagull...."

"Count yourself lucky," said Arvarodd. "It's a damn sight better than
'Arvarodd of Permia.'"

"I suppose so," said Hildy sadly. "Even so..."

"Even so nothing." Arvarodd sighed. "I had dreams, you know, once. Poet-Arvarodd, or Arvarodd the Phrase-Maker, was what I wanted to be called. And, instead, what am I remembered for? Bloody Permia. At least," he said, brightening slightly, "my saga survived. That's one in the eye for King Gautrek. I told him when he showed me his manuscript. Illiterate rubbish for people who move their lips when they read."

Hildy nodded. She did not have the heart to tell him that *Gautrek's Saga* had made it through the centuries as well, and was regarded as the masterpiece of the genre. Men die, cattle die, only the glories of heroes live forever, as the Edda says.

"But I was never satisfied with it," Arvarodd continued. "Needed cutting." He fell silent and blushed.

"What is it, Arvarodd?" Hildy asked. He looked away.

"I don't suppose," he said suddenly. "No, it's a lot to ask, and I don't want to be a nuisance."

"What?" Hildy leant forward.

"Well," Arvarodd said, and from inside his mail shirt he drew a thick scroll of vellum manuscript. "Perhaps, if you've got a moment, you might..."

Hildy smiled. "I'd be delighted," she said. She glanced at the scrawl of runes at the top of the first page. "Arvarodd's Saga 2," it read, "The Final Battle." Out of the bundle of sheets floated a scrap of fading papyrus. Hildy caught hold of it and ran her scholar's eye over it. "Dear Mr Arvarodd, although I greatly enjoyed your work, I regret to say that at this time..." Hildy felt a tear escaping from the corner of her eye; then a sudden inspiration struck her.

"When did you write this?" she asked.

"Just before the battle of Melvich," said Arvarodd. "I was greatly influenced at the time by..."

Hildy thought fast. The manuscript was twelve hundred years old; carbon dating would verify that. No one would be able to doubt its authenticity. And if she was quick she would just be in time for the next edition of the *Journal of Scandinavian Studies*.

"What you need," she said, "is a good agent."

"Checkmate," said the sorcerer-king.

"Sod it," said Prexz.

"That's nine games to us," said King Hrolf, "and none to you. Mugs away."

"You're cheating," said Zxerp angrily.

"Prove it," said the sorcerer-king.

"What I still don't understand," said Starkad Storvirkason, "is how it manages to move without oars."

Hildy scratched her head. "Well," she said desperately, "it's magic."

"Oh," said Starkad. "Why didn't you say so?"

"Starkad," said Brynjolf, "why don't you go and get Vel-Hilda some more seagull?"

"Actually," Hildy started to say, but Brynjolf kicked her under the table. Starkad got up and went to the great copper cauldron that was simmering quietly on the hearth.

"I'm very fond of Starkad," said Brynjolf, "but there are times..."

At the other end of the table, Danny was telling the sleeping Angantyr all about his President Kennedy theory. Hildy sighed.

"I wish you all didn't have to go," she said. "There's so much you haven't seen, so much you could do. We need you in the twentieth century."

"I doubt it," said Arvarodd. "There aren't any more wolves to kill or sorcerers to be overthrown, and I think we'd just cause a lot of confusion."

"Let's face it," said Brynjolf, "if it hadn't been for you, Vel-Hilda, I don't know what would have happened."

Hildy blushed. "I didn't do much," she said.

"No one ever does," said Arvarodd, smiling. "What are the deeds of heroes, except a few frightened people doing the best they can in the circumstances? Sigurd had no trouble at all killing the dragon; it was a very old dragon, and its eyesight was starting to go. If he'd waited another couple of weeks it would have died of old age."

"Or take Beowulf," said Brynjolf. "Weedy little bloke, got sand kicked in his face on the beach as often as not. But he just happened to be in the right place at the right time. It's not who you are that matters, it's what you do."

"No," said Arvarodd, "you're wrong there. It's not what you do, it's who you are."

"Whichever." Brynjolf frowned. "Or both. Anyway, Vel-Hilda, what I'm trying to say is that we couldn't have managed without you. Well, that's not strictly true," he added. "But you helped."

"That's right." Arvarodd nodded vigorously. "You helped a lot."

"Any time," said Hildy. "I'll miss you. It won't be the same, somehow."

"Sorry, Vel-Hilda," said Starkad Storvirksson, returning with an empty plate, "but Bothvar Bjarki had the last of the seagull. There are still a few baked mice, if you'd like some."

"No, thanks," said Hildy, "really. I couldn't eat another thing."

Starkad breathed a sigh of relief and went off to eat them himself.

"I'm quite partial to a bit of baked mouse," said Arvarodd, leaning back in his seat and pouring himself a hornful of beer. "I remember when I was in Permia...."

"Checkmate."

Zxerp glared at King Hrolf with deep hatred. "You two," he said at last, "deserve each other."

King Hrolf rose to his feet and banged on the table for silence. He poured a horn of beer from the decanter and drank it, then cleared his throat. Even Angantyr woke up. The company turned their heads and listened.

"Friends," said the King, "our work is done. Despite the perils that threatened us, we have overthrown the power of darkness and saved the world from evil."

"Steady on," said the sorcerer-king.

"Now our time in this world, which has been unnaturally long, is over, and it is time for us to go to feast for ever in Odin's golden hall. Roast pork," he added before Angantyr could interrupt, "and all the mead you can drink. At the head of the table sits Odin himself; at his right hand Thor, at his left Frey. With her own hands Freyja pours the mead, and the greatest of heroes are the company. There we will meet many we have known, many of whom we have sent there, in the old wars which are forgotten. They say that in Valhalla the men go out to fight in the morning, and at night all those who have fallen rise up again to go to the feast, and fight again the next day. There is also, I am assured, a swimming-pool and a sauna. Personally, I think it all sounds very boring being cooped up with a lot of dead warriors all day, but don't let me put you off. I intend to take a good book with me. Anyway, tomorrow we sail across the great sea. Long will be our journey, past Iceland and Greenland and into the region of everlasting cold, until we pass over the edge of the world and see before us Bifrost, the Rainbow Bridge."

Hildy scratched her head. If they followed the route the King had described, it sounded to her as if they would end up at Baffin Island. But she had stopped doing geography in fourth grade, and only recently found out where Hungary is.

"Sorcerer-Eric and I have settled our differences," continued the King, "and he will be coming with us to Valhalla." A murmur ran round the table, but the King held up his hand. "That is settled," he said firmly. "He has been an evil man and our and the world's enemy, but in Valhalla all earthly enmities are put aside, for all who go there, so it is said, are soon united in common hatred of the catering staff. Besides, there is always a place at Odin's table for men who are brave and have fought well, however misguided their cause, and who can play a good game of Goblin's Teeth."

The murmur subsided. That, after all, was fair enough.

"Behind us," went on the King, "we leave one who has deserved a place in the company of heroes, our sister Vel-Hilda Frederik's-daughter. But for her... Well, she helped, and it is not by blows or good policies alone that battles are won."

That didn't leave much, Hildy reflected, but presumably he meant it kindly. She blushed.

"In our day, the skalds would have sung of her deeds; but now, it seems, the skalds sing no more at the feasts of kings. In our day, her story would have been told by the fireside, when the shadows are long and children hear ghosts when the sheep climb on to the roof to eat the house-leeks. But of our last fight no songs will be made; no one will ever know that we have been here or done what we have done. So it will be for all of us at the world's end, we who thought to cheat death by living for ever in the words of men. Nevertheless." The King smiled and made a sign with his hand. Arvarodd rose to his feet, and drew a harp out from under the table. "I wrote it in the car coming up," he whispered, as Hildy's eyes started to fill with tears. "Hope you like it."

"Vel-Hilda," said the King, "you have deserved a song, and one song you shall have. Arvarodd of Permia," he commanded, "sing us your song."

"The name of this song is Hildarkvitha," proclaimed Arvarodd. "Any unauthorised use of this material may render the user liable to civil and criminal prosecution." He drew his fingers across the strings, took a deep breath and sang:

"Attend!
We have heard the glories
Of god-like kings,
Heard the praise
And the passion of princes...."

Hildy stifled a sob and reached for her notebook.

The young lieutenant was excited. He had never been in this sort of situation before.

"We've found them," he said. "They're back in that fortified position on the cliffs above Farr. God knows why we didn't leave a unit there; they were bound to come back. Anyway, that's where they are. Do we go in, or what?"

The man in the black pullover scowled at him.

"Oh, go away," he said.

Young Mr Fortescue stared in disbelief at the While-You-Were-Out message on his desk.

> *Message from Eric Swenson, Chairman and Managing Director, Gerrards Garth group of companies.*
>
> *Expansion programme scratched owing to unforeseen difficulties, so no China for you. Consolation prize chair, managing directorship of entire shooting match, try not to cock it up too much, why am I saying this, that's why we've chosen you. Written confirmation follows, good luck, you'll need it, suggest you get out of electronics entirely.*
>
> *Message at 10.34.*

It would, of course, be a challenge, and it was nice to think that the boss had such confidence in him ("that's why we've chosen you"). Nevertheless, it would have been better if he had known he was being groomed for greatness rather earlier. He could have taken notes.

"All aboard," said Danny Bennett cheerfully. "Move right down inside please."

The entire company was embarking. They were going on a long tour of the kingdom of Caithness and Sutherland, just for old times' sake and to fill in the hours before it was time to set sail; down Strathnaver to Kinbrace and Helmsdale, then up the coast to Wick and across to Thurso, and on to Rolfsness. The tank was full of petrol, magically produced by the wizard from peat.

"Danny's in no fit state to drive, you know," Hildy whispered. The King smiled.

"For some reason he wanted to," he said. "Insisted that it was his bus, he'd captured it single-handed, so he was going to drive. The wizard's put a spell on him, so we should be all right."

Hildy shrugged. "Oh, well," she said, "if you're sure. I've done enough driving these last few weeks to last me, anyway."

These last few weeks... How long had it been since her adventure started? She could not remember. It had been the same with holidays when she was a girl; week merged seamlessly with week, and soon she had not known which day of the week it was, or what month, or what season of the year, except that the sun always seemed to shine. It was, of course, shining now; strong orange evening light that made even the scraggy brown sheep look somehow enchanted.

"Hrolf," she asked, "what am I going to do once you've all gone?"

"As little as possible for at least a month," replied the King. "First, you're going to have to help Danny Bennett explain all this to the rest of the world—only for God's sake don't let him tell them the whole truth. Have you still got that bit of jawbone Arvarodd gave you? That ought to do the trick."

"Shouldn't I give it back?"

"Certainly not," said the King. "It makes him insufferable. We'll see just how long his reputation as a wise counsellor lasts without it. Anyway, after you've done that, I advise you to go away for a while and persuade yourself that none of this ever happened. It'll be for the best, in the long run."

"Oh, no," Hildy said, "I couldn't do that. Even if I wanted."

"And you don't."

"No. I've had"—Hildy searched for the right words—"the time of my life," she said.

"Funny," said the King. "Oh, well, it takes all sorts. I'm not exactly overjoyed at the prospect of going to Valhalla itself, but I haven't got much of a choice."

"Shall I see you there?" Hildy asked suddenly. "Eventually, I mean?"

"I haven't the faintest idea," said the King. "But don't be in any hurry to find out."

"I won't, don't you worry," said Hildy, grinning. "I guess I've had my adventure. And I know what I'm going to do. I'm going to publish the saga that Arvarodd gave me, and become the world's leading authority on the heroic age of Scandinavia. They'll make me a full professor before I'm thirty."

"Is that a good thing?"

"Probably. Anyway, it's what I want to do, and I reckon I'll do it rather better now that I know what it was really like."

"What was it really like, Vel-Hilda?"

"Just like everything else," said Hildy, "only there were less people, so what they did mattered more at the time."

"You could put it like that."

"I will," Hildy assured him, "only with plenty of footnotes. Of course, I won't be able to tell them about the magic, so most of what I say will be totally untrue. You won't mind that, will you?"

"Nothing to do with me," said King Hrolf.

"It'll be strange, of course. When I'm giving a lecture on Bothvar Bjarki and speculating on whether he was really just a sun-god motif imported from early Indo-European myth."

"Is he?"

"Undoubtedly," Hildy said. "The parallels are conclusive."

"I'll tell him that," said the King. "He'll be livid."

"So are you," she said, "probably. Or you're an amalgamation of several pseudo-historical early dynasties, conflated by oral tradition and rationalised by the chroniclers. Your deeds are a fictionalised account of tribal disturbances during the Age of Migrations, and you have no real basis in historical fact."

"Thank you, Vel-Hilda," said the King. "That's the nicest thing anyone's ever said about me."

"What about me, then?" said the sorcerer-king, leaning over from the row in front.

"Oh, you're just a personification of bad harvests and various diseases of livestock," said Hildy. "No one's ever going to believe in you."

"I believe in me," said the sorcerer-king.

"And look where it's got you," said King Hrolf.

"True," said the sorcerer-king. "But aren't I in Arvarodd's saga?"

"Like he said himself, it's heavily influenced by the *fornaldarsögur* tradition. You're symbolic."

"Allegorical?"

"Very."

"Oh. Fancy a quick game, then?"

"Later," said the King. The sorcerer-king leant forward again and scratched the wolf behind the ear. It growled resignedly.

"That's sad, in a way," said King Hrolf. "I wouldn't have minded being forgotten, but I'm not so keen on being debunked."

"Men die," Hildy quoted, "cattle die, but the glory of heroes lives for ever. It's just that these days people hate leaving well alone. They can't bear anything to be noble and splendid any more. But who knows? In a couple of hundred years or so, they may start believing in the old stories again. That'd be nice, wouldn't it?"

"Like I said," replied the King, "nothing to do with me. There was a man at my father's court who had been a very great hero in his youth. He'd been with King Athils, and he'd killed frost-giants, and he'd wrestled with Thor himself. Unfortunately, he made the mistake of surviving all his adventures and becoming old. Nobody believed he was still alive any more, and when he used to tell stories of his youthful feats, people used to think he was wandering in his wits and either pretending or believing that he was one of the heroes out of the fairy-tales he'd heard as a boy. So he stopped telling his own stories, and had to sit still in the evenings when the poet sang songs about him, which were always inaccurate and sometimes downright slander. In tle end he did go mad and started telling everyone that he'd created the world. Nobody took any notice, of course. It's a terrible thing to be a legend in your own lifetime."

"What was his name?" Hildy asked. "Maybe..."

"Can't remember," said the King. "It was a long time ago."

Suddenly the King and the entire bus disappeared, and Hildy could see the ground moving below her at about forty miles an hour. She started to shriek, then realised that the wizard had made the bus invisible to get them past the soldiers. She started to laugh; she would never get used to magic, but she would miss it when it wasn't there any more. She said as much to where the King had been. He agreed.

"I've never given it much thought," he said. "It's like winter, or all these new machines of yours. You don't know how they work, but you accept them as part of life. We used to enjoy our magic rather more than you do. In fact, we enjoyed everything rather more than you do, probably because the conditions of life were rather more horrible then than now. I'm starting to sound my age, aren't I?"

"You don't look it," said Hildy.

"That," said the King, "is because I'm invisible."

The surveyor opened the door of his car.

"Hold on," he said, "I'm just going to take a leak."

A still night on the Ord of Caithness, with only the pounding of the sea on the rocks below to disturb the silence. God, how he hated this place!

Suddenly, round the bend of the road came a number 87 bus. That was strange enough at half-past one in the morning, but what was stranger still was the fact that it appeared to be full of Viking warriors, plainly visible in the pale ghostly glow of two points of light that shone from inside. The warriors were singing, although he could not hear them, and passing a drinking-horn from hand to hand; and there, sitting on the back seat, was that female archaeologist he had taken up to Rolfsness just before she disappeared so mysteriously. The surveyor stared. The archaeologist—or her spectre—was waving to him. He shuddered, and remembered the old tales of the phantom coach taking the souls of the dead to Hell that he had always been so scornful of as a boy. The bus moved silently, eerily on, and suddenly vanished from sight.

Trembling, the surveyor returned to the car.

"I've just seen a phantom bus," he said. "An eighty-seven, with Rolfsness on the front."

"Time you got a new joke, Donald," said his companions, who hadn't been watching. "That one wasn't even funny the first time."

Past the new wind-generator high above the road ("Look, Prexz, electricity on draught!"). Past the turf-roofed houses of Ulbster and Thrumster, looking exactly as their predecessors had done when Hrolf's subjects had built them as Ideal Homes twelve hundred years ago. Past Gills Bay and Scarfskerry, where Bothvar Bjarki had watched the circling cormorants and given the place its name. Past Dunnet Head and Castletown, the slate fences with broom twigs tucked into them to frighten away the deer. Past Scrabster ("I could tell you a thing or two about Scrabster," muttered Hring Herjolfsson), and the strange complex of buildings that Hildy said was a power station and which made Zxerp and Prexz suddenly feel thirsty. The flat coastal strip dwindled away into moorland and rock, and Ben Ratha was visible against the night sky. Across the little burn called Achadh na Greighe ("I never could cope with those damnfool Gaelic names," said Angantyr. "Why not call it something straightforward, like Sauthajarmrsfjall?"). Ben Ruadh. Rolfsness.

"It was nice to see it all again," said King Hrolf. "Godforsaken place, Caithness, but what the hell, it was my kingdom."

"I like it," said Hildy faintly. "It's sort of—"

"You would," said the King. "Come to Caithness, they said to my grandfather, the Soft South. Agreed, it's a bit less bleak than Norway or Iceland, and there are bits of Sweden I wouldn't give you a dead vole for. It's all right, I suppose. In its way."

The moon mirrored in the waters of Loch Hollistan. A rabbit scurrying for cover as the company approached. The sea.

"Well," said Angantyr, "here we all are again." He slapped Danny Bennett violently on the back. "It's been fun. Thanks for your help, and remember—you don't add the fennel until the meat is almost brown."

"I'll remember," said Danny. He suspected a bone was broken. "Remember, if in doubt, stop down. Better to be a stop over than a stop under."

The great mound was covered over and wired off, a slice cut out of it by the archaeologists. The King shook his head. "I don't know what they're all so excited about," he said, as she saw the signs of their scrupulous and scientific work. "It's just a mound of earth, that's all."

The ship. The moon flashed on the gilded prow, the gilded shields along its sides. As they stood and gazed at it, the west wind started to blow.

"I hate to mention this," said the King, "but how the hell are we going to get it down to the beach?"

"Same way we got it up, I suppose," said Hjort cheerfully. "Starkad, get the ropes."

"Couldn't we all go in the bus instead?" pleaded Starkad. "It's so nice and comfy."

Patiently, Biynjolf explained that the bus wouldn't go over water. "Why?" asked Starkad.

Brynjolf thought for a moment. "Because it hasn't got any oars, Starkad," he said.

"Oh," said Starkad Storvirksson. "Pity, that." He disappeared into the hold of the ship and emerged with several huge coils of rope. "They're all sticky," he said.

"That's the preservative they've put on them," said Hildy. "Lucky they didn't take them back to the labs."

Starkad passed ropes underneath the keel and called to the heroes, who took their axes and set about demolishing the mound and the trellis of oak-trunks. In a remarkably short time, the work was finished, and the heroes took their places at the ropes.

"Better get a move on," said the King, looking at the sky. "It'll be dawn soon, and I want to catch the tide."

With a shout, the heroes pulled on the ropes and the ship rose up out of the ground. Starkad tied a line round the figurehead and, exerting all his extraordinary strength, dragged the ship off the cradle of ropes on to the grass. The other champions joined him, and, with a superhuman effort and a great deal of bad language, hauled Naglfar down the long slope to the beach. As the keel slid into the water, Starkad gave a great shout.

"Is that his battle-cry?" Hildy asked.

"No," said Arvarodd, "the keel went over his foot."

The first streaks of light glimmered in the East, and the heroes saluted the coming dawn with drawn swords. The wizard stepped forward and, sounding like a hierophantic lawn-mower engine, blessed the longship for its final voyage. Bothvar Bjarki hauled on the yards, and the sail rose to the masthead and filled as the west wind grew stronger. On the sail was King Hrolf's own device, a great dragon curled round a five-pointed star.

"I told the sailmakers Earthstar," he explained, "but they had to know best. That or they couldn't read my writing."

"So this is goodbye," said Hildy.

"About my manuscript," said Arvarodd. "The middle section needs cutting."

"I'm sure it doesn't," said Hildy. There were tears in her eyes, but her voice was steady.

"I'm appointing you my literary executor," Arvarodd went on. "I know you'll do a good job. And I want you to keep those things I gave you—you know, the jawbone and the pebbles and things. I won't need them again, and..."

He turned away and went down to join the other heroes.

"Right, Vel-Hilda," said the King, "it's time we were going. Kotkel wants you to keep the seer-stone, and we both think you should hang on to these."

He handed her a bundle wrapped in a sable cloak. She took it.

"That's the Luck of Caithness," he said. "After all, you never know. There may be new sorcerers one day. And we're letting Zxerp and Prexz stay behind; they've earned their freedom, and they've promised to be good."

"We're going to go and live at the hydro-electric plant on Loch Shin," said a faint light at Hildy's feet.

"But the condition of their freedom is that, if ever you need them, they'll be ready and waiting. Won't you?" said the King menacingly. "Because if you don't Kotkel has put a spell on you, and you'll end up in the National Grid so fast you won't know what's hit you." The lights flickered nervously. "Oh, and by the way," added the King, "thanks for the Goblin's Teeth set."

"You're welcome," snarled Zxerp. "We were bored with it anyway."

"Also in the bundle," said the King, "is the sorcerer-king's sword, Ifing. It's lighter in the blade than Tyrving, and easier to handle. That's also just in case, and he won't be needing it. He's a reformed character, I think. And this, Vel-Hilda Frederik's-daughter, is for you, in return for that lovely glass thing and all your help."

From round his neck he took a pendant on a fine gold chain. "The kings of Caithness never had a crown," he said. "This passed from my grandfather to my father to me. Once it hung round the neck of Lord Odin himself. To wear it is to accept responsibility." He hung the chain around Hildy's neck. "I appoint you steward of the kingdom of Caithness and Sutherland, this office to be yours and your children's until the true king comes again to reclaim his own. Which," he added, "I hope will never happen. Look after it for me, Vel-Hilda."

Hildy bowed her head and knelt before him. "Until then," she said.

"And now I must go, or they'll all start complaining," said the King, and there were tears in his eyes, too. "Think of us all, but not too often."

He put his arms around her and hugged her. Before she could get her breath back, he was gone.

"There he goes," muttered Zxerp, "taking the game with him."

"Cheer up," said Prexz, softly. "It could be worse."

"How?" asked Zxerp.

"I could have forgotten to swipe their chess-set," chuckled Prexz.

Hildy ran down to the beach. Already the ship was far out to sea, the oars slicing through the black-and-red water. As a dream slips away in the first few moments of waking, it was slipping away towards the edge of the world, going to a place that had never been on any map. Yet as she stood and waved her scarf, she thought she could still hear the groaning of the timbers, the creaking of the oars in their rowlocks, the gurgle of the slipstream as the sharp prow cut the waves, the voices of the oarsmen as they strained at their work.

"I don't suppose anybody thought to pack any food." Could it be Angantyr's voice, blown back by some freak of the wind? Or was it just the murmuring of the sea?

"You said you were going to pack the food."

"I didn't."

"You did."

"I bloody didn't."

And perhaps it was the cry of the gulls as they rose to greet the new day, or perhaps it was the voice of the King, just audible over the rim of the sky, telling the sorcerer-king about rule 48. Hildy stood and listened, and the sun rose over the sea in glory. Then she turned, shook her head, and walked away.

About six months later, Hildy sat in her office at the Faculty of Scandinavian Studies at Stony Brook University. It was good to be home again on Long Island, thousands of miles away from her adventure, and she had her new appointment as professor to look forward to and the proofs of *Arvarodd's Saga* to correct. Around her neck was an exquisite gold and amber pendant; a reproduction, she assured all her colleagues, but she knew they had their suspicions. Still, she would continue to wear it a little longer.

She leafed through the day's mail. Three circulars with details of conferences, two letters from universities in Norway asking her to go over and give lectures, yet another flattering offer from Harvard, and a postcard with a stamp she had never seen before. She stared at it.

It had been readdressed from St Andrews and was written in Old

Norse. She turned it over; there was a picture of a tall castle. Her heart started beating violently. She screwed up her eyes to read the spidery handwriting.

"Food awful, company worse," it read. "My window marked with X (see photo). Arvarodd sends his regards. Hope this reaches you OK. See you in about sixty years, all the best, Hrolf R."

She lifted her head and looked out of the window. "Until then," she said.

Acknowledgments

Rick Katze, for scanning the original work.

Gay Ellen Dennett, Pam Fremon, and Tony Lewis, for their help in proofreading.

George Flynn, for the most amazingly thorough and helpful final proofs that anyone could ever hope for.

Mark Olson, for his assistance in formatting and answering bazillions of iterations of the eternal question "Why?"

This book was typeset in Adobe Garamond (with titles set in Goudy Medieval) using Adobe Pagemaker, and printed by Sheridan Books of Ann Arbor, Michigan, on acid-free paper.

— Deb Geisler
December 2001

The New England
Science Fiction Association (NESFA)
and NESFA Press

Recent books from NESFA Press:

- *Entities* by Eric Frank Russell $29
- *Quartet* by George R.R. Martin* $15
- *Strange Days: Fabulous Journeys with Gardner Dozois* $30
- *From These Ashes* by Frederic Brown $29
- *Frankensteins and Foreign Devils* by Walter Jon Williams* $14
- *First Contacts: The Essential Murray Leinster* $27
- *An Ornament to His Profession* by Charles L. Harness $25
- *Shards of Honor* by Lois McMaster Bujold $22

The Complete SF of William Tenn
- *Immodest Proposals* (Vol. 1) $29
- *Here Comes Civilization* (Vol. 2) $29

The Essential Hal Clement:
- *Trio for Slide Rule & Typewriter* (Vol. 1) $25
- *Music of Many Spheres* (Vol. 2) $25
- *Variations on a Theme by Sir Isaac Newton* (Vol. 3) $25

*Indicates trade paperback.

Details and many more books available online at: www.nesfa.org/press

Books may be ordered by writing to:
    NESFA Press
    PO Box 809
    Framingham, MA 01701

We accept checks, Visa, or MasterCard. Please add $3 postage and handling per order.

The New England Science Fiction Association:

NESFA is an all-volunteer, non-profit organization of science fiction and fantasy fans. Besides publishing, our activities include running Boskone (New England's oldest SF convention) in February each year, producing a semi-monthly newsletter, holding discussion groups relating to the field, and hosting a variety of social events. If you are interested in learning more about us, we'd like to hear from you. Write to our address above!